D0439950

Danaus and I cut down one naturi after another but still they kept coming . . .

We were painfully outnumbered and the enemy was too close for me to start lighting fires. I needed space and time to concentrate. Shelly managed to keep the approaching alligators off my heels but we were quickly becoming overwhelmed. Behind me, someone screamed in pain.

I turned my head to see who had been injured but the distraction cost me. A blade plunged into my chest, clipping the edge of my heart. I gasped, every muscle tensing in pain as precious blood poured from the wound.

Danaus . . . I whispered, reaching out for the hunter.

"Mira!" he cried, not far from where I was slowly sinking into the ground. The naturi pulled the knife from my chest while I crumpled to my knees, then grabbed a clump of my hair and jerked my head back so that my neck was exposed. Closing my eyes, I focused on setting the naturi on fire. But I was weak and doubted I would be able to kill him.

And then Danaus's powers rushed into me. Energy flowed through every vein and burned in every muscle. I screamed.

And the naturi holding me exploded in flames.

By Jocelynn Drake

The Dark Days Novels

NIGHTWALKER
DAYHUNTER
DAWNBREAKER

ATTENTION: ORGANIZATIONS AND CORPORATIONS
Most Eos paperbacks are available at special quantity discounts
for bulk purchases for sales promotions, premiums, or fund
raising. For information, please call or write:

Special Markets Department, HarperCollins Publishers,
10 East 53rd Street, New York, New York 10022-5299.
Telephone: (212) 207-7528. Fax: (212) 207-7222.

dawnbreaker

THE THIRD DARK DAYS NOVEL

JOCELYNN DRAKE

An Imprint of HarperCollins*Publishers*

This is a work of fiction. Names, characters, places, and incidents are products of the author's imagination or are used fictitiously and are not to be construed as real. Any resemblance to actual events, locales, organizations, or persons, living or dead, is entirely coincidental.

EOS
An Imprint of HarperCollins*Publishers*
10 East 53rd Street
New York, New York 10022-5299

Copyright © 2009 by Jocelynn Drake
Cover art by Don Sipley
ISBN 978-0-06-154288-6
www.eosbooks.com

All rights reserved. No part of this book may be used or reproduced in any manner whatsoever without written permission, except in the case of brief quotations embodied in critical articles and reviews. For more information, address Eos, an Imprint of HarperCollins Publishers.

First Eos paperback printing: October 2009

HarperCollins® and Eos® are registered trademarks of HarperCollins Publishers.

Printed in the U.S.A.

10 9 8 7 6 5 4 3 2 1

If you purchased this book without a cover, you should be aware that this book is stolen property. It was reported as "unsold and destroyed" to the publisher, and neither the author nor the publisher has received any payment for this "stripped book."

To Stephen
Thanks for keeping me young.

Acknowledgments

I'd like to give a special thanks to the dynamic duo that sees me through every book. To my amazing agent, Jennifer Schober, and my brilliant editor, Diana Gill, thanks for all your help and support. I would also like to thank the Florence, Kentucky, Geek Squad for seeing me through some unexpected computer-related trauma. Thanks for your patience and hard work.

dawnbreaker

ONE

The tires squealed.

We took the corner going close to fifty miles per hour, skidding into the turn. I braced myself against the driver's seat and clenched my teeth, swallowing yet another curse as Knox narrowly missed a parked car as he whipped us down another residential street. A second set of squealing tires followed close behind as the Ford Mustang barreled toward us with increasing velocity.

"Get us out of the city, damn it!" I shouted at Knox. At this speed, we were going to hit someone, and with the naturi gaining ground, we couldn't afford to slow down. We had to get out of the city before we killed someone or the Savannah cops finally noticed a pair of cars rushing around the city at breakneck speeds.

"It's not that easy!" Knox shouted back. Both of his hands gripped the wheel tight enough to make his knuckles white. "We're coming from downtown and you said lose them, not get out of the city."

"Well, I'm saying it now. Get the hell out of the city. You're going to kill someone," I snapped.

"Namely us," Amanda added from the backseat. The

blond nightwalker sat next to Tristan, who seemed to be taking it all in stride. Of course, Tristan had been in far worse situations with me and survived. "I'm not going to kill us," Knox snarled as he took another turn going far faster than would be deemed sane. "This is a BMW M3. It's a race car for the rich and bored. The car can handle it."

"No, Knox, tell me what you really think," I growled. The BMW was my car. I had decided to let him drive when I noticed the naturi following us along River Walk—I knew I might need my hands free if we didn't succeed in losing them. I pulled my gun out of the glove compartment and checked the magazine.

"You know what I mean." The nightwalker glanced at me briefly, one corner of his mouth cocked in a weak smile.

"Rich and bored," I repeated drily.

"Are we really having this discussion now?" Amanda demanded as Knox skidded into another turn and clipped the bumper of a parked car.

"Knox!"

"Mira!" he shouted back. "Let me drive or you do it!"

But it was too late for that. The naturi were gaining with every turn. They didn't care who they hit along the way, which was why we had to get them out of the city.

I relaxed a little when we turned onto Montgomery Street. The on ramp to Highway 16 was close by. We would finally get out of the city and into more open ground.

"Mira," Tristan said in a calm voice, grabbing my attention as I looked at him in the rearview mirror. "Is leaving the city the wisest choice?"

Some of the tension might have drained from my shoulders, but a knot of worry still tightened in my stomach. I knew what he was asking. We were leaving the relative safety of the city and potentially taking the fight into naturi territory by heading into the open countryside. Controlling nature was their strength.

Tristan had already fought the naturi with me in the woods, and the fight didn't go well. He had nearly been shredded by a naturi from the animal clan, and I was impaled by members of the wind and earth clans. And this time we didn't have Danaus or Sadira around to help save our respective butts.

"We have no other choice," I admitted, frowning at him because I could understand his fear. "I'm not willing to fight this war in front of the humans like the naturi want."

"Can't you set them on fire or something?" Amanda demanded, fidgeting in the backseat. The nightwalker was anxious to get to the fighting because running wasn't her style. She was all claws and fangs in any situation, leaving behind shredded flesh and a spray of blood. It was what made her a good enforcer among the fledglings, but not the most reliable nightwalker, as she didn't always think things through.

"I have to be able to see or sense what I'm setting on fire, and I can't sense the naturi," I said, turning my frown into a frustrated glare.

"How about the car?"

"Only the parts I can see."

"Then the tires. Set the tires on fire. That'll slow them down."

"That might work," I agreed, rolling down my window with a nearly silent electric hum. "Who taught the naturi how to drive like this anyway? Or hotwire a car?" I muttered under my breath, but in a car full of nightwalkers, everyone heard me.

"The Internet is full of amazing information," Knox said sarcastically.

"The Internet?" I added it to my list of gripes. "These are Old World creatures. They don't drive, hotwire cars, or surf the Web."

To my surprise, Tristan chuckled, stopping me as I grabbed the exterior frame of the door. "There are moments when you sound really old, Mira. Is it any stranger than a nightwalker your age doing all those things and more?"

"Shut up, Tristan." I was barely over six centuries. I wasn't that old.

Turning my attention back to Knox, I said, "Slow down just a little bit and hold the car steady." Gripping the exterior of the car door, I slid out of the window and sat on the frame. It was a somewhat awkward balance, but it made it easier for me to see the tires of the red Ford Mustang following us. Focusing my thoughts, both the front and back passenger side tires exploded into flames. The car swerved twice before finally flipping over onto its top on the side of the road.

I slid back into the car and grabbed my gun from where I had set it on the floor. "Pull over. We have to finish this."

My feet were on the gravelly side of the road before Knox managed to put the parking brake on. I flipped the safety off the Browning that was now my constant companion and paused, looking down at the gun, which was identical to the one Danaus had given me in Venice. Nightwalkers were not in the habit of carrying guns—most of our enemies couldn't be killed by a bullet, and being shot just tended to piss them off. But the naturi could be killed by a well-placed bullet, so now I carried a gun no matter where I went, along with a blade. The rest of my companions hadn't necessarily gotten into the habit.

Tristan? I mentally reached out to him.

I've got a gun, he confirmed without my needing to ask. The young nightwalker had been with me when I fought the naturi in England and again when the naturi appeared in Venice. He was well aware of what it took to kill these resilient bastards.

"Knox," I called, putting the safety back on the gun. "Take this." I lightly tossed the gun to him over the top of the car as he stood. "Just don't hit me with your crappy aim." I was one to talk. We all had crappy aim. Not one of us had ever bothered to learn to shoot. But then, guns hadn't been that reliable five centuries ago—the last time nightwalkers faced the naturi on a regular basis. Times change and we had to learn to change with them.

Pulling a knife from the sheath at my waist, I walked over to where the car was balanced on its top. Three naturi had crawled out, while the fourth was still behind the wheel, not moving. They were cut and bruised but mending from their little fender bender. The naturi had the ability to heal from any wound almost as quickly as a nightwalker. However, a bullet to the head was successful in stopping them. A bullet in the heart slowed them down long enough to reload and take another, closer shot.

"Where's Rowe?" I called when I was within a few yards of the closest naturi.

"Coming for you, Fire Starter," replied the naturi.

I twirled the knife in my hand, letting the long silver blade capture the light from a nearby street lamp. "Tell me something I don't know."

"He wants you dead," the naturi said.

Again I shrugged. Rowe had won at the Palace of Knossos when he managed to break the seal that bound the naturi, but he still had to open the door. He knew that I was going to come after him again with everything I had, so he had been sending a continuous barrage of minor skirmishes my way during the past month, trying to wear me down.

With a twirl of the knife, I returned it to the sheath with my right hand while my left hand shot out, palm open toward him and the other two naturi. They exploded into three enormous candles of fire burning brightly in the night. I stopped them before there was even a chance for the fight to take place. I wasn't willing to risk the lives of my companions for more information. Rowe would either come after me or I would meet up with him at the next sacrifice location.

A shot rang out followed by two more in quick succession. I twisted around, extinguishing the fire with a wave of my hand. Tristan and Knox faced the opposite direction, holding their guns with both hands and firing at the half-dozen naturi running from the forest surrounding us on all sides. They had been waiting for us to finally appear outside the city limits.

To my surprise, two fireballs appeared in the open hands of one of the naturi and were launched toward Knox and Tristan. A light clan naturi. *Shit.* Focusing all my attention on the flames, I captured the two fireballs and pulled them to myself before extinguishing them completely. Fire as a form of attack had now been taken out of the equation, since the light naturi could counter all of my moves.

Redrawing my knife, I ran at the approaching naturi. Gunshots filled the night as Tristan and Knox tried to level the playing field. As we closed on the group, the sound of wings filled the air. A flock of starlings flooded the night sky. I dove to the ground, my bare arms skidding along the rough, rock-riddled earth as I tried to escape from the sharp talons of the birds. Before I could regain my feet, the light naturi with her golden hair and bronze skin was on me, short sword drawn. I rolled to my left, narrowly missing the blade as it came down where I'd been only a second earlier. I created a wall of fire between us, hoping to slow her down for a second so I could regain my feet.

The light naturi wiped away the fire with a wave of her hand. As she took a step closer, I threw my knife at her, burying it deep within her chest.

Stumbling backward, the naturi gapped at the knife sticking out of her chest. She swiped blindly at me with her sword, but I easily dodged it. With a swift kick, I knocked the blade from her weakening grip. I smiled as I stepped forward and pulled my knife from her chest. My maker, Sadira, had made sure that I was an accomplished fighter without my powers. The sucking sound filled the night air followed by her cry of pain, cut short as I separated her head from her shoulders in a single, clean blow.

I was running to face the rest of the naturi before she hit the ground. A quick count revealed that only three remained of the six that had attacked. The birds were gone, indicating that the animal clan naturi had been killed.

Overhead, the clouds began to churn as an unexpected storm blew in from the east. The wind shifted and picked up, blowing my long red hair into my eyes. It appeared that the remaining naturi were members of the wind clan. This was bad. I couldn't stop a lightning bolt, and not one of us was likely to survive being struck.

"Pull back," I shouted. "Pull back." I gathered my powers as I screamed at the nightwalkers. I couldn't set any of the naturi on fire if they were close to the nightwalkers; there would be no way of protecting those important to me once the fire started.

Tristan and Knox hesitated for only a moment, but then pulled back, running toward my car. However, Amanda was trapped by a naturi slicing at her, backing her steadily toward the woods and away from the road. Concentrating, I set the two naturi that had been battling Knox and Tristan on fire and ran toward Amanda.

Out of the corner of my eye I saw another car pull off to the side of the road behind the naturi car. I didn't need a bigger audience and could only guess our new friend was another naturi since we had the whole area magically cloaked.

Take care of the new arrival, I directed Tristan telepathically as I ran to Amanda's side.

The wind naturi with the light brown hair paused a few feet from Amanda and raised one hand up into the air as if reaching to pull down a piece of the heavens. Amanda watched him, her hands trembling from exhaustion and possibly fear. She had no idea what she faced. I did and it wasn't pretty. I had seen Rowe take the exact same stance just before a hailstorm of lightning bolts pelted the ground.

Digging my feet into the ground, I launched myself at her, tackling her to the ground just before a lightning bolt sizzled to the earth exactly where she had been standing only a moment earlier. Pain sliced through my abdomen, but I ignored it as I forced Amanda to roll several feet as we searched for safer ground. Once on my side, I directed a fireball at the offending wind naturi, bathing him in orange and yellow flames before he could call down another bolt.

With the naturi burned to a blackened crisp, I lay back on the ground and closed my eyes in relief. The naturi were dead and no one was seriously hurt.

Mira! Tristan shouted telepathically at the same time more gunshots rang out.

Twisting to look up, sending a fresh stab of pain through my abdomen, I saw three more naturi running toward us. Somehow I had missed them in my count—or they had run from the woods when I crashed to the ground with Amanda, trying to take advantage of a vulnerable moment.

Amanda pushed to her knees, moving in front of me in an effort to protect me, but I grabbed her elbow and pulled her to the side. I couldn't have her block my field of vision. Lifting one shaking, bloody hand, I tried to set them on fire, but I struggled. Each movement of my body sent a fresh sliver of pain screaming through my frame, shattering my concentration. The naturi were gaining ground, faster than Tristan or Knox could. With a snarl, I dug deep, reaching past the pain, searching for the fire that burned bright where my soul was supposed to reside.

The three naturi slid to a halt a few feet away from me. Their gurgling cries filled the nearly silent night air. Dropping their weapons heedlessly to the ground, they clawed at their skin, which had begun to undulate strangely.

It was then that I felt the familiar touch of warm power in the air. I knew before turning my head that Danaus was there. Finally distracted from the pain and the fear, I waved my hand at the three naturi that were being boiled from the

inside out and set them on fire. They were instantly incinerated under our combined power.

"Oh, God! Mira!" gasped Amanda beside me. "I'm so
sorry. I didn't mean to . . . it's just . . . you tackled me . . . I
didn't—"

I looked down at where she was staring with a horrified look. The handle of a knife stuck out of my stomach.
Blood was soaking into my shirt and beginning to fill the
waistband of my jeans. That explained the sudden slice of
pain when I'd crashed into Amanda. I impaled myself on the
knife she had been holding.

"Figures," I grumbled as I slowly pulled the blade out
of my stomach with a low hiss of pain. I escaped being
wounded by a naturi only to be hurt by one of my own. The
embarrassment was worse than pain in my stomach as my
body struggled to heal itself.

A whisper of running footsteps told me that Tristan and
Knox were fast approaching to make sure that we were both
safe. Refusing to allow them to see me wounded by Amanda's blade, I pushed into a sitting position, wincing at the
pain it caused.

"Are you all right?" Tristan demanded before coming to
a complete stop.

"I didn't mean to—"

"I'm fine," I quickly interrupted.

"You're bleeding," Knox countered.

"I'm fine. It's just a scratch." If he had seen some of the
"scratches" I'd had in the past, he would have fainted dead
away.

"But—" Amanda tried to continue, but a familiar rumble
cut her off.

"She's fine," Danaus said with a smirk as he extended his hand to me to help me off the ground.

A matching wry smile touched my lips as I grabbed the hunter's wrist with my left hand and hauled myself back to my feet. While painful, this was a little bit of nothing. "Go gather up the bodies and throw them on the car. We need to destroy the evidence before someone finds them," I directed as I handed Amanda back her knife.

It took only a few minutes for us to gather up the bodies that I hadn't completely incinerated. The cloaking spell we had all thrown over the fight, and the fact that it was three in the morning, helped hide the scuffle from the eyes of humans, but we still needed to get rid of the evidence that the naturi existed.

Once we were all settled in the car again, I set the Ford Mustang on fire. I must have managed to hit the fuel tank because the whole thing went up in this beautiful ball of fire. We lingered long enough to be sure the bodies were completely incinerated before driving back toward the city, with Danaus following us in the other car. No one had yet commented on his sudden appearance, though the questions hung in the air like a pink elephant suspended by fishing line.

Knox was the first to break the silence weighing on the occupants of the car, using his ubiquitous dry sense of humor. "While I enjoy a night out with you as much as the next nightwalker, I assumed you had something else in mind besides playing with the naturi."

"Can we please not talk about them?" Amanda said in a shaky voice from the backseat. I was stunned by her soft, almost broken tone. Nothing had ever rattled her as far as I knew, but then, this had been her first run-in with the naturi, and she'd barely survived. She had also managed to stab the Keeper of the domain she inhabited. Amanda wasn't having the best night.

"I didn't call you together to talk about the naturi," I said with a sigh. "I wanted to invite you both to be a part of my family."

Only now I was beginning to question the wisdom of it.

Two

The study in my private home was a classic Old World library with floor-to-ceiling bookshelves lining three of the walls. Lighted curio cabinets were interspersed among the shelves, holding odds and ends. This was the first home I had maintained for more than a couple of years, and I had begun to allow myself to collect things since I no longer feared the need to pick up and run. Savannah was my home, and I was prepared to defend it.

Leaning against the front of the desk, I found Tristan watching me with hooded gaze as he lounged in a high-backed leather chair. He had grown more comfortable living within my domain during the past month, but then, we were still slowly trying to work out our own relationship of mistress and . . . child. I had stolen him from our maker, Sadira, in an attempt to protect his life. I'd made no plans for such a thing. I had never intended to create my own family, especially with one of the children that once belonged to my hated maker.

Yet, Tristan needed me. Sadira had created and kept him weak so he could never escape the way I had. When he had tried to escape, Sadira tricked me into returning him to her. I knew what it was like to be under her evil, twisted control and I understood his need to finally be free. While in London, I promised to help him find a way to do that, but never expected to become his mistress as part of the bargain.

Once I returned to Savannah from Crete, it had been on the tip of my tongue to set him free; to renounce my ties to him and let him live his own life as a nightwalker. But my conscience wouldn't let me. He was still weak, making him easy prey for anything that set its sights on him. I wouldn't let him get himself killed the first minute he was away from me. For a century Jabari trained me to protect myself, and taught me what it meant to be a nightwalker. I could at least pass along some of that knowledge to my newfound ward.

For now, Tristan seemed content to stay. But there were times when I would find him watching me, a sad look in his eyes. I wondered if he was staying for an entirely different reason. Was he looking for a way to protect me?

Danaus was also there, sitting in one of the high-backed chairs before the desk, his eyes never leaving me, like a lean jungle cat watching its intended prey. Both he and Tristan had fought the naturi beside me in London and again at the Themis Compound, and Danaus stood with me when the seal was broken in Crete. While I'd known both Amanda and Knox longer, I felt a strange closeness to the two newcomers to my domain.

Amanda and Knox wandered slowly around the room, their footsteps echoing in the silence as they stepped from the thick Persian rug to the dark hardwood floor. It was the first time either of them had been in my home outside the city limits. I kept a town house within the city, which was where I held some of my meetings and social gatherings, but the house outside the city was for my own private use. It was also where I spent the daylight hours. Gabriel, my bodyguard, was familiar with my home, and now Tristan, because it was his home as well.

"Mira," Knox murmured, his gaze still taking in the room for a moment before settling on me. "I'm honored that you've brought us here."

I smiled at him, appreciating his Old World charm and manners. He was more than a few centuries old and had been raised by an Old World nightwalker named Valerio, whom I admired and detested in nearly equal amounts.

"You can repay me by promising to never drive my car again," I said with a smirk. He smiled in return, knowing I was not entirely serious. He had done what was necessary to keep us alive. And while I loved my car, it was still just an object.

"I'm guessing you're serious about what you said in the car," Amanda said, turning from a curio cabinet that held a series of daggers from the twelfth century. "About joining your family."

I nodded once, my gaze shifting from Amanda to Knox.

"Then I acc—"

"No!" I said, holding up my hand and halting Knox before he could complete the thought. I pushed off the desk and stood with my hands out and open to both of them, wishing for a moment to be able to find the words to express both my fears and my gratitude adequately. "I appreciate your enthusiasm, Knox, but I don't want either of you to accept or deny this blindly, particularly in the name of loyalty."

"Besides, this isn't your typical family," Tristan interjected, drawing my gaze to him. A wicked smile tweaked the corners of his mouth, but he was just needling me, trying to break the tension that had drawn the muscles in my shoulders taut.

A family among nightwalkers was usually an arrangement where an elder nightwalker agreed to protect a small flock of nightwalkers. Typically, the elder nightwalker had created the others, but not always. Living in a family was a source of protection, like living within a particular mob family. However, life within the family could be just as brutal if not fatal. And in most cases there was no leaving the family alive once you were accepted.

"My arrangement with Tristan is different than what I am offering you," I started, leaning against the desk again in an attempt to resume my relaxed posture. "My arrangement with Tristan will always be different because of the circumstances. That is no one's business but ours. The same goes for his future here in Savannah."

"We have no problem with Tristan," Amanda said with a shrug. "He's welcome here." I didn't miss the tiny smile she shot him over her shoulder before looking innocently back up at me.

Something in my stomach twisted and I reflexively clenched my teeth. That would not do. A pairing of Amanda and Tristan wouldn't be a good thing, would it? I mentally shook my head at myself and my silly thoughts. I was acting like a protective mother hen with Tristan. After what had happened with Sadira and the court of the Coven in Venice, I was wary of anything that could potentially harm my ward. He was still healing from his latest trauma, and I didn't see Amanda as the best influence or the sanest choice for a love interest. But then, such a thing had to be Tristan's choice, not mine.

"We're getting off topic," I sighed, briefly trying to remember what the topic was as I rubbed the bridge of my nose with my thumb and index finger. "The world is changing, as you've obviously seen tonight. The naturi are openly hunting us now. For the most part, they are searching for me, but that doesn't mean they won't take down any nightwalker they run across along the way. As a result, there is a good chance the order that we have established here may begin to fray."

"Like following the attack at the Dark Room," Knox said. He leaned up against one of the bookshelves, folding his arms over his broad chest. The blond-haired nightwalker had been there when a pair of naturi and several lycanthropes ripped through the exclusive nightclub in search of me. Ever since, tension had been running high between the shifters and the nightwalkers.

"And the Docks," Danaus added solemnly. Several humans had been killed at the human nightclub that evening as the naturi attempted to track down Danaus and myself.

"Yes."

"But things have gotten better," Amanda countered.

"It's not enough, and things are going to get a whole lot worse in the coming months," I said. Crossing my arms under my breasts, I resisted the urge to pace the Persian rug. "What I am offering is the protection of my name, in a sense. In an unspoken way, you both have been my representatives within the city, but by joining my family, it makes it more official. If you are a part of my family, your actions are the same as what my actions would be. Your words are my words. But by that same token, if you do something in my name that I don't approve of, I will rip out your heart. No hesitation. No quarter. No questions asked."

I paused and looked at Amanda and Knox. Both seemed to shrink back from my gaze, but they said nothing. I didn't expect either to ever cross such a line, but then, the words had to be said. The warning had to be allowed to hang ominously in the air, if only to give them reason to pause when in the middle of a somewhat questionable act.

"Besides that, being in my family changes nothing else. You will not be required to sleep within this house—"

"Not like that would be such a bad thing," Amanda muttered. I tried to glare at her for the interruption but failed rather miserably. My home was a beautiful, antebellum three-story house, with rich dark woods and a grand winding staircase. It was magnificent, and it was a shame that I spent more than half my hours of the day locked within the basement.

"Nor will you be required to answer to me in any way other than you do at this moment," I continued.

"Interesting," Knox began, sliding his hands into the pockets of his navy trousers.

I arched one brow at him, daring him to continue. There were moments that he truly reminded me of his maker, Valerio.

Knox took a step away from the bookcase and cocked his head at me, sending a lock of short blond hair down in front of one eye. "You're offering us all the benefits of a family without any of the usual drawbacks."

"Yes, I do."

"What's the catch?"

"The Coven," Tristan answered for me.

The Coven. The ruling body that oversaw all of my kind consisted of four nightwalkers called Elders. And now I was considered one of them, after a moment of desperation in Crete. To make matters worse, the second that Jabari agreed to my request to take the open seat on the Coven, he blasted it telepathically to any nightwalker within the vicinity that I was now a member. He ensured that there was no way I could weasel out of it after we defeated the naturi that night. *Bastard.*

"I am now considered a member of the Coven," I admitted, hating to say the words out loud, as if they carried a type of slow-acting poison. "There are many who would have trouble accepting such a fact. If someone decides to strike at me and take my seat, the first place they will strike is at my family. Being in my family puts a target on your forehead."

"Any more so that being a nightwalker when it comes to the naturi?" Amanda asked, perching on the arm of the chair that Tristan sat in.

"In that case, you are simply being hunted by the naturi," Tristan said before I could reply, "and for now, they are content to hunt Mira alone. Tonight, we simply got in the way. Join Mira's family and you will be singled out by very powerful nightwalkers. You will be hunted by two sides instead of just one."

Amanda shrugged off his warning, but I noticed that the smile she forced on her lips didn't quite reach her blue eyes. "It's the risk you take when joining any family."

"Not quite, but similar," I corrected. "Go home and think about it. Tristan will take you back to the city. I'll come to you in a few nights for your answers."

Neither looked happy about the sudden dismissal, but at

this point there was nothing else I was willing to discuss. They were receiving an option that Tristan had not been given, and it made me extremely uncomfortable. I wished I could give the same choice to Tristan, but if he said no, I knew I would not have the strength to let him go yet.

"And Knox, if for some reason you should hear from Valerio, please pass along the message that I need to speak with him as soon as possible. That's an official invitation into my domain, if he should ask."

"I haven't heard from him since I left him, but I will keep your message in mind should something change," Knox said before leaving the library, followed by Amanda.

Tristan pushed out of his chair and walked over to stand before me as I continued to lean against the desk. My shoulders were slumped, weighed down by too many questions and too many solutions that I found unacceptable.

"That went well," he teased, drawing my narrowed gaze to his face.

"Don't push me, Tristan. Our arrangement could easily change." I tried to threaten him, but his grin only grew. Neither of us believed my hollow threat.

"You're not Sadira," he murmured. He took my left hand in his and rubbed his thumb over the silver band I wore on my ring finger. "And you've not offered them a sugar-coated death sentence. This is for the best."

I woodenly nodded, hoping he thought the same about our own arrangement. "Get out of here."

I pulled my hand from his and walked over to one of the bookshelves. Picking up a large silver hourglass, I turned it over so the white sand inside poured into the empty container. Time was slipping away from me. We hadn't located Rowe yet. I had half expected the naturi to appear in my territory looking to remove my head from my shoulders after all the chaos I'd added to his life. But he hadn't appeared, and a part of me was glad.

A sigh passed over my parted lips as I walked over to another hourglass in my extensive collection and turned it over. *Danaus . . .*

The hunter and I had parted ways long before I reached Savannah. He flew with me from Crete, but got off the plane in Paris. I knew he had returned to Themis. It wasn't so much the researchers that worried me, but the leader of Themis, Ryan, and his misinformation. During our time together, I felt as if Danaus was finally beginning to learn the truth about nightwalkers; he had begun to understand that we were more than bloodsucking monsters from human mythology.

Standing in my study with the hunter now staring at my back while the naturi lurked in my domain, I found myself grateful that he was back in town. He was as much a loose cannon as the naturi, but under most circumstances we had the same goal—destroy the naturi. And together we were an unstoppable force. The naturi had no defense against us.

Prior to his arrival, I had felt completely defenseless against the naturi. I couldn't sense them the way I could humans and lycanthropes. I couldn't tell if they were closing in on my secret sanctuary outside the city. Within my own domain, I had begun to feel both alone and trapped.

Reluctantly, I turned back around to face the hunter after turning over a third, silver-plated hourglass with black sand. Danaus had not changed since I'd last seen him, except that his black hair seemed a little longer. His face was nearly ageless. A rare smile shone on his features, making him appear in his mid-twenties, while the perpetual frown that crowded his eyes and tugged at the corners of his mouth put him in his late thirties to early forties—the visage of a time-worn warrior.

"I'm afraid to ask what has bought you back into my domain. Ready to continue our dance?" I asked, referring to our promise to one day fight to the death. Yet after all we'd been through, even that had the feel of a pathetic running gag. However, I knew without a doubt that we would indeed one day find ourselves on the opposite sides of the same battlefield.

"Themis sent me," he replied. He shifted in his seat, from stretching his legs out before him to sitting on the edge with one elbow leaning on the arm of the chair.

"What does Ryan want?" I nearly growled. I knew I shouldn't be so hostile. He had helped us fight the naturi in Crete. He had also attempted to protect us when the naturi threatened us in England. But this was also the same man that brought a helpless human named James into a known battle with the naturi. He had needlessly risked James's life, and I found that unacceptable. It also didn't help that Ryan was an extremely powerful warlock, making him a special kind of dangerous.

"He wants me to stop threatening the researchers at Themis," Danaus replied.

A wide grin spread across my mouth and I returned to my spot in front of my desk. I crossed my left ankle over my right as I folded my arms over my newly mended stomach. "Danaus, have you gone rogue?" I taunted. "Finally come over to the dark side?"

"Hardly," he said with a snort. "The naturi are hunting me. They attacked a safe house in Paris, another in London, and the Compound twice. Three of my hunters were killed along with a couple of researchers." His tone grew angrier and more frustrated with each word, and his hands tightly gripped both arms of the chair.

A part of me wanted to gloat over the loss of his hunters, but I wasn't that coldhearted. They might have killed nightwalkers for some misguided notion, but they were still human, and no human deserved to die at the hands of the naturi.

"So you decided to lure them here?"

"It looks like they're already here," Danaus pointed out. "How are they finding you? They shouldn't be able to sense you."

"I don't think they can. It could be Macaire pissed at me and telling them where to find me at any given moment," I complained, hating the Ancient with a fresh passion. Macaire had instigated a bargain with the naturi, which in turn got me stuck on the Coven in an effort to break the bargain. Without a doubt, the nightwalker was not one of my bigger fans. "Mostly, it's been a matter of luck," I finished with a shrug. "I have to make appearances around town, conduct business. Naturi are crawling all over my city. It usually doesn't take long for one to spot me. However, they generally attack only in a pack."

"Ryan believes that may change if Aurora is freed." Danaus paused as he sat back again. "He seems to think the naturi will grow in power if she returns to the earth."

"Moving them from just a shadow to a full-blown nightmare," I finished. Pushing away from the desk, I stood in the middle of the room, dropping my fists to my sides. "Fantastic. They're enough trouble now. We don't need them as a major powerhouse."

"Since it's too dangerous to let the naturi hammer against Themis, I thought I would come here," Danaus said.

"And let them hammer against Savannah instead," I snapped. "You may not believe it, but keeping the people of Savannah safe and alive is my job as well."

"Then why stay? Your presence here endangers them as much as mine does."

"Because I have nowhere else to go. Do you honestly think any other nightwalker would welcome me into their domain with the naturi snapping at my heels?"

"There is always Venice."

Yes, there was always Venice. Home of the nightwalker Coven. It was said to be the one place that naturi would not go, but even that theory had been destroyed recently when Macaire and Elizabeth elected to side with the naturi. Venice might protect me from the naturi, but it would not protect me from Macaire. I suspected my maker, Sadira, was also there, and she would not welcome me with open arms either.

"There is nowhere to go," I said firmly, leaning back against the desk again as my gaze fell to the floor. "This is my home, my domain. The naturi will not force me from my home."

"We're stronger together," Danaus said. That he would admit such a thing aloud surprised me. But there was a catch to his plan.

"So are the naturi." My gaze snapped back up to his face and I frowned. "Their attacks could become more violent with you here now. If they can kill us both at once, we will have no way of closing the door if it is opened."

"Would you rather I left?" he asked, pushing to his feet.

I stepped forward and nearly laid a restraining hand against his chest, but stopped myself just before I touched him. His warm, vibrant energy danced across my open palm and down my bare arm. It was unbelievable that I had managed to forget what it was like to come into contact with his powers. The warm energy blanketed me, wrapping around me like a pair of flannel pajamas.

"No," I murmured, lowering my hand back to my side. I opened and closed my hand, flexing my fingers to rid myself of the lingering feel of his energy. "You're right. We are stronger together."

"But . . . " he prompted.

"You can't hunt nightwalkers while you're here," I growled. "I can't worry about protecting my kind from both you and the naturi. If you cause problems, I'll gut you and send your charred entrails back to Ryan in a doggie bag."

"Mira—"

"Non-negotiable, Danaus. Penelope's death proves that you can't be trusted to protect a nightwalker ally. You have to swear to me that you won't attack another nightwalker."

"And if I'm attacked?" he said, narrowing his beautiful blue eyes at me.

"Defend yourself. I'll keep the nightwalkers here from harassing you," I promised, leaning against the desk behind me.

"Like Venice." His tone sounded skeptical and his expression darkened.

"I got you out of Venice unharmed and no humans were endangered in the process. What more could you ask for?"

Danaus merely grunted at me. Unhappy with my less than enthusiastic welcome into my domain, he returned to his chair. What did he expect? Last time he was in Savannah, five nightwalkers had died and he brought news of the naturi. His appearance wasn't exactly a good omen.

My other concern was becoming too dependent on his presence when it came to taking on the naturi. Danaus could sense the naturi nearly as well as he could sense me. It gave us an edge in tracking them down and fighting them. I was willing to believe it was why either of us had survived as long as we had. Of course, my fire manipulation and his ability to boil blood also helped.

Pushing off the front of the desk, I walked around, turning over one of the small hourglasses on the desktop before sitting down in the chair. I grabbed a pen and a notepad so I could quickly scratch out an address and some quick directions about the security I'd had installed.

"Here is a place you can stay while you're in town. Just don't trash it. It's my town house in the city," I said as I ripped the paper from the pad.

Danaus stood but didn't take the paper. "I can find a place."

"This makes it easier for me to find you," I said, throwing him a set of keys I had grabbed from the top drawer of the desk. "I've also written instructions for arming and disarming the security system. It's safer than a hotel," I added, waving the piece of paper at him.

With obvious reluctance, he took it from me. I followed him to the front door. Dawn was approaching and I needed to get settled before the sun rose. I felt surprisingly comfortable with the idea of Danaus knowing where I spent my daylight hours. I'd felt more ill at ease letting Knox and

Amanda wander around my house for a brief period of time. Of course, Danaus had proven time and time again that he never attacked a nightwalker while he or she slept. He gave the creature a chance to defend him- or herself. He and I saw eye-to-eye on few matters, but I respected his deep sense of honor.

The hunter paused at the open door, a frown on his lips as he stared down at the paper. But his concern had nothing to do with brief residence I was offering him.

What's wrong? The question escaped me telepathically, traveling along a silent road that we used with growing frequency. Danaus was the only human I could talk telepathically with, and it was disturbing. With my bodyguard Gabriel, I could send thoughts and read his reply, but Gabriel could neither send me thoughts nor read my thoughts and emotions.

Danaus flinched at the unexpected whisper touch of my mind, but didn't snap at me as I had expected. Instead he replied silently, *Rowe?*

The leader of the naturi had yet to show his face in my domain, as I'd expected him to. I had thought the naturi would come there directly after defeating us in Crete so he could personally claim my head and safely welcome his wife-queen back to earth.

Not yet.

He'll come now, Danaus replied, confirming both my hope and my fear. If word leaked to Rowe that Danaus and I were in the same place, I had little doubt that the one-eyed naturi would pass up the opportunity to come hunting us both. We were all that was standing between him and the door opening. After endless centuries of waiting, his lifelong goal was now within his grasp. There was no way the naturi prince would allow us to stop him yet again.

Let him come. I had no desire to have him within my domain, but I wanted this to finally be over, and the key to that was defeating Rowe.

Three

Tristan found me later in my private chambers in the lower levels of the house, preparing for the morning. Dawn was less than an hour away, but my mind was still whirling over thoughts of the naturi and Danaus. I had yet to come across any brilliant answers.

As I tied the sash of my robe, I turned to look at him standing in the doorway, a smile teasing the corners of my mouth. He was wearing only a pair of black pajama bottoms with little white skulls and crossbones scattered across them. He apparently had a penchant for flannel pajama pants no matter the season.

"You don't seem very relieved to have Danaus back in Savannah," Tristan commented. "I thought his assistance would please you."

To him, it was simple. With Danaus, we would be able to easily wipe the naturi from the city. And that was true. However, I never forgot that Danaus was, first and foremost, a hunter. He had killed five other nightwalkers within my domain a month ago while searching for me. Then he killed Penelope, with little warning and no real hesitation.

The area was in turmoil. The naturi were here. The lycans

were affected by the presence of the naturi. The nightwalkers were on edge because of the naturi and the lycans. Introduce the hunter into the mix, and this powder keg would blow.

"We could have managed without the hunter," I said, though it felt like a lie.

"We shouldn't have to 'manage.' I saw what you and Danaus did at Themis. You destroyed those naturi. You can do it again," Tristan pushed, taking a step into the room.

I still didn't want to think about what we had done at Themis. We destroyed their souls. No matter how much I hated the naturi, I would never do such a thing again. Kill them, definitely. Torture them, possibly. But destroying another creature's soul was beyond evil, and that was a road that I would not willingly go down.

"It's not that simple," I sighed. "Danaus is a hunter. What's to stop him from killing nightwalkers while he's in town? If the naturi are killing nightwalkers, do you honestly think he cares?"

"He cares about you," Tristan countered, to my surprise.

A flutter in my stomach made me pause. But then I remembered that it wasn't me that Danaus cared about, but what I could do. I was the weapon of the triad. I was the only one who could possibly reform the broken seal and keep the naturi locked in their cage.

"Danaus is like Jabari. Both are keeping me alive until this whole naturi thing is settled," I grumbled. Tightening the sash of my robe again, I collapsed into one of the comfortable chairs not far from the foot of the bed. "We just have to push on as we have been. We'll find Rowe. He needs me dead, so I'm sure the bastard will come hunting for me himself soon enough."

"That's not particularly reassuring, Mira."

Tristan wasn't happy with my plan, but then I wasn't happy with my plan either. I couldn't sense the naturi, so I was looking for new ways to sniff them out that didn't include wandering through the woods. At the same time, the naturi couldn't sense me, so I was trying to keep a low profile. I was just trying to survive until Jabari determined when and where the next sacrifice would occur. I hated the idea of waiting until the last minute to defeat the naturi when so much was hanging in the balance, but what choice did I have?

I watched Tristan as he stood near the door, his eyes downcast. He had something else gnawing at him and I had a feeling I knew what it was.

"Go ahead. Spit it out," I muttered, knowing I was asking for trouble.

"I . . . what do you mean?" he stammered. His blue eyes widened with surprised innocence and I nearly laughed.

"You've got something else on your mind. You can tell me or I can go digging in your brain for it." But we both knew I was bluffing. I wouldn't read Tristan's mind. He deserved what little privacy I could give him. Wasn't it enough that I was his mistress?

"H-How free am I?" he asked after nearly a minute of silence.

I frowned, hating his question because I hated my answer even more. "As free as I can let you be," I replied. "I have to look out for your best interests, make sure that you are safe. I'm sorry, Tristan. I wish I could set you free, but I can't as long as Sadira is alive. I don't want to free you until I've taught you how to defend yourself a little better."

"I'm not looking to leave you, Mira," he said, smiling as

he finally came into the room. He knelt before the chair I was sitting in and placed one hand on my right knee. "The naturi might be breathing down our necks, but living here has already proven to be better than being under Sadira's thumb. I was curious if you would permit me to become involved with someone."

Tristan's presence in my life had reminded me that we were physical creatures. Whenever he was close, he would lay a hand on my arm or shoulder. He wasn't coming on to me in any way. The physical contact was reassuring to him, so I permitted it as best as I could. Unfortunately, I had not been close with my own kind in a very long time. I was out of the habit, and his touch had both a calming and unnerving effect.

A groan escaped me as I shifted in my chair, pulling my knees out from under his touch. "Please don't say that it's Amanda," I muttered as I shoved one hand through my hair in frustration.

"What's wrong with Amanda?" he demanded.

She's dangerous, Tristan. She has a violent temper and she'll eat you alive. She's the Alpha among the fledglings."

"Then why do you keep her around if she's so dangerous?"

"Because she's good at keeping the fledglings in line. She knows better than to cross me. I'll stake her out in the sun."

"So you're not going to let me see her," Tristan said.

I stared at him for a moment, frowning. I briefly wondered if he would see her behind my back if I did say no, and mentally shook my head. After surviving nearly a century at the hands of Sadira, I had no doubt that he would do exactly as I said, even if it made him miserable. Of course, I had no doubt that Sadira would have denied his request in the name of protecting him from a bad influence.

"Has there been no one else since Violetta?" I asked, my voice barely drifting over a whisper. We had never talked about his wife, from when he was a human. She'd died more than a century ago during childbirth. Of course, we didn't have to talk about his past because I already knew it. The moment I claimed him as my own, I took his blood and mind, drawing in his essence and all of his memories. At one time Tristan had been married to a beautiful young woman. That happy life crumbled when she died, allowing Sadira to easily move in and stake her claim over the weakened man.

"Only Sadira. And now you," he replied.

"Wouldn't you want to start with someone more . . . "

"More like Violetta," he supplied, his voice crusting over with ice. "There is no one like her. There never will be. I know that. It's something that will always haunt me throughout this long existence."

"I was thinking someone more considerate, gentler. Someone more like you."

A tender smile lifted the worry and pain from his large eyes as he stared up at me. I got the feeling that on the inside he was chuckling at me. "I don't think there is anyone like me either."

Reaching over, I ran my fingers through this brown hair, pushing it away from where it was starting to crowd his eyes. "True."

"If you don't want me to see her, I won't," he volunteered.

"I can't do that. I can't take all your freedoms away from you. I might not be happy about it, but I can't stop you from seeing Amanda if it's what you want," I said, dropping my hand back to my side. Despite my reluctance, I knew that Amanda was a good person and might prove to be a valuable teacher. She knew how to take care of herself, and I secretly hoped she would pass some of that knowledge on to Tristan.

"I may see her?" he asked, unable to hide his shock.

"Yes, if she's willing to put up with you," I teased.

Tristan leaned forward and brushed a quick kiss across my temple, his joy rushing through me in a quick burst of energy. I couldn't help but smile as well. After more than one hundred years, he was finally getting his life back. My only hope was that I wasn't giving it back to him in time for the naturi to steal it away.

As he stood, he stretched his arms above his head and blinked a few times. Night was giving its last straining gasps of life as he and I prepared to settle in for the day. The night-walker lay down on the bed and then turned on his side so he could look at me.

"Do you think they will join the family?" he inquired.

I frowned, releasing the warmth and happiness that had filled the room just seconds earlier. "Yes," I whispered. "I think they will." Establishing a family would benefit me, as it would help strengthen the control I had over the night-walkers in the city. Of course, this came at a high price. It would put a target on the chests of both Knox and Amanda, and I was worried about my ability to protect them from the Coven and the naturi.

FOUR

Danaus found me the next night standing barefoot in my backyard with fire swirling around me. A thick bank of trees encircled my house, blocking the show I was putting on from the view of my closest neighbors. And a show it was. For the past hour I had been conjuring up balls of flames and streaks of fire so that it looked like my body had attracted its own comet. I was trying to replicate what happened on Crete, but to no avail.

At the Palace of Knossos the swell of power from the earth had been so great it pushed into my body and I was able to use it to create fire. That had been different than my usual fire manipulation. Before, the power came from within me, and with time it became exhausting. On Crete, the power came from another source—the earth.

I needed to learn to tap this power source if I was going to have any hope of defeating the naturi. Unfortunately, I was having no luck so far.

I could feel Danaus's eyes on me as I went through dozens of different martial art stances I had learned over the long centuries. I struggled to find a center of peace while calling on my ability at the same time. But there was no peace within the fire. It was pure energy that jumped and burned, full of passion and barely controlled excitement.

"If you move your hand fast enough, I bet you could write your name," Danaus said when he was only a few feet away from me.

Smirking at him over my shoulder, I folded my hands over my chest while my name flared to life in jagged, flickering letters before me. It hovered in the air for a full five seconds before it finally went out.

"Show-off," he muttered, threading a lock of hair behind his ear as the wind picked up.

My long black skirt swayed in the breeze and I let all the fire I had called up dim and then finally go out, plunging the backyard into complete darkness. Only a little light drifted down to us from the house where Tristan was sitting at the computer up on the second floor. Last I had checked, the nightwalker was exploring the world of iTunes with my credit card.

"Practice?" Danaus asked.

"Not quite," I said, looking down at my empty hands. Frustration beat at me until I was nearly clenching my teeth. I couldn't do this alone. I needed help. "Do you remember what happened on Crete? When I used my ability?"

"Yes, the power from the earth consumed you." Danaus cocked his head to the side as he looked at me, taking in my bare feet for the first time. "You're trying to replicate it. Mira, you couldn't control—"

"I know, but I have to learn how to. There has to be a way."

"I thought you said that nightwalker couldn't do earth magic or even sense the earth because your human form died."

"Yeah, well, nightwalkers aren't supposed to be able to control fire either," I said, snapping my finger so that a little teardrop of fire hovered in the air for a second before I extinguished it. "It seems that I'm the exception to more than one rule. I'm a conduit for the powers of the triad, and I can also be a conduit for the powers of the earth. I have to learn to control one of them. As long as Jabari's alive, I don't see it being the powers of the triad, so that leaves me with learning how to control the power I receive from the earth."

"Are you getting anything now?"

I shook my head, causing my red hair to cascade around my face. "Nothing." It was true. I felt nothing whatsoever. There was only the cool grass beneath my feet. There wasn't even the pulse of life.

"Maybe you can only use the power when it is near its height," Danaus said.

I gazed out at the blackness of the yard, staring out toward the trees. For a moment I wondered if there were any naturi watching us, but then released the thought just as quickly. Danaus would have told me. "If that's true, this power won't do me much good even if I learn to control it." I started walking back toward the house with him at my side.

"It could help when we go against the naturi at the next sacrifice."

"Any word on when and where that will be?" I asked as I slowly mounted the stone stairs to the patio. With a wave of my hand, I lit a handful of candles I kept outside for Danaus's benefit. His eyesight was nearly as keen as mine, but I imagined that he would feel at least a little more comfortable in the circle of candlelight.

"No word from Themis yet. The fall equinox is coming up, and our theory is that they will strike then."

"I thought as much." I slumped into a chaise and stared into the candlelight while Danaus chose a chair across from me.

"If you're going to learn how to control the power you get from the earth, you're going to need a teacher," he said, thoughtfully scratching the dark stubble on his chin.

"I doubt I'm going to find someone listed in the yellow pages," I sneered, shoving one hand through my hair to push it out of my eyes.

"True. You need an earth witch."

"Hmmm . . . yeah, that would be a great idea if all the earth witches weren't already sided with the naturi. I'd rather not get a mentor that was trying to kill me at every turn."

"Not all of them are."

Grabbing both arms of the chaise lounge, I pulled myself up until I was sitting on the edge of the seat. "You know of someone," I announced softly.

"Yes."

"Is this person associated with Ryan in any way?" I asked, dreading the answer. I didn't want the head of Themis involved in my training, if it was at all possible.

"No, she's outside of Themis. I met her months ago when I was looking for you. She lives just north of here in Charleston."

"Girlfriend?" I demanded, leaning in close for his answer, but he only snorted and crossed his arms over his chest. "That's right. The powerful Danaus doesn't participate in such base human emotions such as love and lust. You just kill."

"Much like you," he countered quickly.

"No, I loved Michael," I whispered as I pushed to my feet. I had loved my bodyguard, and the naturi stole him from me. "Sometimes living is about taking ugly risks that don't have a snowball's chance in Hell. But all in all, those are the risks truly worth taking."

"I take risks."

"Calculated ones."

"Working with you is a calculated risk?" he demanded, arching one eyebrow at me.

A smile finally teased at my lips as I looked down at him. It was a calculated risk, but one that was only slightly in his favor. We both hated the naturi and we both had a deeply ingrained sense of honor. Beyond that there was little else keeping us from killing each other. "Please contact the earth witch for me. See if she will come to Savannah. I have some questions I would like to ask her."

"Do you want me to bring her here?"

"No!" I caught the panicked flare of my temper and cleared my throat. "Take her to my town house in the city. I'll meet you both there when she arrives. My secret home outside the city is starting to feel significantly less secret than it had before."

It was nearly an hour later before I finally shed my dark shadow so I could travel to my next meeting alone. While I appreciated Danaus's presence when there were so many naturi wandering around, I needed to take care of this next matter alone, though I still had mixed feelings about it.

I meandered through the cemetery with the heels of my boots sinking into the soft earth. The rains that summer had been heavier than usual, leaving the earth feeling like a damp sponge. The graveyard was outside the city limits, but judging by the headstones, was as old as the city herself. Angels wept, their faces streaked with time and wear. Grave markers were worn to the point that the names could be made out only by touch now. I wandered toward the back of the expansive graveyard and crossed a small stone bridge that led to an isolated island in the middle of a large lake.

With the death of my first bodyguard, I had purchased all the plots on the island. Here, I would give my guardians their resting place. Upon reaching the island, I paused before the gravestones of Thomas and Filip. Neither had served me long, preferring to pick fights with creatures they had no business tangling with. There had been nothing I could do to stop their unfortunate deaths.

And then I came to Michael. The last of my bodyguards to die. After he had been hired, I referred to him and my current bodyguard, Gabriel, as my guardian angels. Michael, with the golden hair and sweet smile, looked after me with an unwavering vigilance. He protected me during the daylight hours and chased away the darkness during the night.

Now I simply wanted to weep for him. I should never have brought him with me to England. After it became clear that the naturi were hunting me down in Egypt, I should have sent him straight back to the United States where he and Gabriel would be safe. But instead I kept him close to me out of my own selfishness. And the result was his death.

To make it worse, I didn't even have his body to bury here among his comrades in arms. According to Ryan, his body had been stolen away by the naturi for some bizarre reason.

I knelt down in the damp grass and ran my fingers over the letters of his name etched into the thick marble slab. My fingertips slid over the smooth edges as I tried to recall his crooked smile or the rough feel of the tiny hairs along his arms. Gabriel had taken care of all of the arrangements once he returned to the United States, and I visited as frequently as I could. I didn't want the naturi to see me here. I wouldn't fight them while standing over Michael's grave. My angel deserved his rest. He had earned it.

Behind me a shoe scuffed along the concrete of the bridge that connected the island to the shore. I had sensed Gabriel coming, but he was being polite by making a little noise to announce his arrival. He didn't want to catch me unaware with his new guest.

While they approached, I scanned the entire graveyard to find that we were completely alone. Well, as alone as we could be. I couldn't sense the naturi, and was beginning to wonder if I should have brought Danaus along for the meeting. This was as good a site as any for an ambush.

You trust this one? I sent the question winging into Gabriel's mind. The unexpected words caused him to nearly stumble but he quickly recovered.

Less than the others before him, but more than any of the others I was considering. He concentrated on making the sentence as clear in his head as possible so I could read it. Gabriel wasn't a telepath, but I had taught him to arrange his thoughts in such a way that I could easily read his response without the clutter of other thoughts and emotions.

"I pray to you do not regret the choices you've made that have brought you to this point," I announced in the air without turning from Michael's empty grave.

"I think I have stepped beyond the point of regrets," came a reply from a soft, even voice I had never heard before. The accent was Asian, possibly Japanese. I hadn't spent a great deal of time in the region, so my knowledge of the dialects and accents was weak.

Wiping all expression from my pale face, I turned and looked at my newest companion. He stood just over five and a half feet tall, with a slender build and short spiky black hair. His age was hard to determine. He looked like he was in his mid-twenties, but the images and memories running through his mind spoke of a life lived much longer. He had to be closer to ten years older, at least.

"As I am sure that you have been told, my name is Matsui," he said with a slight bow of his head.

"Yes, Gabriel also told me that you came looking for me and that you already know what I am," I replied, keeping a comfortable distance between us. "How do you know of me?" As I asked the question, I sat within his mind. I could not read many of his thoughts, as I didn't understand the language, but I saw the images in his head. He had known other nightwalkers.

"You are a legend around the globe. Even to the Soga Clan," he replied.

"A clan of nightwalkers?" Gabriel asked, coming to stand beside me.

"Similar to a family, but larger and more complex," I said, folding my arms over my stomach. "The system of honor and politics is more . . . complicated in the East, so the Coven has been largely content to let them cling to their old ways so long as it doesn't spread to the rest of the world."

"And even in my small part of the world, you are known," Matsui commented.

"The Grim Reaper in known the world around, but I would still not seek him out. Why have you come looking for me?" I countered.

"I wish to join those who guard you during the daylight hours. I heard of Gabriel's position a couple years ago and hoped that you would be in need of another guardian. I served in a similar capacity to the Soga Clan. I am well-versed in various fighting styles—"

"I'm not concerned about your ability to defend yourself or me. If Gabriel wasn't convinced of your skills, you would never have made it this far. I want to know why you would leave the Soga Clan to join me."

"Word reached the Eastern nightwalkers of the naturi and their attempts to break free, yet few are willing to help," he said with a frown and a slight shake of his head. "Only three nightwalkers that I know of have gone to the Coven. I came here looking for you. It is said you defeated the naturi in the past, and I wish to help you defeat them now."

"Does the Soga Clan know you are here now?" Gabriel demanded, shifting his weight from his left foot to his right. I could feel his anxiety rolling off him in thick waves. He didn't trust Matsui.

"I have their blessing."

Gabriel looked up at me and frowned. In the past, he had carefully hunted down the other bodyguards, selecting them from retired Special Forces members of the United States armed forces. He had even found bodyguards in former club bouncers skilled in various fighting styles. But each one he hunted down he personally selected for a specific reason. Matsui was the first to ever come looking for him, and it set him ill at ease.

"You may have a misunderstanding of this particular position," I explained. "Gabriel does not fight the naturi. He protects me during the daylight hours when I travel. He protects me from other humans that would harm me if I was discovered." It was a partial lie. Gabriel had fought the naturi in England, but he was never meant to. He should have never been in that position in the first place, but I screwed up, resulting in Michael's death.

"Protecting you as you strive to defeat the naturi would be an honor," he said with another bow of his head.

I frowned. "All my bodyguards begin and end where you are standing. I've buried more than I care to count, all of them dying in some fight or battle. It's a short life and a violent end."

"But it is my life and my right to spend it how I wish, no matter how short it is," Matsui replied, giving me almost verbatim the same answer that Gabriel gave me years ago.

I smiled and Gabriel snorted, shaking his head beside me as a reluctant smile lifted his own lips. "Very well," I agreed with a nod. "You've got the job. For now, you take orders from Gabriel. You sleep and eat when and where he tells you to. And if at any time he thinks you are a threat to my existence, he will not hesitate to eliminate you. No questions asked."

"I understand. Thank you for this opportunity. I will not disappoint you."

"Go ahead back to the car," Gabriel ordered.

Matsui nodded and headed back across the bridge as Gabriel and I turned toward the headstone with Michael's name on it.

"I found the angel that you were looking for, and the marble sculptor has begun working on it," Gabriel softly said. "He said that it would take a few months."

"That's fine. We're in no hurry," I murmured, sliding my hand into the open hand of my angel's.

Gabriel squeezed my hand once, his thumb brushing across the top. "Michael would not have any regrets about what happened. Don't make him your regret."

"He was slipping, Gabriel," I whispered, finally giving voice to the guilt that had been eating away at me. "I should have seen it happening. Or maybe I did and just hadn't been willing to admit it until it was too late. He was losing his focus, getting too wrapped up in me. He shouldn't have been there. Neither of you should have been in England."

"We were at your side, which is where we should always be," Gabriel firmly said.

A soft sigh escaped me as I squeezed his hand before releasing it. "Maybe Matsui will last a little longer than some of the others. At least he has been around other nightwalkers in the past."

"Do you trust him?"

A little laugh escaped me as I bumped my shoulder against his. "Not at all."

"I was just checking. Afraid you'd lost your mind for a moment."

"No, I don't trust him, but then there hasn't been a single one that we trusted at the onset."

"It seems that you're becoming more popular. A Japanese nightwalker clan has heard of you. Am I going to be fighting off guardian wannabes with a stick?" Gabriel teased, but I could tell by his tone that he was partially serious.

"The Soga Clan sent Matsui. He's not here because he wants to be here," I said with a shake of my head. "I'm sure they've heard of me. I'm the only nightwalker in existence that can manipulate fire. I'm also six hundred years old. They didn't just hear about me. But I'm sure they just heard about me joining the Coven."

Gabriel paced a couple steps away from me, his heavy steps sinking in the soft earth. He crossed his arms over his strong chest while bending his head to look at the ground in thought. "I don't understand."

"I think this is their way of throwing their support behind

the dark horse on the Coven. When all hell finally breaks loose, I'm the one they expect to survive. Matsui is an emissary, a gift, in a way."

"And you think he will do a good job protecting you because he's been ordered to?"

"He will for the honor of his people. He may be my bodyguard, but he will always be a part of the Soga Clan in some fashion. Matsui will do everything he can to protect me."

"If you're so sure that he will protect you, why don't you trust him?"

"Because I'm not sure that he actually wants to be here, that he wants to be my bodyguard. I like my men to be dedicated, mind, heart, and body. His heart's not in it yet."

"Hopefully that changes fast . . . "

"Or he gains a spot on my little island," I finished, my eyes sweeping over the headstones one last time. There was still room for more.

Five

Nicolai was in the graveyard.

I lingered behind on the island after Gabriel had left, thinking about my last days with Michael. Yet, when I started to cross the bridge to the back of the graveyard, I sensed the lycanthrope's unexpected presence. I halted, my stomach twisting into a knot. He was not supposed to be there. He wasn't supposed to be anywhere near me unless he called ahead of time. With the naturi overrunning the area, the lycanthropes had agreed to leave the city and keep a wide distance from the nightwalkers after the sun set each night. It was the only way we could think of protecting both sides. It wasn't a perfect plan. So far, six nightwalkers and four werewolves had been killed from fighting, including one of Barrett's brothers. The Savannah Pack Alpha was still mourning his loss.

Licking my lips, I turned and headed west, moving away from the werewolf, but Nicolai also changed directions, heading toward me. Yeah, he was looking for me. It was a silly hope, but I had to try.

I didn't sense anyone in the graveyard with us. There was a chance that Nicolai had simply come looking for me over some matter. We'd hardly spoken since I returned from Crete. He had settled in, finding a job at the local college and a new apartment with relative ease. From what Barrett had told me, Nicolai was still struggling to find his place within the local pack, but then this was supposed to be a temporary arrangement. But with Jabari lurking around and the naturi breathing down my neck, I wasn't sure when I would be able to allow the lycan to safely return to his own life outside of Savannah.

Digging in my heels, I changed direction again and started walking toward him. At worst, the naturi had gotten control over the lycanthrope and sent him to kill me. If it was at all possible, I would try to knock Nicolai out and kill the naturi. But my hopes weren't high considering that I would be painfully outnumbered in this situation. I should have brought Danaus along.

I stepped onto one of the winding gravel roads when Nicolai finally came into view. He hadn't changed since I last saw him, my Adonis with an ugly past. His golden blond hair brushed at the collar of his shirt, and his skin seemed a perfect bronze, as if he had been worshiped by the sun. I kept him in Savannah to protect him from the naturi and Jabari, but we both knew that I was only extending his life span by a matter of days.

"Long time no see," he called to me when I stopped in the middle of the road. His pace had slowed to almost a shuffle but he was still drawing closer, his hands shoved into the pockets of his khaki pants.

"Yeah, well, I didn't see much of a future for us," I said, shrugging one shoulder as my eyes continued to sweep over the immediate area, searching for anyone else that might be drawing close for the ambush.

"It's hard to compete with the hunter. He's so determined to have your heart," Nicolai replied, stopping when he was still several yards away from me.

A snort escaped me and I weakly smiled at my companion. "On a pike," I replied, finishing the thought. Danaus's only interest in me was how to finally kill me. "What are you doing here?" I demanded, ending the lighthearted banter we had forced into the tense air.

"He wants only to talk," Nicolai murmured.

"Rowe?"

"No."

"Shit," I hissed, the muscles in my shoulders instantly tensing.

"Me," Jabari said directly behind me.

Spinning around and into a crouch, my skirt flaring out around me, I snarled at Jabari, exposing my fangs to the Coven Elder. I positioned myself between the lycanthrope and the Ancient, ready for the attack. "You can't have him," I growled.

In Venice, Jabari had sent Nicolai to kill me. I knocked the werewolf unconscious and later claimed him as my own in an effort to protect Nicolai from Jabari and the rest of the nightwalker Coven. However, both Nicolai and I knew that I wasn't strong enough to protect him from Jabari should the Ancient ever return to claim him. My only goal had been to extend his life for a little while.

"I can take him back at any time I should choose," Jabari said with a smile. His pale Egyptian robes wavered in the breeze sweeping through the city that night.

"Nicolai, get out of here!" I commanded as I lifted my right hand and conjured up a fireball. The sight of the dancing flames brought a growl from the back of Jabari's throat, forcing the Elder to realize that I was ready to take the defense of the werewolf seriously. The nightwalker seemed too tall, too strong, with his dark brown skin and fierce black eyes. I was in over my head, but I had promised to protect Nicolai with my life, and I was prepared to keep that promise.

"No! It doesn't have to be this way," Nicolai countered. I could hear his footsteps growing closer. I needed him out of there, but he wouldn't leave.

I threw the fireball at the Ancient nightwalker so it landed just before his feet, forcing him to take a couple steps backward. As he moved, I launched myself at him. But he was ready for me. There was no surprising him. Jabari was constantly in my head, he knew my thoughts if he wanted. He grabbed my wrists just before my fingers could reach his neck and tossed me aside like a bag of garbage. My feet slid across the walk, sending up a spray of gravel. The second I stopped sliding, I was moving toward him again. I spun in a roundhouse kick, hoping to get him off balance again, but he caught my ankle and pushed me backward. Landing on my butt, I snarled up at him, preparing to push to my feet. But I couldn't.

Jabari raised a single hand toward me, and I could no longer move. The nightwalker had the power to physically control me like a puppet on a string. He had just been toying with me before, allowing me to get my hopes up that I actually had a chance in defeating him. Now he was ready to crush me.

"You can't have him," I growled, still fighting his control over me. Jabari was too strong, though. I could feel his power sliding through my entire frame, soaking into muscle and tissue until he was a part of me.

"I could make you kill him for me if I wanted it," he taunted, taking a couple steps closer to where I sat. "I could force you to rip his heart out and set him on fire." As he spoke, a surge of power rushed through me, sending a wave of pain through my frame. At the same time, a voice in my head commanded that I create fire. I tried to fight it, but there was no fighting it. A ring of fire sprang up around Nicolai.

"Stop it!" I screamed, fighting his will. The flames shrank, but I couldn't completely extinguish them no matter how hard I tried. The ring of fire closed in around Nicolai until it was only a couple feet away from him on all sides, and still he said nothing. He knew that we were both trapped by Jabari's will. "Stop it, Jabari! Your fight is with me. Not him. Leave Nicolai out of this."

A secretive little smile appeared on the Ancient's full lips for a moment as he stared down at me. And then the fire disappeared, as well as his presence within my body. "I didn't come here to take Nicolai from you," he admitted with an indifferent shrug. "I can take him at any time, but for now my concern is with the naturi."

"What! You came here with Nicolai to talk to me about the naturi, not to steal him back?" I demanded, shock keeping me from pushing back to my feet.

An evil smile twisted Jabari's full lips and danced in his dark eyes. "Yes. You're the one that started this fight. Not me."

"You're a real asshole, you know that," I snapped, pushing back to my feet and dusting off my black skirt. "I've been under attack here since leaving Crete and then I have you pop into town with Nicolai in tow. I don't need this kind of torment, Jabari. My hands are already full."

"You should have returned to Venice as I commanded. You would have been protected from the naturi and had none of these worries," he calmly stated.

"But my people in Savannah would not have been. They are my responsibility."

"You're on the Coven now. Your responsibility extends beyond a single city to all of our people."

I shoved both of my hands through my hair and paced a couple steps away from Jabari in frustration before I screamed. There was no winning with him, in a fight or in a discussion. It was never enough. I didn't want to be on the Coven, but I'd had to take the open seat in order to break the bargain that Macaire made with the naturi. Macaire struck a deal that would have the nightwalkers kill the naturi queen, Aurora, so long as the naturi killed Our Liege, stopping him from releasing the Great Awakening early.

"Besides the need to drive me insane, what do you want?" I finally demanded when I had my temper under control.

"The next sacrifice is going to be in a few days. You need to be there to stop it."

"The fall equinox, right?"

"Yes."

"Do you know the location?"

"Machu Picchu."

I nodded. I wasn't surprised. That was just how my luck ran. Machu Picchu was also one of only two holy sites south of the equator. In Peru at this time of year, winter would be drawing to an end, making the holiday the spring equinox there instead of the fall. The spring equinox was a time of rebirth and new beginnings. Peru was also the sight of the last great failure of Aurora's people to come through the door. There was no better time or place for her to make her grand reappearance.

"Is there a plan?" I asked, almost afraid to hear the answer. The last plan the Coven had come up with to defeat the naturi was to use me as bait in an attempt to draw at the leader of the naturi.

"I would like you to be there early. Hunt Rowe. Stop him."

"Will you be joining us on the hunt?" I inquired, knowing the answer before he gave it.

"Eventually."

I closed my eyes and shook my head. Yeah, Danaus and I were to be the foot soldiers in this attack. We would sweep in and take on the naturi. And then when Rowe was preparing to complete the sacrifice, Jabari would appear and help to take down the consort king of the naturi, stopping the arrival of Aurora. At least, that's how I'm sure he envisioned it. But then I doubted any of this had happened the way Jabari had envisioned it so far.

"Mira!" Nicolai cried, causing my head to snap up. The first thing I noticed was that Jabari was gone, but then, he had the ability to pop in and out of a place at will.

"What's wrong?" I demanded, briskly walking toward him.

"The naturi," he called back, causing my feet to come to a sliding halt. I seemed doomed to have someone forever shouting those two words at me.

I forced myself to take a step closer to him as I looked around the night-drenched cemetery. "Are they here?"

"No," he said, pressing the palm of his right hand against his temple. "They're calling us."

Biting off a curse, I rushed to his side. I cupped his cheeks with both of my hands as he slowly fell to his knees. He was gritting his teeth as beads of sweat dotted his forehead. His pounding heart and ragged breathing filled the night air.

"Are they close?" I demanded, tilting the werewolf's head so he was forced to look up at me.

"N-No . . . in the city."

"Can they read your thoughts? Are they searching for me?" I barely resisted the urge to give him a little shake when his attention seemed to drift away from me.

"No, just calling. Want us to come to the city . . . Forsyth Park."

"Listen to me, Nico," I murmured, kneeling on the ground before him. "You don't have to obey them. They don't own you. They aren't your masters. You *don't* have to go to them."

He sucked in a deep, cleansing breath through his nose and pushed the air out again through his clenched teeth. He was trembling beneath my hands as sweat started to cover his body. He was fighting it as best he could, but if there were any naturi close by, Nicolai didn't have a chance at avoiding them. I had watched the Savannah Alpha give in to the call, and I knew few lycanthropes that were stronger or more stubborn than Barrett.

"They're miles away. You're stronger than they are," I continued, desperate to free him from their siren song. Kneeling beside him on the ground, I was so close now and he was holding on by a thread. If that thread snapped, he would have his fangs into my throat before I had a chance to move.

Nicolai blinked and looked up at me with copper-colored

eyes. I was losing him to the animal inside. I swallowed back the fear that was rising in the form of a lump in the back of my throat.

"Stay with me, Nico. Think of Venice," I said, trying to conjure up a purely human memory for him to cling to as he fought the naturi's hold on him.

"Venice . . . ?" he bit out between clenched teeth. He closed his eyes and shivered. "Nightwalkers everywhere. Air was thick with blood." His upper lip curled and I caught a flash of his right canine as it started to lengthen.

"No, not that part of Venice," I said, running my thumbs over his cheekbones. "I meant where it was just you and me together, alone in the hotel. No naturi. No nightwalkers."

Nicolai's eyes opened and I watched the copper recede to brown. He was coming back to me, fighting their hold as he recalled the memory of us having sex following a narrow escape from both the Coven and the naturi. Neither of us had spoken about that night since it happened. In fact, after returning to Savannah myself, I had gone out of my way to avoid Nicolai, and not entirely because of the naturi. I hadn't been quite sure what to say after our extremely brief encounter, particularly since the night before that, Nicolai had tried to kill me.

"You were beautiful that night," he said in a low, rough voice. He lifted his left hand and laid it over my wrist, his thumb caressing the inside of my arm.

"I like to think I still am," I replied with a smirk. I needed his mood to lighten, needed to be sure he was completely with me before I released my hold on his face.

"You were a long, pale line of white light," he continued, ignoring my comment. His eyes traveled over my face slowly, as if he was suddenly becoming reacquainted with me, before finally meeting my gaze again. "You've avoided me."

"It was for the best. The . . . the naturi," I said, trying to swallow the last word. I had just won him away from that dark race, I didn't want to lose him all over again. "They're making it difficult for everyone."

"You don't even call. You send Gabriel with all your messages," he countered. The hand encircling my wrist tightened, as if he was preparing to hold me in place in the event that I tried to quickly move away from him. "You started acting cold and distant while we were still in Venice. It's because of what my sister did."

I flinched at the mention of his sister, and I know he felt it in my hands, which were still cupping his face. It wasn't his sister so much as him. While in Venice, I discovered that Nicolai had come into Jabari's keeping because his sister and a few others were aiding the naturi. Nicolai traded places with his sister when Jabari demanded to take one of the traitors as a servant. Of course, I didn't discover any of this until after we'd had sex. I believed Nicolai when he said that he didn't help the naturi, but a part of me wondered if he had worked to protect his sister by keeping what she was doing a secret. While I could understand it if he did, I knew that a part of me would never forgive it. The result was an uneasy coldness I felt around Nicolai that I struggled to overcome.

"It's not your sister," I said in my most reasonable tone. "I have no doubt that she has paid for her crimes, and I won't make you pay for them as well."

I released my hold on his face and shoved my free hand through my hair in frustration. How was I supposed to delicately put this? *It was just casual sex. We both needed to blow off a little steam. Baby, you were great in bed, but I'm not looking for anything long-term.* I preferred to not hurt his feelings, but I also didn't have time for this.

"Venice was great," I lamely started again, inwardly cursing my ineptitude. You'd think after living for six hundred years, I'd be better at this.

"Venice was amazing. I thought we were great together. I also thought that since you sent me to your domain, you would want to continue what we started."

"Nicolai, I—" I started, then stopped. "My main reason for sending you here was that it would be easiest to protect you from my own domain. It's not that I don't like you, it's just that . . . " My voice faded as I noticed the lines from the corners of his eyes growing, while one corner of his mouth quirked in a smile. He was laughing at me. "You're just playing with me, aren't you?"

"Totally," he said, his head dropping back as a bark of laughter finally escaped him. I punched him in the arm and then fell back to sit in the middle of the gravel graveyard road, chuckling at myself. Nicolai sat up, his shoulder still lightly shaking as he released my wrist. "You were so serious and scared shitless," he teased.

"Asshole."

"Mira, sweetie, you're great and I appreciate you bringing me here, but it was just sex," he said, stretching out one hand toward me.

I batted his hand away, trying very hard not to smile at him. I felt like such an idiot. "No kidding it was just sex."

"You're just not my type. I prefer to date women that can't kill me with a snap of their fingers," he said, grabbing my hand when I tried to smack him away a second time. "I'm hoping this means you'll at least stop avoiding me."

A sad smile finally lifted the corners of my mouth as I

looked at my handsome companion; a ray of golden sunlight in a dark, dreary cemetery. If he thought I'd been avoiding him because of our brief encounter, I wasn't about to disabuse him of that notion when the truth was far darker. "Not until the naturi have been taken care of. It's too dangerous," I said, giving his hand a light squeeze as if to soften the blow of my words. It wasn't his fault that he lost control when the naturi were around. The race had the natural ability to control all lycanthropes when they were close. The only reason Nicolai was able to fight it that night was because they had been several miles away.

"Speaking of which," I said, suddenly recalling what had started this conversation in the first place, "I'm assuming the naturi are no longer calling you, since you've gotten this good laugh in."

"Yeah, they stopped a little while ago," he confirmed, pushing to his feet. He extended his left hand to me and pulled me up as well.

I dusted off the back of my skirt as my gaze scanned the area once again. As far as I could tell, we were completely alone in the graveyard. But then, I couldn't sense the naturi, nor could I sense Jabari. "Do you know what they wanted?"

"It sounded like a hunt of some sort in Forsyth Park. They didn't want us in human form. I had an overwhelming urge to shift and . . . hunt."

"Hunt nightwalkers," I growled, looking down at the ground. Closing my eyes, I reached out, searching the night for Tristan. Some part of me needed to know that the young one was safe and away from the naturi. I didn't get what I wanted.

Mira! My name reached me as a frantic scream as I made

contact with my ward. *Help! Naturi . . . shifters . . . every-where! Hurry!* Tristan broke off contact, but not before I caught a flash of the large white fountain at the center of Forsyth Park. Tristan wasn't alone. There was another night-walker with him and it felt like Amanda, but I wasn't sure. I knew now that the naturi had summoned up the lycanthropes to hunt down Tristan and whatever other nightwalkers were currently in Forsyth Park.

"I have to go. The naturi are hunting nightwalkers in the city. Tristan!" I said, turning toward where I had parked my car near the entrance to the cemetery.

"Go," Nicolai called after me, but the word had already begun to fade when it reached my ears as I started running.

Tristan was in trouble, and I was going to happily tear apart anything that dared lay a hand on what was mine.

Six

The fight was over by the time I drove the twenty minutes back into the city from the cemetery, but the damage left behind turned my stomach. I parked my car more than a block away from Forsyth Park, as the entire area had been ringed by flashing blue and red lights from the police cars and ambulances. Cloaking myself from prying eyes, I slipped between the police cars and entered the area.

I flinched at the sight of the first body. Naked, he had been disemboweled before his head was torn from his body. He was one of the unlucky lycanthropes that answered the call of the naturi. The moment he died, his body had naturally changed back into human form. I suppressed a shudder as a white cloth was laid over the body and pushed on, moving deeper into the park.

Tristan? I hesitantly began. I had not tried to contact him earlier for fear of distracting him at a critical moment. But now that I knew the naturi were gone from this place, I needed to hear his sweet voice in my head.

Here . . . he whispered. His mental touch was weak and thready, but it was close. I followed the feeling toward a small cluster of EMT workers who knelt around a person leaning up against a tree. The bark above their heads had been gored by long claws, scoring it down to its pale, pulp interior.

"Tristan." His name escaped me in breathless relief before I could stop myself, revealing myself to those close by that could hear me. Two of the three human heads popped up in surprise to find someone unknown standing so close to the injured victim.

"Do you know this person?" one man inquired, pushing to his feet.

"Yes, he's . . . my brother," I said, hesitating for only a heartbeat. I looked too young to pass myself off as his mother, even though I technically was, within the family. "Let me see him." I followed the command up with a slight mental push to all three of the EMT workers, who then rose to their feet and took a step away from Tristan.

Kneeling before him, I discovered that the nightwalker was covered in blood. His dark navy shirt was shredded and large patches of white gauze and tape were placed over his neck, arms, and chest. Another patch was placed on the thigh of his left leg. Just by the look of him and the destruction wrought within the park, it appeared as if he and a few others had been attacked almost solely by lycanthropes.

"What happened?" I asked, grabbing the arm of the closest EMT worker. I put all three of the workers under my mind control so Tristan could feed in peace. I appreciated their tender ministrations as they undoubtedly helped to slow his blood loss, but both he and I appreciated their blood donation more.

"We were cutting through the park, heading toward the

Dark Room, when the naturi attacked us," he said in a low voice, accepting the EMT worker's wrist I offered him. "There were only two of them, and then the shifters attacked. There had to have been at least a dozen, all in wolf form. We didn't have a chance."

"Who is this 'we'?" I asked, then frowned as I caught him the moment his fangs sank into the man's wrist, effectively catching him with his mouth full.

Four of us. Amanda, me, Kevin, and Charles. I could also feel a small sigh escape him as the blood rushed down his throat. It would go a long way to speeding up his healing. *We were headed to the Dark Room to meet up with Knox.*

Stay here. Feed. I ordered, pushing to my feet. Tristan took over mind control of the three EMT workers while I wandered through the carnage. Park benches were smashed, deep furrows were dug in the earth from where bodies had been thrown to the ground. And across everything were claw marks.

I quickly walked the entire length of the park, searching for every body, every wounded fighter. Six lycanthropes and a blond-haired nightwalker by the name of Charles were killed. Amanda and Kevin were nowhere to be found. Neither were the two naturi that Tristan said he'd seen.

Tristan, where's Amanda and Kevin? I asked, trying to steady my thoughts.

Kevin ran to the Dark Room for help. The lycans followed. The naturi took Amanda. There was a hopeless note to his thoughts. He didn't plead with me to find her, to bring her back, though I know that request was hovering on the edge of his thoughts. We both knew that if the naturi had bothered to take her, then they planned to use her to get to me. It was also highly unlikely that the young nightwalker was going to survive the encounter, even if the naturi were trying to keep her alive for some kind of exchange.

Finish feeding, and then take my car back to the house. I'll be in contact, I instructed, trying to deaden the anger boiling over inside of me.

She was going to join the family. She planned to tell you tonight, Tristan said, twisting the knife that I felt buried in my gut. I knew that she had planned to regardless of the danger to herself. I had warned her about the naturi and the threat of the Coven, but never thought the naturi would stoop to kidnapping another to get at me. I thought they would simply kill anything that stood between them and me.

I . . . I will find her, I found myself telling him, if only to ease some of the pain I could feel radiating off of him. Tristan truly did like Amanda. He liked her smile and the joy she got out of waking each night and finding that she was still a nightwalker.

And I knew that I would eventually find her. I just couldn't promise him that I would find her alive.

With Tristan settled, I set about adjusting the memories of the police, detectives, and emergency workers that flocked to the scene. I posed as a detective, giving orders and mental shoves where needed. It was the biggest massacre I had tried to cover up in recent years under the watchful gaze of so many humans. I was desperately trying to convince a horde of people that a group of teenagers had been attacked by a pack of rabid dogs. Lucky for me, these terrified humans were willing to believe anything that made more sense than things like nightwalkers and werewolves.

After close to an hour of work, my eyes finally fell on a familiar face: Archibald Deacon, coroner for the city of Savannah and the surrounding county. He would help me cover up this mess before someone started running blood tests.

"Why am I not surprised to find you in the middle of this nightmare?" Archibald said, running one hand over his balding head as he narrowed his dark brown eyes at me. I noticed a fine trembling to his fingers as he lowered his hand back down to his side. Savannah had never seen such destruction before, not since the days of the war.

"I wasn't a part of this mess, but I will need your help cleaning it up. We need to get these bodies back to your morgue before anyone starts demanding tests and shipping the dead to the hospital."

"No one is shipping anyone to the hospital who belongs in my morgue," he said, his large round body seeming to puff up at the very notion of anyone invading his domain of the dead. "What about the police? The evidence?"

"I've adjusted memories where possible and I've already called Daniel. He'll keep an eye on things for me," I replied. Detective Daniel Crowley had worked with me in the past to settle small matters like the questionable death of a nightwalker or a lycanthrope that got to the police before reaching me or Barrett. But this was bigger than anything we had dealt with before, and it was going to take most of the night.

While Archie pulled his team together and got the bodies ushered off to the morgue as quickly as humanly possible, I finished up with the cops and any of the onlookers that had wandered too close for my liking. There was nothing I could do about the local news crews that were camped just beyond the perimeter. Their cameras caught every body bag and every ambulance and meat wagon that pulled away from the scene. I caught only snippets of what the media was being told, but by their tone, it didn't sound as if the cops were completely buying the story of the roving pack of rabid dogs. I know it didn't sound very believable, but it was the only thing I could think of that would account for the claw and fang marks slashed across the bodies.

Sunrise was only a few hours away when I finally reached the morgue with the last of the bodies. Archie got them settled in the examination room in the basement and sent all of his assistants home for the night with the promise that they would start the tests later that morning. I slid into one of the hard plastic chairs, resting my elbows on my knees and my face in my hands. It felt like my entire body was shaking from exhaustion. So many minds infiltrated and altered throughout the night, so many memories tweaked so that the carnage was blurred and the horror dulled. I wished I could forget about it all as well.

Six lycans and one nightwalker killed. A second nightwalker missing. Tristan wounded. It was only from a call from Knox while I was looking over the park that I discovered Kevin had made it the Dark Room, but there were still questions as to whether he would survive the next few hours.

"Mira, it's late. You can go home. I'll keep things under control here," Archie said as he eased into a cushioned chair behind the battered desk to my right. He sighed heavily and then began shuffling around different sets of papers. The coroner would run the blood tests himself, using human blood he had in stock already so that no one would discover the true identity of the vampire and lycanthropes within his custody. As soon as it was possible, all seven of the bodies would go into the oven and be cremated.

"I wish I could," I muttered. I still had one more meeting

that night, and it wasn't going to be pretty. In fact, he was already there, and I could sense his temperament before he even entered the basement. "It would be best if you left here for a little while."

"I need to start these tests," Archie argued.

I lifted my head and frowned at him. We were both exhausted and I could understand his desire to start what was going to be a long list of doctored tests just to protect the identity of my people and those of the lycanthropes. However, I knew it would be best if he was not around at the moment. "Barrett is here to identify the victims. You need to leave."

"Oh," he whispered, then pushed to his feet. Just before Archie could escape, the double doors exploded open and Barrett entered the room, his face a mask of barely contained fury. And I couldn't blame him. During the past month, four members of his pack had been slaughtered by the naturi, including one of his own family members. And after tonight's massacre, their numbers had been decimated.

"M-Mira will take the names," Archie said in a low voice as he slid around Barrett and out the door.

Normally, Barrett was a calm, even-tempered werewolf. He was a good, strong leader, a steady protector of his people. But the recent deaths had shattered his control and left him snarling at anything that moved. I had called him on the ride over to the morgue. The conversation was brief simply because I knew we would have a longer one when he arrived.

Barrett walked from table to table, pulling back the bloodstained white sheets that covered each body. His fist grew tighter with each death he was forced to look in the face, their sightless eyes closed but still seeming to stare through us both. A low growl rumbled from his throat as he reached the final body. I had expected it. It was Will, the youngest of his three brothers and the second brother to die in the past two months.

I remained silent, watching him, wishing I could remain unnoticed while he inwardly grieved for his dead brother and the other members of his pack. He shoved both hands through his chocolate brown hair and sucked in a deep breath in an effort to regain control of his emotions. Reluctantly, he moved toward a covered table that was somewhat off to the side.

"That one doesn't belong to you," I said in a low voice, drawing his narrowed gaze to my face for the first time. I barely suppressed a shiver.

"So, you've finally lost one of your own," he growled.

"One is dead, another lays dying, a third was severely injured, and still another was kidnapped and is most likely being tortured as we speak," I replied, hating myself for being drawn into the argument. He was hurting from the deaths that had plagued his people recently.

"Two of my brothers have been slaughtered in as many months! A third of my pack has been decimated by nightwalkers. My own mother and sisters have been forced to hide in another city while we die at your hands!" he shouted, finally losing his temper.

"Your pack attacked us," I said evenly. I wished I could show him more sympathy and compassion, but I had my own people to protect. I was afraid of saying something here and now in a moment of compassion that would only trap my people at a later date.

"Because we've been under the control of the naturi."

"And what do you expect us to do? Let you kill us because it's not your fault?"

"I thought you were supposed to be doing something about the naturi. I've talked to the other packs and not one has had the trouble we've had. Some lycans have gone missing, but the body count is nothing like what we've experienced."

I stepped away from the desk and closed the distance between us by a few feet. "Barrett, they're trying to separate us," I said softly. "They want us fighting amongst ourselves instead of fighting them."

"We are fighting each other, and my people are losing! We're trapped, fighting you, fighting the naturi. Why? Why here? Wh—" Barrett's rant was suddenly cut off as he stared at me. In that horrible moment he realized exactly why his people were being slaughtered. The naturi were hunting me, using the lycanthropes as cannon fodder. In my battles with the lycans, I had managed to avoid killing any of them, but it was becoming more difficult. The naturi were growing desperate, throwing more and more shifters at us in an attempt to overwhelm us with sheer volume.

"They're still hunting you, aren't they?" Barrett demanded in a low voice that scraped across my skin like sandpaper. "They were hunting for you at the Dark Room two months ago, and they've been hunting for you since you returned here more than a month ago."

"They need me dead," I admitted, balling my hands into fists, hating to say the words aloud. "I can stop them from opening the door that will set all of their kind free."

"But why come back here? Why not stay surrounded by your own kind? Can't your Coven protect you?" he countered, taking a step toward me.

"I'll not be run from my home by the naturi," I snapped.

"But you're killing my people!"

"Don't do this to us, Barrett," I cautioned, feeling myself getting boxed into a corner, though he had yet to move. "We've worked well together over the years. Our people have learned to respect each other."

My only warning was a low growl before Barrett crossed the distance between us in a couple long, quick strides. He grabbed both of my upper arms and kept walking until he slammed me into the cinder-block wall behind me. Stars exploded before my eyes as my head hit the wall, just before darkness threatened to swamp me.

"Respect! Why haven't you shown my people a little more respect? You're responsible for each and every death because you've—"

"Because I've what? Refused to lay down and die for you? My death won't stop the naturi. It won't save your mother or your sisters or your pack."

"It would buy us some time," he snarled, his brown eyes turning the same shade as liquid copper.

"To do what? Fight back?" We both knew how effective that would be.

His hands tightened on my arms for a moment, threatening to break bones before loosening again. "Why did you have to come back?" he whispered. He was beyond frustrated. His people were dying and there was little he could do to stop it.

"This is my home. I have nowhere else to go," I admitted, feeling as if something was tearing in the back of my throat. It was a truth I'd been reluctant to face. I no longer had a safe haven from the world other than my home in Savannah. Two of the other three members of the Coven wanted me dead, and the third member simply wanted to control my every move and thought. The naturi were hounding my every step. I had more enemies than I cared to count, and too few allies.

"Leave here, Mira. Find some other place to hide and take the damned naturi with you," Barrett bit out. His hands once again tightened on my arms, bruising my pale flesh.

"You can't force me out," I said through clenched teeth. "This is my home and my people are here. I have a right to protect them."

"As much as I have a right to protect my people from you and the naturi. You have the power to save both my people and your own—leave here," he argued, anger growing in his voice, thickening his beautiful southern accent so that the vowels collided with one another.

"I can't leave yet. The naturi have a member of my family. I won't leave her in their hands to be tortured. I have to at least try to get her back." It was a suicide mission, but I had to try. I owed Amanda that much. I had offered her a place in my family, waved my so-called protection in her face.

"Then do it without killing another one of my people. We've died enough for you. Why don't you try getting rid of the naturi instead of hiding from them?"

"I'm no coward, if that's what you're implying, were-wolf," I snarled, shoving him off of me. Barrett stumbled backward a few steps before turning and curling his upper lip so that I could see his elongated canines. "I've fought the naturi more times than I'd care to remember. I've fought them and suffered. My people have died protecting your kind and humans."

"So now you're looking for my gratitude?" he incredulously demanded.

"No, I'm looking for a little patience."

"My patience ran out when my brothers started dying. Find your missing vampire. Kill all the naturi. Leave here and never return. I don't care what you have to do, but if another one of my pack dies, the naturi won't have to call us any longer. It will be open season on you and all nightwalkers within Savannah."

Barrett then stalked out of the morgue without looking back at me and his dead brethren.

I slid down the wall until I sat on the cold linoleum floor. Wrapping my arms around my bent legs, I rest my forehead on my knees. He was right. I was as much responsible for the dead bodies surrounding me at that moment as the naturi. I should never have come back. I should have found another way to deal with the naturi while we waited for the next sacrifice and hunted for Rowe. I had just been afraid that if I went to the Coven, they would have been happy to use me as bait in an effort to draw out the one-eyed naturi.

Barrett wanted me to leave, and I planned to abide by his wishes. I had no choice. The next sacrifice was only a few nights away. But I couldn't leave my beloved Savannah yet. I had to find Amanda first. If I could save her and exterminate the naturi in just one quick foray, I could leave my city with a small feeling of peace. However, I still had to first convince Danaus to help me.

Seven

A sigh escaped me as I slipped out of the taxi and walked to the Dark Room. Sunrise was growing close and I was tired. Fortunately, this was my last stop of the night, and then I could go home for some rest.

The line to get in the Dark Room was gone, and the night-walker bouncer was seated on a black bar stool outside the entrance, with a handheld game system gripped between his two meaty fists. The Dark Room had become a quiet place during the past couple of months. The lycanthropes had stopped attending and fewer nightwalkers appeared, fearful of being trapped in one place should the naturi suddenly show up. When the bouncer finally saw me, he jerked to his feet and shoved the game into the back pocket of his jeans. I only smiled and patted him on the shoulder as I walked by.

In the entrance, between the two coat checks on either side of the room, there was a splatter of blood on the floor. I followed the trail across the dance floor, which was currently empty, toward one of the back rooms. The half-dozen nightwalkers in the club were ensconced in the dark booths, whispering about the latest naturi attack. Before heading into the back, I paused to order the bartender to mop up the blood before it dried. Spilled blood might not have been a problem to a bunch of nightwalkers, but I preferred not to leave our unique DNA lying around. I had spent too many years protecting our secret to lose everything now to a stupid mistake.

Gritting my teeth, I entered the room where I already sensed Knox. He stood over the dying nightwalker with his hands on his hips and a dark frown on his lips. His black shirt was soaked with blood and clinging to his tense frame. There was also a smudge of blood across his left cheekbone.

"There's nothing that we can do," he announced when I shut the door behind me. I looked around the room to find three other nightwalkers in there, lining the back wall. Six humans were collapsed on the floor near them, a sickly shade of white. The blood donors. The humans were breathing heavily and their heartbeats were sluggish from their blood loss.

"Get them in cars," I ordered. "Take them to at least three separate hospitals. They need blood." I didn't need a bunch of humans dying because of this naturi attack as well.

The nightwalkers jumped into motion, picking up the unconscious humans and carrying them out of the club while I turned my attention back to Knox and the dying Kevin.

"There's nothing we can do without some medical help from the humans," Knox admitted, rubbing his chin with one bloody hand. "His heart was nearly ripped from his chest. His wounds are too deep and too numerous. We can't keep enough blood inside of him to get him to heal."

In other words, Kevin would never survive the daylight hours. When the sun rose, his soul would fly from his body while the blood that Knox had fought to get into Kevin finished leaking out. When the sun set again, Kevin's soul would be unable to find its way back to its body and he would be officially dead.

I didn't bother to ask if there was any other way, or if Knox had tried everything. There was no reason to try to keep a steady stream of blood donors marching through the door until the sun finally peeked over the horizon. Both Knox and I had seen enough mortal wounds in our long lifetimes to know when the end was near and fighting it was futile.

Kevin didn't stir on the blood-soaked sofa where he laid. I could feel the faint flutter of his soul within his fragile frame. His skin had already turned an ugly shade of gray under the coating of blood. Towels had been pressed to his chest and stomach to slow the blood, but they were already saturated. There was nothing we could do now but watch him die.

Shoving one hand through my hair in frustration, I paced away from this nightwalker to the opposite side of the room. Helplessness ate away at me, filling me with nervous energy. Not for the first time, I wondered if my return to Savannah had been a mistake.

Sitting in one of the chairs positioned near the sofa, I leaned forward and rested my elbows on my knees. I would stay as long as I could. I would hold this death watch with Knox. Unfortunately, we couldn't leave Kevin's body laying around during the daylight hours. If someone broke into the Dark Room while we were sleeping and found the body, we would all be in trouble of discovery. If Kevin didn't die within the next hour, I would have to finish the job so we'd have enough time to get his corpse to Archie before the sun rose. I would have to kill Kevin. It was my responsibility.

"You don't have to stay," Knox said, settling in the chair next to me.

"It's the one place I belong tonight," I murmured. "I will be the one to finish this if necessary."

"He mentioned Tristan when he was still conscious. If Tristan was with them, I think you should be with him right now," Knox said.

I frowned, looking at my bloodstained hands. "Tristan wasn't wounded that badly. He'll survive the morning with no trouble." I paused and licked my lips, wondering how much Kevin had told him of the fight. I still didn't know much, but there was potentially one piece of the puzzle that Knox was ignorant of. "Amanda was with them as well. She was taken by the naturi."

"What do you mean 'taken'?" he demanded, pushing to the edge of his chair.

"I mean taken. Kidnapped. Captured."

Knox jumped to his feet and paced away from the chair to the opposite end of the room. His rage beat against me in that small room even though he never said a word. He was a smart guy. He knew that Amanda had been taken as bait to get at me. He also knew that I couldn't risk my life for one nightwalker when I still had to go to the site of the sacrifice and save all nightwalkers from the threat of the naturi.

"I liked her," he finally said into the air, his back still to me. There was the sound of defeat in his voice. "She was always a bit impulsive, but she was a good person, followed orders."

"Don't talk like that!" I snapped, getting him to jerk around to look at me. "She's not dead yet. I plan to—"

A sharp knock at the door broke off my words. Before I

could say anything else, the bartender poked his head into the room.

"Mira, Barrett is here to see you."

Surprised by the lycanthrope's unexpected appearance, I automatically did a quick scan of the bar to discover that he had not come alone. At least a dozen lycanthropes accompanied him. This wasn't going to be pretty.

With a frown pulling at the corner of my lips, I rose and followed the bartender back into the main room with Knox close on my heels. The lycanthropes were spread out around the room, while Barrett stood in the center of the dance floor. Apparently, phone calls had been made and the pack called together. Nicolai stood off to one side, looking somewhat uncomfortable. I had a feeling that he was afraid he would be forced to choose between the pack he was now a part of and the debt he owed me for saving his life.

The nightwalkers that had been in the booths were on their feet and gathered on the opposite side of the room, looking just as aggressive as the lycans. No one was speaking. Even the music had been turned off, leaving the nightclub encased in an uncomfortable silence.

"Barrett," I said with a nod of my head as I stepped onto the dance floor with him.

"We've come to escort you from the city," he announced. "You're the only reason why the naturi are here. You're the reason that my people are dying. It's time for this to stop."

"I'm not leaving."

As I spoke those three words, a growl rose from the shifters that lined two of the walls, while a matching hiss went up from the nightwalkers. Tension in the room spiked to mind-crushing levels, leaving us all balanced on the edge of a knife as we waited for someone to flinch first.

"Stop!" I shouted, holding out my open hands to both sides. "Going this route will also end in more deaths, and neither side can stand to lose another person. This is my home, Barrett. My people are here and I need to be here to protect them."

"You being here is killing your people," he barked at me.

"I'll be leaving Savannah in a couple days. I have some business that needs to be taken care of first. One of mine has been kidnapped and I need to get her back," I argued. My hands dropped back to my sides and tightened into fists. "When I leave for the sacrifice, the naturi should follow me."

"It's not soon enough. I want you out of town tonight and I want you to never return," Barrett snarled.

A brittle smile lifted my lips as I looked at my shifter companion. I tried to remember that he had lost two brothers and was in pain. I tried to remember that he had lost a third of his pack to the naturi. I tried to remember that his people were helpless when the naturi attacked, but still, he was asking for the impossible.

"This is my home," I calmly stated. "I will not be forced out."

Barrett growled at me, his upper lips curling so I could see his fangs dropping into place. His deep brown eyes shifted to copper as the animal inside of him demanded control of his body.

"Do you really want to do this?" I asked. "You're going to lose more of your pack, when I am willing to take the naturi with me in a couple days."

"But you'll be back and they will follow behind you until you're finally dead. If necessary, we'll finish the job for them and deliver your body."

Mira! Knox shouted in my brain.

He doesn't mean it like it sounds. He's upset, I quickly replied. Barrett had made it sound like he was siding with the naturi, which was forbidden among the races. I knew him better than that. He would never side with the naturi. He was just looking for a way to get the naturi off his back, and the best way to protect his people was to get rid of me.

"If you want me dead," I said, "then you do the deed. Don't include the rest of your pack. They've lost enough." A rumble went up around me as the lycans immediately opposed the arrangement.

"Silence!" Barrett shouted, and quiet immediately settled over the room.

This is suicide! Knox snapped at me. *The sun will be up soon. You're weakened.*

I'll be fine.

"Just you and me," I said to Barrett. "Beat me. Kill me. And Savannah will be free of my presence for as long as the naturi walk the earth."

"And if I were to lose?" Barrett countered.

I smiled broadly at him, exposing my fangs. "I'll think of something. The key is that no one interferes on either side no matter what happens. Agreed?"

"Agreed."

Barrett had barely gotten the word out before he lunged at me. His fist went immediately for my heart, aiming to end the contest as quickly as possible. I dodged the blow and delivered one of my own to the left side of his rib cage, breaking two ribs. He hissed in pain but didn't let it slow him down. He twisted, punching me in the jaw hard enough to snap my head around. Taking advantage of my momentary confusion, he came down on the side of my left knee. I howled in pain as I crumpled to the floor.

For the first time, fear beat within me. I was too slow, too weak, and I had severely underestimated Barrett and his need to have me dead. However, the pain quickly overwhelmed the fear that had briefly blossomed, waking up the monster that squatted behind my soul. Where I had been calm before, a new blood lust swelled within my chest, lighting my lavender eyes.

Barrett punched at my face again, but I caught his fist this time. Tightening my grip, I fractured at least two of his bones while pushing to my feet and forcing him back to the far wall that lined the dance floor. I kept most of my weight balanced on my right leg as my left knee slowly healed. Hobbled as I was, I stepped away and waited for him to come at me again.

The lycanthrope pushed off the wall and came at me with the amazing speed of his people, surging across the open space in a blur. With my wounded knee, there was no moving out of the way. I blocked a succession of blows aimed at my face, stomach, kidney, and ribs. Nothing got through, causing his frustration to grow.

Sweat beaded on his forehead and his eyes began to glow with a copperish light. He was losing what little control he had. Soon he would be forced to shift, and I'd easily have him. But I didn't want it to go down that way. I would be forced to kill him then, and I knew that his pack needed his leadership.

Unfortunately, I was beginning to lose my own battle with the monster inside of me. It growled and spit as it clawed its way up my chest, and was now wrapped around what passed for a heart within my chest. It wanted Barrett's blood and it was the only way I could satisfy it.

I knocked him away from me again, sending him back across the room to the far wall. This time he paused long enough to break a leg off of one of the tables that encircled the dance floor. He finally had a weapon he could use against me—a wooden stake.

A smile once again graced my lips as I waved for him to attack. If he was going to up the ante that way, then I had no problem taking his blood. He was not looking to just beat me. He obviously wanted me dead.

Barrett came back swinging. I easily slipped beneath his blows, which were aimed to take my head off. I was tempted to set the piece of wood on fire but resisted. I promised myself that I would keep this a fair fight, and the use of my unnatural ability would tip the scales too much in my favor. He deserved a fair fight.

Around me, I could feel the night waning. I was growing weaker. It was less than two hours until the sun finally set. We would all need to reach sanctuary soon or be at the mercy of the lycanthropes, whom I no longer trusted to let us be. My people needed to be safe, and I knew only I could give them that safety.

With a low growl, I approached Barrett, slowly backing him toward the wall. He swung the stake at me, trying to knock me unconscious. I raised my left arm as he aimed a particularly hard blow. The hunk of wood shattered in his hand, sending shards flying across the room. He took the opening, plunging the remaining piece of wood in his hand for my heart. But at the last second I caught it with my right hand, halting it before it could puncture my skin. With a quick twist, I was suddenly standing behind him. The piece of wood was now pressed to his chest just over his heart. We both held onto the wood, struggling for control.

He was strong and he was fast, but I was centuries older than him. I would always be faster and stronger. It would have taken little effort to overpower him at that moment and plunge the stake into his chest.

"Would you like to know what it feels like to be staked?" I whispered in his ear. His only response was to growl at me and struggle for control of the stake of wood. With a dark chuckle, I grabbed a handful of his hair with my free hand and jerked his head back. The blood lust was now in control. I sank my fangs into his throat, bringing a scream from his lips. His blood poured down my throat, filling me with a new strength while I stole his away.

Around us I could feel the lycanthropes closing ranks, preparing to rush me. I had their leader in a death grip. I could easily drain him to the point of death and they knew it. A ring of fire sprang up around us, keeping both the nightwalkers and the lycanthropes at bay. Unfortunately, the fire set off the fire sprinkler systems, sending down a thick wall of water. But the fire never went out completely as I drank from Barrett. No one moved, becoming statues in the downpour.

The water helped to clear my head, and I released Barrett when his grip on the stake finally grew limp and his hand fell harmlessly back to his side. He dropped to his knees before me, slowly shaking his head as he attempted to clear the fog and remain conscious. I doused the flames, but the water continued to fall, drenching all of the nightclub's occupants.

"This fight is over. I could have killed him, but chose to

spare him," I proclaimed. "Everyone leave, except you." I pointed to Barrett's remaining brother, Cooper. "You stay and help your brother. We have business to discuss."

I watched as everyone slowly filed out of the nightclub. The bartender was the last to leave as he paused long enough to turn off the sprinkler system. There was only Cooper, Barrett, Knox, and myself left. Time was running out for the night, but I needed to know that things were settled between Barrett and me before I continued. There were still other ways that the shifter could betray me and my kind.

Eight

Cooper put Barrett's arm over his shoulders and helped his brother walk into the back room, where he settled in him one of the few chairs. Barrett blinked a couple times until his eyes finally focused on Kevin. A low wheeze escaped the nightwalker and I saw him make a fist with his left hand. He was struggling to hold onto his soul, but it was a battle he couldn't win.

"Is he from the park?" Barrett asked.

"Yes," I replied, coming to stand near Kevin's head. I wished I could ease his pain, I wished I could end his life now so he would no longer be washed in this agony, tortured with the knowledge that the end was hovering so close. But I couldn't. He deserved these last seconds of his life—we all needed every second we could get.

"I won't feel guilty over him when I still have to bury my brother," Barrett said, clenching his teeth as he looked up at me.

"I'm not asking you to. I wanted you to see that you're not the only one with a body count."

"And you're the only one that can end this." Barrett tried to push to his feet but immediately wobbled and sat back down as he struggled to remain conscious. "You're the one killing both nightwalkers and lycans."

"The naturi are killing them. Not me. I'm trying to get rid of the naturi forever. What are you doing to help me on this front? What are you doing to save not only your own people but also the lives of nightwalkers and humans?"

"Just leave, Mira. Save us all by just leaving Savannah," Cooper said wearily with a shake of his head.

"Would you leave, Barrett?" I asked, drawing the shifter's dark eyes from the dying nightwalker to me again. "If our roles were reversed, would you leave?"

"Of course."

I smiled down at him and shook my head. "We both know that's a lie. Savannah is as much in your blood as it is in mine. This is home, the only home either of us has ever known. You would make a stand and fight, regardless of the potential loss of life."

"Mira," Knox suddenly said. I looked up at my companion, who was leaning against the door, his hands shoved into the pockets of his soaked slacks. "He's gone."

My gaze jumped back down to Kevin. I did a quick scan of his body to find that his soul had completely left him despite the fact that we still had more than an hour before the sun finally rose on this nightmarish night. I couldn't feel his soul in the room with us. Kevin had died.

"Take him to Archie. Tell him—" I started, then caught myself. The coroner wasn't mine to command. He was a friend that did me favors for the protection of my people. "Ask Archie to cremate the body immediately."

"What about . . . ?" he asked, his eyes moving over Barrett and Cooper, who was hovering just behind his brother's shoulder.

"I'll be fine. Barrett won't be strong enough to attack me for another couple hours, and Cooper knows that if he takes a single step toward me I'll set him on fire."

Knox was still frowning when he picked up Kevin and carried him out of the room, shutting the door behind him.

I sat on the arm of the sofa and looked at Barrett. We had been friends since he was only twelve years old. I had known his father, his grandfather, and his great-grandfather. I had worked with each of them to maintain strong ties between the nightwalkers and the lycanthropes. I was unwilling to lose everything we had gained during those years tonight. Unfortunately, it meant putting my good friend in a very awkward position.

"Tomorrow night I go to rescue a nightwalker that has been kidnapped. The naturi will pull everyone back in an effort to end my life. And I will do everything within my power to wipe out as many of them as I possibly can. Not long after that I will go to Peru to fight them again, to preserve the barrier that has blocked the naturi horde from the rest of the world. Any remaining naturi in Savannah will follow me."

"But what about when you come back?" Barrett asked.

A small laugh escaped me and I smiled at him. "There's only a slim chance that I will survive Peru and return home again. But if I do, it is unlikely that the naturi will follow me. I like to think that if I return to Savannah, it means that we won and the remaining naturi have been scattered to the wind. They won't dare to take me on again."

Barrett shook his head, looking down at his open hands where they rested between his knees. "I'm sorry about this, Mira. We've been friends a long time. I hate what the naturi have ruined between us."

"Yes, this damage may never be repaired," I agreed. A lump grew in my throat as I stared at him. He looked so defeated, and it wasn't over yet. "I won this battle, Barrett. It means you at the very least owe me a boon."

His head snapped up and he straightened in his chair. "Are you going to ask me to leave Savannah?"

"I had thought about it, but that wouldn't solve my current dilemma."

"I thought that's why you sent that Gromenko to me. He's obviously the Alpha from another pack. You want him to take over the Savannah pack."

"I never considered that. Nicolai is here for his own protection. It has nothing to do with you and your pack. It's between me, Nicolai, and another nightwalker. It will never extend to the rest of your pack."

"But we have to protect him if he's attacked," Barrett countered.

"No, you don't, and we both know that you wouldn't. You've never accepted him, never welcomed into the fold. You and your people wouldn't raise a finger to help him if he needed it. I'm no fool, Barrett. Nicolai is fully aware that I'm the only one that has his back."

Barrett looked away from me, shame eating away at him. He had created an outcast of Nicolai because of his own lack of security. "He doesn't belong with us."

"Only because that's how you want it to be. But that's your choice. I'm not here to tell you how to run your pack, the same way you won't tell me how to manage my nightwalkers. What you do with Nicolai is your business, but you have to understand that it is my duty to protect him from all threats."

"So he is to come between us as well. Isn't it enough that we have the naturi between us?"

"Nicolai will only come between us if you let him," I said, rising to my feet. "Besides, we have other problems to discuss. My boon. From you, I simply want the truth."

His brow furrowed and a frown pulled at the corners of his mouth as he again shifted in his chair. "I've never lied to you."

"But you would have a very good reason to lie to me now. I want to know how deep your betrayal of me has gone. How deep the betrayal of your people runs against nightwalkers."

"Betrayal?" Cooper demanded, taking a step toward me. I cocked one eyebrow at him in warning, and he took a step backward again. "We've never betrayed you or the other nightwalkers."

I looked back down at Barrett, who was watching me with angry eyes. "Tonight you offered to hand me over to the naturi. We have all vowed to not aid the naturi in any way. You seemed more than willing to break that vow tonight," I said, crossing my arms over my chest against the chill that was creeping into my frame. The warmth I had gotten from his blood was starting to fade, and the sunrise was growing close. I would need to leave soon if I hoped to find sanctuary against the sun.

"I—I—I didn't mean it like that," Barrett stuttered, growing ghostly pale.

"We've never willingly sided with the naturi," Cooper argued. His right hand rested on his brother's shoulder and squeezed. "We're not traitors."

"Give me the truth, Barrett. Would you hand me or any nightwalker over to the naturi?"

"No!"

"Would you order someone from your pack to hand a nightwalker over to the naturi?"

"No!"

"Would you hand Nicolai over to the naturi?"

"No! No! No! I wouldn't do anything that would help the naturi. I wouldn't side with them no matter what was being done. I know, Mira, that they are at the root of our problems. They are not a solution."

"The naturi aren't our only problem," I said, causing some of the anger to leak from Barrett's frame. "This past summer I asked you to retrieve evidence from the Daylight Coalition database, evidence that could expose me as a nightwalker. I never asked you about that, but I'm asking now. Was the evidence retrieved as I requested?"

"Yes, of course."

"Was it destroyed?"

He was silent.

So I thought. I'd feared that his people had downloaded the information, wiped the Coalition database clean, and kept a copy for themselves. A little insurance for a rainy day. Well, it was raining now and I couldn't afford to be fighting the Coalition at the same time I was fighting the naturi. The Daylight Coalition was a group of humans who took it upon themselves to hunt down and destroy anything that wasn't human. We all believed that included all the races, but so far their focus has been exclusively on nightwalkers.

"You're not willing to betray me to the naturi, but you have no problem betraying me to the Daylight Coalition," I snarled at him.

Barrett shoved to his feet and managed to remain standing. "I haven't betrayed you!"

"Then destroy the evidence. We're in this together—against both the naturi and the Coalition. We've all promised to watch out for each other against the Coalition. What have I done to earn this animosity?"

"Nothing. I—I was just trying to protect my own people. You're powerful, Mira. You're an unstoppable force, feared across all the continents. What if you suddenly decided to turn on my people? How would I protect them?"

"So you chose the Coalition? So you came in here tonight and threatened to hand me over to the naturi? Until now I had no reason to turn on the lycanthropes. I handed you Nicolai, who is important to me, because I trusted you to watch out for him."

"I'll destroy the evidence!" Barrett quickly said. He reached out to take my hand, but I took a step away from him, unwilling to bear his touch at that moment.

Since taking his blood, I had been in his thoughts, reading his emotions without his knowledge. He was telling the truth. He was also terrified I would report him to the other packs that he was potentially making deals with both the naturi and the Coalition. He was on thin ice and we both knew it. I had never wanted to put him in this position, particularly since the Coven already tried to make a bargain with the naturi. Our hands certainly weren't clean. However, I still needed Barrett's assistance.

"I believe you," I murmured, wishing I could give him some other kind of reassurance, but I wasn't feeling too forgiving at the moment. "But I have one last request."

"Name it."

"Someone among the lycanthropes has already begun to deal with the Coalition."

"Are you sure?" Cooper inquired, his brow furrowed in confusion.

"While I was in London, I ran across a witch and a lycanthrope traveling with a member of the Coalition. They both attacked Tristan and me. They could have walked away, but didn't. They had chosen a new side. I want you to look into what's going on."

"I'll see what I can do," Barrett agreed.

"The lycan was called Harold Finchley. I want to know who his pack was. I want to know if there are others like him. I want to know if we've been betrayed."

"I'll find out."

"We'll find out," Cooper corrected, coming to stand next to his older brother.

"Good. You handle the Coalition and I'll get rid of the naturi. Now get out of here. I need to rest."

Barrett nodded and allowed his brother to lead him out of the nightclub and out into the slowly dying night. I slumped onto the sofa the moment they were outside the club, the last of my strength seeming to drain from my body. Sunrise was but an hour away. I had just enough time to catch a taxi back to my home outside the city. I'd endured enough blood, pain, and betrayal for one night.

Nine

It was a couple hours after sunset the next night before I was able to meet up with Danaus. Dawn had been too close when I finally left the Dark Room the previous night to try to see him. Besides, I still had to make sure that Tristan was comfortably settled and healing before I climbed into bed myself at daybreak. There was simply too little time to handle it all. The only cold comfort I did find before succumbing to the dawn was that Amanda would be safely out of the hands of the naturi during the daylight hours. They might have her body, but her conscious mind was beyond their reach, making torture worthless for at least a few hours.

But they were waiting for her when she awoke tonight. I heard her screams in my mind when I woke at sunset. Reaching out with my powers, I found Amanda was to the south of the city, out in the marshes. I connected with her mind long enough to discover that she was on an island. By what I could quickly pick out of her thoughts, I was willing to bet that she was being held out on Blackbeard Island. Knox and Tristan had been sent ahead to procure us a boat. It was my job to convince Danaus to come along for the hunt.

However, standing on the front porch outside my town
house, my hand on the doorknob, I was beginning to wonder
if I would be able to convince him to join us in this insane
venture. It was obviously a trap. The goal of the naturi was
to get to me, and I was willingly walking into it because the
bait was one of my own. Common sense said that the naturi
would kill Amanda either before I arrived or just as I set foot
on the island. I had little hope of actually saving her. The
risk I was taking didn't make sense, and yet I felt that she
was one of my own. I had offered her entrance into my family and couldn't turn my back on her now because it wasn't
convenient to my own plans.

Unlocking the front door, I strolled in through the foyer,
but my footsteps quickly dragged to a halt when I sensed
that Danaus wasn't alone. There was a woman with him. My
teeth clenched and my hands balled into fists as I forced myself to step into the front parlor. Both he and the pretty blond
woman jerked to their feet at the same time as I entered the
room, their low conversation falling silent.

"I'm sorry," I apologized snidely, my dark gaze lev-
eled on the hunter. "I didn't realize that I had left you with
enough time to go out on dates. Apparently, I hadn't properly explained the seriousness of the situation in which we
find ourselves."

"She's not a date. This is the earth witch I told you about,"
Danaus said. "She's agreed to help you."

"Hi!" the woman exclaimed. "I'm Michelle French, but
you can just call me Shell, or Shelly. That's what all my
friends call me. Except my dad. He calls me Seashell when
he thinks he's being funny."

It was all I could do to keep my mouth from falling open
during this exuberant introduction. She was the epitome of

perky, with her upbeat attitude and sunny disposition. Even her clothes shone, a pale yellow shirt and white shorts. I was willing to bet that she'd been a cheerleader during high school, maybe even through college.

"Yeah," I drawled while dragging my gaze back to Danaus, who was looking at me levelly. Shelly was not the type of person either of us typically associated with. Most of our encounters were with other dark creatures that understood our world revolved around the basic tenet of kill or be killed. "Can I have a word with you in private?"

"Oh sure," Shelly said in her sweet, chipper voice. "I'll just run upstairs to my room and finish unpacking while you and Danaus talk." With a bounce in her step, Shelly swept by me and skipped up the stairs to the second floor. I waited for the bedroom door to close before I opened my mouth.

"Have you lost your mind? Where the hell did you get her?" I snapped, shoving both my hands through my hair.

"Charleston," Danaus simply replied, further fueling my anger when he refused to elaborate.

"Is that how they are in Charleston?"

"Sweet and happy is not a crime, you know."

"It is in our world. Why did you bring her here?"

Danaus sat back down, watching me pace back and forth through the room, weaving between the sofa and the coffee table. "You said that you needed someone to teach you how to use earth magic. She can do that."

"*She's* an earth witch?"

"She's an earth witch and one that *hasn't* sided with the naturi. That type of earth witch isn't easy to find, particularly when your name comes up. She's willing to help you."

A snort escaped me as I paused in my pacing to face him,

my arms folded over my chest. "I find it hard to believe that she will be able to help me."

"And I find it hard to believe that she's willing to help you," Danaus lectured, pushing to his feet again and coming to stand directly in front of me. "Outside of Savannah, you're seen as a walking pestilence. Savannah has become a war zone and no one is willing to come here. But she was, so I would get off your high horse and give her a chance."

"This isn't about my ego, you ass," I snapped. "It's about her getting killed in the first five minutes of being here. It is a war zone, and she's not equipped to handle something like this. I don't want to worry about watching over her when I've got bigger problems to worry about."

"What's happened?" Danaus demanded, ready to put aside our argument and jump back into the business of surviving.

"Tristan and some others were attacked late last night by some naturi and lycanthropes. Two were killed and Amanda was taken hostage. She's still alive and being held on an island out in the marshes," I explained, then paused, looking away from him. I couldn't look at him when I continued. "I have to go get her."

"Mira," Danaus murmured, but when he spoke again, his voice was hard and firm. "You can't do this. It's a trap."

"I know it's a trap!" I exploded, more frustrated with the situation than I was with the hunter. "Do you honestly think that I don't? Of course it's a trap, but I can't leave Amanda to them. She belongs to me. She is a member of my family and I have sworn to protect her. I have to go after her."

"And if you die, we're all damned. We won't be able to reseal the doorway between the two worlds. The naturi will escape and they will kill us all."

"I have no choice," I whispered.

Danaus gripped my shoulders with both hands and gave me a little shake, forcing my eyes back up to his face. "You have a choice. You can choose to walk away from this. You have to choose between saving one nightwalker and saving all nightwalkers."

"This is more than saving just one nightwalker," I said, stepping backward out of his grasp. "This is about eliminating all the naturi within my domain. A number of lycanthropes have been killed during the past couple of months because of the naturi. Nightwalkers have died. It has to stop. I have no doubt they've pulled back to the island, where they're waiting for me. We can kill them all tonight, cleansing the area before we leave for Machu Picchu."

"Machu Picchu?"

I nodded, a frown pulling at the corners of my mouth as I sat on the edge of the sofa while Danaus returned to his seat opposite me. "Jabari appeared last night with Nicolai. The Ancient said that the next sacrifice is to take place on the night of the equinox, and that it is to be at Machu Picchu. Naturally, we are being dispatched."

"Naturally," he grumbled, resting his elbows on his knees.

"Come with me, Danaus. Help me rid my home of the damned naturi. Barrett and his pack have lost enough because of them. So have my people," I said. I knew it wasn't my best argument. Danaus would be happy to see all of my kind wiped out, but right now we were the best defense against the naturi, who were infinitely worse than nightwalkers. The problem was that I couldn't do this without him, and we both knew it.

Danaus gave what sounded like an unhappy but affirmative grunt. He would be happy to leave me to this suicide mission to save one nightwalker when we both knew I should just walk away. But I couldn't. Jabari, Tabor, and Sadira saved me years ago from the naturi's clutches. Sure, it was because they all wanted to control me and use me as their own personal weapon, but I didn't know that at the time. All I knew was that someone came to save me. Amanda deserved that now, and I wasn't about to abandon her. And neither would Danaus.

"I'll help you," came a soft voice from where Shelly stood in the doorway.

"No! Absolutely not!" I exclaimed, quickly pushing to my feet.

"She might be of some help," Danaus suggested.

"I can be of help," Shelly interjected before I could argue. "You're not the only one who knows how to manipulate fire." With a snap of her fingers a small ball of fire hovered above her hand. No magic words, no special wave of her hand or pause so she could summon up the power from the earth. She simply snapped her fingers and it was there. Maybe I *had* underestimated her abilities.

"There are going to be numerous naturi there with the single goal of trying to kill you," I said. "Have you fought the naturi before?"

"No, but I have been in magical fights before with other witches who were aiming to kill me. I survived those. I can survive this one," she commented, straightening her shoulders and standing up a little taller than before.

Frowning, I looked down at Danaus, still seated in the chair behind me. He was frowning as well, but he wasn't denying her request to go along. This felt like a mistake, but so did rescuing Amanda, and I was determined to do that. At least with Shelly accompanying us, we had one more fighter against the numerous naturi that were waiting for us. And I was looking for anything that would even the odds.

"Go put on some jeans. We're going to be slogging through the marshlands," I said with a shake of my head. Shelly flashed me a brilliant smile before she jogged up the stairs. I just prayed that I didn't live to regret this decision.

Ten

A single lamp lit the landing where Knox and Tristan were waiting for us. A motorboat on the black waters floated silently as its would-be passengers impatiently milled around the concrete landing. Tristan was far too eager to be headed out into the night in search of Amanda, while Knox leaned against a post, his face expressionless as he stared out at the waters lapping at the shore.

The car ride to the landing with Danaus and Shelly was oppressively quiet, each of us lost to our own thoughts as we prepared for the battle that loomed ahead. The introductions to Shelly were brisk and solemn as we loaded up in the boat.

Knox claimed the helm, steering us out into the dark waters while I took the point, since my night vision was the strongest of the group. Danaus hovered close at my side, his powers washing through me and out into the marshlands.

"How many?" I asked, my voice barely drifting above the sound of the motor.

"At least a dozen. Some are approaching the boat," he replied. I looked at my companion to find him removing one of his knives from its sheath on his waist.

"Harpies?" I asked, recalling the wind clan naturi that attacked us in Venice and Crete.

"No, they're in the water."

I swallowed a curse and instantly returned my attention back to the seemingly calm waters before us. I had yet to face a member of the water naturi—I'd hoped to go my entire existence without encountering them, but that wasn't going to happen.

My thoughts stumbled into one another as I struggled to come up with an appropriate warning for the threat that was approaching. But there was no time. An unexpected wave swelled off to the starboard, and Knox jerked the wheel in time to keep us from capsizing. Shelly was tossed to the floor and Danaus stood to help her back into her seat. It was what they were waiting for.

A spout of water shot across the boat, hitting Danaus square in the chest and knocking him off balance. I made a grab for him but came up with only empty air. The hunter tumbled over the side of the boat and into the dark water, which instantly swallowed him up.

"Kill the engine!" I shouted a second before I dove over the side of the boat. Despite the warm night air, the cold water bit deep, momentarily stealing away my concentration. But a second later I sensed Danaus just a few yards away from me. The water wasn't deep, but it was enough for the hunter to drown in if the naturi were able to hold him under for an extended period of time.

I couldn't see Danaus, but I could sense him. The only problem was that I couldn't see or sense the naturi that were in the water as well.

Danaus? I called out mentally, hoping to reach him in on our unique telepathic link as I swam toward his location.

Hurry! was his brief angry reply. He was going to run out of air soon.

How many?

Two with me. One with you.

I barely resisted the urge to stop and look over my shoulder for the naturi. I kept swimming, confident that I wouldn't be able to see the naturi until it was already on top of me.

A thrashing in the water before me indicated I was close to it, yet as I reached out, a pair of claws raked across my back. I swam to my left with a jerk, twisting around so I could spot my attacker, but the water was too murky to see much of anything. Grabbing my blade from my waist and slipping it between my teeth, I swam, desperate to reach the hunter before his air supply ran out.

As I turned back, the claws ran over me a second time, raking across my shoulder blades. But I was ready this time. Pulling the knife out of my mouth, I reached my right arm behind me, catching the naturi as it swam by me. A garbled cry filled the water, indicating that I'd scored a hit. Kicking, I turned to find the naturi clutching its side. The creature looked human in the faint light except for what appeared to be webbed hands and feet—not exactly the mermaid I was expecting to find lurking in these waters. Gills on his neck opened and closed with each labored breath. With the naturi just in reach, I had a chance to use my unique ability. I didn't stand a chance in an underwater fight. I was too slow. The only reason I had scored a hit already was due to surprise, and that element was now gone.

The water naturi came at me again, claw-tipped webbed hands reaching for my face in an effort to scratch my eyes out. I dodged its grasp, resulting in it getting just a handful of hair. Its fist tightened in my hair, jerking my head back. It opened its mouth, revealing rows of sharp teeth that would have made a piranha proud. Gripping my knife, I plunged it deep into its stomach. I immediately pulled the knife free and plunged my hand into the open wound before the naturi could release its hold on my hair. With my fingers wrapped around its insides, I put all my concentration into starting a fire, burning anything that I touched. The naturi jerked and kicked, desperate to be free of my fiery grip without ripping its burning organs from its body. It swiped one final time at my face while landing a kick to my stomach, loosening my hold on it. Then it kicked a couple few away before finally going completely still. It slowly floated to the surface.

Mira! Out of air! came Danaus's panicked cry in my head.

Boil their blood! I commanded, swimming back toward him again.

Can't.

Do it. I can't see you. I had little chance of being able to fight off both naturi before Danaus finally passed out from a lack of oxygen. We were running out of time, and the longer he waited, the less strength he was going to have.

As I once again neared his position, there was a great commotion in the water. I was reluctant to strike—I couldn't be sure which of them Danaus was but I could feel his power swelling in the water. He was killing the two remaining naturi by boiling their blood. I swam close, only to have someone kick me in the ribs. And then the water went completely still.

Danaus? I inquired. I could still sense him, but the feeling was becoming faint and thready, as if he was drifting away from me. *Danaus!* I repeated when he didn't immediately reply. I kicked both feet, crossing the remaining distance toward where I could sense him. The water was too dark to make out anything beyond his large form.

Here came a whisper across my brain. He was exhausted and out of air. Grabbing his wrist, I swam to the surface, dragging him along. As he surfaced, he sucked in a lungful of air before coughing up the water he had swallowed.

"Are you all right?" I asked as I waved to Knox to bring the boat over to pick us up.

Danaus nodded, still struggling to catch his breath.

"Why didn't you immediately boil their blood once you hit the water?" I demanded angrily. He had nearly been killed, and there was little I could have done about it.

"Wasn't sure you'd jump in after me . . . " he said breathlessly, still struggling to draw enough air into his lungs. "Knew I wouldn't have the strength to swim back to the surface if I used my ability."

A part of me wanted to kick him. How could I not jump into the water after him? We needed him. I hadn't even thought about not going into the water after him.

Knox halted the boat beside us while Tristan helped us climb out of the water. A breeze cut through the air, chilling the clothes that now stuck to my frame. I paused at the side of the boat to wring out my hair before resuming my seat at the point.

"Your back!" Shelly gasped when I walked past.

"It's healing," I said with a shrug. "Let's get going."

Taking my spot at the front of the boat, we continued the rest of the way to the island unmolested. Knox beached the boat on the sandy shore between two other boats that had been used by the naturi and killed the engine. I glanced over my shoulder at Danaus to find that his breathing had finally evened out. I wished I could give him more time to recover, but I knew the naturi would never allow it.

"Let's go," I announced, pushing to my feet.

"They're waiting for us," Danaus said, halting me. "Close by."

"I have no doubt," I muttered under my breath as I jumped over the side of the boat. My feet sank into the wet sand, leaving me feeling momentarily trapped. I had walked only a couple feet from the boat when I noticed several alligators creeping closer.

"Shelly, take care of the gators," I ordered as I continued toward the interior of the island.

"Wh-What do you mean?" she asked, landing in the sand behind me.

"They're going to attack from behind. Kill them before they have a chance to kill us. Knox and Tristan will cover you," I said, my eyes locked on the figures I could see stepping out from the tree line.

"But—"

"Just do it! Knox!"

"I'm on it," he called, jumping down from the boat. As we all stepped onto the island, a great splash came from behind us. I turned to find a woman standing within a geyser of water. Her skin was a pale bluish-green while her long hair was the shade of green algae. To my surprise, she stepped out of the water and onto dry land. Around her was a thick wall of mist so she could continue to breathe outside of the water.

"I just came to get what belongs to me," I said, fighting the urge to pull the knife back from its sheath.

"We were counting on that," the female naturi replied. Her voice was garbled by mist.

"Do yourself a favor and swim away." I smiled at her so she could see my fangs. It was her last chance; I honestly didn't expect her to take me up on my offer. That would have been too easy. I was simply stalling in an attempt to give Danaus a chance to regain his strength.

"No," the naturi said.

I grabbed my knife and reached down into my powers, ready to ignite anything that moved, but the attack didn't come from the front I'd been expecting. The sound of birds suddenly filled the night, as if thousands had cried out at once as they lifted into the air. At the same time, I heard the distinct sound of jaws snapping together. The alligators were on the move.

Find the animal clan naturi, I ordered Danaus as he stepped forward with a long knife in one hand, ready to take on the naturi as they approached. For now, they were content to hang back and let the animals under their control do the dirty work.

"Easier said than done," he growled at me.

It was on the tip of my tongue to make a snide comment in return, but I didn't get the chance. Birds burst from the trees and dive-bombed us, beaks and talons ready to rip, tear, and shred. With a wave of my hand, a wall of flames washed through the water fowl, burning feathers in an instant. The air was filled with an enormous cloud of orange and yellow flames, followed by black smoke. Their small bodies plummeted to the earth before us, their cries piercing the air.

"No!" Shelly screamed, drawing my eyes back to her. Knox, Tristan, and Shelly were circled by a low wall of flames, keeping the alligators at bay. Yet Tristan and Knox were trapped as well, keeping them from helping in the battle. Shelly's tortured gaze was on the birds dying at my feet.

"Kill the alligators and help us!" I shouted at her before turning my attention back to the naturi.

They had left the tree line and were now rushing to attack us. I moved to create a wall of fire between us and the naturi, but Danaus was already on the move, ready to engage them. I couldn't risk cutting off the hunter's ability to retreat. With a grunt, I stepped forward and swung my knife at the first naturi to approach me. A knot tightened in my stomach. We were painfully outnumbered and the enemy was too close for me to start lighting fires. I needed space and time to concentrate on what I was doing. If I paused now, there was a good chance I would end up with a knife in my back.

Danaus and I cut down one naturi after another, but still they continued to come. Shelly managed to keep the approaching alligators off my heels, but it locked both Knox and Tristan at her side. We were quickly becoming overwhelmed.

Behind me someone screamed in pain. I tried to turn my head to see who had been injured, but the distraction cost me. A blade plunged into my chest, clipping the edge of my heart. I gasped, every muscle tensing in pain as precious blood poured from the wound.

Danaus . . . I whispered, reaching out for the hunter.

"Mira!" he cried, not far from where I was slowly sinking to the ground. The naturi pulled the knife from my chest while I crumpled to my knees. He grabbed a clump of my hair and jerked my head back so my neck was exposed. Closing my eyes, I focused on setting the naturi that held me on fire. I was weak and doubted I would be able to kill him before he was able to remove my head.

And then Danaus's powers rushed into me, filling me so there was no escaping the energy that flowed through every vein and burned in every muscle. I screamed, and the naturi holding me exploded in flames.

Seconds later Danaus was kneeling beside me, his hand pressed to my chest as he tried to stop the bleeding. I opened my eyes to find the naturi taking a couple steps back as they watched us anxiously. We had finally caught them by surprise, and we had to take advantage of their confusion if we were to survive this fight.

Help me destroy them, I pleaded as Danaus started to withdraw his powers from my body. The relief was intense, but it wasn't what I wanted. I wanted to be free of the pain, but I wanted to be free of the naturi more.

Not like this, he replied.

It's the only way, I said. I laid my hand on his, holding him connected to me, my blood seeping through both of our laced fingers. *They're killing my people. They're killing the lycans, and soon it will be the humans. I'm not strong enough without you. We won't destroy their souls. Help me end this tonight.*

Mira . . .

Please, my friend.

The power exploded through my frame like a torrent of water rushing through a narrow canyon. My body bowed forward under the force of the energy that ran through me from Danaus. My head fell back and my eyes closed, but I could sense them, all the naturi in the area, just like when we hunted them down in England. Gathering up the energy, I focused on their bodies with the sole intention of setting them all on fire. But it didn't work. I reached out again, my grasp encircling their frantically beating hearts, and still I could not set them on fire.

I tried again and again, beating back the energy that was demanding to be used. I didn't want to destroy their souls as we had in England. There had to be another way, but I was out of time. The energy that Danaus was pouring into me had to be used before it destroyed me, destroyed us both. Hating myself, I reached for the wisp of energy that floated in every naturi and set it ablaze.

There were no screams of pain. The end came and went for them too fast. With Danaus's power still flowing through me, I reached out past the marshlands and killed all the naturi within my domain. My people would be safe for at least a few nights, and the Savannah Pack would be safe from the reach of the naturi for now. Two dozen naturi died that night, and I felt the touch of every soul as it was extinguished. Two dozen new reasons for me to be damned to Hell when this existence was over.

Danaus jerked his hand out of my grasp and I fell forward in the sand, landing on my stomach. I was too tired, in too much pain, to try to catch myself. The world went black around me and I welcomed the emptiness.

Eleven

I opened my eyes to find Knox kneeling beside me, one hand sweeping across my forehead. His clothes were torn and there were a collection of scratches and bite marks on his body, which were slowly healing. I looked around to find Tristan sitting in the sand near me, looking much the same. They both had been wrestling alligators. Shelly stood off to the side, her face pale and streaked with tears. Her hands trembled. I had made a horrible error in allowing her to come along.

"Are you okay?" Knox asked, drawing my gaze back to him. I had yet to see Danaus, but I could feel he was close by, his anger boiling silently on the inside.

"I've been better," I grumbled, slowly sitting up. "Let's go find Amanda and get the hell out of here. I'm going to need to feed tonight."

Knox grabbed my elbow and helped me to my feet. The nightwalker remained close to my side as we walked deeper into the island, as if waiting for my knees to give out on me. I appreciated his concern but it put me on edge. I didn't like being this weak around other night-walkers, even though Knox wouldn't try to take advantage of the situation and stab me in the back. It wasn't his way. I almost felt as if he was attempting to protect me from either Shelly or Danaus, since he was careful to keep his body between myself and the hunter, while his eyes continuously drifted back to the earth witch on the other side of me.

"There's someone over there!" Tristan called before darting ahead, anxious to finally have Amanda back in our safe keeping.

"It's not her," I murmured, my brows drawing together over the bridge of my nose. I could see the creature's hair color, and it wasn't Amanda's bright blond.

"It's naturi!" Danaus said, and I understood his surprise. We had killed all the naturi within the region, reduced them to gray ash. Surely there couldn't be one still alive and in one piece.

When we got close to the naturi curled on the ground, we could see that she was covered in a blue dome of energy. Beside her in a hole in the ground was Amanda, curled up and unconscious.

"Is she still alive?" Tristan asked, ready to jump in the hole the moment I deemed that it was safe.

"She's asleep," Shelly said, her voice soft and wavering. The earth witch stepped forward and looked down on the two women, as different as night and day. Amanda was pale and blond, while the other had dark hair and tanned skin. "This is a sleep bubble. It keeps whoever is inside in a deep, protective sleep."

"Why keep a naturi asleep with a nightwalker that you're holding prisoner?" I asked as I knelt down across from the naturi, keeping a safe distance from the bubble. "Is the naturi torturing Amanda in her sleep?"

"Unlikely. They're both asleep. A deep sleep. There's no thought, no dreams. It's like being dead."

"It's two prisoners," Danaus suddenly said. "Look at her wrists."

The naturi was curled into the fetal position, with her hands pressed against her stomach, but there was no missing the iron bands wrapped around her slender wrists or the chain connecting them together. This sleeping creature was a prisoner, an enemy of my darkest enemy. A smile flitted across my lips.

"That's interesting," I murmured, mostly to myself.

"What do you plan to do?" Tristan asked, taking a step away from Amanda for the first time. The situation had become more complicated. It wasn't as simple as waking Amanda up. I had a feeling that in order to remove Amanda, we had to get rid of the bubble, which meant waking them both up.

"I haven't decided yet," I truthfully replied. "A naturi has just fallen into my lap. What should I do with it?"

"Besides kill it?" Tristan snapped. "Is that . . . that spell hurting Amanda?" he demanded, turning his attention to Shelly. The witch had bent down to examine some marking in the dirt around the bubble.

"No, she's perfectly safe. She's simply asleep."

"A healing sleep," I added. "Something she needs right now. There's no telling how long the naturi tortured her before we were able to get to the island. Let her sleep while she can."

"Are you planning to keep her like this because of the naturi?" Tristan demanded, taking a step toward the hole that held Amanda as if he planned to jump in and grab her up, spell be damned.

"No, of course not. But a few more minutes won't harm her." I rose and walked over toward Tristan. I grabbed his hand and pulled him back a couple steps away. "We need to think this through. We have an interesting opportunity before us and we need to make the most of it."

"What do you mean?" he said, his hand slipping from my grasp.

"Yes, Mira," Danaus said with a hiss. "What exactly do you mean?"

"We have a naturi prisoner at our fingertips. Don't you think it would be within our best interest to try to get some information out of her?"

"You're not going to kill it?" Tristan shouted, pointing at the sleeping naturi as if it were a snake slithering toward them on the ground.

"Of course I'm going to kill it, but it's all a matter of when."

"Is it the same 'when' that has Danaus's life hanging by a thread?" Knox asked, bringing a frown to my lips. I had been saying for months now that I would kill the hunter, and it had yet to be accomplished. I still had too much use for him. I didn't expect the naturi to be quite as useful.

"Not quite," I growled. Walking back over toward the naturi, I crouched down low so I could closely look at it. She seemed young; a teenager somewhere between the age of fifteen and seventeen, but then that was just her appearance. The naturi aged slowly if at all. She could be centuries old and not look it. Her clothes were dirty and there was a bruise on her temple. While she hadn't been treated as poorly as Amanda, she was no precious cargo either.

"She could be a plant," Danaus said, breaking into my thoughts. "The naturi knew she would be of interest to you like this and took a chance that you might try to get some information out of her. She could prove to be nothing more than a spy."

Dusting off my hands, I stood and turned to face the hunter. It was an angle I hadn't considered. We certainly couldn't trust her if we did bother to awaken her. "True, but who is she going to report to? We killed all the naturi within the immediate area. She has no one to report to even if she does find something out."

"You think nightwalkers are the only telepathic creatures?" he retorted. "I bet she could talk to any naturi she wanted to, regardless of the distance."

"And tell them what? Where to find me? They already know Savannah is my domain."

"It's worth the risk," Knox said, sliding his hands into his jeans pockets. "Any information that we can gain at this point would be of value."

"You expect her to tell the truth?" Tristan asked.

"Not at first," Knox replied. He shrugged his wide shoulders, a dark grin lifting one corner of his mouth. "But I'm sure under enough pain she'll talk."

"Shelly, wake them up," I said, taking a step back from where Amanda and the naturi were encased in the glowing blue dome of energy.

The witch stepped up to the bubble and paused to look over her shoulder at me as if questioning one last time if this was what I truly wanted. I nodded once, prodding her on. Drawing in a heavy breath, Shelly reached her right foot forward and with the toe of her shoe smudged the circle in the dirt that surrounded Amanda and the female naturi. There was a small pop in the air as the bubble over the two completely disappeared.

"That was it?" I asked in surprise.

"Sure. It's just a sleep spell," she replied, stepping back at the sound of Amanda beginning to stir within her hole in the ground.

"Could you replicate it if necessary?"

"It's been a while, but I think so."

"Brush up on it. We may need it," I said, returning my attention to the two creatures at my feet.

A low moan escaped Amanda as she slowly awoke and shifted in the hole. Keeping one eye on the naturi that had yet to move, I walked over to the hole so Amanda could see me. Her beautiful blond hair was matted with dirt and blood. Her clothes were torn and the visible skin was crusted with dried blood. She had briefly walked through Hell and survived, but I was solely concerned about how it would change her. My time with the naturi had not left me a better person.

"Mira?" she whispered over cracked lips.

"I'm here. The naturi are gone," I said in a low, soothing voice. She had not yet opened her eyes, yet when she did, she let out a wounded whimper at finding herself in what amounted to a freshly dug grave. Knox leaned down, extending his hand to her while Tristan took her elbow, both men bringing her slowly to her feet. Amanda wobbled once, and then took a long sniff of the air. She had picked up either Shelly's or Danaus's scent, and she was hungry. Her blue eyes glowed as they focused on the young witch and a smile curved her lips.

I stepped forward and placed a restraining hand on Amanda's shoulder. A low rumble of warning rose from the back of her throat but I ignored it. "Amanda, you can't feed here. Knox and Tristan will help you." I then directed my attention to Knox, who was standing on her right. "Take the boat and get her back to Savannah. Let her hunt there. We'll take one of the other boats back."

"Do you need any help with . . . ?" Knox nodded toward the naturi that still lay on the ground.

I shook my head, a frown teasing the corner of my lips. "No, we'll be fine. Get going."

The female naturi finally began to stir when Amanda was being helped back to the boat with Tristan and Knox. She jerked into a sitting position, the manacles jangling as she raised her hands to ward me off. Her wide green eyes swept over the area, quickly taking in me, Danaus, and Shelly.

"They're all gone. Dead," I confirmed, in what I thought was my most threatening voice. I must have been off my game because she actually sighed in relief. "And you're left with us," I continued, waiting for the fear or at least the burning hatred to kick in.

"Who are you?" she inquired in a soft voice that somehow reminded me of the wind. "Could you help me take these off?" She lifted her chained wrists to me and I laughed.

"I'm a nightwalker," I said, causing her face to crumple.

"Oh, I guess not," she murmured, lowering her hands back to her lap.

I stood before the naturi with my hands on my hips and my legs spread wide. "Who are you?"

"My name is Cynnia. Did you come to rescue the nightwalker they were holding?"

I ignored her question. I thought it was obvious why we were there. "Why are you bound? Are you a prisoner?"

"Yes."

"Why?" I repeated between clenched teeth when she didn't say anything else.

"They accused me of being a traitor," she softly said, dropping her eyes down to the iron manacles around her slender wrists.

"Mira!" Danaus snapped. I understood why he was suddenly upset. Her words had left me ill at ease as well. It was too convenient. A traitor to the naturi in the hands of the enemy. It seemed like a dream come true, but it felt like a trap.

"Scan the area!" I replied without looking over my shoulder at him.

"Mira?" the naturi asked, her head popping up again. "Mira? As in the Fire Starter?"

"The one and only," I said with a devilish grin. She got a good look at my fangs and lurched backward a couple feet, trying to edge away from me, but there was nowhere for her to go.

Danaus's power swept over the island and over the surrounding marshlands. I flinched inwardly, my body still sore and aching from our earlier connection. I was in no hurry to feel his powers again.

"There aren't any naturi in the area," Danaus replied.

"Where's Rowe?" I demanded, taking a step closer to Cynnia.

"Rowe?" Her voice wavered as her gaze darted from me to Shelly and then to Danaus.

"Yes, Rowe. Where is the one-eyed bastard?"

"I—I don't know. I've never met him," she said with a shake of her head.

I was on her in a flash. Kneeling next to her, I roughly grabbed a chunk of her hair and jerked her head back. I pressed my knife blade into the long line of her throat, drawing a bead of blood that slipped down her neck. "Where is Rowe?" I growled.

"I'm telling the truth. I don't know," she said.

"Mira!" Danaus sharply said, snapping my head around to look at the hunter. A low snarl rumbled in the back of my throat, and my upper lip curled so he could see my fangs. It was a warning. "What if she doesn't know anything?" he asked, his right hand on the handle of the blade attached to his waist. He was ready to attack if he thought I pressed things too far.

"Then she's going to die in agony," I said, tightening my grip on her hair, causing her to let out a little whimper.

"Please . . . I—I don't know anything," Cynnia said. "I just arrived here and they said I planned to betray my sister. I've been held captive for days." The words flowed from her like a river.

"Your sister? Who's your sister?" I asked, lowering the knife slightly.

"Aurora," she whispered.

I lurched to my feet and took a couple steps away from the naturi. At the same time, Danaus stepped forward so he was now standing beside me. I suspected that his thoughts were whirling away in the same direction as mine. Could it be possible? Were we truly holding the sister of the queen of the naturi? I couldn't be that lucky, but even as my doubts mounted, I couldn't get over the fact that she looked familiar. And now I knew why. She looked like Aurora. I'd caught a brief glimpse of Aurora centuries ago, when we battled the naturi on Machu Picchu and her frighteningly beautiful face had been burned into my brain. I would never forget it, and now I saw kneeling before me a younger, more vulnerable version of the queen.

"You're Aurora's sister?" I demanded slowly, needing to say the words aloud.

"Yes," she winced, possibly realizing her vulnerability now. "Please, I love my sister. I would never do anything to harm her. I came here looking for my brother. This war needs to be stopped, and I thought my brother would be able to help me."

"Who's your brother?" I asked, swallowing a smile. I felt like Alice slipping down the rabbit's hole. It all seemed too fantastic.

"His name is Nerian, and he has brown hair like me. He—"

"Had," I interrupted coldly. "Nerian is dead."

She lifted wide green eyes to my face, a frown pulling at the corners of her mouth. "You killed him, didn't you?" she asked, though the question wasn't accompanied by the splash of tears I had been expecting. In fact, she seemed quite calm about the news.

"Yes," I hissed, grinning from ear to ear. Nerian had been my tormentor at Machu Picchu, my constant waking nightmare. I couldn't begin to express the relief I felt at wiping his existence from the face of the planet.

Cynnia shook her head and looked back down at her hands. "I never knew him."

"Count yourself lucky. He was a cruel, sadistic bastard. Completely insane."

"A good soldier," Danaus added, to my surprise. "He believed in your sister's cause. He would never have helped you."

"Why here? Why were you being held here?" I demanded, drawing her attention back to me.

"I don't know. I was brought here from across the ocean. They seemed to be following someone."

"They were following you," Danaus said. I looked over my shoulder to find the hunter's intense gaze locked on my face. "They followed you from Europe back to your home."

It was an interesting theory. "Why?" I murmured, sliding my hands into my back pockets as I stared down at the naturi once again. She was a strange puzzle piece that I had to figure out if we were to survive the next few nights.

"For two possible reasons," he said. Danaus walked forward so until he was standing beside me, his arms folded over his strong chest. "They expect you to kill her."

"Which would not be out of the ordinary for me," I said with a nod. I tended to kill the naturi and ask questions later. The naturi were better off burned to a crisp, not running around causing problems. "And as the sister of their queen, it could definitely work to unite the splintered factions within the naturi host. The evil nightwalker kills the sweet, innocent younger sister of Aurora, unifying them against a common evil. Of course, that's assuming she's telling the truth."

Cynnia's head popped up and her mouth fell open to argue with me, but the words halted in her throat when I pointed my blade at her.

"Or they expect you to take her hostage and torture her for information," Danaus continued.

"That wouldn't be out of the ordinary for me either," I admitted with a nod. "But then they could be counting on me wanting to have control of Aurora's so-called sister as a bargaining chip. We take her with us, and she kills us all in our sleep."

Frowning, I slid the knife back into the sheath on my side as I stared at the naturi, turning over the different options facing me. Killing her now would rid the world of one more naturi. But leaving her alive gave me that chance to garner a little information out of her. And what better source of information could I ask for than Aurora's sister?

What's more, it might actually draw Rowe to my side, at long last. The naturi had been happy to appear in Venice when it looked like a naturi was being held by the Coven. If word reached him that I was holding a naturi hostage, especially if it was his wife-queen's sister, then he might finally come running. And ending this standoff between the naturi and the nightwalkers was dependent upon Rowe finally meeting an untimely demise.

We could use her to draw out Rowe. I pushed the suggestion into Danaus's brain, preferring to keep my plans private from both Shelly and Cynnia. The earth witch had turned a sickly shade of green when I put the knife to the naturi's throat. I was reluctant to count on her to keep her mouth shut when it came to the well-being of my new captive.

Do you think he will come for her?

Don't know. But he hasn't come gunning for me, so why not try something new?

We have to leave for Peru soon. We're out of time.

I frowned. He was right, we were running out of time. But I was unwilling to waste this unique opportunity. Cynnia was the first naturi I had met that didn't seem to immediately want to kill me or use me. I had to find a way to get a little information out of her before I finally killed her.

"Do you still have that house? The one with the basement?" I asked, looking over at the hunter from the corner of my eye.

He shook his head, a frown pulling at his lips. "No. Burned down."

I wasn't surprised. I had killed Nerian in that house. It would have been a perfect place to keep Cynnia locked up for a day or two, but I suspected that Danaus had seen to it that the house burned down in an effort to wipe away all evidence of both his and Nerian's existence.

"Then we'll take her back to my town house. Shelly, can you replicate the sleep spell that they used?"

"Th-The sleep spell?" she stammered, suddenly nervous. She wrung her hands together, her eyes darting from me to the naturi watching us. "Yes, I can duplicate it. It's an easy enough spell."

"It's your lucky night," I sneered at Cynnia. Reaching down, I grabbed the chain linking her manacles together and jerked her to feet. "You're going to live awhile longer. And the longer you live depends on how useful you prove to be. Lie to me and you'll wish I killed you now."

Mira, you don't have to be so cruel. She's terrified as it is, Danaus chastised, following close on my heels.

I laughed. *You haven't even begun to see cruel.*

Twelve

Danaus parked my car and sat with his hands gripping the steering wheel. I sat in the backseat with Cynnia, splitting my attention between my captive and Danaus, who was growing angrier by the minute. The long silent drive had given him ample time to stew about what had happened on the island.

"We need to talk," he bit out, still staring straight ahead. It was clear to even Cynnia that he was talking to me. I looked up and met his blue gaze in the rearview mirror. This wasn't going to be pretty. I opened my mouth to argue that we still needed to see to Cynnia when he snapped, "Now!" There was no avoiding this confrontation.

"Shelly, take Cynnia inside. Get her something to eat and drink," Danaus directed in a hard voice that left no room for argument, but that didn't stop me from hissing at the back of his head. I didn't want the naturi to feel as if she were suddenly a guest in my house when she was really a prisoner.

While Shelly escorted Cynnia inside to the comfort of my home, Danaus and I walked across the street to one of the many small parks that dotted the city. For the first time in more than month, I didn't glance over my shoulder, looking for a naturi ready to put a knife in my back. For a brief time they were gone and my city was safe again. I just had to deal with Danaus's anger over what I had convinced him to do.

"You lied to me!" he snarled. "You were so desperate to convince me that nightwalkers aren't evil, and you lied to me. You destroyed their souls."

"Don't put this all on me. You knew what was happening. You could have stopped at any time, but you didn't because we were desperate," I argued, taking a couple steps away from the hunter. We were both still armed. I didn't want to be the one to throw the first punch, but I would be ready if it came to that.

"You said we wouldn't destroy their souls. The goal was to kill them!" he ranted, pacing away from me and back again.

"I didn't want to. I tried. Couldn't you tell? You were in my brain. You've got the power to control me. Can't you tell that I tried?" A sickening feeling grew in the pit of my stomach as I replayed in my head that brief moment of panicked indecision. I had been left with an ugly choice of destroying the naturi souls or the chance that Danaus would destroy me if I fought him. Or worse still, he could have withdrawn his powers before killing our opponents, leaving us both weak and vulnerable.

But Danaus was right in his outrage. The decision to destroy their souls was growing too easy. There had been too little hesitation on my part when my attempt to burn their hearts failed, and no hesitation to reach out into Savannah and kill all those within my domain.

"This has to stop!" he proclaimed.

"I know," I said in a wavering voice. I closed my eyes

and sucked in a deep shuddering breath. "But what if there's more that we can do if we only learn to control this?"

"Control this?" Danaus stepped forward and grabbed both of my shoulders. "There's no controlling this, Mira! It's a curse from Hell. I'm trying to save my soul, not damn myself further."

"You're not going to Hell because of what you are," I snapped, knocking his hands off me and walking away from him.

"Prove it."

I couldn't, but that didn't matter. I believed you didn't get marked for Hell when you were born. You were marked for the choices you made, and we had made some really bad decisions so far.

"We had no choice," I said in a low steady voice, desperate to convince myself as much as I was trying to convince him. "If we hadn't done what we did, we would be dead right now. No one would be able to stop Rowe at Machu Picchu in a few nights, and the naturi would be walking free once again."

"We shouldn't have gone there in the first place!" he shouted, pointing back toward the south and the marshlands. "We knew it was a trap and we nearly got ourselves killed in the process. To make matters worse, we're paving our way to our own private section of Hell with convenient phrases like 'we had no choice.'"

"Don't talk to me about choices," I snarled, standing on the tips of my toes so I could clearly look him in the eye. "You didn't have to go. You're not the one that made a promise to Amanda to protect her. I did, and I was not about to abandon her to the naturi because it was inconvenient to our plans."

"You left me with no choice. If I had let you go without me, you would have gotten yourself killed and then we'd all be screwed!"

"I refuse to regret what we did tonight!" I screamed at him, the last of my composure cracking like an eggshell under his boot. "You don't know what it's like being held by them. Night after night, the endless pain and torture. And then never knowing if anyone is going to come for you, wondering if anyone even knows how to find you. Until you're no longer sure why you are even trying to survive."

Bloody tears streaked down my face, but I couldn't bring myself to wipe them away. Rage and old feelings of complete helplessness boiled up inside of me, leaving me clenching my shaking fists at my sides. I hated myself for losing my composure in front of Danaus. I hated him for seeing me in this moment of weakness when I needed to always be strong in front of him, in front of all the others who looked to me for some kind of direction in this moving disaster.

To my surprise, Danaus wrapped his arms around me and pulled me against his chest, breaking down the last of the walls that surrounded the memories of my captivity with the naturi. In all the long years, I had never allowed myself to cry. Not when Jabari saved me on that distant mountain or during the long centuries that passed. But now I buried my face in his strong chest and let the tears slip unchecked from my clenched eyes. I opened my fists and held onto his sides when my legs no longer wanted to support me under the weight of the memories that danced through my mind. Too many nights spent under the knife with Nerian, too many blank spaces in my mind that either I couldn't or didn't want to remember—the horrible things that happened to me.

"I hate them," I groaned past the fist-sized lump in my

throat. "I hate them all so much. I hate them for what they did to me. I hate them for what they are doing to my people."

Danaus said nothing as I stood trembling in his arms. He didn't have to. He had held Nerian captive for roughly a week, and the naturi had been happy to regale him with stories of all that he'd done to me. The hunter knew how long I had been held and how I was tortured. The hunter knew more of my horrible past than any other living creature on the planet, had even seen the scars carved into my back. With Danaus, there was no hiding for me.

After several minutes I finally stepped out of his warm embrace and walked a few feet away from him as I wiped the tears from my face. I could smell his scent on me now, the scent of sea and the sun. Clean and clear and peaceful. Some of the weight that I had been carrying for more than five hundred years finally lifted from my shoulders and the ball of anger in my chest had diminished somewhat.

"What are you going to do with her?" he softly asked when I finally had my wits about me again.

It was on the tip of my tongue to say that I was going to do to her what they did to me, but I couldn't utter the words because I knew it wasn't the truth. Torture was a dark path I had left behind me some years ago. Now, when I killed something, it was a quick and merciless action. There was no torture, certainly not like what I endured. I liked to think that I no longer had the stomach for it.

"I plan to see if she has any useful information to give us and then I'm going to kill her. Nothing more," I said, turning back around to face the hunter. However, I couldn't quite meet his gaze. I simply shoved my hands into my pockets and stared at the sidewalk in front of me. "I can't imagine that she can honestly be used as a bargaining chip with the naturi."

Danaus placed his hand under my chin, forcing me to raise my eyes to meet his piercing gaze. "What if she truly doesn't know anything at all?"

"Then she'll die a quick death."

"And if she is what she says she is, a traitor to the naturi?"

"Then we might finally have something interesting on our hands," I said, forcing a smile onto my lips. I slowly took a step backward, removing my chin from his light touch. "Watch her for a while. I need to see to something."

"Will you be back tonight?"

I glanced up to the night sky, catching glimpses of starlight as the dark clouds floated by. We still had a few hours until sunrise. "I honestly don't know."

Danaus nodded and stepped aside so I could walk past him to the car. As I reached it, he handed me the keys, a worried look passing over his stony features. It felt as if something was hanging unsaid in the air. I didn't know what it was that he wanted to say to me, but he never spoke a word as he climbed the front stairs and entered the town house.

Heaving a soft sigh, I got into my car and drove quickly to my home just outside the city limits, where I knew Tristan would be waiting for me. I had only to briefly touch his mind to realize that the night was not going well for the young nightwalker.

As I pulled into the garage, I opened my mind and followed the path back to him. He was standing in front of one of the windows on the second floor looking out on the front yard, his emotions a mass of pain, anger, and confusion. The naturi might have taken only Amanda, but they had hurt Tristan as well.

The only light in the room poured through the window, giving his pale skin a faint glow. His arms were crossed over his chest and his shoulders were rigid as tension hummed through his entire body.

Frowning, I watched the young nightwalker in silence. I couldn't leave him brooding over whatever dark thoughts plagued him. Since coming to my domain, I had yet to see him actually happy. Sarcastic, bitter, worried, and melancholy were the emotions he seemed to be limited to despite my efforts to make him feel welcome. Yet, it was understandable. He was still dealing with his new position in Savannah, as well as his past with our maker, Sadira. We all had ghosts that haunted us in some manner, and most were not that easy to eradicate.

"How is Amanda?" I asked, knowing she was somehow at the root of his dark mood.

"I have no idea. You would need to ask her or Knox." He refused to look at me as he spoke.

"What happened?" I stepped farther into the room, to stand beside the large king-size bed that had never been slept in.

"The naturi happened," he snarled at me. "I've gone from having Sadira ruin my life to having the naturi mucking up this too-long existence."

"What did she say?" I pressed, inwardly dreading the response.

"She won't come near me," he said. Tristan whirled around to face me, his blue eyes glowing in the darkness. "She would allow only Knox to help her; only Knox could touch her.

"She's been through a lot, Tristan. Knox is familiar to her," I coaxed, trying to calm him down.

"No! It's because I failed to protect her from the naturi and the shifters. When they attacked, I should have been able to handle the situation and stop the naturi. But I couldn't. I failed her and she was taken."

He picked up a delicate snow globe from the end table near him and hurled it across the room, aiming to smash it against the far wall. I took a quick step to my left and caught it awkwardly before dropping it safely to the bed.

"Sadira kept me weak," he continued to rage, his hand shaking before him.

"You're still young," I countered.

"I'm weak for someone my age. Don't deny it!" he said, pinning me with his angry gaze.

"I won't deny it," I replied with a shrug. "You are weak for a nightwalker of your years. But that's not your fault. That's Sadira's doing. She wanted to keep you weak because she got burned by me."

Tristan shoved both his hands through his shoulder-length brown hair and turned back toward the window. "I'm useless," he murmured. "She made me useless."

"Stop it!" My voice cracked across his shoulders like a whip, causing him to flinch. "That's nonsense and you know it. You're not useless. I don't waste my time with useless creatures."

"Why?" he said with a shake of his head as he turned back toward me. "Why did you save me from Sadira? I've never understood it."

"Because I saw in you the potential to be something great and I wanted that person on my side," I admitted, with a cocky smile lifting one corner of my mouth. I thought he had great potential if he could finally escape Sadira's long reach. But we were all damaged in our own unique ways. Tristan had to find a way to use that damage to his advantage.

"What about Amanda?" he asked. The glow had faded

from his eyes, and his shoulders slumped under the weight of his concerns. The rage was gone for now.

"Give her time. The naturi are still haunting her thoughts," I said, sitting down on the edge of the bed.

"And if she can't forgive me?"

A heavy sigh slipped past my lips as I looked down at my empty hands. It was a possibility. "If she understands you that little, then she doesn't deserve to have you in the first place, and you're both better off."

"I hope you're wrong."

"So do I, because if I'm not, it means I sorely misjudged her."

Tristan gazed back out the window, the fingers of his right hand pressed to the glass. The only sound for several minutes was the gentle hum of the air conditioner pumping cold air through the house. Both of us settled into our own thoughts.

I could understand why Amanda was so important to him. It was more than finally meeting a creature that was interested in him and he was interested in as well. It was the ability to make that choice to pursue or walk away. It was the excitement of slowly developing an emotional bond with someone over time. Sadira had directed all of his interactions—told him who to kiss, touch, and sleep with. In the end even our relationship had been forced upon him. Amanda represented his first choice as an individual in more than a century. I could understand why he didn't want to lose his chance at that.

"Did you kill it?" he suddenly asked, crashing into my thoughts. It took me several seconds to realize he was talking about the naturi we had found captive with Amanda.

"No, not yet," I said, shaking my head. Laying my left

hand on the bed comforter, my fingers aimlessly traced over the pattern.

Tristan turned away from the window, his brow furrowed in confusion. "You're kidding, right? How could you have not killed it?"

"She's a potential source of information. She may be able to tell us something about the naturi's plans."

Taking a few steps closer to me, he leaned forward, bracing his hands against the back of a chair that stood between us. "You expect her to tell you the truth?"

"Not really." I admitted with a slight shrug.

"Then why take her? Why risk the naturi coming after her?" I smiled at him, finally bringing a snort of laughter from the young nightwalker. "Bait."

"The naturi aren't the only ones who know how to set a trap," I said. "Danaus and I cleared the area of naturi tonight. We've got a small window of time to use her as bait to draw out Rowe or simply kill her."

"You expected him already, didn't you?"

My smile faded into a frown as my eyes returned to the blue and gray comforter. I had expected the one-eyed naturi more than a month ago. I expected him to be hounding my every step. Instead he sent a small army to harry my every waking moment, destroy the local werewolf pack, and winnow down the number of nightwalkers within my domain. Rather than attacking me personally, he was trying to turn my allies against me. Soon I would have no safe haven within this world, and I believe that was his ultimate goal.

"Rowe's not coming here. Not without a little added incentive like my new captive," I replied.

"That's assuming he wants her back."

"True," I sighed as I pushed to my feet again. "Did Amanda say anything about the naturi?"

"No, not really. She asked if you were going to kill it. I told her yes. Are you going to prove me wrong?"

"I wasn't planning on it. How did Amanda react to the news of the naturi's imminent demise?"

"She didn't. Just stared straight ahead. She might have nodded. What are you thinking?"

"The water naturi at the island wasn't the leader," I slowly said, mostly thinking out loud. "She might have ordered the attack while we were in the water, but she wasn't shouting orders once we got to the shore. No one was."

"What are you thinking?"

"What if we have their leader?"

"The naturi? The one held with Amanda? Their leader? Are you thinking they turned on her?" Tristan said, straightening from his leaning position.

"No, I'm thinking she's a spy. I need to check on Danaus and Shelly. If you talk to Amanda before I return, ask her if she knows anything about the naturi that was being held with her," I said, heading toward the door.

"What do you want to know?" Tristan asked, following me out of the room.

"How was she treated? Who was giving the orders on the island?"

"If I see her, I'll ask," he called as I rushed down the stairs.

Around me, I could feel the night decaying, showing its age, and I was growing tired. After the fight on the island, I needed to feed, but there wasn't time. I pushed down my rising hunger and tried to ignore the fatigue gnawing at my limbs. I had to get back to Danaus and Shelly.

Thirteen

A s I reached the ground floor and turned toward the back door and the garage, I sensed someone walking up the front stairs to the house. I paused in the rarely used kitchen and cocked my head to the side as my senses probed farther from my body. It was Amanda.

Jogging through the house, I jerked open the front door as she raised her hand to knock. Tristan had sensed her as well because he was now standing at the bottom of the curved staircase, his emotions a ball of tensed anxiety.

The young nightwalker stood alone on my front porch in a clean change of clothes, but she had yet to bathe. Her blond hair was still dirty and matted from her ordeal, while dirt smudged both of her cheeks as well as her bare arms. There was no expression on her pale face, as she seemed to stare blankly through me.

"Amanda," I murmured, motioning for her to enter the house. "Where's Knox?"

She stepped inside and gave a slight shake of her head. "He's gone. I told him to go home."

I could no longer sense an overwhelming hunger in her, so I felt it safe to assume that Knox had stuck around long enough to help her feed, ensuring that no unfortunate mistakes were made before he gave her a little space. However, I couldn't begin to guess why she had decided to show up on my doorstep so close to sunrise.

"You should be resting," I chided, closing the door behind her.

Amanda frowned, and I could feel the first bubble of anger rise within her. "I came to tell you that I accept your offer. I want to be a part of your family."

At first I thought she simply felt obligated to join my family because I'd risked my life to save her, but there was something buried within her tone that made me doubt it. "But . . . ?" I said, causing her head to snap around to me. I arched one eyebrow at her, questioning. "You don't want to be."

"I'm a target now because I've been seen with you, with Tristan. Why shouldn't I join your family when it's the only way I'm going to be protected from the naturi?" she said in a voice so low it was nearly a snarl.

"She warned you that you would be a target of the naturi when we met last night," Tristan said. While I appreciated his defense, "I told you so" wasn't going to help Amanda right now.

"Last night, you were eager to join my family. Now you've had a taste of the naturi in the area, and you're unsure of what you want," I said, walking toward my study.

"I know what I want!" she shouted, losing her temper finally. "I never want to be touched by the naturi again. You have no idea what it's like to be held by them! To be tortured, drained, and taunted while you wait for an even more painful death."

The distance closed between us in a flash as fury consumed my every thought. Wrapping my fingers around her throat, I threw her into the wooden railing of the staircase, causing the wood to crack and groan. I then slammed her into the marble floor, earning a whimper from her.

To my surprise, Tristan stepped forward and placed one foot on her stomach while wrapping his right hand in her hair. He was preparing to hold her still for me so I could continue to knock her around. Punishment was something he had come to understand during his time with Sadira. He was ready to put aside what feelings he had for Amanda and hold her down because of his loyalty to me. Tristan was stronger than anyone gave him credit for.

Struggling to get a grip on my anger, I balled my shaking hands into fists at my sides. "Let her up," I growled at Tristan, and then turned my attention to Amanda. "You will never question the depth of my understanding of the naturi. I know better than any exactly what they are capable of."

"I have no choice," she complained, which brought a chuckle to my throat. It was a common complaint.

"No one is forcing you to join my family, and I would prefer it if you didn't join because you felt trapped into doing so," I said, some of the fury and tension sliding from my frame.

"But if I don't, I leave behind my position in the community. I lose your protection," she countered.

"True, but your other choice is to leave Savannah." Out of the corner of my eye I saw Tristan flinch, taking a jerky step forward as if he could stop my words from reaching her ears. "Leave here and I'm sure the naturi won't follow you. You wouldn't be the first to leave here because of the naturi."

"I'm not leaving," she stubbornly said.

A smile tweaked the corner of my lips. I wasn't the only one clinging to this city, a place I called home. "Now you have to decide whether you want to be a part of my family. Are you willing to serve and obey me? Are you willing to face the naturi again?"

"I want to join your family," she said, pushing slowly to her feet again.

"I don't want you if your only reason is to protect your own skin."

"It's not. Being in the family will enable me to protect others from the naturi," she quickly said, her eyes briefly drifting to Tristan and then back to me.

An ugly smirk twisted my lips as my eyes narrowed at her. "Tristan doesn't need your protection. He's strong enough to face the naturi. I will personally see to that." I shook my head and turned my back on her. "I've changed my mind. You're not the person I thought you were. I rescind my offer."

"No!" she cried.

"Mira, please!" Tristan shouted. I turned to find him standing between me and Amanda. "She's been through something terrible. She needs time to recover. She's not thinking clearly. Please, reconsider. She belongs with us." The nightwalker reached out and clasped my right hand in both of his.

"Then she should have stayed in her home and recovered from her encounter instead of coming here and insulting our family," I snapped.

"I'm sorry," Amanda murmured. "I—I—"

"Which naturi was giving orders while you were being held?" I demanded, quickly changing subjects. I didn't want to hear her apologies right now. She had insulted both

Tristan and me, coming to my home with her whining complaints and feelings of entrapment.

"I—I don't understand," she replied, shoving one hand through her hair to push it away from her face.

I resumed my trek into my study, their footsteps following me across the marble and hardwood floors. "If you're going to be in this family, you're going to be of use to me," I said irritably. "Who was giving orders?"

"I'm not sure. Knox said that you killed everyone on the island," she said.

I glanced over my shoulder to find her hovering in the doorway. Where she had been eager to explore and soak in every inch of my house last night, she was now equally hesitant to enter my world and endure my gaze. She feared me again, which was something I needed since I no longer had her absolute loyalty, like Tristan.

"Nearly," I admitted. "The naturi that was being held prisoner still lives. Was she a prisoner when you arrived?"

"Yes. They beat her every time she spoke. She always wore manacles. They tried to get me to drink her blood," Amanda quickly explained.

Standing beside my desk, I turned over a silver-plated hourglass. It was possible that what Amanda saw was the truth, but then it could just as easily have been an act. I didn't trust Cynnia or my luck when it came to the naturi. It was too much to hope that I had managed to get my hands on someone that could actually help me get closer to Rowe and potentially Aurora.

The black sand poured from the upper glass chamber in a steady stream, building in the lower chamber in a spent pile. We were all running out of time. The night was wearing down, and I needed to make some decisions about Cynnia before Danaus and I left for Peru. I also needed to make some serious attempts to learn some earth magic before I climbed to the Incan ruins.

At the same time, I felt as if I needed to put Tristan and Amanda on a healing path. What if I didn't come back from Machu Picchu? I wanted to know that Tristan would be safe and happy in Savannah, and that would only happen if Amanda respected him. Too much to do and too little time.

My fingers drifted over the glass bulb of the hourglass, wishing I could slow those seconds down. "Stay here, today. Tristan will find a safe place for you to sleep. I have some business to complete."

"It's getting late, Mira," Tristan reminded me. "Can't it wait until tomorrow?"

"I'm running out of tomorrows," I said with a frown as I lifted my hand from the hourglass. "I'll be back before the sun rises."

"I am truly sorry, Mira," Amanda said, trying to draw my gaze back to her form, but I refused to lift my eyes from the surface of my desk. "I didn't mean to insult you. It's . . . it's the naturi. I—"

"I'm not the one you should be apologizing to," I said, then silently slipped out of the room, leaving Tristan and Amanda alone to finally face the battle they had both survived in different ways.

I had dipped into Tristan's mind when I found him in Forsyth Park, watched it replay the battle in gory detail. He had held his own, killing several of the wolves that overwhelmed him. They had surrounded him, separating him from Amanda when she was grabbed by the naturi. He had performed well, but it wasn't enough to save Amanda.

He blamed himself for his capture when there were few who would have been able to save her. She needed to understand that he had been there for her, argued for her rescue when common sense said to abandon her. I had a feeling this was their only chance, and I wished them luck.

Fourteen

Summer was in its last days but you wouldn't know it in Savannah. The air was still hot and heavy with the scent of flowers and earth. It was well after midnight now and the traffic had slowed to the point of being nearly nonexistent. I was sure the bars down along the riverfront were still seeing some action. Yet I remained away from the buzz on River Street, returning to the one place I thought I wouldn't see again tonight: my own town house. When I left Danaus, I had sworn to myself I wouldn't return until tomorrow night; that I needed more time to relax from the battle, to think and detach myself from the naturi that was now in my grasp.

On the drive over I knew I was being drawn back to my town house for more than just my need to talk to Cynnia and to see that my companions were safe. I needed to talk to Shelly. Standing outside the front gate, I scanned the house. Danaus was in the front living room with, I assumed, Cynnia.

Pausing there, I mentally reached out along the well-trod path between my mind and Danaus's. The more we mentally touched, the easier it became. While I wished it wasn't so, I couldn't deny that the ability to communicate with him this way was useful.

Is the naturi with you? I demanded suddenly in his brain.

Yes. What's wrong? His reply was instantaneous, as if he were expecting my touch.

Nothing, I thought with a faint sigh. *We'll talk more soon.*

I wasn't particularly happy about the arrangement, but this was the best option for all those involved. I would have preferred to keep the naturi locked up in the warehouse I owned downtown, but it was inconvenient for all those involved. Danaus would be stuck there during the day guarding her, and I couldn't guarantee his privacy. I just had to remind myself that this was an extremely temporary arrangement.

Shelly, on the other hand, was alone in the backyard. Slipping silently past the iron gate, I walked around the house to find her seated on the ground with her face in her hands.

"I hesitated," she announced into the air before I could start to approach her. I hadn't made a sound and yet she knew I was there.

"You choked," I corrected, shrugging off the trick. Maybe something in the earth had told her I was coming. I entered the backyard, coming to stand several feet away from where the witch sat on the ground.

"I'm sorry," she murmured, twisting around to look up at me. Her large eyes were red-rimmed and her face was flushed from crying. My stomach twisted with guilt and regret when I looked at her. My instincts had told me she was not ready for a fight with the naturi, but I let my need for manpower override my common sense, and her presence had endangered everyone. If I was to survive the upcoming battle at Machu Picchu, I needed to be more aware of who comprised my team and less worried about the numbers. But then I wasn't the only one there with a hard lesson to learn.

"I'm not the one you should be apologizing to. Your hesitation and inability to handle the situation put Tristan and Knox in serious danger. They could have been killed trying to protect you when their main concern should have been saving Amanda," I explained.

"I know. It won't happen again," Shelly affirmed, wiping the last of the tears from her face. She turned on the ground so she was facing me.

"I know it won't. Your assistance is no longer needed here," I firmly said, shoving my hands into the front pockets of my leather pants. "You're free to go back to Charleston or wherever Danaus brought you from."

"What? I don't understand."

"I can't allow you to endanger my people."

She unfolded her legs so she could push to her feet. "But I thought you needed me to help you learn how to use earth magic. I can still help you," she argued.

"I need to learn how to use this magic in an aggressive manner, for fighting. I don't get the impression that you even know how to do that."

"I do!"

"Prove it," I growled. In the blink of an eye my hand slipped down to the knife in the sheath on my belt. With a flick my wrist the knife spiraled through the air toward her. I was careful to aim it to land a foot in front of her, but to my surprise she deftly rolled out of the way of the approaching blade and got to her feet. With a wave of her hand, three balls of fire appeared before her and shot toward me.

"Normally a nice move," I said, raising my hand to catch each of the fireballs as they approached me. "But I'm the Fire Starter. Fire isn't about to stop me."

"True, but this might," Shelly said between clenched teeth. She moved her left hand in another sweeping motion, but no fire appeared. I prepared to pitch my own ball of fire at the little witch when vines broke out of the ground and wrapped around my ankles. The plant quickly thickened so they were like ropes snaking up my legs to my knees, holding me trapped to the spot on the stone patio.

"It's a nice start, but it still won't hold me for long," I said with a smirk. Fire ate at the vines, and with a little tug, I pulled free again.

Shelly gave out a little grunt of frustration and took a step back for every step I took toward her into the yard. When the fight started, I had cloaked the yard from the view of any neighbors that might decide to look out their windows. I didn't want to waste my evening wiping the memories of my darling neighbors because they saw fireballs, or plant life, crawling across my back lawn.

"It's a nice effort, but you don't have it in you to attack a person with the skills you have," I commented, stopping when we were both in the center of the yard. "You have to be willing to kill the creature that is trying to kill you. Not everyone has that instinct."

"You're wrong," she sneered.

I hadn't a chance to react. Vines burst out of the ground, wrapping around both my arms and legs in the blink of an eye. My entire body was lifted up and my back was slammed into the trunk of the nearest tree. Stars exploded before my eyes and my vision briefly swam, destroying my ability to concentrate. Before I could conjure the thought to burn the vines, I felt a sharp point pressing against my chest just over my heart. I looked down to find a fifth vine shaped like a sharpened staff and pointed directly at my heart. A wrong word from me, a flinch, and Shelly would have me staked.

"Admit it," she shouted in an angry voice. "I've got you."

Instead of conceding like a sane person would, I started to laugh. My head fell back and hit the trunk of the tree behind me as laughter poured from my throat. "Yes, you've got me! Why couldn't you have done this sooner?"

"They attacked with animals! Helpless animals. It wasn't their fault they were attacking us."

"So your answer is to let them kill us?"

"I believe that you should find another way besides killing when it comes to fighting your enemy. Isn't there another way?"

"No, there isn't," said a sad voice from the house. We both looked up to find Cynnia standing in the open doorway and Danaus on the patio with a long knife in his hand. "Mira is right in that there is no other way to deal with my kind. Aurora believes that the only way to save the earth is through the total extermination of all nightwalkers and humans," she continued, closing the door behind her as she came to stand on the patio beside Danaus.

"What are you doing out here?" I snapped, ignoring the fact that I was still held completely defenseless and in absolutely no shape to start shouting orders.

"She said that she felt someone using a great deal of earth magic out here," Danaus replied before Cynnia could speak up. "I thought it might be a good idea to check it out."

"Shelly, put me down."

"Can I stay?"

Instead of answering, I closed my eyes and concentrated on the vines wrapped around my arms and legs as well as the one that still pressed against my chest. I didn't like being in this position. I wasn't sure what Cynnia was capable of, but there was the potential that a single thought from her and I was dead. The vines immediately went up in flames around me, but neither my clothes nor my skin were singed.

Dusting off the last of the debris, I looked over at the earth witch who stood clasping both of her hands before her. She had the power I needed in someone who could handle themselves with the naturi, but she seemed to lack the killer instinct of Danaus or the nightwalkers that surrounded me. There was a time in my life when I wouldn't have seen that as a bad thing, but in my world as it stood now, it was positively fatal. If she wasn't willing to kill a creature whose only goal was to kill her, she was undoubtedly going to end up dead, and it would be on my shoulders.

Yet, if she knew what was at a stake and still wanted to stay, I could only hope that she would learn to take care of herself before it was too late. There was only so much protection I could offer her.

"Mira?" Shelly pressed softly.

"You protect when I tell you to protect and kill when I tell you to kill. Endanger another one of my people and I'll kill you myself," I threatened. It was the closest she was going to get to an acquiescence out of me.

Walking back toward the house, I paused at the edge of the patio and stared at the naturi.

"I heard stories about you," she volunteered when she realized that I was staring expectantly at her, waiting to hear whatever thoughts were churning away in her brain. "I thought you were a myth, a scary tale my sister Nyx made up to frighten me. I never expected you to be real."

"Nyx? How many sisters do you have?" I demanded, irritated. I wasn't exactly pleased to discover that I was a bedtime story for the naturi.

"Two. Aurora and Nyx."

"And Nerian was your brother," I said in a low voice that seemed to crawl across the distance separating us.

"Yes," she replied with a frown marring her young face. "Nerian was the one that hurt you. He's the reason that you hate us all so much." My gaze automatically swung up to Danaus, but Cynnia spoke before I could utter the accusation that rested on the tip of my tongue. "No one told me. I can hear it every time you say his name. I've only known one other person to speak with such hatred."

"Who?"

"Aurora, when she's talking about you."

I smiled at the young naturi, my eyes undoubtedly bright with my contained laughter. The queen of the naturi not only knew who I was, but she hated me. It was a pleasantly uplifting thought.

"What am I to do with you?" I said aloud, though I was mostly talking to myself.

"Set me free," Cynnia suggested, raising her chained wrists. The sight of the iron bindings reminded me that while she was a naturi, she had also been a prisoner of her own kind. While I wouldn't call this an "enemy of my enemy is my friend" kind of situation, it did mean that she might be willing to provide me with some interesting information in an effort to prolong her own life.

"Why were you manacled and spellbound by your own kind?" I demanded.

"They called me a traitor. Said I wanted to betray our kind to the humans and the nightwalkers," she reluctantly admitted. She dropped her gaze down to her hands, where her long fingers fiddled with the iron chain connecting the two wrist irons.

"Is it true?" Danaus asked before I could.

"No! It's not like that!" she cried, her head snapping up again to look at him and me.

"What is it? How did you get here if you were trapped in the other world?"

"Aurora discovered during the past few years that the walls between our worlds were growing thin and weak. Some of our magic weavers could create a temporary hole in the barrier. We could send one or two people through, but we weren't sure they were actually arriving here," she explained.

"So you came alone?"

"No, there was another," Cynnia said. She wandered over to a chair and plopped down into the thick cushion. "She was a spell weaver, a powerful one. I trusted her. I thought she was going to find a way to help me, but it was all a lie. She dumped me with those naturi you found me with. She told them to kill me."

"But they didn't," Danaus prodded when she seemed to pause.

Cynnia shook her head slowly. "They were afraid to, I think. I am sister to the queen, after all."

"So they decided to leave the job to me," I said, folding my arms over my chest. "It's an interesting theory, but it only explains how you got here. Now what about why you're here?"

"I think Aurora is wrong," she whispered, as if afraid one of her own kind was listening in.

"About what?"

"This war."

"I don't believe you," I snarled, taking a step closer to her.

"Mira—" Shelly started, but I held up my hand, halting the comment in her throat.

"It's too convenient. A naturi that wants to end this war winds up in the hands of the nightwalker that can potentially destroy their hopes of freedom," I said. "It's a trap."

"Are you sure?" Danaus asked, surprising me.

"She gets close because I believe her tale of woe, and she kills me," I argued, turning my attention to the hunter, who was now standing beside me.

"It can't be a trap because their plan has already failed," Cynnia said. "You were supposed to kill me back on the island when you rescued your friend."

"There's still time," I reminded her, which only made her smile at me.

"Yes, but if you kill me, I can't help you."

"Why would you want to do that?"

"Other than the fact that I believe there is a better way to end this war than killing everyone?" she asked, arching one thin eyebrow at me. "I think that my sister is trying to kill me."

"And I'm to be your protector?" I asked, my voice jumping in shock.

"Of course, you're the Fire Starter. She can't beat you."

I looked over at Danaus, who seemed to be struggling to keep a straight face, not that I could blame him. It all sounded pretty ridiculous, but it was all I had to go on for now.

Frowning, I was suddenly unsure of what to do with the

naturi. I didn't believe her, but there was this nagging question in the back of my mind. What if? What if it was the truth, and I had the power to destroy the naturi nation with this young naturi and her idealistic hopes for something other than war?

"If I'm going to help you, I'm going to need your cooperation," I said slowly.

"I'm not going to help you kill my kind. I'm not a traitor."

I smiled and took a step toward her. "We can avoid killing them if we can avoid them completely. How many naturi are in my city?"

"I'm not sure," she said, lifting her wrists. The iron manacles were blocking her ability to sense her own kind.

"They're not coming off, and you're becoming less valuable to me by the minute."

Cynnia released a heavy sigh before she stepped around me and walked into the yard. Sitting on the ground, she pulled off her worn brown boots and placed her bare feet in the grass. Her green eyes fell shut as her smooth brow furrowed in concentration.

"There aren't any close by," she murmured after a minute. "Not for a great distance—in the west and to the deep, deep south, across an ocean."

"Danaus?" I prompted, turning to the hunter in hopes of getting some confirmation.

"My reach isn't as strong as hers," he hedged, his deep voice close to a low growl.

Yet, before he finished talking, I felt him reach out with his powers, sending the warm wave of energy crashing through me. The touch was soothing, easing away some of the tension humming through my taut frame.

"There are no naturi within the immediate area," he said at last.

"So what do you hope I will be able to do for you?" I asked Cynnia, standing over her as she continued to sit in the grass. "Let me guess. You want me to allow the door to open so I can kill your sister." It was a story I had already heard before from another set of naturi, as well as from Macaire, one of the three Elders on the Coven.

"No! Absolutely not!" Cynnia awkwardly pushed back to her feet and took a step closer to me. "I want the door to stay shut. If she is forced to stay in her own realm, then she can't wage a war here."

"So Aurora will be stuck in her world and you'll be stuck here," I said, raising one eyebrow at her.

"Assuming that you let me live."

"Not likely," Danaus interjected before I could speak.

A smile haunted my lips as I wandered back into the yard and sat down in the grass not far from where Cynnia had sat only moments ago. I threaded my fingers through the cool grass, an interesting thought rolling around in my head. I could feel Danaus's censure before I even spoke my first word. The plan definitely had a few flaws to it.

"You've charged me with a difficult task," I drawled. "Not only must I stop Rowe and his plan to free your sister and the naturi horde, but I must also protect you from Rowe and Aurora because you have some grand idea of bringing a peaceful end to this fight. I'm the Fire Starter, not a god. You're expecting the impossible."

"Can't you raise an army?"

"An army will be raised to defeat Rowe. They will not do anything to protect your hide."

"Then what? What do you want from me?" she cried,

extending both her hands to me, palms out and open. "I'm offering you a chance for peace. Why are you fighting me?"

"I'm not. I'm being realistic. I've fought Rowe twice now and barely survived both encounters. I need an edge."

Cynnia took a step backward, the chains on her manacles jangling slightly as she raised one delicate hand to her throat. Her wide green eyes never wavered from my face. "What do you want?"

"Teach me how to use earth magic," I said with a grin.

The naturi gave a soft little laugh and dropped her hands back down to dangle before her. "That's impossible. Nightwalkers can't use earth magic."

I rose bonelessly to my feet, standing only a couple feet away from her. With a thought, a ball of fire blossomed between us. It slowly circled around Cynnia then came back to loop around me, forming a perfect figure eight—drawing us together. "I shouldn't be able to manipulate fire, but I can. I can lock the naturi away in a separate world. And just a few weeks ago I discovered that the well of energy from the earth can push itself into me like lightning through a conduit." I stepped closer, so the fireball now circled around us, keeping the others at a distance. "I heard the great earth mother roaring in my head, angry and powerful."

Cynnia tried to step back, but the ball of flames circling around us kept her close. She stared up at me, her mouth forming a perfect O.

"I can access the power of the earth when I am at one of the swells, but I have no control over it. If I don't learn to control this soon, I'm going to kill everyone around me, regardless of whether we are on the same side or not."

"And controlling it will give you the edge you're looking

for to defeat Rowe?" Cynnia softly asked, a frown marring her sweet young face.

"Rowe wants Aurora free. He will do whatever it takes to see that accomplished. From what I've seen, he's already mastered blood magic to find a means to his end. I have no doubt that he will kill everyone that stands in his way—human, nightwalker, and naturi alike."

"He's weaving blood magic?" Cynnia gasped, mindlessly taking a step backward. I roughly grabbed her arm and jerked her forward to keep her from getting burned by the fire that continued to circle us. She didn't seem to notice. "That's forbidden."

"I'm willing to guess that he's desperate and doesn't really care what is forbidden at this point."

"But if I'm to teach you earth magic, you'll have to remove these," she said, raising her manacles to me yet again.

I simply chuckled and shook my head. "Nice try. No, you'll be instructing me through the lovely Shelly here," I said, motioning toward the earth witch hovering on the edge of the patio, watching the entire conversation. "She was hired to help me with a little earth magic, and now we're both going to get a crash course in how to use earth magic, naturi style. And if that doesn't work, I'll kill you."

Cynnia glanced over at Shelly, who flashed her a somewhat sheepish grin while wagging her fingers at the naturi. There was nothing intimidating about Shelly, which was disheartening because I needed her to be an intimidating figure right now. Instead she came off looking like that sweet college roommate everyone loves.

"I—I don't know," Cynnia stammered, her gaze shifting from Shelly to me to the ground.

"You've got some time to think about it. We fly to Peru

in two nights. We begin lessons before we leave or I kill you in Cuzco."

I turned my attention to Shelly, who was staring at me with a stunned look on her face. She had just realized that my plan not only included her after her major screw-up on the island, but that she was now traveling to Peru to help me with the naturi. I wasn't pleased with the plan so far, but I hoped to keep her as far from the fighting as I could. I needed a tutor, and Cynnia and Shelly would just have to do.

With a wave of my hand, the fire that had been circling Cynnia and me disappeared. "Shelly, take Cynnia inside and put her back in the sleep spell. You are not to wake her until either Danaus or I say so."

I watched as the two walked across the patio, a new thought beginning to gnaw at the back of my brain when I caught a glimpse of Cynnia's solemn profile.

"Wait!" I called out, stopping Cynnia at the door. "Your sister, Nyx. Is she here as well?"

"Nyx? I . . . I don't think so," she slowly replied. She paused, nibbling on her lower lip in thought before she spoke again. "I arrived here with only the spell weaver. Nyx and Aurora didn't know anything about my coming here. Do you think she's come for me?"

"Would she side with you or Aurora?" Danaus inquired, slipping his hands into his trouser pockets.

"Aurora," she whispered. "My sister Nyx is the defender of our people. She would follow Aurora to the ends of the earth to protect my people and do what is best for them."

"Does she look like you?"

"Why? Have you seen her?" Cynnia demanded, coming back down a stair toward me.

"How can I have seen her if I don't know what she looks like? I want to know in case we meet up with her in Peru."

Cynnia paused, a frown playing on her lips. She finally sighed and walked back toward the door into the house. "No, she doesn't look much like me, and nothing like Aurora. Tall and thin like a willow, with perfect white skin and midnight black hair. Her eyes are slate gray like the color of storm clouds."

"And is she of the wind clan? Like you?"

"How did you know I was—"

"Your coloring and build. It was also a guess."

"Yes, we're both from the wind clan. Aurora is of the light and Nerian was from the animal clan," Cynnia tightly said, finally becoming irritated by my invasive questions. "Anything else?"

"How is it possible that four siblings were born of three different clans?" Danaus demanded. "Did you all have different parents?"

"No!" Cynnia gasped, her lovely features twisting momentarily in anger. "My father was of the earth clan and my mother was of the light clan. Which clan we are born into is not determined by our parentage. It's determined by the need of the earth. If mother earth is in need of more wind clan members, then the next children born will be of the wind clan and so on."

"That will do. Sweet dreams," I taunted.

Danaus and I stood in silence outside that house as we listened to Shelly and Cynnia moving to one of the bedrooms on the second floor. I kept my focus tightly on Shelly, my mind a shadow in her thoughts, which were racing a mile a minute as she reviewed everything that had happened to her that evening. Since I couldn't sense the naturi, this was the safest way for me to keep an eye on Cynnia while Shelly cast the spell. At the same time, I knew that Danaus was focused on Cynnia, making sure the naturi didn't try to pull a fast one.

"Is taking either of them that good of an idea?" Danaus asked after Shelly had completed her spell, knocking Cynnia safely out for a while.

"We'll try to keep them both in the city, out of the Sacred Valley. Shelly might be able to teach me a few things before the sacrifice. At this point, any new knowledge will help me when it comes to dealing with the power swell at Machu Picchu."

"And the naturi?"

"Bait for Rowe."

"You think she's going to actually teach you anything?" he asked, shoving one hand through his shoulder-length hair, pushing it out of his face. His brilliant blue eyes reflected some of the light coming from inside the house, reminding me of the first night we met. I had not expected our association to last this long.

"Not really. Even if she does want peace for her people, she's not going to risk making a stronger enemy for them to face."

Danaus dropped his hand back to his side and stared up at the stars for a moment. The night was nearly done. I needed to get back to the safety of my home. As it was, I was exhausted and the blood lust was gnawing at my insides like the fires of hell.

"Do you believe her?" Danaus asked, pushing aside my thoughts of blood and sleep.

"About wanting peace?"

The hunter gave a soft grunt that I took for a yes.

"It doesn't matter whether I believe her or not. Our plan is set for when we arrive at the sacrifice at Machu Picchu in a few nights. We stop Rowe. We stop the sacrifice. We finally reform the seal. Thoughts of peace and war—we don't have the luxury of debating such things. We have to stop Rowe."

"I agree, but you didn't answer my question. Do you believe her?" he repeated.

It was my turn to stare up at the stars that were winking out above me as daylight approached. Dawn was coming. Did I believe Cynnia?

"No, I don't," I murmured.

But the problem wasn't that I didn't believe her. It was that for the first time in my life I truly wished I could believe that the naturi was telling the truth. I wished she did want peace and was seeking a way for naturi and nightwalkers to coexist on this planet without the constant fighting. I wished it were a possibility. But it wasn't. Not so long as creatures like Aurora and Rowe existed. Not so long as I existed would there ever be peace between the nightwalkers and the naturi.

Fifteen

I arrived at my town house the following evening to find Danaus with his various weapons spread out across my parlor coffee table. He was running a check over his equipment, which seemed to have multiplied since his arrival in Savannah. Standing in the doorway to the parlor with my hands on my hips, I stared at the spread—an unfortunate reminder that we had to fly to Peru tomorrow night.

"Don't scratch up the table," I said by way of announcing my arrival.

"They're in the kitchen," Danaus replied, not even looking up from the gun he was cleaning.

"Magic lessons begin tonight. Pack up your toys. I want you to come along."

A smirk lifted one corner of his mouth as his eyes shifted up to me for the first time. "Wouldn't miss it for the world."

I shook my head at him as I continued down the hall to the kitchen. "Well, isn't this coz—y," I said, choking on the last syllable when my gaze fell on James, who was sitting at the table with Cynnia and Shelly, sipping iced tea.

The Themis member immediately jumped to his feet, his left hand smoothing his tie. A wobbly smile perched on his lips. James was the last person I expected to see sitting at my kitchen table. I could only guess that the warlock Ryan was up to something.

"Mira—"

"Is Ryan here as well?" I asked, rudely cutting off whatever he was going to say.

"No, I came alone."

"With me," I snapped, motioning for him to follow me down the hall to the office, where I shut the door behind him sharply. Turning on my heel, I quickly closed the distance between us and gripped him in a hug. I felt him flinch at my touch but ignored it.

"I'm so glad to see that you are safe. Have you healed completely from Crete?" I demanded, my hands resting on his shoulders as I held him at arm's length from me.

"Y-Yes, I'm fine," he said, his eyes wide with surprise behind his gold, wire-rimmed glasses. "There were no complications and I healed quickly."

"Ryan is such a bastard," I growled, releasing James as I paced away from him to the desk at the opposite end of the room. "He had no business bringing you along to Crete. You could have been killed."

"I wanted to go," James firmly said, but I just shook my head.

"Ryan knew how dangerous it was, and you're in no way trained for such a situation." I paced back away from the desk and plopped down in one of the chairs, motioning for James to take the seat next to me.

"It wasn't just about the naturi," he said, slowly taking the seat beside me. "I should have been the one to tell you about Michael."

I shook my head, balling my fists in my lap. "You weren't

his keeper." The thought of Michael's dead body being taken still angered me beyond rational behavior, but I was getting control of my temper. "Least of all, you weren't the keeper of his corpse."

"It was my job to see to them while they were on the Compound grounds," he said.

"You're absolved," I said with a wave of my hand. "My main concern is the naturi now. It is unfortunate, but as Ryan said, Michael is dead. They can't hurt him now."

"Thank you, Mira," James said, straightening his glasses on his long, slender nose.

"What are you doing here anyway?" I demanded, shrugging off his comment. I didn't deserve his thanks—the disappearance wasn't his fault.

"I came to tell you that the next sacrifice location is going to be at Machu Picchu, Peru," he said, leaning forward in his excitement.

"So I've heard," I muttered, falling back to rest against the back of the chair while I stretched out my legs to cross them at the ankle.

"You've heard already?" he softly said, looking positively crestfallen.

"Two nights ago, Jabari dropped the news on me."

"Oh."

"Though I do appreciate the confirmation from Themis," I said, forcing a smile. "It's nice to know that the Coven isn't lying to me."

"You're welcome," he said, though he still looked a little disappointed that he wasn't the bearer of important information, as he had assumed.

"Of course, you could have just called and told us this information. What's the other reason for your appearance?"

A blush stained his cheeks as his brown eyes dropped down to his slender hands. "I also brought Danaus a fresh change of clothes as well as some additional weapons that I thought he might need for his trip to Peru. He's been on the road for a while now. I thought he could use some fresh items."

A smiled toyed with my lips, but I smothered it before he could see it. While James was a full-fledged researcher for Themis, his main role was assistant to both Danaus and Ryan, which included seeing to their random needs, such as fetching weapons, researching, and making travel arrangements. James was eager to be a part of the fray with Danaus, but his biggest stumbling block was that he was simply a human playing in the realm of powerful creatures out for blood. There was only so many ways he could be of assistance in our world, and right now he was limited to errand boy.

"I'm sure he's grateful for the fresh items," I said, hooking a stray stand of hair behind my right ear. "Is Danaus frequently away from the Themis Compound?"

"He spends more time away from it than at the Compound. He doesn't like to be settled in one place for too long," James admitted, sitting back in his chair as well.

"Where does he go?"

"Ryan usually has him on one mission or another," James said with a shrug of one shoulder.

"But Danaus hasn't been sent to kill that many night-walkers. If he had, I would have heard about him much sooner than I did, and he would have come after me much sooner." Unless, of course, Ryan had hidden my existence from the hunter for some reason—not that I currently found that strand of logic likely. "He must have somewhere that he goes when he's not on a mission for Themis."

A smile lifted James's lips and he shook his head at me as he sat up in his chair. "If you're trying to get some little tidbit of information regarding Danaus from me, you're not going to get anything interesting. Danaus doesn't talk to me. He doesn't talk to anyone. I'm sure there is plenty of time when he's not on a mission, but I don't know where he goes. I'm still trying to get him to carry a cell phone so I can locate him when he's needed."

I sighed and stared straight ahead at the desk that rested before me. Beyond it was a large window that looked out on the square, which was filled with enormous live oaks whose leaves blocked most of the street lamps. Night had settled in around us, and I was wasting it trying to pry information out of James regarding Danaus. It was nothing more than curiosity since I was willing to bet I already knew more about Danaus than the man that sat beside me.

"It's getting late," I announced, pushing to my feet with my powers. James jumped to his feet as well, moving a fearful step away from me as he saw the boneless way I rose. "We need to get going."

"Is there any way I can be of assistance?"

"You're not going to Peru," I snapped. The man's life had already been threatened and nearly taken in Crete. I wasn't about to risk it again.

"I didn't think so," he said with a little half smile. "I was thinking more along the lines of transportation, weapons, lodgings, etcetera."

"I have someone that can arrange all of that," I said with a shake of my head, then paused and looked over at him, scratching the tip of my chin with an index finger. "However, if Themis could convince the Peruvian government to close access to the mountain, it would be greatly appreciated. I would prefer it if I didn't have to worry about the naturi grabbing a bunch of tourists on their way up to the ruins."

"I'll see what we can do," he said, then extended his hand toward me. "I wish you luck. I hope that we have a chance to work together again. I feel there is a great deal that I could learn from you."

An evil grin lifted my lips and narrowed my eyes as I took his hand in mine. "You'd be stunned at what I could teach you, my friend. Have a safe journey home."

James followed me to the front door, but as I opened it, I discovered that I had a new visitor preparing to knock. Barrett stood there, looking somewhat haggard. If my heart still beat within my chest, it would have been racing. The Alpha of the Savannah pack was on my doorstep, and I had a naturi sipping tea in my kitchen. This wasn't something I could easily explain away—at least, not in any way that I was sure he would believe.

"Barrett!" I said, my voice jumping in surprise. The lycan shouldn't have surprised me. I should have sensed his arrival, but I'd been so focused totally on James and his unexpected appearance that I hadn't scanned the area around my home.

"I need to speak with you," Barrett said, nodding briefly to the other man, who stood next to me.

"Of course," I said, then said a quick good-bye to James before ushering Barrett quickly into my office. The lycanthrope seemed to sniff the air once before I managed to quickly shut the door and motion for him to take one of the chairs before the desk.

"What can I do for you?" I inquired, leaning against the front of the desk. A part of me inwardly prayed that Cynnia and Shelly remained happily ensconced in the kitchen until I managed to get the werewolf out of my town house.

"The naturi are gone from Savannah," he said, unable to hide his shock or relief.

"All but one, yes. They are gone," I hedged. If he did end up seeing Cynnia here, I didn't want to be caught in the middle of a lie, particularly when I so artfully manipulated him just the other night. I still needed him cooperating with me.

"You did this?"

"Danaus and I, yes."

"Why didn't you do this earlier?" he demanded, his relief giving way to frustration. I understood his anger. He had already lost two brothers to the naturi in the past couple of months.

"Because of the cost," I said softly, looking down at my feet, which were crossed at the ankle. "We attacked them last night to retrieve Amanda. We were outnumbered and nearly killed. A spell was cast in desperation, which wiped out almost all of the naturi in the region. It's something I hope to never do again."

Barrett frowned as he looked away from me and gazed out the window to the street beyond. He knew I wasn't going to provide any more information than I already had. And in fact I wasn't going to tell the lycanthrope that I was risking what was left of my soul and the soul of my companion. It wasn't any of his business.

"Did you have anything else?" I inquired, trying not to sound like I was rushing him.

"That name you gave me, Harold Finchley," Barrett said, his dark gaze snapping back to my face. "We don't have any record of a lycanthrope existing with that name."

"He may not have been from the U.S."

"I checked the database for both the U.S. and Europe. There's no record."

"So it must have been an alias," I murmured, talking to myself.

"Or he was a shifter that wasn't a part of any pack. A rogue acting alone."

I frowned at Barrett. It would make for a nicer, prettier explanation of what had happened. If this was just a case of a rogue shifter acting alone, it meant there wasn't a greater conspiracy against nightwalkers with the Daylight Coalition. It meant that lycanthropes weren't betraying the promise we had all made to protect each other from discovery and extermination.

Unfortunately, the witch that had been traveling with the lycan and the Coalition member made me doubt whether the lycan was acting alone or a part of something larger.

"Keep an ear to the ground for me," I said around a darkening frown. "I've got someone checking into the witch."

"Is there any chance of being able to speak with Finchley?" Barrett demanded, arching one brow at me.

"Not without a mystic," I said with a shake of my head. "I was in a hurry and I couldn't wait around to hand him over to someone who could take care of him properly. The laws are clear. Working with the Coalition is a death sentence."

"I'm not questioning your actions," Barrett said, raising both his hands as if to ward off my defensive statement. "However, this all could have been cleared up much easier if you had left him alive."

"Yes, well, it wasn't a possibility at the time." A knock at the door broke off my train of thought, snapping my attention to Danaus standing outside the office.

"What?" I rudely demanded, growing more anxious the longer Barrett was in my house.

Danaus opened the door and poked his head inside. "We need to get going. It's getting late."

"I know. We're almost finished. Pack up," I said with a nod. I appreciated Danaus's polite prod. I had no doubt that he could sense my anxiety and took the easy excuse to look in on me.

Unfortunately, I was out of time. Barrett took a long sniff of the air now that the door was open again. Damn the lycanthropes and their strong sense of smell! A low growl rumbled through the werewolf, and his eyes glowed when he looked up at me again.

"That last remaining naturi, it's here!" he snarled, jumping from his chair. He stalked out of the room, pushing roughly past Danaus while I followed on his heels.

"Yes, the naturi is here," I admitted, following, making a grab for his arm, but he jerked loose of my fingers.

He burst into the kitchen where Shelly and Cynnia were still seated at the table. Both women looked up and seemed to shrink in their seats at the sight of the rage twisting Barrett's face. The werewolf made a grab for Cynnia, but Danaus got there first and threw him across the room, where Barrett crashed into the wooden cabinets.

"Stop it, Barrett!" I shouted, coming to stand between the naturi and the lycanthrope. "I need her alive."

"You've just accused my race of siding with the Coalition, executed one of my people, and here you are harboring a naturi!" he shouted as he pushed back to his feet again. "How deep does your betrayal run?"

"I haven't betrayed you, Barrett." Reaching behind me, I grabbed the chain that linked Cynnia's manacles and pulled her to her feet so he could see the irons. "She's a prisoner. She's going to help me get close to Rowe, get me close to the people that can finally end all of this. If necessary, she's going to get me close to Aurora."

"Why is she so willing to help you?" Barrett asked. "Why is she so willing to turn on her own people? How can you trust her?"

"I don't trust her, but then again, I'm not giving her any choice. She has to help me if she wants to take her next breath."

"I don't trust you," he finally said, pushing away from the counter he was leaning against.

"You think I'm going to help the naturi?" I demanded, releasing Cynnia's chain. "After all the naturi that I've killed, after everything that I've survived at their hands, you think I would turn on my people? That I would turn on you?"

"Yes."

Danaus reacted before I could. The hunter grabbed Barrett by the collar of his shirt and slammed the man into the stainless steel refrigerator, hitting it hard enough to dent the front. "She's going to die in Peru for you in two nights," he snarled in a frightening low voice. "She's going to die for your worthless hide. She's going to die for every worthless vampire and werewolf that walks the earth because she sees it as her duty. Mira's willing to do whatever it takes to protect her people, even if it means enduring the presence of a naturi. What are you willing to do for your people?"

I took a jerky step backward at Danaus's words, a strange feeling twisting in my chest where my soul should have been. A part of me had always known that it was highly unlikely I would return to Savannah after the final sacrifice at Machu Picchu. I knew I would do whatever it would take to stop Rowe, even if it meant sacrificing my own life. But to actually hear the words aloud was a different matter. It seemed to crush the last of the flickering hope that burned inside of me, leaving me feeling cold and hollow. It bothered me to know that Danaus was aware that this was most likely our last battle together.

He released Barrett, and the werewolf slid to the floor, his knees buckling beneath him, but his gaze never wavered from my pale face. "I—I didn't know."

"You weren't supposed to. No one's supposed to know," I said with a shrug. "Do you think I want chaos in my domain? Besides, there's a slim chance I might actually survive this." I had no doubt that my brittle smile was completely unconvincing, but I had to try. I didn't want his pity. I just didn't want him causing problems while I was trying to take down the naturi nation by starting rumors like the nightwalkers were making bargains with the naturi. I could only fight one war at a time.

Stepping over to Barrett, I extended my hand to him, offering to help him to his feet. He hesitated, staring at my ghostly white hand for a few seconds before finally taking it and allowing me to help him up.

"I know this looks bad, but we've been friends for many years," I said, refusing to release his warm hand. "I've never betrayed you. I'm not about to start now when I need your friendship the most. If things go bad in Peru, there is a chance that everything could fall into chaos here. I expect Knox to take my place as Keeper of this domain. I would like to leave here with the knowledge that you will have his back."

"I'll stand by Knox. But who will have your back?"

"The hunter."

Barrett shook his head. "You're the only person I know who would surround herself with her enemy as a way of protection. Survive this, Mira."

The werewolf pulled his hand free and silently walked out of the house, slamming the door behind him.

My knees trembled and I wished I could crumple to the floor. My nights were undoubtedly numbered and my life was going to end in pain. And my closest companion, the one I would depend on to protect my back, was a man that had killed more nightwalkers than I cared to count. Why did I find such easy companionship with those that wanted me dead? Danaus. Jabari. I even seemed to have more in common with Ryan, despite the fact that the warlock had ordered my death. Maybe I had developed some secret death wish. Too many years on this earth had made me weary of this heavy coil. Whatever the reason I surrounded myself with people with such a lust for my blood, the result was going to be the same in the end. I would go to Peru and stop Rowe with Danaus at my side and Cynnia under my heel.

Sixteen

The car ride out into the Georgia wilds was painfully silent. Danaus sat in the backseat with Cynnia, while Shelly occupied the passenger seat beside me. A couple times the perennially sunny witch took a breath to make a comment, but seemed to quickly release the air again when the words continued to elude her. It was better this way. I didn't need the idle chatter to annoy me when my thoughts were solely focused on what lay ahead.

We were venturing out into the woods, where I could be as close to nature as possible, in hopes of someone being able to teach me something about earth magic. In my mind it was my last hope in gaining an edge over Rowe and the other naturi; it was my only chance of survival if Aurora was actually released from her cage. But by the mood in the car, I was beginning to have my doubts as to whether what I wanted would be enough to save myself and those around me.

I pulled the car off the expressway and drove for more than an hour along one winding rural road after another until there were only trees and farmland for as far as the eye could see. At long last I pulled off onto a rutted dirt road that seemed to burrow down into a grove of trees. Once the car was off the road and unlikely to attract the attention of anyone who might randomly drive by, I put the car in neutral and killed the engine.

"Everyone out. We're here," I announced, opening my car door.

"Where exactly is here?" Shelly said as she got out of the car and looked over the roof at me.

"Middle of nowhere, middle of the woods," I said, flashing her a wolfish grin. "I thought this would be the best place to practice in the event that anything caught on fire or worse."

"Good logic," Cynnia muttered behind me as she shut her door.

The trio of oh-so-happy campers followed me deeper into the woods. While Danaus, Cynnia, and I had perfect night vision, Shelly wasn't quite so lucky. She lagged behind the group, stumbling over broken branches as she struggled to see in the pitch-black darkness. Finally, Danaus took her elbow so he could guide her through the woods.

I halted the hike by a narrow stream filled with ankle-deep water that flowed over smooth, algae-covered stones. Standing in the middle of the stream, I tried to ignore how my feet cooled as the water flowed over my leather boots while I lifted my arms over my head. My eyes fell almost completely shut in concentration as I reached deep within myself. Around us, five balls of fire flickered into existence and hovered overhead, beating back the darkness.

"This is my power—the creation and control of fire," I announced to my companions. My strong, steady voice seemed to echo through the empty woods. "I've been able to do this since I was human. The power is fueled from the energy created by my soul. If I use it too much, I grow tired."

"And you retained this ability even after your conversion from human to nightwalker," Cynnia stated, settling on the bank of the stream, her eyes staring up at the fireball closest to her.

"I retained my soul, so I retained the ability." I lowered my arms back to my sides while I extinguished two of the five fireballs. "But then, all nightwalkers are limited to soul magic, or blood magic as it is commonly known among my kind. We lose our connection to the earth when we're reborn."

"I'm confused," Shelly said, speaking up. She carefully stepped down the bank to the edge of the stream so she was standing only a few feet away from me. Only Danaus remained higher up on the rise, looking down on us three, half hidden by the shadows. "If nightwalkers are limited to blood magic, why have you asked us to teach you earth magic? By your own admission, it should be impossible."

"But then so is my unique ability in both human and nightwalker form," I added, arching one brow at her. "What human have you known that could create fire? That's the realm of witches and warlocks, and only the more skilled. I was breaking the rules the day I was born."

"That logic doesn't mean you can break them all," Danaus called down at me, a smirk filling his tone.

"But I've already broken this next one," I said, my gaze sliding from the hunter to Cynnia. "At the swell on the island of Crete, I could feel the energy from the earth. It pressed against my skin, and when I used my ability, it entered me. I could use that power from the earth to fuel my fire, instead of using the energy from my soul."

"Amazing," she breathed.

"Yes, but I couldn't control it. It was pure raw energy that had found an outlet. I couldn't stop it, and I couldn't push it into any other kind of spell. There was only the need to create fire."

"Do you know any other spells?" Shelly inquired.

"No."

"Well, that's part of your problem," Shelly chuckled.

"But I'm not even sure how I technically control fire," I countered. "I woke up one day and I could. Time and practice have made the ability stronger and more dynamic, but I don't understand it any better."

"Mira," Cynnia slowly said, backing away from the edge of the water and up the bank toward Danaus. "At the risk of my own life, I was wondering if you considered that maybe, by some slight chance, you weren't born human."

"I was human," I snapped, taking a step toward her.

"But as you said, humans can't control fire like you do."

With a wave of my hand, the last of the fireballs were extinguished, plunging the woods into total darkness. "And if I wasn't human, what do you think I was?"

"Maybe you should have been a witch," Shelly quickly interjected.

"We both know witches and warlocks are trained; they're not born," I briskly said, my gaze not wavering from the naturi that seemed to be cringing near Danaus's feet. "No, you've got something else in mind."

"What you're describing is very similar . . . to how . . . light clan members manipulate fire," Cynnia said haltingly.

I was out of the water in a flash, coming up the hill, but was immediately halted by Danaus's long knife. He had lurched forward into a squat, hovering over Cynnia as he held the knife to my neck, holding me at bay. I had simply reacted to the horrid suggestion, no real thought crossing my brain. I wasn't naturi. There was no part of me that held a strain of naturi.

"Mira?" Danaus inquired, his steady voice helping to draw back the veil of rage at the very suggestion. I had no doubt that he would like for it to be true. It would leave me with my own dark secret, much like my dear Danaus and the secret of his own powers.

"It's impossible."

"A lot of things about you are impossible," he said in a low voice. "Why is this?"

Gritting my teeth, I stepped backward down the hill until I was in the water again, letting the cool feeling soothe my anger and ease the tension that hummed through my body. With a wave of both my hands, the five fireballs reappeared in the air. However, this time they were somewhat larger and crackled a little louder, as if matching my lingering anger.

"If I possessed any naturi blood within my system, it would have killed the nightwalkers that made me," I explained, starting to get my emotions back under control as I logically thought about it. "Naturi blood is poisonous, even in its most diluted form. Besides, you're saying that it's possible for a naturi and a human to have a child together, which is not only highly unlikely, it's impossible. The closest thing to a naturi half-breed is a shapeshifter, right?"

"That's true," Cynnia softly admitted, her eyes dropping down to the grass at her feet. "The whole thing is nigh impossible, but you have to admit that the similarity is striking."

"Striking," I growled, kicking a rock out of my way. "But impossible. I knew my parents. They were both human."

"Then it's just some kind of genetic mutation," Shelly suggested, clearly trying to smooth over the tension.

I bit my lip, holding in another snide remark. She was trying to be nice, but making it sound like I was a freak of nature wasn't much of an improvement. "I'm not naturi. Making me into a nightwalker would have killed my creators." Sadira, Jabari, and Tabor would have been instantly poisoned by my blood, resulting in their deaths. I would never have been turned into a nightwalker.

Shoving both of my hands into my hair, I pushed it out of my eyes as I turned to look at my companions again. "But we're getting off topic. My heritage has nothing to do with what I want tonight. Teach me how to use earth magic. Teach me how to control the energy that comes up out of the earth."

"Can you feel the earth's energy now?" Cynnia asked, starting to scoot back down to the bank again now that I was acting like a rational creature again.

"No."

"Take off your shoes," she instructed.

With a huff, I waded to the bank and sat down in the soft earth, ignoring that fact that I was getting mud on the seat of my leather pants. Barefoot, I flinched at the coldness of the water as I returned to the stream. I closed my eyes and reached out with my senses. I could feel Danaus and Shelly near me. I could sense other humans miles away and nightwalkers clustered together to the east, back in my domain. But there was no feeling of energy similar to what I had felt on Crete. The only flow beneath my feet was the cold water in the stream.

"I still don't feel anything," I sighed, letting my eyes fall shut as I concentrated harder, but there was only nothingness where there should have been energy.

"What if I fed you some earth energy?" Shelly said, causing my eyes to snap open.

"How?"

She rose to her feet and snapped her fingers, creating a small ball of fire just above her fingertips. She was going to throw the fire at me and I would catch it. It was similar to what had happened to me in London with the earth witch that had attacked me. At that time, I had sensed a flow of energy, but couldn't identify it or understand it.

"Bigger."

With a wave of her hand, the ball of fire grew until it was the size of a basketball. I nodded and she flung the fire at me. Reaching out my right hand, I caught it then let it flow down my body like a snake until the fire hit the water and was extinguished. For a moment the connection of the fire and water caused a dull roar in my head. I could hear the flow of power beneath the surface of the earth. It tingled through my toes for a second and then completely vanished. It lasted for only a second, but I felt it.

"There! I felt it! It was faint, but I felt something," I cried. Stepping out of the water to the opposite bank, I shouted, "Do it again!"

Shelly repeated the spell and I allowed the fire to wash down my frame until it was absorbed by the earth. The feeling was stronger this time, but it was still only a feeling. I didn't feel a part of it in any way as I had in Crete. It was as if the earth was indifferent to my existence.

"I can feel it, but I can't tap into the power itself. It just flows right past me."

"Beneath your feet?" Cynnia asked.

"Yes."

"You don't feel it in the air?" Shelly inquired, crinkling her nose as she stared at me.

"No."

"Mira, earth magic users draw their power from the air. Only the oldest and most skilled can actually draw it from deep within the earth, where it is the strongest and hardest to manipulate," she explained.

"Also, only naturi have been known to consistently draw their power directly from the flows in the earth," Cynnia added. "The fact that you can feel it means you're sensitive to only the strongest points of power. The odds of you being able to learn how to use earth magic is extremely slim, if not impossible. Unless you're at a swell, you won't be able to sense the magic to use it."

With my teeth clenched in frustration, I flopped down on the opposite bank and looked over at my companions. Yes, the similarities between my abilities and the naturi light clan were striking, but that's all it was. I wasn't a naturi, didn't have any ties to the naturi, thus I didn't have any ties to nature. For some reason, the earth could use me as a weapon of destruction, but I couldn't use it.

"Then teach me a new spell," I said in a low, weary voice.

"But you can't use earth magic," Shelly countered, her gaze dancing from me to Cynnia.

"I saw a warlock do a protection spell. It created a physical barrier between him and his assailant. Can you teach me that? If I can learn to do it using blood magic, maybe I can channel the earth magic into it when I'm in Peru."

Again Shelly looked over at Cynnia, who shrugged one shoulder. Both women looked skeptical but seemed willing to try.

And try they did for more than four hours. We worked through the night until I was shaking with exhaustion. I had used up much of my soul energy to create this magical barrier that was strong enough by the end to stop Danaus's blade. Its strength was never consistent, but it was a start. I suspected that it might be easier to manipulate when I had an excess of energy flowing through my frame.

By the end of the evening, I threw the car keys at Danaus and settled into the passenger seat, trying to ignore the mud that was being smeared across the leather seats. But in truth I was too exhausted to care. Danaus drove us back toward my domain, back to the protection of my city and away from the dark, indifferent woods.

Did you get what you wanted? his voice whispered through my head, and my eyes grew heavy.

No, but it's a start.

Mira . . .

I'm not part naturi, Danaus. They would never have survived the transformation, I replied, thinking of my three beloved makers and the care they had taken in making me into a First Blood nightwalker.

The similarity is . . .

Creepy, I finished. Too creepy.

I was confident that I wasn't a naturi, that I had no relation to the naturi race. Yet, for the first time in my entire existence I was forced to wonder, had I truly been born human? Unfortunately, I doubted I would have the chance to find the answer to that question, since we flew to Peru tomorrow night.

Seventeen

Upon waking, I hit my head, banged my knee, and stubbed my toe all at the same time. I had forgotten that I was curled up in a trunk and not stretched out on a bed in Savannah. We had been somewhere over the Atlantic when I finally curled up in the trunk I brought along before hopping on a plane just outside the city. I hated the thing before I even climbed into it. It was cramped, and the only lock was on the exterior. I preferred my metal alloy, fireproof box with its double interior locks and silk lining. Unfortunately, I was once again traveling without my bodyguards, and I didn't want to worry about Danaus trying to maneuver the coffin while trying to keep an eye on Shelly and Cynnia at the same time. Gabriel had offered to come along, but that would mean bringing Matsui along as well, and I wasn't prepared to be asleep around my newest guardian. Trust came with time.

Now I was stuck with a trunk that Houdini would have felt at home in. I, on the other hand, needed to get the hell out of the thing before I developed an acute case of claustrophobia. Shifting as best as I could in the tiny space, I put my back into the lid and slowly pushed, testing to see if it was locked. I had the strength to force open the trunk anyway, but no desire to break the one lock on my only protection during the daylight hours for the next couple of days. Luckily, the lid offered no resistance.

Sighing as I stood, I instantly banged my head against a metal rod and wooden plank. Barely stifling a string of curses that were perched on the tip of my tongue, I hunched down and rubbed the top of my head as I looked around. The room was positively tiny, with an extremely low ceiling and a pair of sliding wood doors inches from my face. The curses escaped me this time in a rough whisper as I realized I was standing in a closet. As if waking up in a trunk wasn't bad enough. No, Danaus had shoved me a closet.

With my teeth clenched, I slipped my fingernails into the crack between the door and the wall. Yet, I froze in the act of sliding the door open when I heard a doorknob turning in the next room. Someone was coming and it wasn't Danaus. The hunter was already in the room, and by the sound of his soft, steady breathing, asleep on the bed. Sliding the door open without a sound, I smiled to see that the room was pitch-black except for the shaft of light that cut through it as the stranger entered.

The man with short black hair blinked against the inky darkness, waiting for his eyes to finally adjust to the gloom. I wasn't about to give him the chance. Sweeping soundlessly across the room, I clamped my right hand on his throat and slammed him into the wall behind him. At the same time, I pushed the door shut, plunging the room back into total darkness. I could still see him clearly, but I knew he could see nothing of me.

"What are you doing here?" I snarled.

"I—I'm sorry I'm late," he stumbled, his speech carrying

a thick accent that made his words difficult to understand. "I had trouble getting away from the bar."

"The bar? What are you talking about? Late for what? Who are you?"

"Let him go, Mira," Danaus's calm voice interjected before the man could speak.

Turning my head to the right, I saw Danaus kneeling on the bed, knife in hand. I hadn't even heard him move.

"He was sneaking into the room," I said. My grip had not changed. A little tighter and I would crush his windpipe.

"He's from Themis."

While not the most reassuring information, it was enough to buy him some time. Releasing the man's throat, I stepped away, flipping on the overhead light as I walked to the opposite side of the room.

"Mira, this is Eduardo, one of the few Themis contacts in South America and the only one located in Peru," Danaus explained.

When I reached the far corner of the room, I turned on my heel to face the man. I knew I didn't look my best, but I hadn't expected the violence of his reaction. Eduardo attempted to back up, but he was already against the wall so all he achieved was hitting the back of his head. His dark brown eyes widened and he quickly crossed himself with a shaking hand. A string of words escaped him, but they were spoken in neither English nor Spanish. I could only guess it was Quechua or one of the Highland dialects, but couldn't be sure. All I knew was that those hushed words teased at memories in my brain of nights spent on Machu Picchu, sounding too similar to the dialect used by the Incans centuries ago. They had watched as I was tortured by the naturi, their hushed conversations swirling around me.

"Stop it!" I screamed, pressing the heels of my palms against my ears, wishing I could just as easily blot out the memories. "Shut up!" I closed my eyes and stepped backward until my back touched the wall. A second later my eyes popped open at the sound of a muffled footstep. Danaus was standing before me, a concerned look on his face.

"What's wrong?" he demanded when I dropped my hands from my ears.

"Why is he here?" I asked, ignoring his question. He didn't need to know I was terrified of old ghosts.

"He was to wake me before sunset," Danaus replied. A frown still hovered over his lips, and I could see the worry in his eyes. I knew his thoughts without delving into his mind. He was wondering if I was finally going insane. And maybe I was. Being able to count the final minutes to your demise had to drive any creature a little mad. In just a matter of nights I would once again be standing on the mountain retreat of the Incans, the naturi on one side and the nightwalkers lined up on the other side, with me standing in the middle. The one hope of the nightwalkers to put an end to this war. My only complaint was that it was likely to kill me in the process.

"Send him away," I whispered, letting my eyes fall shut. No words were spoken. The only sounds were the quick shuffle of feet, the rattle of the doorknob, and finally the slam of the door. Opening my eyes, I pushed away from the wall. Danaus stepped away from me, allowing me to walk over and slump in the only chair in the room.

Sitting in the sagging cushion chair with the faded green fabric, I let my eyes slowly take in the tiny room as he sat on the edge of the bed. Next to the closet was a rickety bureau that I had a feeling was made of pressboard instead of the oak it was supposed to resemble. A matching nightstand squatted next to the bed that dominated the room with its loud striped spread. There was one other door in the room, which I presumed led to the bathroom. The room was neat and clean, but it had a worn and weary feel to it, as if it had seen too many occupants in its long history. The one appeal it seemed to possess was the fact that there were no windows.

"You look like hell," Danaus announced, shattering the silence. My eyes jerked back to his face to find him frowning at me.

"You sleep in a trunk shoved in a closet and see how you come out looking," I snapped, not caring how bitchy I sounded. My gaze fell down to my T-shirt and leather pants, and I absently tried to smooth the wrinkles, but it was a futile gesture. I had a feeling they were now permanent.

"That's not what I meant," he replied calmly, unruffled by my tone. I could well imagine how I looked. I needed to feed again. I should have fed before we boarded the plane in Savannah, but there was a problem with getting my jet off the ground. I'd been forced to make a series of unplanned phone calls to get everything in line again so we could quickly leave, which left no time for feeding. It had been too long since I last fed. It also didn't help that I had been injured on Blackbeard Island, leaving me feeling drained and edgy, in addition to the magic training I'd endured the previous night.

Fear also had its talons deeply embedded in my flesh. If I were still alive, I would have been hyperventilating while my heart raced within my chest. As it was, I fought the urge to rub my palms on my knees, but I no longer sweated. I knew what Danaus saw. I was ghostly pale and my lavender eyes were wide with a near permanent glow. And if he looked close enough, he'd see the slight tremble in my fingers.

"I need to feed," I admitted, trying to shrug off the feeling that was like a conflagration building in my veins and blotting out rational thought. With a somewhat extravagant sigh, I put my left elbow on the arm of the chair and rested my head in my hand. "Where are we?"

"Cuzco."

"What?" Bolting upright, I lurched to the edge of my chair. The sudden movement caused Danaus to jump to his feet, his right hand instinctively reaching for a weapon. I flinched at the defensive move and forced myself to slowly sit back. Either my earlier outburst or my appearance had the hunter on edge despite our continued truce. Or worse, he could feel my starvation. He had admitted as much when we were in Crete together, commenting on how the hunger burned through his mind as well when we were together. We were both dancing on the edge of the knife now, working together simply because we were desperate, but trust was thin on the ground.

"We are supposed to be at the lodge at the foot of the Machu Picchu ruins," I continued in an even voice when he sat on the edge of the bed again. "Or at the very least in Aguas Calientes. We should be closer to the mountain."

"We're lucky we're in Cuzco," he said, his shoulders slumping wearily. "The plane was redirected to Lima at the last minute due to storms in Cuzco. After a three-hour delay, we left for Cuzco. The landing was rough due to high winds. It took another hour to get out of the airport. By then it was late afternoon. All the trains into the Sacred Valley were on their way back to Cuzco."

"And nothing else was headed toward Machu Picchu?"

"This isn't America," he reminded me grimly. "There are only two trains to Aguas Calientes, and both leave before seven A.M."

"What about renting a car and driving?"

"I checked. The road goes only as far as Ollantaytambo. From there you have to take the train the last two hours to Aguas Calientes."

"How can you run a country like this?" I shouted, pushing out of my chair. I shoved both of my hands through my tangled hair as I paced the room. The heels of my boots tromped across the wood floor, sending the noise banging against the thin walls, so I was now sure that our neighbors in the next room could hear my growing anxiety.

"Mira, you've got the Andes on one side and the Amazon rain forest on the other. We're lucky we're here," Danaus patiently stated.

I dropped my hands back to my sides. "You're right." We had another problem brewing that needed to be taken care of anyway. "Where are Shelly and Cynnia?"

"In the next room," he said with a jerk of his head.

"Any problems?" I asked as I headed for the door, Danaus following close behind me.

"None. Both were perfectly behaved. In fact . . . " His voice faded before he could finish the thought.

I stopped in the hallway beside him, my body blocking him from heading to the room that held our two companions. "What?"

Danaus frowned and looked away, his gaze traveling the length of the hallway before finally settling on a point just over my shoulder. "I had no choice. At one point I had to take off her shackles in an effort to get her through security. My bigger concern was making sure that they didn't search your trunk. Shelly couldn't shield their minds from both the iron shackles and the trunk."

"So you freed her?" I gasped, struggling to keep my voice down in the public area. I wanted to shake him. Had he lost his mind? I could understand the circumstances that he found himself in, but still, he set free our prisoner! I fought the urge to shove my fingers through my hair and stomp down the hall. Instead I settled for just curling my hands into fists at my sides and gritting my teeth.

"I had no choice. She was well-behaved the entire time. She helped cloak us. We got through security faster with her help."

"And I'm sure that she also alerted her own kind to her presence in Cuzco," I snapped irritably.

"Possibly," Danaus admitted with a shrug as he pulled another hotel room key out of his pocket. "But I thought that's what we wanted. A confrontation with Rowe before the sacrifice? If she's alerted them that she's in the country, then they should come running for her."

"And have they?"

"The naturi are close. In the city, but not one has come close to the hotel from what I have been able to tell."

"You were also asleep."

"Because I don't think she told them she's here."

"Why?"

He knocked once on the thin hotel room door before inserting the key. As he turned the knob, he looked over his shoulder at me, a dark look filling his deep blue eyes. "Because she looks worse than you."

Surprised by his comment, I wordlessly followed the hunter into the small hotel room that looked identical to ours with the exception of a small window in the wall opposite the door. Shelly sat on the bed with her back against the headboard, a fingernail file slowly sculpting each nail on her left hand. Cynnia sat on the ground in the corner, as far as she could get from both the door and the window. Her arms were wrapped around her bent knees, and her shoulders were painfully stiff. The iron shackles once again graced her slender wrists. There was the slightest jingling of metal in the air, as if her hands were trembling.

"You're still here," I said with a note of surprise filling my voice.

"Where else would I be?" Her soft voice was little more than a whisper of wind. Her normally pale, pearlescent skin was sallow now, almost gray, and her bright green eyes were flat as they jerked from one end of the room to the other.

"From what I hear, you could have run off to meet up with your own kind. They're crawling all over the place like a bunch of cockroaches. You could have rejoined your herd."

"For what purpose? Fall in with another group that wants me dead? What if Rowe believes what they are saying about me? He'll kill me on the spot. Or worse . . . " She paused, pushing one shaking hand through her stringy brown hair. " . . . he could hand me over to Aurora when she makes it through the door."

"First off, Aurora is not getting through the door. That door is staying closed!" I said, walking to stand in front of her. When I was less than a foot away, I knelt down and leaned forward on the knuckles of my left hand, causing her to press farther into the corner. "And second, why would you want to stay with a group that plans to kill you as well?"

"Because at least you still need me," she said, lifting her chin slightly.

I backed off a bit, but remained kneeling in front of her, a frown toying with the corners of my mouth.

"Not at the risk of my own life," I said. "I've no reason to protect you at the risk of my own life, and so far, you've given me little reason to keep you alive."

"I protected you while you slept!" she cried, leaning forward. "The sun was high and those men would have demanded to check the trunk Danaus was carrying if I had not cloaked you."

"Why do it?"

"You mean other than the fact that Danaus would have cut my heart out the moment I revealed your location?" she said, her mouth twisting into an ugly frown. "I need you. I need your protection from the rest of my kind. Particularly Rowe. He's my sister's mate. If she's trying to kill me, I expect that he would happily follow her orders."

My grin spread slowly across my face, stretching to reveal my perfect white fangs. "Then I'm going to need more from you than a simple cloaking spell."

Cynnia sighed heavily and lowered her head so her forehead touched her knees. Her voice was muffled when she spoke, but I could easily make out what she said. "There are dozens of naturi here. More than a hundred. They're in the city and out in the mountains. They are everywhere."

"And you felt that when Danaus took off the manacles?"

"I can feel them with the manacles on. I sensed it the moment my feet touched the ground." She raised her head and met my gaze, revealing glassy green eyes. She was looking at me, but I had a feeling that she didn't actually see me. "The earth is saturated with power here. I can feel it everywhere. In the earth, in the air, in the animals that lurk in all the shadows and in the surrounding forests. Rowe has more than enough power to open the door between the two worlds. He has the power to completely tear down the walls and destroy the cage that held us. The mountain called Machu Picchu may be the pinnacle, but the entire valley area is overflowing with energy. The nightwalkers haven't a chance if you expect to take on the naturi directly here."

I sat back on my heels for a moment, staring at my captive. She didn't look triumphant like I would expect when someone was prophesying the complete annihilation of my kind when we attempted to take on the naturi. Instead she looked sad, almost broken, as she sat on the floor, her shoulder slumped and her eyes nearly closed as tears shimmered there in the faint light.

"Danaus, do you still have those tree pictures that you showed me?" I asked, not looking up from Cynnia. She seemed willing to talk, and it honestly felt like she was telling me the truth.

"What?"

I twisted around to look at the hunter, who was staring down at me with a confused look on his face, his fists resting on his hips. He looked as if he was prepared to attack, but at the moment I wasn't sure who he intended to protect—me or Cynnia.

"Months ago in the bar, you showed me a stack of pictures with symbols in trees. Do you still have them?"

"Yes, in my bag," he said, jerking his thumb toward the room we were currently sharing.

"Go get them."

Danaus looked at me strangely for a moment, then left the room to fetch the pictures. Behind me, I heard Shelly slide off the bed and walk over to where Cynnia and I still sat on the floor.

"Is there something that I can do? After we arrived at the hotel, Danaus said that I wasn't to use a sleep spell on Nia."

"Nia?" I asked, looking from Shelly back to Cynnia, who gave me a weak smile, shrugged one shoulder.

"It's a family nickname," she admitted, then gave a soft sigh and shook her head a little. "Actually, only Nyx ever used it. I don't mind Shelly calling me Nia," Cynnia continued. "She's been nice to me."

I gritted my teeth and closed my eyes to keep from snapping irritably at both of them. Cynnia was a prisoner. I kept repeating this, but it seemed like I was the only one who was actually listening to this tale. She wasn't a puppy or a goldfish that we were keeping. We didn't need to be establishing a friendship with a creature that I ultimately planned to kill.

"If you didn't use a sleep spell, what's the magic that I can feel in the air?" I asked Shelly when I was sure I could keep my voice even and calm.

"A cloaking spell."

"It's not working. I had no trouble spotting her when I entered the room," I said with a frown.

"It's not a cloaking spell against nightwalkers. It's only supposed to work on the naturi," Shelly corrected. "It's like a special kind of glamour."

"That doesn't make sense. Glamour doesn't work on naturi. And when did you learn a spell that worked specifically against the naturi?"

"Nia taught it to me."

My head snapped back to look at the naturi that was still seated in front of me, a tentative smile touching her pale lips. "She needed help," she said, "and I can't rely on you completely to protect me. I know a few tricks. If I can't use them, I don't see any harm in teaching Shelly."

I wasn't entirely comfortable with the idea of Cynnia teaching Shelly magic when I wasn't around. But then, it wouldn't really matter if I was present or not. I didn't know enough magic to recognize whether Cynnia was truly teaching Shelly a cloaking spell or possibly a tracking spell. Much to my chagrin, I actually had to trust Cynnia, and I didn't like it.

Danaus chose that moment to enter the hotel room again, saving me from making a rude comment.

"Are there any naturi in or near the hotel?" I demanded as soon as he closed and locked the door again. I felt his powers rush out of his body and fill the room before pushing out to encompass the entire structure. Closing my eyes, I reached out with my own powers, connecting with his in such a way that I rode the energy out of the hotel. I couldn't sense anything beyond the scattering of humans and the nightwalkers in the city, but for now I needed the feel of his warm energy to soothe my frazzled nerves.

You need to feed, he said in my mind while our powers mingled.

Soon, I whispered back, not needing the reminder.

It's becoming a distraction.

I can handle it.

You're not the only one that's being distracted.

A part of me wanted to smile at the reminder that Danaus could sense my hunger as well. The stronger the blood lust grew, the more difficult it became for him to be around me. He never told me exactly how it affected him, but I was willing to bet that the consequences were not happy ones. For me, it fed my more predatory side, making me more violent and more willing to take unnecessary risks. And then the feeding itself frequently turned into something sexual with the right partner, though it wasn't necessary.

Without the blood lust clawing at the inside of my brain, feeding was nothing more exciting that grabbing a hamburger at a local fast-food location. However, when the world before you was covered in a haze of blood, the act of feeding could be positively orgasmic. It definitely made me wonder about my dear Danaus.

"There are a few naturi a couple blocks away, but Cynnia is the only naturi that I can sense in the hotel," he finally said. "And I can't technically sense her."

"The pictures?" I asked, reaching over my shoulder toward him.

Danaus slapped the sheaf of color pictures into my open hand. The edges were wrinkled and worn from their journey. So far, they had traveled from Savannah, Aswan, London, Venice, Heraklion, and then back to Savannah again. It was amazing they had survived.

"Danaus, I want you to take Shelly to find some food for her and Cynnia. The naturi is starting to look a little pale, and I don't need her dying before I'm ready," I said, my gaze never wavering from Cynnia as she watched me.

"I don't like this, Mira," he said, making no effort to hide his disapproval. I could feel his worry and anger beating against my back as he stood near me.

"I don't expect you to," I snapped. "Just do it and be quick about it. I promise not to kill her without you here."

"Mira, please don't talk like that. Nia has been cooperating with your every request," Shelly argued. "Maybe we can find another way."

"Shelly, get out of here. Take Danaus with you. If you

want to be sure that 'Nia' remains safe, then I suggest that you don't dawdle."

No one spoke again. There was only the sound of two pairs of footsteps and the slam of the door. I smirked at Cynnia, who was watching me, no expression on her weary face.

"Alone at last," I said.

"You're not going to kill me," Cynnia boldly announced, lifting her chin in a moment of bravery.

I laughed at her, tossing my head back as I resettled myself on the floor with my legs crossed before me. "Of course I'm going to kill you eventually. But for now, you seem willing to help me, and if you haven't guessed yet, I'll take all the help I can get to keep your sister Aurora locked in her own realm. I'll also take any help I can get against Rowe, so it seems we're on the same side."

"Like you and Danaus. He's a nightwalker hunter, isn't he?"

"Yes, but there's a very distinct difference between you and Danaus." Smiling again, I leaned forward so my elbows rested on my knees. "I don't hate Danaus with every fiber of my being. What happens between Danaus and I is still up in the air. When this is over, I'd be willing to let him walk away. You? Not so much."

"So, what can I do to prolong my life?" Cynnia asked.

"Take a look at these." I handed over the pictures of the trees that Danaus had shown me just a few months ago, the ones that started me down this long horrible journey. There were twelve different pictures of twelve different types of trees. Each tree had a different symbol carved into it. Neither Danaus nor I had been able to figure out what it meant, but now we at least had a naturi at our disposal. The mystery might finally be solved.

Cynnia slowly moved, crossing her legs before her as well so she could more easily spread the photos out on the floor before her. She flipped through each one, her eyes pausing over a symbol for less than a second before moving on to the next.

"Trees," she murmured. That had pretty much been my reaction, but I hadn't expected it out of the naturi. This was their handwriting. It had to mean something to her.

"I noticed that the pictures were of trees as well," I said between clenched teeth as I struggled to keep my temper under control. "I was hoping you could enlighten us as to what the symbols meant." If I hadn't known better, I would have said that she was toying with me.

"I'm not sure."

"What do you mean you're not sure? How can you not be sure?" I grabbed up a few of the photos and shook them at her. "This is your language, isn't it? Your writing?"

"Yes, but some of them are just symbols used in spells. I'm not that strong a spell weaver. I know enough to protect myself, it's all I was ever taught."

And suddenly that struck me as odd. Why hadn't Aurora seen to it that her youngest sister was well-versed in their own magical arts? Cynnia had never tried to physically attack us, and she had cooperated with Danaus during her one chance to escape when her manacles were off. Had Aurora purposefully kept her little sister weak? It was a thought I was content to let stew for a while.

Spreading the twelve pictures out between us in three neat little rows, I drew in a slow, steadying breath. I caught a whiff of her own unique scent this time over the stale scent of dust and some kind of cleaning product from the nearby bathroom. She smelled of spring rain and yellow tulips. "Can you read any of this?" I asked, feeling a little calmer.

"Yes, some of these are words, but I don't know what order any of this goes in." She picked up one picture that looked like a birch tree. "This one means 'open,' and this one means 'welcome,'" she continued, picking up another picture of what appeared to be a type of palm tree. Cynnia put those two pictures aside and scanned over the rest. "This one over here refers to a 'weary traveler,'" she said, putting aside a picture of blue spruce.

As she pulled pictures out of the three rows, I carefully rearranged them before her so she could clearly see each one. None of it made sense to me so far, but I was hoping that as we identified more pieces of this puzzle, a picture would become clear.

"There isn't a clear translation for this one between our two languages," she said, pulling up one that looked like a maple tree.

"Can you give me something close?"

"Maybe . . . 'forgotten path.' Or 'hidden road.'"

That didn't feel particularly reassuring, and a knot twisted in my stomach. I had yet to guess what the naturi were up to with this assortment of pictures, and I felt more anxious the closer we drew to the evening of the equinox and the coming sacrifice. Rowe had something special planned up his sleeve.

With the pictures whittled down to two rows of four, I noticed that Cynnia had stopped picking them up, her brow furrowed in concentration as she stared at each one. Every once in a while she would rearrange them into a particular order and then shake her head again, as whatever she was looking for failed to appear.

"Is there anything else here that you recognize?"

She sighed, her eyes slowly traveling over the remaining eight pictures. I noticed that her hand trembled slightly when she reached for one picture that was on my far left. I had always hated that picture. It was hard to tell from the darkness of the image, but it looked like the symbol had been carved into the dark, thick bark of a live oak tree, just like one of the hundreds of live oaks that dotted the historical district of my beloved Savannah.

"This one means 'home,'" she said, then shook her head. "But not just the idea of home as the place where you live. It's home as in Earth—our home."

Nodding, I took the picture from her and added it to the pile that she had already identified. "What about the rest?"

"Just magical symbols. They don't equal words, ideas, or phrases to me. They're used for some kind of spell."

"Spell? Not message?"

"I doubt it's a message of any kind unless the naturi on this side have developed their own kind of shortened language or base of symbols. It's possible, but it looks like these trees are from all over the globe. You would need to see most if not all of the message to make sense of it. I've seen it all and it doesn't make sense to me," she admitted. She picked up one of the pictures that she couldn't identify and shook her head before putting it back on the floor. "I've thought about the symbol and what it resembles, and the potential relation to the type of tree that it's in, but I'm coming up with nothing. Why are some easily identifiable words and the rest is just nonsense?"

"I need answers, Cynnia, not more questions," I snapped, resting my head against my hand while placing my elbow on my right knee.

"Sorry."

I glared up at her, curling my lip up to reveal one of my fangs. She quickly held up her manacled hands as if to ward me off.

"I'm serious. I'm sorry that I can't help you with this. Helping you means that I get to stay alive a little bit longer."

"So you're willing to sell out your own kind just so you can live a little while longer?"

"No," she quickly said, then frowned as she looked down at the iron manacles on her wrists. "Not really." She drew in a slow breath and closed her eyes, holding back tears that I saw suddenly rise to the surface. "I've not told you anything that would endanger my people. They've cast some kind of spell using symbols in trees, but I can't tell you what the spell is. It's honestly beyond my knowledge."

"And if it wasn't? If you could identify the spell, would you tell me?" I asked, straightening my back as I watched her closely.

"I—I don't know," Cynnia replied. "I don't know what I would do. Yes, they're my people and I know I should do everything within my power to protect them. And according to our laws, that means killing any nightwalker or human that we come into contact with. Yet, they've called me a traitor when I've done nothing to betray them." She shook her head and a tear slipped out from beneath her right eyelid, which she quickly wiped away with a jangle of chains. "They left me for dead, to be killed by the infamous Fire Starter, because they were too afraid to kill their queen's sister. They left you to do their dirty work, sure you would give me a tortured and gruesome end."

"So the question becomes, why protect them?" I asked. It was a question I'd had to answer myself on more than one occasion during the past couple of months. And every time I did, I was left wondering if I had made a mistake.

"Because it's the right thing to do."

I smiled at her and shook my head. "And what exactly is the 'right thing'? That's the true sticking point in this mess. I truly wish you luck in figuring that out. I'm still looking myself."

There was a knock at the door, and my hand instantly went to the knife at my side even though I had already sensed Danaus's approach down the hall, with Shelly following directly behind him.

"Mira, I won't lie to you," Cynnia quickly said before Danaus could come into the room. "If it comes down to telling you something that would betray and hurt my people and lying to you, I will simply refuse to tell you."

"And then I'll kill you."

"There are worse reasons to die," she said.

Eighteen

After Shelly and Cynnia were settled with food, Danaus followed me back to the other hotel room we were occupying. I was reluctant to say that we were actually sharing it. He had the bed and I, obviously, was stuck in a trunk in the closet. Hardly a fair setup, but unfortunately a necessary one.

"I need some weapons," I announced after he closed and locked the door behind me.

With a nod, he pulled out his handy black duffel bag from under the bed and dropped it on the mattress with a small bounce. He unzipped it and began sorting through the items, coming up with an assortment of knives with matching sheaths that I could attach to my waist and ankle under my pants.

"Where are we headed?" he asked as I pulled my pant leg back down over the last knife.

"I'm headed out for a bite to eat," I said, looking up at him. Danaus frowned, his fingers nervously fiddling with a small silver throwing knife as he stared down at the bed.

"Mira, I don't know if I . . . " he started, but his voice quickly faded. I knew what he was about to say. He wasn't sure that he could accompany me on a hunting expedition since he was still struggling with the idea of what I was. And yet, he felt that he had to stay by my side in an effort to keep me alive.

I smiled as I walked over to him. I carefully took the throwing knife out of his nimble fingers and laid it on the bed, more out of an effort to keep it from accidentally injuring one of us. Danaus stared down at me, his dark blue eyes narrowed with mistrust.

"I wasn't inviting you along," I murmured. "I don't want to worry about you trying to keep up with me."

"I've had no problem keeping up with you, vampire," he bit out, but there was no real fire behind his anger.

"So far, but then you've never been around when I've been hunting," I teased. Reaching up, I brushed aside some black hair that had fallen forward on his forehead and was threatening to block his vision. Danaus caught my wrist and squeezed tightly so I wouldn't be able to easily free myself.

"This isn't about you hunting," he said, his voice softening.

"I know."

"It's about Rowe hunting you."

"I'm counting on it. I want him outside waiting for me. He and I need to talk again," I said, twisting my wrist slightly, but he refused to release me, though he did lighten his grip.

"And I don't want you meeting with him alone. He could kill you before you get a single word out."

I shook my head at his assessment, though I appreciated his concern. "That's not Rowe's style. I'd be willing to bet that he wants me to stay alive to see his triumph on the mountain at the Machu Picchu ruins. My only problem is making sure that I'm not present as a prisoner, and Cynnia will be my guarantee that I'm not. Rowe will be willing to talk with me."

Danaus slowly released me, his thumb rubbing along the tender flesh on the inside of my wrist, caressing the veins that would have held my pulse had I still been alive. The hunter wasn't happy with my plan, but he was going to let me go alone. At least, he would say that, but I didn't trust him not to be lingering at a distance, protecting my back. I had to keep him otherwise occupied.

"After I feed and meet with Rowe, I will need to meet with all the nightwalkers in the city," I announced.

"Locals?"

A soft chuckle escaped me and I shook my head as I took a couple steps away from the hunter. When I looked up at him, a ghost of a smile flitted across my pale face. "There's no such thing in South America. No nightwalker that I know of calls this continent home. This is naturi territory. Always has been."

Around us I could feel nightwalkers awakening and beginning to move about the city. They had all been sent by the Coven for one purpose, which explained the overwhelming feeling of anxiety. Unfortunately, fear easily shifted to anger and violence. I needed to get this group reined in before people started dying.

"We need to get moving," Danaus said, shoving his hands in his pockets. After his more casual attire in Savannah, he was back in his durable black pants, but his black T-shirt looked new.

"Do you know of a place I can call the nightwalkers together? Somewhere very large and public?"

"There's a bar a couple blocks away called Norton Rat's.

It's just off the main plaza and should be big enough. It's where Eduardo works."

"Good." I nodded, pacing over to the edge of the bed and then back. "Head over there and see if Eduardo can help you get some vans or a bus. We can at least drive part of the way to Machu Picchu tonight."

"And you?"

"I'll hunt, take care of my business with Rowe, and meet you at the bar in less than an hour," I said.

"Are you sure?"

"We both know you wouldn't allow me to feed, and I must hunt tonight. I go alone. I can handle Rowe and whatever the naturi decides to throw at me," I firmly said.

Whatever he planned to say died in his throat. I knew what he was concerned about. The naturi were in the city. I couldn't sense them, but I believed Cynnia when she said there were more than a hundred. The whole area was crawling with them.

"I'll be fine. Trust me, if I'm in trouble, you'll know it." I flashed the hunter an evil grin full of fangs and menace. If I had to, I'd set half this town on fire to rid the earth of a handful of naturi.

"The bar is off the Plaza de Armas. You have to go through the Hostal Loreto to reach it," Danaus explained, finally accepting my decision. He then wordlessly left the hotel room. I didn't ask how many naturi were in the city and he didn't offer. Obviously, he thought it was better that I didn't know exactly how many were close by.

Once the door was closed, I jerked open my bag of clothes and dumped its contents onto the bed to see what I had grabbed in a rush before running out of the house to catch my painfully late flight. Jerking off my T-shirt, I pulled on a

V-neck, long sleeve shirt that clung to me like a second skin before pulling on a second button-up black shirt. While fall was just beginning to give birth back in the States, Peru was still in the last days of winter, waiting for the official arrival of spring. The cold wouldn't bother me, but it would tighten up my muscles, and I needed to be as nimble as possible if I was going to take on Rowe.

I quickly ran a brush through my hair and piled it on my head to keep it out of my eyes. Just before leaving the room, I paused in front of the pile of clothes I had created when I rummaged through my backpack. Why bother even to pack again? The fight on Machu Picchu was coming soon. There would no longer be any need for clothes or worrying what I would wear to return home. Oh, I planned to fight back against the naturi, Jabari, and, if I had to, Danaus as well. But the odds were stacked against me.

With a growl, I turned back at the last second and shoved all the clothes back into the bag. Stranger things had happened. Hell, the naturi were waltzing around the Coven's main hall. Maybe I could survive this mess.

It wasn't yet eight o'clock when I hit the streets. The night was young and I was starving. Every instinct within my body begged that I fall back into my typical hunting style of slowly stalking my prey. Ordinarily, I would wander through the crowds of people that still lingered on the streets and listen to their thoughts until something finally caught my attention, but I didn't have that luxury tonight. Rowe would be lurking somewhere within this crowd, waiting for a glimpse of me, I had no doubt. I needed to feed quickly and carefully tonight. My only concern was not grabbing a naturi in my haste and drinking their poisoned blood.

Out of pure necessity, my "hunting" was condensed down

to settling as comfortably as possibly in a dark shadowy niche between a pair of tall stone building and mentally calling to one human after another. My only requirements were large men in their mid-twenties to early thirties. I needed to be sure they wouldn't pass out from a little blood loss. I fed from four different men and they all walked away without a mark or a memory of the event. On the other hand, I felt more than a little dirty from the whole affair, but pushed my qualms aside.

Flushed with fuel again, I leaned against the wall, running my tongue over my fangs as I sent my last victim on his merry way without a memory of the encounter in his head. The wind had picked up and was whipping through the city, causing flags to snap and flap in an angry frenzy. Trees swayed and the clouds overhead churned and swirled through the sky, completely blotting out the stars. The earth seemed angry.

Upon leaving the hotel and setting foot on the street, I instantly felt the power that Cynnia had warned of. It wasn't as strong as at the Palace of Knossos on Crete, but it was there, beating against my flesh, trying to find an entrance into my body. We were still many miles from the ruins of Machu Picchu. I didn't think I should be feeling this energy here, but there was no denying that the mother earth was fueling the power nearly crackling in the air around me. If anything, I had a feeling that it made the naturi more dangerous than normal. They had a new power to feed off of.

While drinking from my victims, I'd picked out a quick map of the city, discovering that I was only a couple blocks from the plaza that Danaus mentioned before I left the hotel. With that in mind, I now wandered in the opposite direction, toward a second, smaller square. I headed away from the crowds and from where I sensed most of my own people were congregated. If I was going to finally draw out Rowe, I needed to be as alone as possible.

And I knew the moment that it worked. I had entered the distant square from the south, my hands shoved in the pockets of my leather pants, trying to keep my fingers warm and nimble against the bitter wind. I skirted the cobblestone sidewalk that led toward the center of the park with its stone monument to some forgotten hero or a forgotten people. The dead grass and sticks crunched lightly under the rubber soles of my boots, but I stuck close to the shadows created by the trees, offering up an obscured view of me as I passed through the darkness.

I sensed no one in the area—nightwalker or human. And naturally, I couldn't sense any naturi in the region. I was half tempted to reach out to Danaus across the vast distance and see if he could scan the area for me, but quickly pushed aside the urge. No need to make the hunter worry more than he already was.

A feeling twisted in the pit of my stomach suddenly as I stood halfway between the entrance of the square and the monument in the center. Freezing where I stood, I slowly turned my head left and then right while my hand slid down to grasp the handle of the knife at my side. There was a whisper of cloth rubbing, and I was in motion in the blink of an eye. Rolling to my left, I jerked my knife free with my right hand and was grabbing for a second knife with my left by the time I was back on my feet, facing whatever creature had managed to sneak up behind me.

Rowe, the one-eyed naturi, smiled at me, pulling his dark black wings close to his body while wielding a long knife in his right hand. The silver blade reflected a sliver of lamplight as he twisted it in his hand, waiting for me to make the next move.

"I've been waiting for you," I said, inwardly wishing I had brought something a bit longer than the trio of short daggers. His long knife was going to make it difficult for me to get in close to do any kind of substantial damage without completely impaling myself.

"I figured as much," he snorted, lowering the blade slightly. "Wandering alone at night in a city dominated by the naturi. You have to suspect that you're completely surrounded right now. You have no way of walking out of here alive."

To his obvious surprise, I placed the dagger in my left hand back in its sheath on my left thigh and turned my back on the naturi, a smile toying with my lips. I walked toward the monument in the center of the square. It was little more than a plaque on a marble slab. I didn't attempt to read it, because all of my senses were focused on the approach of the curious naturi.

"You fell while we were at Knossos and didn't get back up," I commented as if making idle chitchat. I could barely make out his footsteps on the stone walkway as he approached me, but my smile never wavered. "They said that you had to be carried away. What happened?"

"I fell and hit my head on the edge of some broken stone," he said in a strange voice. He stopped when he was a few feet away, standing almost directly across from me at the monument. His brow was furrowed in confusion and his full lips were twisted in a frown that seemed to deepen the scars that stretched across what I could remember being a handsome face.

To add to his confusion, I very carefully placed the knife

in my right hand back into its sheath on my waist and snapped the guard over it so I wouldn't be able to quickly draw it. While it would be a lie to say I was completely unarmed, I could honestly say that I was not holding a single weapon at that moment. In response, Rowe tightened his grip on his knife and took an unsteady step backward.

"You're surrounded, you know that," he said in a loud, hard voice. As he spoke, his wings disintegrated into fine black sand that spread across the paving stones.

I cocked my head to the side, seeming to listen to the wind. But deep down I knew that he was bluffing. Every time Rowe had faced me, he'd been alone. Regardless of whether we were trying to kill each other or just wanting to talk, it always came down to just him and me. I was beginning to think that he had it in his head to succeed where Nerian had failed; he wanted to break me personally.

"Maybe from a distance," I conceded with a shrug of my slender shoulders as I shoved my hands into my pockets. "But in this square, right now, there's just you and me."

"What game are you playing, Mira?" he snapped, shaking his blade at me. "Do you seriously think I won't kill you right now?"

"Killing me would solve so many of your problems, wouldn't it?" I taunted, starting to walk around the monument to my left. Rowe matched my movements, maintaining the same distance between us. "I wouldn't be around to stop you from opening the door between worlds. I wouldn't be around to form yet another seal, keeping Aurora safely locked away. I wouldn't be around to ruin any more of your brilliant schemes. Why, I bet you'd be able to locate your missing princess if I weren't around!"

A snarl erupted from Rowe and he quickly tried to close

the distance between us that he had been so eager to maintain. I chuckled as I stepped back and created a circle of fire around me about five feet tall and only a couple feet wide in diameter. I wanted to make sure there was only enough room for one within that circle.

At once, the energy that had been filling the air pushed harder against my skin, trying to gain entrance into my body. Lucky for me, the power in the air wasn't as strong as it had been in Heraklion. Yet, I was in a dangerous situation, beyond just my baiting Rowe. If the energy from the earth entered my body as when we were in Crete, I had no way of stopping it, no way of turning off the flow. It was likely to kill me just as easily as Rowe could with his blade.

"Take a step back, Rowe," I warned in an even voice. "I came here to talk. Let's continue our little chat in a civilized manner, if you please."

"Where the hell is she?" he growled. The point of his blade wavered as it penetrated the flames to come within inches of my heart. I stood still, smiling at him, daring him to plunge the blade into my chest. But I was making a dangerous wager. I was willing to bet that Cynnia was more important to him alive than I was to him dead—at least for the moment.

"Back off," I repeated.

Rowe snarled one last time as his blade sliced through the flames and returned to his side, yet not before leaving a small cut on the side of my throat, a reminder that his patience was extremely limited. The one-eyed naturi paced away from me, his knife tightly clenched in his fist, ranting in a language I didn't understand.

In the flickering firelight his tanned skin took on an almost swarthy complexion, while his scars stood out as white lines crisscrossing one side of his face before disappearing beneath a leather eye patch. His dark black hair swung down past his shoulders, nearly obscuring his face when he turned away from me for a second then paced back again.

"Did I do that to you?" I softly asked, bringing his pacing to an abrupt and uneven halt. He stared at me with a confused look until I touched my cheek, mirroring his, which had been brutally scarred.

"What? Why do you care?"

"I don't, but there's so much I obviously don't remember about you, and when we last met, you seemed all too eager to jog my memory. Tell me, did I do that to you?"

"No, you didn't," he snapped, then turned his body so I could clearly see only the unflawed side of his face. "Are you surprised to find that there are more dangerous and evil things in this world than you?"

"No, relieved actually," I said with a half smile.

"Where is she?" Rowe demanded, returning to our previous conversation. He seemed a little calmer than a few seconds earlier.

"Somewhere safe."

"The only place that she will ever be deemed safe is with her own people," he said, and was about to continue when I started laughing at him. My head fell back and for a moment the flames actually flickered as my laughter broke my concentration.

"I truly doubt that little Nia is safe with your people," I mocked, purposefully using her nickname to drive the proverbial knife even deeper into his stomach. "I honestly wonder if she would be safe in your hands, or the hands of her loving sister Nyx. That's who I saw you with back at the Palace of Knossos just moments before the seal was broken.

Thin creature, dark hair, silver eyes—Cynnia's sister Nyx, right?"

Rowe said nothing, but he began circling me again. His full lips were pressed into a hard, unyielding line of hatred as he watched me, looking for a way to get at me through the flames without risking complete immolation himself. I knew he was fast, but he had to count on me being equally fast. And then, if he killed me before he discovered Cynnia's location, what would happen to the young naturi in the meantime?

"You see my quandary, don't you?" I said, smiling broadly at him, loving every minute that I could let him twist in the wind. Only months ago he had tormented me in much the same fashion, and now the shoe was on the other foot. And I loved it. "She fell into my hands quite neatly. I was supposed to kill her when I found her, and yet I didn't out of sheer curiosity. And now I wonder—just who is trying to kill this young naturi?"

"Like you care for her well-being! Give her to me!" Rowe raged. He took a reckless step closer to the flames and then back again, pacing like a caged tiger ready to leap at any second.

"Or what?" I chuckled a bit hysterically. "You'll kill me? Torture me like Nerian did years ago on that forsaken mountain? Why should I not do the same to Cynnia?"

"Because she's a child, damn it! She's just a child," Rowe shouted, slicing through the flames with his knife though he came nowhere close to hitting me.

"So was I," I bit out, suddenly fighting back a well of tears I had not expected to spring forth. With my teeth clenched, I drew in a steady breath and strengthened the flames around me so they snapped and crackled angrily between us. "But then again, I don't think she's the child you claim she is. I think the main concern is that she is of royal birth, the same bloodline as your beloved wife-queen. And we've already seen how I treat the royal family."

Nerian had died at my hands months ago, though his death would have come centuries sooner if I had not been so concerned with the rising sun. The only brother to the queen, he died in a dingy, crumbling basement with his throat in my hand. He had been raving madness right up until the end. I hoped I never saw the same madness light Cynnia's eyes.

Gritting his teeth so the muscle in his jaw jumped and throbbed, Rowe stabbed his long knife back into its sheath at his side. He threw open his arms, showing that there were no weapons in his hands, but I only laughed and shook my head at him.

"You are as unarmed as I am at this moment," I taunted.

"What do you want from me?"

"I want you to walk away from Machu Picchu." Rowe shook his head, but I ignored him and continued. "Walk away from Machu Picchu and your plans to open the door. My people and I will reseal the doorway and there will be no more talk of freeing Aurora. Enough of your people have snuck through the weakening walls. We will stop hunting you and you will stop hunting us. Both races will endure in silence."

"And what about Cynnia? Would you then hand her over to me?"

"I would set her free." I carefully attempted to evade his question, but it didn't work.

"Would you give her to me?" he angrily repeated, dropping his hands down to his sides.

"If that is where she wanted to go, I would let her go to you."

"Why wouldn't she want to go to me? What have you been telling her? What lies have you been spreading?"

I shrugged lightly and placed my hands into my back pockets. "None that I know of."

"What have you told her?" Rowe demanded, once again taking a step closer to the flames. I increased the power going into the flames and a pain shot through my temple. I was wearing down, and the power from the earth was working harder now to find a way into my body. I had to end this conversation soon or there were going to be bigger things to worry about than one pissed off naturi, however powerful.

"I told her that you are a loyal soldier to your wife-queen. That you follow her direction. She told me much the same of her sister Nyx, calling her the defender of your people. Was any of that wrong?"

"No," Rowe murmured, taking a couple steps away from me.

"Good. Now I think we have come to an understanding, or at the very least, you and Nyx have a lot to discuss during the next couple of nights," I said, lowering the flames slightly. "I will take Nia to Machu Picchu the night of the equinox. If you're not there and there is no sacrifice, then I will set her free. She will be free to find her own way in this world, with or without you, that is her choice. If you continue with the sacrifice, then she will die with the rest of the naturi on the mountain ruins."

"You can't do this!"

"You've left me no choice."

Rowe shoved his left hand through his hair, pushing it out

of the way of his eyes as he angrily marched away from me and back again. "I can't turn my back on centuries of work for the life of one person."

"No, I can't imagine this is what Aurora would want either, but then again, after talking to Cynnia, I'm beginning to think this may have been a part of her master plan after all. I'd just be wary of how Nyx fits into all of this."

With a wave of my hand, I extinguished the flames that separated us, plunging the tiny plaza back into total darkness. Rowe growled softly at me, and the hiss of the blade as it left its scabbard warned me of his attack. I ducked low and drew my own blade. The naturi scored a hit on my upper right arm while I made a shallow cut across his chest before we both separated again.

He crouched several yards away from me as wings exploded from his back—the trademark of a member of the wind clan. With a span at least nine feet long, they were perfectly black with an almost leathery texture. They were kept low to his body as he prepared to take flight on the wind still whipping through the city.

"Don't bother to have me followed," I called to him, still tightly gripping my knife. "I'm going to see my own kind. I'll not see Nia again until the night of the equinox. And if I suddenly disappear, Danaus will kill her."

His only answer was a low grunt, and then he threw open his wings, allowing them to catch the wind and pull him up into the black night above me. I had been partially lying. I was just hoping that he at least believed the lie, as it would buy me a little more time.

Putting the knife back in its sheath, I leaned back against the monument and inspected the cut along my arm that was still bleeding. Normally it would have healed already, but all naturi weapons contained a poison that slowed the healing process and burned like the fires of Hell.

"Don't hurt her," commanded a soft voice from the darkness. My head snapped up, and I was surprised that I hadn't actually been alone with Rowe. Flinging my arm out, I sent five fireballs speeding out into the surrounding darkness, not caring who saw me—naturi or human. I needed to see who my new companion was.

The naturi stepped between two fireballs as they went speeding past her. She was still dressed in the same soft gray clothing that I had seen her in at the Palace of Knossos. Her black hair danced in the wind and her pale skin seemed to glow in the lamplight. Cynnia's sister Nyx.

"Abide by my wishes," I told her, "and I promise that Cynnia will be safely released."

To my surprise, the woman nodded and said, "I'll see what I can do." She then threw out her own black wings, but these were different than Rowe's. Nyx's wings were not made of the same leathery material, but covered in glossy black feathers. Once again the wind rushed through the park, and then she was gone into the night sky.

Nineteen

My upper arm had stopped bleeding by the time I reached the Plaza de Armas. A good portion of my sleeve was soaked in blood, making the minor cut look much worse than it actually was. If I was lucky, Danaus would overlook the little scratch. He hadn't been in favor of me traveling through the city alone, and the blood covering my arm didn't exactly argue my case.

I was struggling to ignore the bite of winter wind. With the city at more than two miles in the sky, the night air had dropped down into the low thirties. I reminded myself that though it was September, in Peru the land was slowly plodding through its winter months. Cold generally didn't bother me, except when I was low on blood. The wound Rowe inflicted had left me needing to feed yet again. However, most of the tourists were now tucked away for the night in their respective hotels, forcing me to wait around in a dark corner for some drunken sot to stumble from one of the local bars so I could drain a pint off of him to keep me warm.

The Plaza de Armas was a large square flanked by a cathedral and two other churches to the northeast, and another, more ornate, church that rose up from the southeast. With a frown, I was forced to cut between the quartet to reach the Hostal Loreto. As I walked, I mentally reached out and tapped the minds of the nightwalkers around me, sending them images of my route and calling them to my side. When I reached the Loreto, I could feel close to forty vampires approaching. It was going to get crowded.

Of course, that concern was temporarily derailed when I passed through the lobby and halted at the entrance to the bar. It was as if I had left Peru and stepped back into the United States. It looked like so many of the places I had visited in the U.S., with its enormous bar, crowded tables, and scattering of televisions flashing whatever sporting event their satellite could pick up. I could only guess that the owner was a motorcycle fanatic because the walls were covered in photographs, posters, and other biker paraphernalia. This theme was evenly balanced against the soccer posters that also covered the walls. Maybe not the exact kind of decoration you would find in an American bar, but close enough to make a traveling Yankee feel at home.

After scanning the room briefly, I located Danaus near the back talking to Eduardo. Weaving through the throng, I joined the pair. However, Eduardo took one look at me and excused himself before shuffling off to the kitchen. I shrugged as I slid into a chair across from the hunter.

"He thinks he may be able to track down a couple of tourist vans," Danaus said. "The drive to Ollantaytambo is about two hours, probably longer at night."

"How many can fit in a van?"

"About ten."

"We're going to need more than two vans," I murmured, my eyes drifting up to the entrance, where a steady stream of nightwalkers poured into the bar and headed over to our table. Not one of them looked like a local. There was no chance of blending in, but then again, I hoped to have them all out of Cuzco before dawn.

I bit back a curse and closed my eyes for a moment when I discovered that Stefan was leading the group across the room. While he was slimmer and a few inches shorter than Danaus, there was something very impressive about the vampire. He was only a few years shy of being considered an Ancient, but you couldn't tell it by the way his powers were pushing against the walls and filling the air. Like me, Stefan had been created with care and patience. He was a First Blood and he carried himself as if he were royalty. Stefan had no idea what it meant to be chum.

To make matters worse, his appearance was absolutely heart-stopping. In general, all nightwalkers are attractive. It's almost like evolution considered it one of the items necessary for our survival, like the white fur of a snowshoe hare. How else would we lure our prey? But Stefan's beauty was so perfect it was almost frightening. At the moment, his dark brown hair was cut short and brushed to the side so it hung slightly over his left eye, which was a cold, heartless shade of pale gray.

And Stefan was as cold as he was beautiful. I'd say he had inspired Oscar Wilde to write his *Dorian Gray* tale, except that I thought Dorian had more redeeming qualities than Stefan.

We'd met only a couple of times, and he had a very reluctant respect for me. In his eyes, we were of the same elite class. We were also both survivors of Machu Picchu, not that I remembered him being here. Of course, I'm sure I managed to destroy whatever grudging respect he had for me through my continued association with Danaus.

"I'm surprised," I said, arching one brow at him when he was standing beside our table. "I never thought I would see you in Peru again."

With an elegant shrug of his slim shoulders, he said, "I have been to the ancient city before. I know its layout." His voice danced around the room, melodious and seductive at the same time. He made it seem as if we were going out for an average night of hunting through the streets of Paris. I knew better. There were no signs of concern in his languid gray eyes or along the corners of his full, soft lips, but I knew. Very few of the nightwalkers that visited Machu Picchu five centuries ago had survived. We were pressing our luck by returning.

"And the Coven ordered your appearance," I said, almost flinching at the unexpected hardness that filled my tone.

"They made the request; I complied graciously," he corrected, with a slight trace of French softening his words. His tone was still bland and bored, but something flashed briefly in his eyes. It was too easy to push his buttons, and I reluctantly relented. There was no time to play.

"What exactly was their request?"

This time a smile of genuine amusement lifted his lips and sparkled in his slumberous eyes. For a moment they seemed to glow in his delight. "To protect you."

"Anything else?"

"Specifically, I have been asked to protect you, Sadira, Jabari, and him, no matter what," he said, his voice hardening when he was finally forced to acknowledge Danaus.

"So I thought," I murmured. Jabari and Sadira had yet to appear, and I had a feeling they wouldn't until the last minute. "Would you care to join us? It seems we may have some logistics to work out."

With a regal nod of his head, Stefan took the empty seat next to me, while a woman with short blond hair sat next to Danaus. A third nightwalker male pulled over a chair from an empty table and sat at the end of the table. I noticed that the other nightwalkers that strolled into the bar had taken up various tables around the room, but were not too far from our location. I had no doubt they would be able to hear everything we said.

"This is George," Stefan said, introducing the vampire at the end of the table and motioning absently with his right hand. The pale, slender gentleman with the narrow face and cinnamon-colored hair nodded toward me and Danaus, sitting back in his chair as if he didn't have a care in the world. As best as I could tell, he had at least three centuries under his belt and most likely had never seen a member of the naturi.

"And this is Bertha," Stefan continued, waving his hand toward the pert little female vampire seated beside Danaus.

My mouth fell open; there was no controlling my reaction. After a while even someone my age will start to buy into some of the nightwalker mystique we had promoted to the humans. Vampires were not named Bertha. We had sleek, exotic names that rang of dead civilizations.

"I know," the nightwalker cheerfully said with a giggle when I finally managed to close my mouth. "It's a horrible name. I've tried to change it, but nothing ever sticks. You can just call me Bert or Bertie. Everyone does." The little blonde had sparkling, wide blue eyes and an adorable button nose. Her cheeks were round and dimpled when she smiled. She couldn't have been more than sixteen or seventeen when she had been reborn. I shoved back my initial reaction of sympathy at the sound of her name and smiled broadly at her. I imagined she hadn't tried too hard to change her name. Her disguise was perfect. Who would suspect that a five-foot-nothing, little blonde called Bertie was a lethal predator?

"A pleasure," I said with a nod of my head.

The smile in her eyes flickered for a moment as she assessed me, weighing me, before the smile widened on her cherry-colored lips. She had my measure. I doubted we would underestimate each other.

"This is Danaus," I said, letting my eyes drift back over to the hunter's grim visage. He didn't move, hardly breathed as the nightwalkers looked him over. When everyone was introduced and settled at the table, I turned my focus back to Stefan. "How many have arrived?"

"Nearly forty nightwalkers, with more promised from Jabari. In addition, more than thirty human guardians have arrived."

"Great. Cannon fodder," I grumbled, but Stefan remained nonplussed by the idea. What did he care? Humans were easy to replace.

"We have to reach the Sanctuary Lodge tonight," I said, folding my arms over my chest. "As soon as the sun sets tomorrow, we have to hit the mountain. I don't know when they will attempt the sacrifice, but the sooner we take out the naturi on the mountain, the better."

"A number of us can fly," Bertie piped up. She sat calmly forward, her fingers threaded and resting on the table.

"How many?"

"Ten."

"That would put only a small portion at the lodge tonight," Danaus interjected with a grim shake of his head. "Do we want to risk making the trip during the day? They know we're here."

My fingers restlessly played with the knife and fork that had been wrapped in a paper napkin when I sat down. I unfolded the napkin and slowly turned the knife over with my fingertips. "A daylight trip is far too risky," I said absently, a part of me wondering how I was going to handle Cynnia in the midst of all this chaos.

"We could double up or make a couple trips," Bertie replied. "It takes an hour at most to reach the lodge. We could have all the nightwalkers to the mountain before dawn."

"The humans could take the first train in the morning," Danaus said, sitting forward so that he could lean his forearms on the table. "They'd reach the lodge well before noon."

"Leaving us without protection deep in naturi territory for more than five hours," George grimly said.

"We have no choice," I quickly put in, before an argument could start. "Stefan, Bertie, organize those nightwalkers that can fly. Everyone doubles up. Nightwalkers go to the lodge first. Oldest and then the youngest. The first set secures the lodge."

"Already done," Stefan said, and looked down his nose at me, giving me a patronizing smile. "The lodge had been closed and emptied due to repairs."

"Excellent. Danaus and I will take a small group in a van to Ollantaytambo. After Cuzco has been emptied, a pair of nightwalkers can come and get Danaus and me. The last of the group can take the train from Ollantaytambo to Aguas Calientes and then secure our luggage on the bus to the lodge in the morning."

"Why are you going to Ollantaytambo?" Stefan demanded.

"There's something I wish to check. It's only a couple hours away by car. By the time the last group reaches the lodge, we should be done and ready to be picked up. Also, it will be a shorter distance to fly for whoever comes for us," I argued. My hands gripped the end of the table as I fought to keep my tone even. I didn't need a fight with Stefan.

"Bertha and George will see to the arrangements," he stiffly said, daring me to contradict him. "I will accompany you and the hunter to Ollantaytambo."

"As you wish," I agreed, flashing him a brilliant smile that took him by surprise. "Select four humans to accompany us. We'll meet you outside this hotel in a couple hours." Pushing out of my chair, I nodded to the three nightwalkers at the table with me. I never raised my voice, but I knew all the vampires within the bar could hear me. "All possessions are to be labeled and dropped off at the train station before you leave town. Your guardians will retrieve them from the bus in the morning."

With Danaus beside me, I walked out of the bar and through the hotel to the plaza.

The hunter didn't speak up until we were several yards from the hostel and safe from being overhead. As we walked back toward the shabby hotel that we occupied along with Shelly and Cynnia, he grabbed my blood-streaked arm and held it up between us. "I see everything went well."

"You're just jealous that you aren't the cause," I teased, pulling my arm out of his grip.

"You could be right." He flashed me one of his rare half smiles before it completely disappeared. "Will we be hearing more from our dark companion?"

"Undoubtedly, but I at least gave Rowe something to think about. He knows we have Cynnia. He also knows that I'll kill her if he so much as breathes in my direction. Of course, I told him that I'd kill her if he went through with the sacrifice, so he's already faced with an ugly dilemma."

"How are we going to protect her during the daylight

hours once we reach the lodge? The naturi could easily hit the place while all the nightwalkers are out for the count. They'd burn straight through any humans that happened to be defending the nightwalkers. Speaking of which, how are we going to protect the nightwalkers during the day?" Danaus suddenly stopped walking and shook his head. "I can't believe I just uttered those words."

Laughing, I threaded my arm through his and forced him to start walking again toward the hotel. "I knew you'd finally come around."

"Mira," he said in a low, warning voice. I was pressing my luck.

"Joke," I said, but still snuggled a little closer to him. Not only was he radiating wonderful body heat, but his powers flared out around him as he constantly scanned the area. "How many?" I asked when we were only a few yards away from the hotel.

"Three within a block. Another dozen are scattered throughout the city. Most seem to be a distance from here. To the north, lower elevation, possibly."

"They're already at Machu Picchu," I confirmed. "It's going to be interesting to see if they let us set up an outpost at the lodge. It rests at the foot of the Incan retreat."

"How exactly are we going to do that?"

"I'm sure it can't be too hard. I mean, we will have a talented naturi and an earth witch with us. I'm sure between the two of them, they should be able to figure out something that would keep us all protected."

Danaus stopped walking again and glared down at me, less than patiently waiting for the real response. I sighed heavily and pulled him along until he was finally walking toward the hotel of his own accord.

"Stefan also knows a couple interesting tricks," I said, "though I would never say as much to his face. The bastard has enough of an inflated ego, and at the moment, I truly doubt that I am his most favorite person in the world."

"Old boyfriend?"

An unladylike snort escaped me before I could stop it, and I clenched my free hand at my side. I didn't like Stefan. I didn't like his kind. He believed that anything weaker than him was put on this earth for his amusement; that included both human and nightwalker. Lycanthropes were a temptation, but since they tended to travel in packs, it was more difficult to pick off just one victim. But that didn't put the occasional shifter beyond his reach.

"Hardly," I sarcastically snapped. "Stefan is nearly an Ancient. I have no doubt that he can practically taste that one-thousand-year mark and it's now eating him alive that I have claimed the open seat on the Coven—the very seat I know he planned to claim for himself."

"So we have a new reason not to trust him," Danaus murmured, gazing down at my upturned face.

I smiled at my companion, feeling silly for enjoying this quiet moment. It was one of the rare times when we weren't yelling at each other. Danaus wasn't cursing me for what I was while we plotted to kill each other. We were a team with a single goal ahead of us—stop the naturi from opening the door. It made me feel as if we were unstoppable. I knew that it wasn't the truth, but at least it was a comforting feeling as we walked together down the cold, dark cobblestone streets of Cuzco with naturi surrounding us.

"Normally, I would agree with you, but at the moment, Stefan is going to be my greatest protector. He's got a direct command from the Coven to protect you and me. Destroying one of us right now isn't going to earn him any points with the Coven. If anything, it's going to get him killed for failing to complete his duty."

Danaus stopped walking and turned his body so he was facing me. The wind flew down the narrow street, slamming him in the back before flowing around him to hit me in the chest. My hair danced about my face as if it had taken on a life of its own, like Medusa's snakes.

"The Coven," he said, and then stopped again. He raised both of his hands, closing them into fists before lowering them back to his sides in frustration. "Why? I mean, couldn't there have been another way? Or could I have . . . " His voice faded as he tried to put into words the maelstrom of feelings that were swirling around inside him. It was tempting to just close my eyes and creep along our connection to try to get a clearer picture of exactly what he was feeling, but I decided against it. There were some things that were better if they remained unknown.

I slowly reached forward and laid my hand over his heart. Its beat was steady and even, a heartbeat that I could spend centuries listening to, letting it lull me into peaceful rest. "There was no other way. Joining the Coven may have been a mistake, but I'm stuck with it now. I'll find a way to make the best of it, *without* being a puppet for Jabari."

"Or a target for Macaire and Elizabeth," he said, laying his hand over mine. "You promised that one day we would finish our dance. I still mean to kill you, nightwalker."

A sad smile drifted across my lips as I rested my forehead against his hand, which was still covering mine. "Afraid of a little competition?"

"It seems like half the world wants you dead."

"Yes, but only after I'm done risking my life for them,"

I said, lifting my head again. "Let's get going. We need to check on the girls." I stepped away from him and started walking down the street again, ending our brief moment.

"Why are we going to Ollantaytambo?" Danaus inquired, at my side again, his hands shoved into his pockets. He had no obvious weapons strapped to his body, but I had no doubt that he probably had a number of knives. It was on the tip of my tongue to ask how many naturi were now close to our location, but I swallowed the words. The hunter was on edge already, his eyes continuously scanning the area. If we were being threatened, he'd tell me.

"Even since you mentioned Ollantaytambo, it's been ringing in my head. The name keeps teasing at some memory in the back of my brain," I said, not bothering to filter the frustration from my voice.

"What?"

"I don't know," I sighed. A bitter wind whipped through the city, pulling at my hair so that a few tendrils danced across my face. I hooked a bit of loose hair behind my ear, but it refused to stay put. "I've been to Peru just once, and I thought only at Machu Picchu. But I feel like I should remember something about Ollantaytambo—maybe I've been there or they mentioned it. I don't know, but I want to check it out."

"So this is just a side trip while we wait for the others to be taken to the lodge?" Danaus replied.

"Possibly," I admitted with a shrug. "Get the van organized with Eduardo. I'm going back to the hotel to get our 'things' and talk to some locals. Maybe I can get some information about Ollantaytambo."

"Mira . . . " he started. I could guess what he was going to say. Something about the number of naturi lurking in Peru, in Cuzco, or in our hotel. They would always be close, but I didn't think that Rowe would be willing to make a move just yet. Or at least, I didn't think that Nyx would allow him to risk the life of her sister. Unless she really did want Cynnia dead, and then I was about to be proven seriously wrong.

"Is one standing behind me?" I sharply asked before he could continue.

Danaus furrowed his brow and frowned at me. "No."

"Then I don't want to know. Don't tell me how outnumbered we are until I ask."

With a nod and half smile, he headed back toward Hostal Loreto to find Eduardo. I trudged back to the hotel, my hands in my pockets and my head down against the wind. I didn't want to tell him that fear twisted in my stomach whenever I heard the word "Ollantaytambo." There was something I was supposed to remember about that place. As best as I could recall, I had woken up one night on Machu Picchu after being in Spain the night before. I don't know how I had gotten to Machu Picchu and I never asked. Pain quickly accompanied consciousness during those long nights, and petty thoughts about how I'd traveled a long distance were unimportant.

Had the naturi spoken of Ollantaytambo during my imprisonment? Or worse? Had I been there but couldn't remember? I had to know. It probably had nothing to do with the sacrifice and the opening of the door, but I knew I would never have another chance to find out. If we were lucky, we'd zip in and out of Ollantaytambo without being noticed and then be flown to the lodge. Of course, Lady Fortune had given me the cold shoulder for much of the past few months. Why change now?

Twenty

Shelly and Cynnia were seated cross-legged on the bed with playing cards when I entered the room using the key I had gotten off of Danaus. Judging by the way Shelly was continuously looking over at Cynnia's cards, it appeared that she was attempting to teach the naturi how to play gin with mixed results.

"We need to change rooms," I said, slamming the door shut behind me. Both women looked at me a little strangely, each tensely clutching their individual hand of cards.

"Come on! Let's move! They could be in the hotel already," I snapped when they didn't move. Taking the cards out of Cynnia's hands, I dropped them on the bed and grabbed the chain linking her wrist irons. She stumbled behind me as I pulled her to her feet, with Shelly following.

"I don't understand," Shelly said. "Who's here?"

"The naturi," Cynnia answered before I could.

"Where's Danaus?"

"On an errand." I halted when we reached the door and looked down at her. "Do you sense them? Are they here?"

"Mira, with the manacles, I can't clearly sense much of anything," Cynnia explained. "I can feel the power in the air, but I can't use it to clearly sense my own kind while I'm in the hotel."

"But earlier you said that you had sensed them."

"It was when I was standing on the ground outside, while we were traveling," she argued. "When I'm in this hotel with concrete separating me from the earth, I can't feel anything but the energy in the air."

"Grand," I snarled, my gaze sweeping around the room to snag on the one window against the far wall. "Shelly, I want to you keep an eye on that window until I say to follow me." The witch nodded, and I moved back to the door with Cynnia in tow.

I opened the door and quickly palmed my knife with my right hand. Peering down the hall to the left and then to the right, I saw that it was empty and felt some of the tension in my chest uncoil.

"Is someone coming after us?" Cynnia asked

"Possibly." I jerked the door open wider and pulled her into the hallway with me and down to the next door, where Danaus and I shared the windowless room. "Shelly, come on!"

"Is that why you're wounded? You were attacked by a naturi," Cynnia said, trying to take a step back from me, but her manacles were tightly held in my grip. Unfortunately, I was out of hands to set the key into the lock. I wasn't willing to let go of the knife either, as I felt safer with it close at hand. Frustrated, I buried the tip of the knife into the wooden doorjamb, earning a gasp from both Shelly and Cynnia as I fished the room key out of my pocket.

Once the door was open, I grabbed the knife and ushered both women quickly into the room. Shelly and Cynnia huddled together against the far wall after I locked the door and conducted a thorough search of the room to ensure that we were truly alone. I liked this room better—there was no window, and only one entrance, only one door to defend if someone had followed me to Cynnia's location.

"What happened?" Shelly inquired when I finally seemed satisfied that we had the room to ourselves. "Your arm is covered in dried blood."

I sat on the edge of the bed, while Shelly took the one good seat in the room, leaving Cynnia to once again curl up on the floor against the wall. "I met up with an old friend of mine named Rowe. He seemed really anxious to find you, Cynnia."

"Does he mean to kill me?" Cynnia said, wrapping her arms around one of her bent legs while keeping the other out straight.

"I don't know, but I gave him an ultimatum. If he walks away from the ceremony, I'll set you free. If not, you're dead. I thought it was what we both wanted."

"Not the dead part!"

"He has to be given a reason to cooperate."

"Couldn't you think of something equally persuasive other than ending my life?"

"No, because I mean it. I have no use for you if I can't use you to stop the sacrifice from being completed. You're just another naturi that wants to kill nightwalkers and humans, then."

"No, that's not true! You know it's not true," she argued. She lurched forward so that she was on her hands and knees before me. "I can help you. I don't want this war. I don't want to fight with the nightwalkers and I'd be happy to find a way to live in peace with the humans."

"Unfortunately, it doesn't seem like Rowe is willing to

put aside his plans just for the sister of the queen. He plans to go forward with the sacrifice tomorrow night."

"No! Mira, please, we can find another way. I can be useful to you," Cynnia desperately argued.

"You are in luck, because someone else appeared before I had a chance to return here," I said, causing her bent head to snap up. "It seems you're rather important to your sister. Enough so that she may be willing to try to stop Rowe's plans in an effort to save your life."

"Nyx wants me alive?" Cynnia whispered. She sat back again, tears slipping down her pale cheeks. "I was afraid that if she was here, she had been sent to kill me as well. But Nyx wants me alive."

"So it would seem," I murmured.

"You have a plan?" Shelly asked, drawing my attention to her. She had been a quiet companion on this trip, seeing to Cynnia's needs while Danaus and I made what plans we could for Machu Picchu. Hopefully, she could block the naturi earth magic.

"If our little Nia wants to stay alive, then it seems that she may have to provide some assistance to us, and by extension, to her sister Nyx." I paused to be sure that I had Cynnia's complete attention. Her wide, wet eyes were locked on my face as she used the sleeve of her shirt to wipe away her tears. "We have to keep the door closed."

"I agree," Cynnia said with a nod. "I don't want to see Aurora hurt, but she can't be allowed to return to earth."

"Then I need you to teach Shelly and me how to use earth magic."

"I already know how to use earth magic," Shelly argued, moving to the edge of her chair.

"Maybe, but not to the powerful levels that are available

to you right now," I said with a shake of my head. "I need you to be able to wield this power. The Sacred Valley is flooded with energy, more so than what I experienced at Stonehenge or the Palace of Knossos. This place is different, and I need you prepared to take advantage of it."

"Besides, nightwalkers can't use earth magic," Cynnia argued. "It's against all the laws."

I smiled and pushed off the bed to walk over to her. "All laws can be broken. Rowe has been using blood magic. I know a warlock that has been wielding both blood and earth magic. I can manipulate fire, which seems to have given me some kind of in when it comes to using earth magic. I need your help in learning to control it."

"There is no controlling it." Using the wall behind her, she pushed to her feet. "It's energy that is there for your use, but to actually control it and wield it is not something we believe in."

"Look, Cynnia, I'm not in the mood to debate semantics with you. I want you to teach me to be able to use this power that is flowing about me. Teach me to be an earth witch, if you must."

"It's not that simple, Mira," Shelly chimed in.

Turning back around, I flopped down on the edge of the bed and put my head between my hands in frustration. "It's like we're talking different languages—we don't have time for this."

To my surprise, Shelly stepped forward. She left the chair and came over to kneel before me, taking both of my hands in her warm hands. "We're not trying to make this difficult, but it *is* a matter of semantics, in a way. I don't know about blood magic, but earth magic comes from one single, living source. The power itself has its own consciousness and identity. You can't control it because it doesn't want to be controlled. You can't wield it the same way that you wield a sword because it's not a thing."

"Then how do you use it?" I demanded, giving her hands a slight squeeze to emphasize my desperation as my gaze darted from her to Cynnia. "You cast spells. You make plants grow. You change the weather. You control animals. All of this is accomplished through earth magic. I need to be able to do these things, or at least understand how these things are done. In this fight, it's not enough that I am an old nightwalker or even that I am the Fire Starter. When I am here at the place of the sacrifice, I am a danger to myself and those around me."

Shelly's hands slid from mine and she sat back on her heels before me, confusion filling her lovely face as her blond hair slipped down around her cheeks.

"I don't understand," Cynnia whispered.

"I can feel the earth's power when I am here," I said.

"Just here or when you're near a swell?" Cynnia quickly inquired, causing my brow to furrow at her word choice.

"A swell?" Shelly asked, her gaze darting over to the naturi.

"It's one of the places on the earth where the crust is the thinnest. It's where the power flows up through the center of the earth to the surface. It's likely these are the places that Rowe has been holding the sacrifices; they would provide him with the power he needs to break the seal and open the door."

"Yes, when I'm near a swell, I can feel the power of the earth," I said with a nod. I threaded my fingers together, twisting them tightly as I continued my story. This was information that I wasn't sure was safe in the hands of the naturi, but at the moment I didn't see that I had much choice. We had already gone over much of this the previous night in the woods, but I was forced to leave that place with only a weak barrier spell in my back pocket. After walking around Cuzco and feeling the power in the air, I knew I was going to need a stronger plan of attack to survive the encounter at Machu Picchu. "It's more than that. I can feel the power from the earth pushing against my skin, trying to enter my body."

"I'm assuming that you allow it to enter," Shelly said, a frown pulling at the corners of her lips.

"No, not intentionally."

"Mira, why not? That's a wonderful gift that you've been given," Shelly said, rising up on her knees with newfound energy. "It's like the earth is reaching out to you. It's not the same for earth witches. We have to reach out and tap the energy in the air that we can find. Being here, with the power so thick in the air, it's easier for me now, but for it to come searching you out . . . it's . . . it's like an honor."

"But I can't feel it when I'm not at a swell," I countered.

"You said that you didn't intentionally allow the power to enter your body, but it has in the past?" Cynnia asked. She had crawled a little way from the wall and was now seated closer to me and Shelly.

"When I create fire at the swells, the earth power rushes into my body. I can't stop it! It fills me, consumes me until there seems to be nothing left inside of me except for this power. The only way to get rid of it is to create more fire, but it never seems to be enough."

"And it never will be," Cynnia said with a sad shake of her head. "How do you finally get it to stop?"

"Blood magic. It pushes the earth magic back out of my

body," I carefully said, avoiding mentioning that Danaus served as my source of pure blood magic, given his bori nature. "I want control of this. I want to be able to use the earth magic that pours into my body, but I also need to be able to shut it off. Can either of you teach me that?"

Cynnia hesitated, but Shelly quickly spoke up, laying her hand on my knee. "I can."

I looked over at Cynnia, who refused to meet my gaze. "Your usefulness is dwindling."

"Please understand my point of view, Mira," she said, slowly lifting her eyes to meet mine. "You're already the stuff of legends among my people. Am I to be the one responsible for making you even stronger? More dangerous not only to my people, but to the entire world?"

"And what happens if we don't?" Shelly snapped, raising her voice toward the young naturi for the first time. "Your sister Aurora will come through and kill us all. I don't always agree with Mira's methods, but at least in her version of the world, there's a place for humans."

"You're food!" Cynnia snapped. She balled her hands into fists and tried to jerk her hands apart, but the chains kept her bound. "You're cattle to them."

Shelly jerked back, looking as if Cynnia had suddenly smacked her. Her mouth hung open but no words came out.

"It's true, Shelly," I gently said. This time I laid a hand on her shoulder. She flinched under my cool touch, but I refused to move my hand away. "Nightwalkers cannot exist without humans to feed upon, but that is not the only reason we seek to protect you. Humans are also our friends, our enemies, and our lovers. No matter how long a nightwalker exists in the shadows, at some time we always find ourselves establishing some sort of relationship with a human. It's where we started as creatures and it's something that we cannot completely escape."

"They've hunted you," Cynnia argued through clenched teeth.

"And we've protected you," I calmly said. "We are neither villains nor saviors. We simply are a part of this world as much as humans are."

Cynnia stood and took a couple steps toward me, her fists trembling in anger before her. "And we deserve a place in this world just as much as nightwalkers."

"I'll agree with that as long as you're willing to share it with the rest of the races. Look me in the eye and tell me that is Aurora's plan."

Cynnia held my gaze for a second then blinked and turned away from me. "She doesn't want to share," she whispered, her slender shoulders slumping in defeat. "She never will share with the humans."

"And because of that I will not stop fighting the naturi. Give me a naturi ruler that understands coexistence and I will consider putting down my sword."

"Consider?" Cynnia asked, turning back to look at me, one eyebrow arched in question.

"Your brother and many others are responsible for much I will never be able to forgive. I cannot learn to forget so quickly," I said in a cold voice.

"I thought the saying was 'forgive and forget.'"

"I know my limitations. There will be no forgiveness."

A sigh from Shelly drew my attention back to the earth witch. She was trapped between two warring races. Her only chance was to pick a race that would protect her survival, which meant siding with the nightwalkers. But Cynnia was right. Humans were little more than cattle to us. Cattle and a bit of violent, ugly amusement when the mood hit us. The lesser of the two evils was still evil.

"From what it sounds like, Mira," Shelly slowly began, moving away from my touch as she kept her eyes on the worn and faded carpet beneath her knees. "You're trying to act as a battery for the energy that is coming into you instead of a conduit."

"I'm not trying to do anything," I admitted, struggling to keep from sounding defensive. "The first couple times it happened, I wasn't trying for it. It just happens against my will."

"Then the earth must recognize you as an outlet because of your ability to manipulate fire," Cynnia volunteered sullenly. She returned to her place on the floor against the wall, her arms wrapped around her bent legs. "To stop this from happening, you can simply stop going to the various swells around the world."

"Nia," I murmured in the gentlest voice I could muster amidst my growing frustration. "I have to stop the door from opening."

To my surprise, Cynnia closed her eyes and a single fat tear rolled down her cheek. "I know." What she also knew was that many of her own kind were going to be killed in the ensuing battle for Machu Picchu tomorrow night.

"As I was saying," Shelly continued, drawing my attention away from the lost and hurting naturi. "You're acting as a battery. It sounds like the power is going into your body and your body is attempting to store the energy until you are ready to use it. Unfortunately, you can store only so much energy before it finally destroys you."

"I'll agree with that assessment," I muttered. At least that explained the excruciating pain I felt whenever the power entered my body, and the relief I felt when I used my powers. It also made me wonder if that was why I felt the same pain when Danaus or Jabari attempted to manipulate me. Was I simply storing up their power within my body until I finally abided by their wishes?

"You need to become a conduit," Shelly said. "You need to allow the energy to not only flow into you, but to also flow out again. When you use earth magic, you are simply tapping into the power that is naturally flowing through you."

"So how do I do that?"

At that question, Shelly bit on her lower lip and looked over her shoulder at Cynnia, who shrugged.

"This is your one chance to prove your value to me, to save your own life, and you're going to say no!" I shouted, pushing off the bed and walking toward her.

"No, that's not what I meant," Cynnia said, throwing up both arms to keep me off of her. "I have no idea how to teach what you're asking. It's supposed to come naturally. Honestly, if I had a clue as to what I could do, I would tell you. I don't want to contemplate how much energy you can hold or the damage you can do once that power is released. I'd rather you become the conduit that Shelly spoke of."

I paused and looked back at Shelly, who was nodding at me. "I've never heard of this problem," she added. "I have to reach for the power of the earth, pull it into myself, and it naturally flows back out again, like a river. When it flows through, I simply scoop up what I need for the spell that I am weaving."

"Damn it," I muttered, walking back over to plop back down on the edge of the bed. I shoved both my hands through my hair, pushing it out of my face in frustration as I desperately sought some solution, any kind of solution, to the problem. I couldn't avoid the swells. In fact, I planned to be haunting each and every one of them until Rowe and his crew were finally taken care of.

The hairs on the back of my neck suddenly began to tingle, and I sent my powers flaring out of my body, running through the hotel like a horde of ghosts until they finally settled on Danaus. He was approaching. I was out of time for now. We needed to leave.

"Maybe you can help me in another way," I began, looking up at Cynnia. "What can you tell me about Ollantaytambo?"

"Nothing," she said with a shake of her head. "I've never heard of it."

"It's a place just outside of Machu Picchu," I pressed. I needed any kind of information she could give me before we left on this fool's errand. "I think there's some sort of old Incan temple or structure there."

Again Cynnia just sadly shook her head at me. "I only know the name Machu Picchu because you use it. It's not our name for this place. I just know that it's the last place that we attempted and nearly succeeded at opening the door."

"What do you call this place?"

Cynnia said something in her own lyrical language that I couldn't even begin to replicate, causing me to frown at her. "It translates roughly to 'Mother's Garden.' It's what we call the entire valley area."

Danaus knocked on the bedroom door. It was time to go to Ollantaytambo. It wasn't that I really wanted to go this site of ancient Incan ruins, but that I felt I had to go. There was something calling out to me from my past here. A door that needed to either be opened finally or firmly shut and locked forever.

Twenty-One

Only the human guardians spoke during the car ride to Ollantaytambo. Even then it was low, whispers in broken bits of Spanish or Italian. I rode in the front seat next to Danaus, who graciously volunteered to drive. At the random intersection, he'd stop, grunt, and we'd silently look at the map Eduardo had given us before we wordlessly continued on. Stefan lounged in the seat directly behind Danaus, vainly attempting to unnerve the hunter. If he succeeded, I couldn't tell, but then again, that was Danaus. As far as I knew, I was the only one who had succeeded in rattling him. And I had every reason to believe he was going to cut my heart out for my troubles.

Stefan's goal was also to remain as far from Cynnia as possible. It had not gone well when I informed the nightwalker that both an earth witch and a naturi would be joining us on our journey to Ollantaytambo. He would have been content to cut Cynnia's heart out where she stood in the middle of the city sidewalk and leave her for the humans to find later, but I deftly talked him out of it, using promises of being able to use her as a bargaining chip later at the battle of Machu Picchu.

So, for now, Shelly acted as a thin, human buffer, sitting between the powerful and brooding Stefan and the all too quiet Cynnia as we headed deeper into the Sacred Valley by a sliver of fading moonlight. I would have liked to ask either of the two women if their sense of the power in the air was getting stronger, but I didn't want to alert Stefan to any of this earth magic nonsense just yet. I preferred for him to think that I maintained a strict captor-captive relationship with Cynnia. He didn't need to know that I was currently depending upon her to give me some kind of guidance when it came to controlling, or at least using, the earth magic that seemed desperate to flow through my body.

As we drove close to Ollantaytambo, hills rose up around us, blotting out what little light the stars had to offer. Naturally, the moon was nowhere to be found. Reduced to a slim sliver of her once great glory, she remained hidden from sight, seemingly content to let us fumble around in the overwhelming darkness. The animals that watched us lumber along the narrow, winding road were silent, cloaked by the rocks and bushes.

After more than two hours of driving, both the mountains and the scattering of trees and brush at last pulled back, opening into what seemed to be a tiny valley. Despite the fact that I didn't breathe, I had to fight back the urge to draw in a deep breath at the sight of Ollantaytambo. The city was small, with only a handful of streets and a few hotels. It wasn't a major stop for tourists. Some would take a short day trip to see the ruins at the edge of the city, but then move on to Aguas Calientes and Machu Picchu.

As we slowly rolled down the main street, I noticed that the four humans we'd brought along had fallen silent. At the back of the van I could make out the sound of cloth rustling and the soft snap of weapon guards being released so knives and guns could be quickly drawn. Before leaving the hotel room, both Danaus and I once again loaded up on weapons. He had a short sword strapped to his back along with a pair of guns that I couldn't readily identify. The hunter had also been kind enough to return to me the same style of Glock and Browning that I'd used at Crete. I didn't like handguns but was familiar enough with these two that I could manage better than starting with two totally unknown weapons. I also had a short sword strapped to my thigh. I was hoping to avoid using my power while we were here, as there was already too much energy crackling in the air to make me feel comfortable.

As we drove into the city, I noted that each block was surrounded by high walls in the traditional Incan design. Inside the walls were a cluster of neat little houses, and a courtyard in the center of it all. It was nearly midnight when we entered the town, and each of the houses was shut up tight and the lights doused.

At the end of the main street, Danaus halted the car and looked at me for direction. Now that we were here, I didn't want to move, didn't want to speak. It had sounded like a good idea while I was sitting in a crowded bar in Cuzco surrounded by my own kind. No, that's wrong. It had sounded like a horrible idea when I was in Cuzco, and now that I was sitting here in the dark, I knew it was disastrous.

"Mira?" he prodded when I still refused to speak.

"The ruins," I replied in a low voice, proud that it didn't tremble. Of course, I was still struggling to loosen the death grip I had on the door handle. "Were we followed?"

There was no reason to ask who I was talking about. Only one group would be able to follow us without being detected by normal means. There was only one group right now that any of us were worried about. The naturi.

"No, but they're not far away," Danaus said. His deep voice was even and calm; a soothing balm despite the ominous words. Since we left the hotel, there had been a steady throb of energy seeping from him as he searched the area for our enemy. The relentless waves washed over and through me, pulling me closer to him. Those waves had both protected and sought to tear me apart in the past. Now I needed their protection not only from the enemy that was drawing close, but also from the ghosts haunting my past.

Danaus turned the grumbling white van down the road and drove the short distance to the ruins. Surrounded by hills, it was easy to make out the ruins rising up before us with the intricate stonework carved out by men centuries ago. The hunter pulled the van into the small, gravel parking lot a few hundred yards from the base of the mountain. Of course, mountain was a relative term considering we were already more than nine thousand feet above sea level. By the looks of it, the hike to the peak of the ruins was less that a quarter of a mile.

"Well, Mira," Stefan started, breaking the silence that was punctuated by only the rough breathing of the humans. "We're here. What is it you wished to see?"

Turning in my seat, I looked back at the naturi huddled as close to the door as she could get, putting as much distance as possible between her and Stefan. "Cynnia? Is there anything you can tell me?" I asked, ignoring the nightwalker for the time being.

"Nothing. I've never been here. I'm not quite sure why it would be viewed as important other than the fact that there is a great deal of energy in the air right here."

I couldn't argue with her there. The air seemed thick with energy, as if it were moisture on a hot and humid day. The energy within the area had become an entity that seemed to demand its presence to be recognized. Well, I was about to.

"We go to the top," I bit out, goaded on by Stefan's insolent tone. If the nightwalker had any special skill, it was his ability to instantly get under your skin like a tick. "The humans stay here and guard the van."

"Mira?" Shelly's voice softly broke the quiet of the van.

"You stay close to Cynnia. Don't let her out of your sight. Don't let her anywhere near the ruins where she might be able to escape us," I commanded, more for Stefan's benefit than for Shelly's. I didn't expect Cynnia to make a mad dash for freedom here, not if she was afraid of the allegiance of any naturi she found. For now, she was actually safer in my hands.

"Are you sure she can handle—"

"She can handle it," I snapped, interrupting Stefan's question.

Without waiting for any additional comment or argument, I shoved open the door and stepped out. I had to get moving. A flock of nightwalkers would be arriving in less than an hour to fetch us and carry us back to the lodge at the base of the ruins. This would be my only chance to see this place. Yet, all well laid plans are nothing without the occasional stumbling block.

The moment my booted foot touched the gravel-covered ground, my knee buckled beneath me. Luckily, I had yet to unwrap my fingers from around the armrest on the door, saving me from landing on my butt. The weight of my body pushed the door all the way open, pulling me out of the van. My other foot touched the ground and a second shockwave of power surged through my body, pulling a soft whimper from my throat. I tightly locked both hands around the armrest and leaned my head against the door, waiting for the feeling to pass. I couldn't get my legs to work. They remained limp, useless noodles beneath me. Pain filled me in massive, endless waves as the power from the earth pushed and pummeled my body from head to toe.

"Mira?" Stefan laid a hand on my shoulder, his voice questioning but without its usually cold indifference. I hadn't even heard the side door slide open when the nightwalker alighted from the van.

"Don't you feel it?" I choked out as I unclenched my teeth.

"Feel what?"

The question startled me enough to force my eyes open. I twisted my body to look over my shoulder and find Stefan standing just behind me, appearing perfectly fine. Then I lifted my head to see Danaus walking around the van. He also appeared unaffected. There was so much energy in the air it was positively suffocating. How could either of the two men manage to be completely oblivious to it?

"Shelly?"

"I feel it, but it's not painful," she said, coming to stand by me. "It feels like a lot of energy just flowing by me, sort of like standing in the middle of a fast-running stream."

"It's not running by her like it should," Cynnia said as she walked toward me. "It's trying to push its way into her. Even with the manacles, I can feel the energy swirling around Mira, swamping her. It wants in."

"What's going on?" Stefan demanded over the buzz of conversation and contemplation. "What energy are they talking about?"

"The energy from the earth," I muttered when no one seemed willing to talk directly to him. "I can sense it."

"Is it going to make you useless to us?" he continued in his usual less than cheerful manner.

"Danaus?" My eyes fell shut again as I concentrated on holding onto the armrest. I didn't need to worry about Stefan and his attitude at that moment. I had to worry about finding a way to function like this. If we were attacked right now by the naturi, I would be useless to the group, a liability.

I listened to the crunch of gravel beneath Danaus's feet as he stepped closer. His broad hand rested on my back and a surprised grunt escaped him. He drew his hand away and I opened my eyes to find my dark companion staring at me in confusion.

"What is that?" he growled.

"The earth," I whispered. "Pick me up." My grip on the door of the van was beginning to weaken and I didn't have the strength to crawl back into the van. It also wasn't an option. We had to get to the top of the ruins before the other nightwalkers arrived.

Without a word of argument, the hunter lifted me up into his arms. Instantly, the surge of energy was gone. For a moment my limbs felt weak and shaky, but even that quickly subsided. Laying one arm around his shoulders, I rubbed my temple with the heel of my other hand, trying to clear the fog from my brain. I didn't have a clue why the energy was so strong there. This wasn't where they would make the sacrifice in order to open the door. We all knew that was going to be at Machu Picchu. But for some strange reason this place was a maelstrom of energy, and I had to know why before we continued on to the lodge. If this place was of value to the naturi, I needed to know why before we left it at our backs.

"Let's get going," I sharply said, feeling awkward giving commands while being cradled in Danaus's arms, but I'm sure I accomplished it with my usual aplomb. "How long until the others arrive?"

"They're already on their way," Stefan stiffly said. Danaus had started walking, and the nightwalker was forced to take a couple jogging steps to catch up. "You can't have him carry you to the top."

"I can't touch the ground here just yet. There's too much energy in the area. It's either Danaus carrying me or you flying us both to the top," I snapped. I didn't trust Stefan. I wouldn't put it past him to fly me to the lodge and leave Danaus to catch up in the morning. I didn't want to be separated from the hunter. Not until after the sacrifice was stopped. He was the only one I knew that shared the same goal: stop the naturi.

"We haven't time for this nonsense," Stefan grumbled, his pale gray eyes flaring with frustration.

"Why are we here?" Danaus smoothly interjected as if sweeping the nightwalker and his concerns under the rug. "What do you remember?"

"Nothing." I shifted my gaze from Stefan to the path ahead of as we wove our way up the mountain. The very air seemed to tingle about us.

"Did they mention this place?" Danaus continued.

"No." I started to shake my head, but something caught my eye. "Stop!" Reaching out, I touched one of the huge stones that comprised the wall. The gray stone had three straight lines scored into the rock. Two lines ran parallel, cutting diagonally across the stone, while the third line slashed through the rock in the opposite direction, running through the other two lines. It wasn't a naturi symbol, but it also definitely wasn't natural.

"Put me down," I said in a hoarse voice, already pushing against Danaus's chest. Slowly, he let my feet touch the ground. Again the power surged into me, causing my legs to buckle. My knees hit the ground, jerking a soft cry from me as I continued to cling to the stone.

Clenching my teeth, I reached out mentally and touched any creature that had a soul within the immediate area. If earth magic was going to push and hammer against my body until it found a way in, then I was going to fill my body with as much blood magic as I could find to keep it out. Around me, I could feel the energy flowing from Shelly and the humans down at the van. More important, I had fired up the connection between Danaus and me. I could feel his emotions so clearly now, as if they were my own. With very little effort, I knew I would be able to hear his thoughts as well, but I was careful to keep that door shut.

The wellspring of power flowed cool and soothing into me, helping me fight back the intense energy that was trembling in my limbs. Pain still filled my joints and caused a heavy throbbing in my temples as the two energies fought for dominance within my slender frame. But at the moment, the pain didn't matter. I finally remembered why Ollantaytambo was so important.

"It's their gateway," I announced, struggling to my feet.

"What do you mean?" Stefan asked. Standing close, he cupped my elbow with one hand, helping to steady me now that I was standing again.

Instead of answering him, I twisted around so I could look at Cynnia, who seemed to shrink from my gaze, shifting so she was partially hidden behind Shelly. "You can travel through the energy, can't you?" I demanded in a harsh voice.

Cynnia nodded to me, her brown hair falling forward to obscure her face. "It's how we can quickly get from one part of the globe to the other part. It takes some practice and a lot of control, but most naturi can manage it, from what I've been told."

"Can you?"

The young naturi snorted at me and took a step away from Shelly. "Of course not. I've not been on earth that long, and no one has bothered to tell me how they work. I'd probably get myself killed in the process."

"I'd stay away from it," I warned. "We would hate to lose you."

"So, there's a gateway up here?" Danaus interjected, cutting short my ominous threats. He really did have a knack for ruining my fun.

"There are great energy flows through the earth like massive underground rivers. The naturi can ride these rivers to travel around the world," I explained, my voice gaining strength as I continued up the path. One hand slid along the rock wall face in an attempt to steady myself. "But there are only a handful of openings to these flows. The closest one to Machu Picchu is here in Ollantaytambo. It's why I've been here; why I remember it."

"It's a way for them to get reinforcements to Machu Picchu," Stefan said, his hand tightening on my elbow. "We have to destroy it."

A bitter laugh escaped me before I could grab it. "You can no more destroy it than you can stop the coming dawn," I sneered. "It's the very life of the earth and all the things that grow upon it."

"Can we block the opening?" Danaus demanded, drawing my eyes back to his face. He stared at me, his cold blue eyes seeming to glitter in some stray starlight. "At least temporarily block it. Buy us some time."

"Maybe. Are they here?" My concentration had been so completely focused on the energy pouring from the earth and the opening that was at the top of Ollantaytambo that I almost forgot that the naturi were on their way there.

"Not yet, but getting close."

Looking over my shoulder, I found Stefan intently listening to our conversation. "How much longer?" I asked him.

"Bertha and a few others should be here soon," he replied.

"Then we have to move now. We won't have another chance at this," I said, picking up my pace a bit. My legs were trembling beneath me and it was hard to keep focused on gathering the energy I needed to fight back the earth magic that was desperately attempting to force its way into my body.

A soft sound of frustration escaping Stefan was my only warning, and it came nowhere close to providing me with enough time to react. Wrapping one strong arm around my waist, he pulled me back so his chest was pressed to my back, and then we were in the air. I envied his ability to fly, to have the freedom to escape the coming dawn whenever he so chose. And under most circumstances I might have said something nice about the feel of the cold air rushing past us. Unfortunately, I wasn't in the mood. He was being an overbearing ass, and I had enough creatures in my life trying to control me.

The second my feet touched the ground I tried to shove my elbow into his stomach, but I hadn't thought about the well of power waiting for me when we reached the top of the mountain. My legs immediately crumpled beneath me, leaving me leaning heavily on Stefan's arm.

"It's worse up here?" he asked.

"Yes," I choked out as I struggled to fight back the power that left my knees knocking. I reached out to every living creature I could find. My mind stretched out to the village of Ollantaytambo and its sleeping population. Their energy swirled around me and swam through my body, seeming to cleanse me once again.

"Why can't I feel it?"

"Because you have not traveled in the flow," I replied, getting my legs beneath me so I could step away from him. It was a lie, but one he would buy for now. I had no idea why I could sense earth magic beyond the fact that I had the ability to manipulate fire. Unfortunately, I had a dark suspicion that my ability to manipulate fire and my ability to sense earth magic had little to do with each other. There was something else that would one day step forward to haunt me on that front, but for now I thought the lie might make everyone a little more comfortable.

Stefan slowly slid his hand from me, as if expecting me to fall to the ground the second he pulled away.

"The flow in the earth is how the naturi were able to get me from Spain to Machu Picchu in a single day," I explained. "It's the only way they could have done it."

I didn't go on to explain that I now remembered our arrival in Ollantaytambo. I could vaguely recall the sun and my body burning as the naturi raced to find a way to protect their prize before it was reduced to a black pile of ash. I remembered screaming and thinking I had finally descended into Hell. But there was no explaining how I came to be awake during the day, beyond the theory that it was just a side effect of the flow.

Yet those delightful contemplations were pushed aside. "The naturi are here," I announced to the cold night air.

"Are you sure?" Stefan demanded, frowning. Before I could answer, a single gunshot shattered the silence. Hesitantly, the earth seemed to take another breath before a barrage of gunfire from an automatic weapon resounded in the valley below.

"Yeah, pretty sure," I said, sarcasm slathered over every syllable. Before the first gunshot rang out into the night, I had felt a disturbance among the humans. They felt uneasiness wash over them, as if something was watching them out in the darkness. Pulling in their energy, I was also attuned to their emotions. I had felt their fear instantly grow to terror when they realized they faced a creature they could not beat.

The silence had sunk back in again. Without checking, I knew the four humans we had brought with us were dead. The naturi would wipe out anything and everything from their path to us. The humans were simply a warm-up act to the slaughter they anticipated on the top of the mountain at Ollantaytambo.

A footstep at the edge of the plateau had both Stefan and I ready to spring into action, but we quickly relaxed at the sight of Danaus jogging over, followed by Shelly and Cynnia.

"How many?" I gruffly demanded.

"Eight," the hunter replied, one of his guns already sliding into his hands. I pulled the Browning from the shoulder holster I was wearing, cradling the gun tightly in both hands as I waited for our adversaries to arrive.

"That's it?" I sounded strangely disappointed by the number. Of course, after having already battled a horde in London and another army while in Crete, I would have thought an army was waiting to destroy me in Peru.

"There are more on the way," he growled, as if to appease me.

"You and Stefan block the gateway. I'll take care of the naturi," I ordered, my eyes darting from the hunter to the nightwalker. Neither one looked particularly pleased with me, but no one argued.

"What about me?" Shelly asked, drawing my attention back to her and Cynnia for the first time. I had forgotten that I dragged the naturi and the earth witch into the nightmare with me. Maybe I should have left them both back in Savannah playing cards, but now wasn't the time for contemplating such things.

"Keep an eye on Cynnia! She's not to leave the mountaintop unless Danaus or I accompany her."

"I'm not leaving here with them, Mira!" Cynnia shouted. "Those naturi most likely belong to Rowe, and I'd rather not see my brother-in-law just yet. Not until at least one of us has a plan."

"Do I protect her?" Shelly asked, leading me to pause in the act of turning back toward Danaus and Stefan. My eyes danced from the naturi to the earth witch, my mind a clutter of thoughts, none of which made sense in that moment when a battle was breathing down our necks.

"Protect each other," I murmured.

Cynnia held up her manacled hands and I shook my head at her. "There's enough energy in the air. I'm sure you'll figure something out."

"Mira!" Danaus shouted, finally drawing my gaze back to Stefan and him. "Where is this gateway that you've been talking about? Where's the opening?"

"Over there," Cynnia said, pointing behind them. Spinning on my heel, I followed Cynnia and Shelly to a depression in the ground a few yards away to the west. "This is it," the naturi confirmed.

Both Danaus and Stefan looked at me, doubting the veracity of anything told to them by one of the enemy. I nodded. It was the exact spot I would have picked out. The energy was the thickest there. The earth was covered in thick green grass, as if it grew from the richest earth and was watered every day. The rest of the surrounding area was dirt with patches of grass and weeds intermixed with large stones. The gateway was here.

Drawing in a deep breath, I focused my powers and attempted to create a ball of fire that would hover over the depression. Instead I got twenty balls of angry, crackling fire scattered about the plateau.

"Whoa," I murmured. I had meant to say something close to "Holy shit" in old Greek, but my mouth wasn't working. I stared at the flickering fires the size of basketballs. Not quite my usually cute, baseball-sized beacons of light. Of course, I was tapped into two different power sources, and both were looking for an outlet. The power from the earth had immediately surged into my frame, but it was unable to tear me apart because I was still pulling heavily from the soul energy in the region. I just had to hope that the naturi didn't decide to wipe out the nearby village before they came to take care of us.

Danaus threw me a dark gaze, but wisely kept his sarcastic comments to himself. He had been around me enough the past several days to know I hadn't intended for that to happen. I walked over with him and Stefan but stopped several feet away, not wishing to draw any closer. The gateway was nothing more than an oblong circle about three feet in diameter that was slightly sunken into the ground, marked by the lush green grass that stood out against the surrounding rock and dirt.

"How do we close the gateway?" Stefan inquired.

"You don't," Cynnia said, taking a half step backward. I followed her lead. Standing so close to the flow sent a feeling creeping over my skin, like thousands of ants marching beneath my clothes.

She held her hands out toward the gateway, as if warming her hands by a fire. I had no doubt that she could feel the energy pouring out, enticing her, but so far she was behaving herself. "You can only block it so the naturi can't use it," she explained.

"Take some of the large stones off the ruins and pile them over the opening. Make a pyramid or something. I don't care," I shouted. I grabbed Cynnia by the shoulder and pulled her away from the opening. I didn't need to worry about her and an abundant source of power, even if the iron manacles were supposed to dampen her ability to use magic. I truly doubted that the iron completely blocked the ability, particularly with this much energy floating around in the air.

"And the naturi won't tear it down?" Danaus demanded, the sarcasm finally slipping out.

"I'm sure they will, but I'm hoping it won't be before the new moon," I growled at the hunter. "You'll just have to get some of the Themis boys down here to protect it during the day."

Danaus opened his mouth to argue, but I was saved from having to listen when a naturi dart shot through the air. He jerked his head back just in time to avoid the poison-tipped mini-arrow.

Three naturi with wrist crossbows crested the plateau first, shooting their bolts in hopes of paralyzing their victims before finally delivering the killing blow. I dodged two arrows aimed for my heart and unloaded the Browning into the three before they had a chance to launch the next phase of their attack.

The naturi were a mess, but still breathing. My aim was pathetic—I had to learn to shoot. Dropping the empty gun on the ground with a hollow thud, I pulled the short sword from the sheath and ran to their side. In a few quick slashes their heads were rolling from their bodies and I was splashed in a fresh coating of blood.

A whimper drew my attention from the edge of the plateau. Cynnia stood behind Shelly, peering out over the witch's shoulder. Her wide green eyes shimmered in the firelight. For a moment something within me felt at peace. She was finally seeing me as the monster I truly was, as the nightmare her people had painted me for countless centuries. Washed in the blood of her people, blade in one hand and fire flickering around me, I was the Fire Starter.

"Watch out!" Shelly cried.

Ducking down as I turned, I managed to block a sword aimed to enter my back. We exchanged a series of blows that I narrowly escaped. I had finally met my match in a swordsman, but that wasn't my greatest concern. My big problem was that the sword fight gave the naturi time to gain purchase on the plateau. One attempted to slip by me and head for Danaus and Stefan. While blocking one blow, I pulled a knife from my waist and threw it at the second naturi. The knife found her back, but I got a long cut across my stomach as I failed to block my adversary's next move.

"You can't win this time, nightwalker," the naturi taunted, coming at me with another flurry of blows that I barely managed to block.

I wanted to make some witty comment, but as I tried to

take a step backward to avoid another blow, my right foot became stuck. Unable to look down, I tugged at it, to find that something had wrapped around both of my ankles. I was trapped where I stood. An earth clan naturi had arrived at the party.

"I've got it, Mira!" called Shelly from behind me.

"No! Stay with Cynnia!" I shouted back, trying to keep my focus on the bastard in front of me who was trying to cut my heart out.

"Cynnia?" he whispered.

I didn't question the distraction. With a quick stab, I plunged the short sword into his heart, catching him by surprise. He dropped to his knees before me, and I relieved him of his head.

"Mira!" Danaus shouted. I turned to find him struggling with a naturi. He had the creature by the wrists, fighting to keep the dagger from being plunged into his chest while another naturi approached from behind. We were being overwhelmed.

"I've got it!" Cynnia shouted, to my surprise. There was no warning, no chance to stop her. A bolt of lightning crashed from what had been a clear sky only a few moments earlier and instantly incinerated the naturi sneaking up behind Danaus. It surprised the naturi who was struggling with the hunter. He broke off and tried to take a few steps away, but didn't get far. A second bolt of lightning struck, burning the naturi to a crisp in an instant.

I turned to find Cynnia on her hands and knees, struggling to breathe. I ran over and knelt beside her, with Shelly on the other side.

"Is she all right?" Danaus called, heading toward us.

"I'll take care of her. You just get it covered!" I shouted, waving him off. Eight naturi, my ass! There might have only been eight naturi in the immediate area, but they'd taken the time to awaken the surrounding wild life on their way to Ollantaytambo.

Behind where I squatted, I could hear a mix of grunting and the crunch of heavy stones being dropped on one another. The pile was building, but they needed more time to finish. I also needed Cynnia back on her feet if she was going to be able to help defend our position. However, at the moment she was on her hands and knees, heaving up her guts. Shelly stood silently by, holding Cynnia's hair out of her face while rubbing one hand gently up and down her back.

"Are you hurt?" I demanded when Cynnia finally drew in a cleansing breath, wiping her mouth with the back of her dirty sleeve.

"I—I killed them," she replied in a shattered voice. "I killed my own people."

I knew that it was a sad commentary on my own existence that my first thought was to tell her to get used to it, but I wisely kept my mouth shut for a moment. Nightwalkers made a common practice of killing their own kind. So did humans. But not every race was quite so heavy into genocide as we were.

"You saved Danaus's life and I thank you," I murmured, causing her to finally look up at me. "Were you hurt casting that spell?"

"Yes," she hissed, as if suddenly noticing what had to be searing pain. We looked down to find that her wrists were burned and blistered where her manacles touched her flesh. The iron hindered their spell casting, but apparently it didn't necessarily stop it under the right conditions. A good thing to remember.

I looked up in time to see more naturi reaching the top of the plateau. Our brief rest was over and I needed to get back to the business of defending my compatriots. "Keep your head down and keep each other alive. Danaus and Stefan are almost done," I said, hoping that I was telling the truth.

I wobbled as I pushed back to my feet. Exhaustion chewed at my limbs and weighed on my shoulders. I was still pulling soul energy from the village and a little from Shelly in an effort to keep the earth magic from entering my body, but it was becoming a losing battle. The fireballs I was maintaining around the plateau to light the battle had grown in size. They crackled and snapped, as if they had developed souls of their own and were angry.

Danaus? Are you almost done? I asked, mentally reaching out to the one companion that I had grown to depend on in more ways than I cared to count.

Soon.

I may need your help.

It was time to let the earth magic in. I was tired of fighting it, and at the moment, it was more powerful and more plentiful than the soul magic I was desperately clinging to. Waving my hand, the large balls of fire hit the ground and rolled to the main path up to the ruins. As they traveled down the path, glomming onto whatever creature they passed, I found myself humming "The Sorcerer's Apprentice," as if the balls of fire had become my broomsticks to command. My head fell back and I stared up at the canopy of stars reappearing now that Cynnia had stopped casting her weather spells. Laughter welled up in my chest as I listened to the naturi scream. It almost made up for the night of torture I faced at their hands centuries ago. It almost made up for the fact that

I knew I would be destroyed tomorrow night by either the naturi or Jabari. Almost, but not quite.

I turned to find that the mountain of stones the two men built had a base more than ten feet wide and was more than eight feet high. Only Stefan could now pile rocks on the top, since he could take to the air.

"Are there any naturi in the area?" I called, a waver threading its way through my voice as I fought to contain the energy writhing within my body, searching for an outlet. I had thought to extinguish all but two of the fire balls that Danaus and Stefan were working by, but the flickering flames were the only way I could keep the power from the earth appeased. Otherwise, it would eventually tear me to shreds.

Danaus shook his head as he wiped his brow with the back of his hand, breathing heavily from the exertion. I was willing to take a wild guess that he had tried to keep up with Stefan. Yes, Danaus was fast and half bori, but Stefan was a nightwalker that was nearly an Ancient.

Do you need me? he asked, taking a step toward me even before I answered, but I shook my head, waving him off. I had to find another way to control the power or it would destroy me. I couldn't rely on Danaus or Jabari always being around to save my ass when I found myself in a situation I couldn't control.

As I stepped toward Cynnia and Shelly, I leaned forward, my arms wrapped around my middle. The grass under my feet curled and turned black. I was a walking flame, and I needed the naturi's help to find a way to extinguish myself.

"Help me," I gasped, kneeling on the ground before them. "I can't stop it. The power. It's inside of me. Running through my brain."

"Let it go, Mira," Shelly said, placing a hand on my shoulder, but quickly pulled it away and stumbled back a step. I knew she must have felt the charge of energy burning away inside of me, searching for an outlet. She shook her hand and stared at me in wonder.

The power continued to grow inside me, and the trees surrounding the plateau burst into flames like dry tinder too close to a crackling fire. A circle of fire sprang up around us, reaching more than six feet into the air.

"Mira!" Danaus called, sounding worried. I could barely feel him on the periphery of my mind, waiting until he had no choice but to intervene. In the past he had pushed his own powers into me, which in turn pushed out the powers of the earth. But considering the energy and pain burning through me then, I wasn't sure that he would be strong enough to help me take control again.

"You have to release the energy, Mira," Cynnia calmly said. "You have to send it back out of your body and into the earth."

"Don't you think I've been trying to do that?" I shouted, my voice broken and fractured under the weight of the growing pain. "I push against the energy with everything that I've got and my only outlet is to create fire, but it's not enough. I would have to set the world ablaze for it to finally be enough."

"Why is the energy getting stuck?" Shelly asked. I looked up to find her staring down at Cynnia, who was frowning at me.

"Because she's a nightwalker," the naturi softly murmured. The pounding of the energy and the crackle of the fire made it nearly impossible for me to hear her. But then it wasn't her words that unnerved me so much, it was her tone. "She doesn't have an outlet for the earth magic to flow through. The fire magic, that little bit of who she is, seems to be drawing it in, and it has nowhere else to go but to leave her through fire. She needs an outlet for the earth."

"How?"

Instead of answering, Cynnia knelt before me and reached over to one of the knives in its sheath on my waist. She slowly unsnapped the safety strap and placed a restraining hand on my shoulder as she pulled the knife out of its sheath. She met my gaze, her wide eyes swimming with fear. "Please don't let them kill me," she whispered, then plunged the dagger into my heart.

Just as quickly, she jerked the knife out again and let it and me fall to the ground. I hit with a heavy thud as new pain radiated through my entire body. The fire around us was extinguished with a sudden whoosh, and both Stefan and Danaus were on Cynnia in a flash, while Shelly stood in the background gasping for air. I lay on the ground, feeling the blood flow out of me and into the grass beneath my chest, and with it, the power of the earth finally flowing out of me.

I turned my head enough so there was no long grass sticking into my mouth. "Don't hurt Cynnia," I murmured, speaking as loud as I could. Luckily, I was dealing with creatures with superb hearing.

"She tried to kill you!" Stefan argued, sounding like he was standing somewhere above me.

"She saved me," I said, wincing as Danaus helped turn me over on my back. A puncture wound to the heart couldn't kill a nightwalker, but it could definitely slow us down. Nothing short of decapitation or the total removal of the heart would kill a nightwalker. As well as immolation, but that fate wasn't for me.

Laying in Danaus's lap, I closed my eyes and focused on the different energies I could now feel in, around, and through me. There was the soul, or so-called blood energy, that made up my existence. It was cool and calming, filling me as it mended the wound in my heart. Danaus's powers also flowed about me, cautious and worried, but not seeking entrance into my weakened frame. He hovered on the outside, waiting for an invitation, or at the very least, a sign that I wasn't healing as he expected.

And I could now feel the earth's power, warm and light, flowing up from beneath me. The energy pulsed around me and through me as if it had its own heartbeat. The power seemed to flow out of me just as quickly as it flowed in, as if recognizing that it had wandered into a dead creature.

"Mira?" Stefan demanded in his cold voice, drawing me back to the present and the dilemma at hand.

I opened my eyes to find him holding Cynnia by her hair, a knife blade pressed so close to her throat that a thread of blood was streaming down her neck. I paused for a moment to wonder if we still needed her alive. She had fixed my problem with the earth magic, and I had a feeling that Shelly could now teach me to use that earth magic. I also suspected that keeping Cynnia alive wouldn't provide me with enough leverage over Rowe to stop him from performing the sacrifice. For that, I had to rely on Nyx.

"I wasn't trying to kill you!" Cynnia cried when I had yet to move. "You needed a tie to the earth. Nightwalkers lose their tie when they are reborn. Your allegiance is based solely on soul magic and the bori."

Beneath me, I felt Danaus flinch inwardly at the mention of the bori, but he didn't move or say a word. The hunter and I still had a few things to discuss about our respective origins, but now was not the time.

"So, blood straight from my heart poured into the earth opened my connection to the earth again," I said, letting my eyes fall shut as I tried to gather my strength. The wound had not been too deep and for the most part had already healed. Unfortunately, the earlier fight, the tug-of-war between the two energies, and the blood loss, had left me exhausted and in need of a fresh meal. "It was a lucky guess," I murmured, one half of my mouth quirking in a smile.

"It was not a guess!" she gasped.

"Stefan, you can release her. She didn't kill me," I said in a weary voice. I opened my eyes to find Cynnia rubbing her neck, her right hand covered in my blood.

"It wasn't entirely a guess," she admitted with a sour look. "I knew you needed a way to give your blood back to the earth. We needed to open the gateway. I was just hoping it wouldn't kill you in the process."

I choked on a laugh, allowing my eyes to fall shut. With a sigh, I scanned the area around me out of habit, keeping a so-called eye on everyone during my weakened state. I realized something odd then. I felt Cynnia move, sensed her stepping away from me and approaching Shelly, putting a comfortable distance between herself and Stefan.

I wanted to scream for joy and laugh like a madwoman. Instead I had to settle for squeezing Danaus's hand and biting my lower lip as I pulled myself into an upright position with my eyes still closed.

What? he demanded in my head.

I don't know what you're talking about, I denied, but the words came across as far too giddy.

You're too damn happy about something.

Possibly that I'm still alive.

No. Tell me, or I'll find it on my own, Mira, he said, threatening to go rummaging around in my thoughts. I wasn't sure if he actually had the ability to do such a thing, but in my weakened state I wasn't willing to put it to the test.

I can sense Cynnia over by Shelly, I admitted, pointedly rubbing my closed eyes.

Danaus remained silent for a couple seconds, then his hand tightened on mine in surprise. *You can sense her? Without my help? Can you sense any others?*

I don't know. I'm too tired and this may be a temporary thing related to these specific circumstances. Then I opened my eyes and turned my head to look at the hunter, a grin growing on my pale, blood-streaked face. *But wouldn't it be wonderful if I could?*

Twenty-Two

Bertha was covered in blood when she arrived at Ollantaytambo a few minutes later. The nightwalker looked pale in the faint starlight, while her eyes glowed a deep blue. Her pretty blond hair was stained with blood and her clothes had a variety of new rips and tears.

"We're being attacked by the naturi. They're trying to take the lodge from us!" she shouted before her feet touched the ground in front of Stefan. A second nightwalker landed directly behind her, looking the worse for wear. It was easy to surmise that the battle for the lodge was not going well.

With Danaus's help, I pushed to my feet and walked over to where the three nightwalkers stood. "What's happening?" I demanded, releasing my hold on his arm so that I was forced to stand on my own. I was weak, but I needed to muster what strength I had left for the fight we still had ahead of us.

"They started attacking shortly after we arrived at the lodge," Bertha explained, her eyes briefly flitting to the bloodstain on the front of my shirt before meeting my gaze again. "They've tried to set the place on fire twice and we've managed to stop it, but they're wearing us down."

"We have to abandon the lodge," interjected the second nightwalker. "Sunrise is only a couple hours away and we have no way to secure it during the daylight hours. We'll be slaughtered while we sleep."

I glanced over at Danaus for a moment, knowing that he would be willing to defend me while I slept. He had protected me during the daylight hours in the past, but the illustrious hunter was no match for the horde of naturi waiting for us. That explained why only eight naturi had been sent to see what we were doing at Ollantaytambo. Their main concern was destroying the contingent sent to the lodge.

"We can't pull back," I said with a wave of my hand. "If we try to maintain any other location outside the Sacred Valley, we'll never reach the top of Machu Picchu in time to stop the sacrifice. That's their plan. To destroy us or delay us."

"Can't we use that one somehow?" Stefan asked with a jerk of his head toward Cynnia. The young naturi took a step backward, hiding both of her bloodstained hands behind her back.

"She's naturi?" Bertha asked. Her upper lip curled with the question, revealing a flash of her white fangs.

"She belongs to me," I said, coming to standing between Bertha and Cynnia. "A bargaining chip I'm hoping to use at a later date."

Bertha instantly backed off, taking a step back and holding up her hands, indicating that she had no disagreement with me. "You may be running out of time. Could it be time to use your bargaining chip?"

"I think she may come in handy," I said, nodding, then looked over my shoulder at Stefan. "I need something from you to make this work."

A cruel smile twisted his lips and he bowed his head. "What do you wish from me, great Elder?"

I matched his smile and bowed my head back to him. I had not meant to invoke my status as a member of the Coven, but if that's how Stefan was going to be, I would play the part.

"I need you to pull a Stain on the lodge as a last resort."

Stefan lurched a step backward, his hands balled into fists at his sides. Bertha also gasped, but I wasn't surprised to see that the other nightwalker didn't react. He was too young to know what a Stain was—I hadn't heard of one being pulled in several centuries.

"Mira, I—"

"I know you know how to do it, Stefan. I studied under Jabari and followed the Coven for centuries. I can name every nightwalker that can perform a Stain. I would do it myself, but I know only the mechanics of it. I've never actually done it. You have, successfully."

His hard jaw was clenched, which made his face appear as if chiseled from stone. "A last resort?" he demanded at last.

"I have a couple more tricks up my sleeve," I said, flashing him a wry grin. "But we need to get going. We're running out of night, and everything must be settled before the sun rises."

"Then let us be gone," he announced, sweeping one strong arm beneath my legs as he gathered me up into his arms.

"Not without Danaus!" I shouted, but we were already airborne. I tried to twist in Stefan's grasp but he held me too tightly and the positioning was awkward.

"Don't worry," he chided, mocking my concern. "Bertha will see that the hunter arrives at the lodge safely."

"And Shelly and Cynnia?"

"All will arrive safely just seconds behind us," he said calmly as he sped through the night sky.

The air was cool. The wind whipped at our clothes and pulled at my hair as we crossed the vast black distance toward the lodge that was currently under siege.

"I'm surprised that you want the others along if you plan a Stain," Stefan said after a moment of silence. "You seem to care for them. Or at the very least, seem to want them to stay alive a little while longer."

"Precautions can be made so they aren't harmed," I said as I wrapped my arms more tightly around his neck and huddled against his larger body in an effort to avoid some of the wind. "It's a risk, but we have no choice in this matter."

"I hear some say that you have the same opinion of your place on the Coven," he said, his French accent thickening as his anger bubbled to the surface. "That you had no choice in the matter."

I snorted at him, drawing his dark silvery gaze down to my face. "I didn't want it. I still don't want it. I did what I thought I had to do at the time to protect our people. If I could hand the chair over to you right now, I would, but I can't. Jabari would never allow it."

"Word was that you and Jabari were . . . separated," he said after a lengthy pause, as if searching for the right word to describe my current loathing for the Ancient.

"We are 'separated,' yet the nightwalker has found a new use for me, as a member of the Coven. And there I will stay, on the Coven, until someone kills me or . . . " I paused, leaving the sentence floating in the air beside us.

"Or . . . ?" Stefan prompted, his hands tightening on me. I

had my answer. I needed to know how badly he wanted that seat on the Coven.

"Or kills Macaire," I finished.

"Ahhh . . . so that is the way the wind blows." Stefan chuckled, his grip loosening on me.

"Are you at all surprised?" I asked. The war between Jabari and Macaire seemed to have lasted for centuries. At least, it was in existence for as long as I had been a nightwalker. And in the end, maybe I was the cause of the rift between Macaire and Jabari. But for whatever the reason, the war would only end when one of the two nightwalkers was dead. My only goal when it came to the Coven was avoiding becoming a casualty of the war, like Tabor, the nightwalker whose seat I now possessed.

Our conversation ended as we approached the lodge in the darkness. Fires flickered around the building and in what appeared to be gardens that looked up at the great Incan city. The Sanctuary Lodge would have been an exquisite oasis in the middle of the lush landscape that surrounded it, but in a matter of a few hours, we had reduced it to a battlefield.

"Drop me here!" I commanded as we flew close to the front of the building.

Stefan instantly obeyed as two naturi on butterfly wings streaked toward him, swords drawn. He didn't need his hands full of me.

As I fell, I quickly pulled my short sword and a small knife, allowing me to slash through the first naturi I encountered while I hit the ground. I had killed two more when I felt Danaus hit the ground near me. We weren't winning this battle. The naturi were too many and too strong. The power from the earth was making them faster, harder to kill than

I remembered. We needed a new trick if we were going to finally end this.

Where's Cynnia? I demanded of Danaus as I dodged a blow aimed to slice off my head.

Shelly is taking her inside.

Go get her. I need to talk to Rowe.

Danaus said nothing, but disappeared from my side, and was surprisingly replaced by Stefan.

"Rowe!" I shouted when I finished off the last naturi to attack me. Placing my hand on Stefan's large chest, I forced him to take a step back. A second later a ring of fire sprang up around the lodge, cutting through the garden and lighting up the gravel parking area. The power came easier than I had expected. Earth and soul energy flowed through me constantly now, causing the fire to burn hotter and brighter than it ever had. The naturi trapped within the ring were quickly slaughtered by my kind, but so were the few night-walkers trapped outside the flames.

"I demand to speak to Rowe!" I shouted again. My voice rang out clear in the crisp mountain air now that the sound of battle had subsided.

"Right here," the one-eyed naturi announced as he walked to the front of the crowd of naturi standing just beyond the boundary of the flames. The fire wouldn't hold out those of the wind clan, since they could easily fly over the five-foot-high flames, but then, this was just a temporary truce so the two sides could make a few threats before getting back down to business.

"I thought I suggested that you should not bring your people to Machu Picchu," I said, inwardly cursing Danaus and his slowness.

"The door will be opened," Rowe said. "And we'll be happy to finish you off tonight if you'd rather. You don't think that a little fire will keep us away, do you?" As he spoke, two naturi with pale blond hair stepped forward and raised their hands. The flames around the lodge flickered and grew low, threatening to go out completely.

With a growl, I reached deep, pulling more of the earth's energy into my body, slowing its flow back into the earth. The flames flared again, reaching back to their previous height and then higher by another foot. I could feel the two light clan naturi fighting me, pushing against the fires, struggling to extinguish it.

My eyes drifted shut and I dug deeper than I had before. The power of the earth swelled within me, combining with my natural ability to manipulate fire. Focusing all of my attention, I dropped the flames around the lodge for only a second. At the same time, I waved both my hands at the two blond naturi. The females with their thin lithe bodies and almond-shaped eyes instantly burst into flames, causing Rowe to shout and jump away from them.

In the next second, the flames around the lodge were roaring again. I had managed to take the two naturi by surprise, as they expected me to expend all my energy on maintaining my defense, not to attack. I hoped that Rowe would be unwilling to sacrifice any more members of the light clan, because I doubted that I'd be able to get them to fall for that trick again. I was stronger now, but not strong enough to continue to take on multiple light clan naturi.

"This fire will keep you out for now," I said with a sinister grin. "Send me your light clan, and I will burn through them like a dry brush."

"You're running out of time!" Rowe countered, deciding to change tactics when he realized that a direct assault would not work now that I had a brand new skill. "The sun will rise soon."

"True," I said, nodding, and then put my hand behind me, grabbing hold of Cynnia as Danaus brought her forward. "And you're ensuring that it will be the last sunrise Aurora's sister ever sees." I jerked Cynnia forward so she was standing next to me, the firelight dancing off her sculptured features and pale skin. She was smeared with blood and her clothes were dirty and torn.

"Nia!" I heard a woman scream. Then Nyx pushed through the crowd to stand beside Rowe, her eyes wide and haunted.

"Nyx!" Cynnia cried, lurching a step forward. I roughly grabbed her by a hunk of her hair and kept her close to my side.

"I offered a trade," I said. "You walk away from the sacrifice and I set little Nia free."

"Mira!" Rowe shouted at me in frustration. The hand holding a blade trembled in his rage, but he said nothing more. I had no doubt that Nyx had been pressuring him to come up with a way to free Cynnia, and I knew his plan the second his eyes drifted toward the sky. He planned to simply wait us out and take her.

Danaus stepped up beside me, a weapon in each hand, ready to resume the attack, but he also knew there would not be another attack until after the sun rose. And then it would be he and Shelly alone against the army of naturi. The naturi would slice through every nightwalker until we were all dead, and then free their wayward princess.

We have no choice. His words danced across my brain like a warm breeze, catching me by surprise. I thought I would have to convince him of it. I thought I would have to beg and plead with the hunter to use our power to destroy the naturi that waited to kill us all.

It will kill Cynnia as well, I found myself saying before I could stop the thought. I had become accustomed to having her around. She had saved my life earlier that evening when she stabbed me in the chest. I'd begun to think that I might actually set her free and let her live the rest of her life in peaceful solitude with some of her other people.

"Take Cynnia back inside," Danaus said, looking over his shoulder.

Shelly led the trembling Cynnia away.

I don't want to do this again, Danaus admitted at last. In both his hands, he still gripped blades, ready to physically attack our enemies if I lowered the flames so much as an inch.

If we destroy them now, there will be no sacrifice. No door to close again.

Danaus dropped his knife from his left hand and grabbed my upper arm. Out of the corner of my eye I saw Stefan take an ominous step forward, moving to come between me and the hunter. A wave of my hand kept him at bay, but only just barely. He would keep his word to protect both me and Danaus, but that didn't mean he couldn't rough the hunter up a bit.

More than Danaus's words vibrated through my brain. I could feel his horror and his revulsion at the thought of what had happened back on Blackbeard Island. We had been desperate. Backed into a corner, surrounded by the naturi, he and I had agreed to make one last push with our powers. He had taken my hand in his, while pushing his powers into my body, wielding me like a weapon from Hell. At Themis, it was an accident. We didn't realize what we were capable of. Yet, on the island, trapped and frightened, we knew what we were doing when we killed them all. We felt each soul being crushed into bleak, cold nothingness. We destroyed their souls.

No. I don't want this either, I softly admitted, dropping my head so I could only see his chest.

Never again.

We can do this, I pressed. I was still confident that there was another way to use the connection between us. There had to be. There had to be a way to use this power beyond just destroying their souls. *It's about control. We have that.*

Mira . . .

I could feel him begin to waver. He knew this was our best and only shot to survive the day. *We have to do this. If we stop them tonight, there's no going to Machu Picchu tomorrow night.*

Danaus released my arm but didn't step away as he continued to stare at me. He didn't want me in his head as he weighed what I had said. He could care less if Jabari or any member of the Coven intended to kill me once I completed the task they had set before me. Sure, he might want the honor of chopping my head off, but dead was dead for him. But I liked to think he also realized that our best chance of defeating the naturi was by attacking them now, not trying to mount an offensive on Machu Picchu.

"We go slow," Danaus finally said.

"No argument there," I said, trying not to sound too relieved.

"Only the naturi in Peru," he continued.

I tried not to laugh at his tone. It was his conscience he was attempting to soothe. "You're the one in the driver's seat. I'm just the weapon," I replied, bitterness slipping between my words.

"Mira, what's going on? What are you planning?" Stefan suddenly interjected. I had forgotten the nightwalker was still standing there. But right now it didn't matter. He didn't matter. There was only Danaus and the naturi.

"We're getting rid of the naturi," I murmured, lifting my hand so it hovered between Danaus and me.

Taking a deep breath, Danaus wrapped his long fingers around mine. For a moment there was only his warmth. The strength of his hand holding me was calming, reassuring in a deeper way that I hadn't felt in a while. For those few seconds, the world and all its threats slipped away because I had someone willing to stand with me.

And then I screamed. The pain was overwhelming, burning brighter than the fire that surrounded me, brighter than the sun I was only now beginning to recall. My back arched and my limbs trembled as the muscles and bones splintered and exploded within me. I could feel Danaus's power, but the earth power was fighting back. The two were burrowed deep inside of me, fighting for dominance. There was no focusing on the wispy souls of the naturi that surrounded us. There was only white, blinding pain.

Focus! Danaus ordered, but I could barely hear him over the roar in my head.

I reached out, could see naturi bursting into flames before me but not how we had planned it. The energy was growing too intense. I wrenched my hand from Danaus and fell to my knees. Stars danced before my eyes and I struggled to stay conscious. The flames before me grew hotter, turning a frightening shade of blue. The energy that flowed within me had to go somewhere.

"What happened?" he demanded, kneeling before me. He roughly grabbed both of my shoulders and forced me to meet his intense gaze. "It felt different. I wasn't in control any longer—something inside of you was fighting me. Did Cynnia do this to you?" He whispered the last bit, but I had no doubt that Stefan had heard it.

"Our last shot failed," I murmured, then tilted my head up to look at Stefan, who was standing behind me. "We've reached our last resort."

"The Stain."

I raised my hand to him. "I'll help you."

Twenty-Three

Stefan's long cool fingers slipped around mine in a slow caress before he pulled me back to my feet. He stood holding my hand in silence for just a breath of time before releasing me. "Preparations need to be made," he said. "The perimeter needs to be walked. The—"

"It will be handled." I suddenly cut him off, fully aware of all that needed to be completed in an exceedingly short period of time. "Danaus, go find Shelly. Tell her to put Cynnia into another sleep spell. It's the only way we'll be able to protect her." The hunter seemed to hesitate and I didn't blame him. The naturi were lingering just beyond the protective wall of blue flames, the sun would soon rise, and I was attempting a strange spell with a nightwalker I wasn't particularly fond of. But in the end Danaus disappeared inside the lodge to find the earth witch and the naturi princess.

Turning to my left, I let the fingers of my right hand dance through the flames as if I were running them through falling water. At the same time, Stefan took my left hand in his hand as we strolled together around the perimeter of the flame-enclosed area. Naturi fighters paced us as we completed our walk. If someone drew too close, the fire between us would flare and snap at the adversary until they backed off again.

As we walked, we trampled the fragile orchids and thick ferns that filled the garden area. We walked everywhere that the fire touched, our individual power from blood magic filling the air as we established a perimeter we hoped the naturi would not be able to cross when the sun finally slipped back above the horizon.

"You realize what this entails, don't you?" Stefan asked as we neared our starting point.

"The spell will leave a marker on my soul," I said with nod of my head.

"A stain for all the bori to see," he said in an ominous tone.

I flashed him the smile that he was trying so hard to win from me with his dramatic tone. The spell we were attempting was technically called a Soul Sucker. It had been created centuries ago by nightwalkers to protect their daytime lair from any naturi that might happen by. Any creature that moved within the set perimeter had the energy drained from its soul until it finally died. The spell fed upon itself—the more souls it took, the stronger it became. In this case, we were counting on that, considering we had a number of naturi waiting to attack the moment the sun rose.

The spell had garnered the nickname the Stain back when there were bori still on the planet. The more that were killed by the spell, the more souls drained, the darker the stain left on your own soul, marking you to the deadly bori as a powerful nightwalker. There was also the theory that the originator of the Stain spell also got a boost of power from the souls of the dead. The creator of the spell became a storehouse for the soul energy, something the bori not only craved, but survived on.

When the bori roamed the earth, the Stain was a spell of last resort. It was cast when you were completely desperate, fearing discovery during the daylight hours. Because while you might protect yourself during the day, at night you could find yourself under the dark gaze of the bori, and that was something no nightwalker wanted. No one wanted to be faced with their creator and the leash they held.

But then, it had been a long time since it was last used. We stopped when both the bori and naturi were locked away and we could find more adequate and safer means of protecting ourselves during the daylight hours. There was also a danger to the Stain spell—it wasn't particular to the soul it attacked. It attacked anything that happened within the perimeter—naturi, animal, or human.

Now, when we closed the perimeter, Bertha stepped over, with George hanging just behind her shoulder. "They say you're performing a Soul Sucking spell," she said, her eyes slipping down to our joined hands for a second.

"It's the only way to protect us during the day. We can't leave here now. Sunrise is less than an hour away."

"What if they set fire to the place?" George demanded.

"I've got something for that too," I replied, catching sight of Shelly coming out of the front of the lodge, with Danaus following behind her. "Can I leave you to prepare?" I asked, looking up at Stefan. "I have a couple of things that need to be taken care of."

"I don't understand what you're going to do with him," Stefan said, sliding his hand out from mine. "Drain them both and pray they don't move until sunrise?"

"Not quite," I sneered, then walked toward the lodge where the others waited.

The tension in the air grew thicker with each passing moment. The sun was creeping close to the horizon, and all of the nightwalkers could feel the coming death of the night. Naturally, those that survived the initial attack of the naturi had begun to wander closer to the lodge, as it offered cover from the rays of the sun, even if it was a deathtrap in itself.

At the same time, the naturi had pulled back their ranks around Rowe, who stood several yards away from the flickering blue flames. His eyes never wavered from me as I moved about the small enclosed area. I wondered if he knew what I was planning. Had he ever seen a Soul Sucking spell? Even if he had, was he willing to throw every naturi he had at us in hopes of killing us when we were at our most vulnerable? I prayed he wasn't. The kind of power created by the spell would undoubtedly shine like a beacon to something dark and scary that lingered on the earth.

Shelly was pale and trembling in the cold night air when I finally reached her side. The nightwalkers that passed her watched the earth witch with slitted, hungry eyes. It had been a long night, a long battle already, and she represented a quick, warm meal.

"Cynnia is safely asleep in the basement," Shelly said. "I thought it best if we put her as far from their reach as possible."

I shot her a wry smile and nodded, resisting the urge to pat the witch on the shoulder. Between the fight at Ollantaytambo and now the war zone that surrounded her at the Sanctuary Lodge, I was willing to bet that she was already on overload. "Good. Don't worry. Your job is almost done. I just need you to complete a couple more tasks for me."

"And then what?" she demanded, taking a step back, so she was partially hidden behind the hulking figure of Danaus.

"And then you get to sleep. Just sleep. It's been a long night and you've earned a little sleep," I soothingly said. My voice dipped down into hypnotic tones, embedding the thought of sleep into the deepest reaches of her brain. I knew I would need to call on that suggestion later that night.

"Oh." The single word escaped her in a whisper, but I noticed that she still didn't move out from behind Danaus's form.

"I need you to do a protection spell over the entire Sanctuary Lodge. I need you to make sure that it won't burn," I said. "I'm assuming you know that spell."

"Of course." Shelly stepped closer again, her chin raised a little higher at the idea that she might not be familiar with one of the most basic of spells. It was simply a couple of magic words and a symbol written in ash over the place you didn't want to burn. It was so basic that even I knew how to perform it. All nightwalkers did. The spell wouldn't allow a structure to burn.

"Good. Go over the entire lodge, from top to bottom. Get a few nightwalkers to help you. We need this done quickly," I said, raising my voice a little so I would be heard by any nightwalker within a few feet. "Don't worry. No one will touch you." At least, they wouldn't now that I'd thrown that promise into the air with an edge of a threat.

Shelly nervously nodded to me, then turned and went back into the dim light of the lodge.

"Will it be enough?" Danaus asked as we stood together in silence for nearly a minute outside the lodge. "The spells you're working?"

"The fire spell will keep them from setting the place on fire, which I honestly think will be their last resort," I slowly said. The growing lightness was starting to wear on me, and I suddenly found myself longing for my own bed back in Savannah. "Their first desire will be to try to acquire Cynnia alive, which will mean getting past the Soul Sucking spell Stefan and I are creating."

"The Stain?" he said.

I nodded, then motioned for him to follow me into the lodge. "The Soul Sucking spell will drain the energy from any creature that enters the perimeter Stefan and I have created with the fire. When the sun rises, the fire will die, but the perimeter will remain."

"Will it be able to handle this many naturi?" he asked, following me as I led him down into the basement.

"It will. It grows in power with each one that it kills. After a while Rowe will catch on and stop sending naturi after us. I figure he'll have no choice then but to try to burn the lodge to the ground, which Shelly is now protecting us against."

I paused in front of Cynnia, who lay curled into the fetal position on the cold concrete floor. Shelly had sketched out a circle around her and made the appropriate symbols in blue chalk. A matching blue dome rose over the naturi, protecting her, keeping her from moving until we finally released her.

"I didn't think that nightwalkers were magic users," Danaus said, standing beside me.

"We typically aren't. We have enough special skills like speed, strength, and night vision to keep us ahead of our enemies. However, we've found it in our best interest to learn some more defensive magic. Most of us know how to protect ourselves from being set on fire during the day or maybe to erect a defensive barrier like the one Cynnia and Shelly taught me the other night. We don't bother to learn magic that is used for attacking."

"Why?"

"Because the magic drains from our souls. It weakens us. Defensive magic is less draining to maintain than an offensive spell. Besides, don't you think a nightwalker has enough of an edge in a fight?"

"Not against a warlock."

"That's why we don't go picking fights with witches and warlocks," I said with a smirk as I gazed up at him.

"Where do you want me?" Danaus asked, his right hand resting heavily on the handle of a knife strapped to his hip. He was ready to take on any of the naturi he believed might get through the Soul Sucking spell. What he failed to realize was that they wouldn't. It was impossible. Oh, the first few might actually get past the perimeter and onto the steps of the lodge, but I seriously doubted that any would actually make it inside. Particularly after the first five or six died, their souls sucked straight from their bodies.

I took a deep breath and slowly released it. With my right hand, I motioned to an empty space on the floor not far from where Cynnia was sleeping. "I need you to be right there," I slowly said, dreading every word as it left my lips.

"You want me to protect the naturi?" His brow furrowed. "Is Shelly going to be down here as well? Are you?"

"Yes, Shelly is going to be down here with you. Most of us are going to be crammed down here, I imagine," I said. My gaze darted away from Danaus for a moment and I licked my lips. I had to just come out and say it.

"The spell won't discriminate between naturi and human. It will attack anything that moves," I explained, looking back up at the man that didn't trust my kind, and yet I was asking him for the ultimate moment of trust. "I want Shelly to put you in a sleep spell like Cynnia."

Danaus's face twisted with horror and rage. "No! Absolutely not!" he shouted, pacing away from me. The sound of his boots hitting the concrete floor rebounded off the walls, filling the room with his anger. "There has to be another way. I will *not* be helpless during the day!"

"Welcome to my world," I said with a tinge of bitterness. "I've been helpless during the daylight hours for more than six centuries and yet I've survived. I'm asking one day of you."

"I'm not a vampire!" he snarled at me. He undid the safety strap on the knife handle he had been holding and drew the knife. I was grateful that we were alone down there, or this could have become an even uglier stand-off. "I've been a hunter my entire existence. I won't lie side by side with my enemy while the naturi come to kill us all."

It was on the tip of my tongue to tell him that he had been a hunter for too long, but then that was for another fight and another time. "We have no choice."

"That's your answer for everything!" He took a step closer to me with the knife drawn, but I didn't move. I wasn't going to do anything to give him the fight that he was currently aching for out of fear. "We're trapped. We're surrounded. The naturi have us beaten at every turn. Let's combine our powers and destroy their souls!" he shouted at me.

"Well, then you should be happy that we've got an alternative this time," I calmly stated. "This spell will only kill them. Their souls are set free to go on to their afterlife the moment the spell has been ended. From my understanding, it's not a particularly painful death either. It's just a need to sleep that can't be overcome."

"How nice! A humane death," he sarcastically snapped.

"Do you have an alternative?" I growled, finally reaching the end of my patience. "We tried to kill them our way and it didn't work. You may get your wish, and it may never work again after what Cynnia did to me. I still don't know. All I do know is that the moment the sun rises above the horizon, all the naturi waiting just beyond the fire are going to come flooding into the lodge with the simple goal of beheading every nightwalker within its confines. You are a master swordsman and a warrior whose equal I have not seen, but you cannot win against that many naturi."

"I won't be left helpless during the day."

"We'll be protected from the naturi," I said, finally taking a step closer to him.

"I'm not completely human. You know that. Maybe the spell won't affect me," he suddenly countered. It was an angle I had thought of and didn't like. There was something else that could happen because of his bori background that I wasn't too thrilled about either. Putting him to sleep was the safest solution.

"You're human enough," I sighed heavily. "It just means that it might take a few minutes longer to kill you, and the more you move, the faster the spell will work. It comes down to this, Danaus. You either let Shelly put you into a sleep spell so you can be protected here, or you try to sneak away from the lodge as it is surrounded by naturi. Your odds of survival are higher if you stay here."

"I won't be helpless!" he repeated, but some of the venom had left his tone.

I closed the distance between us and laid my hand over the hand that was still tightly clenching the knife. When I touched him, I could feel fear radiating through him, similar to the terror I had felt the first few nights I spent alone as a nightwalker. Helpless during the daylight hours, at the mercy of anything that happened to stumble across you while you slept. "We will all be protected from the naturi."

"And what about when the sun rises?" he inquired, his grip on the knife loosening somewhat under my hand.

"Then you'll awaken," I reassured him.

"Not like you will. I'll be trapped within a sleep spell. Someone will have to wake me up."

"No one will touch you!" I snarled suddenly, finally getting to the root of his problem. It wasn't just that he was afraid of being surrounded by naturi while he slept during the day, but that he feared being helpless against the nightwalker enemy when we awoke the following night. I reached up and cupped his face with both my cold hands, threading my finger through his thick black hair. "No one will touch you! I forbid it. You belong to me and me alone. I will be among the first to awaken and I will wake you. No nightwalker or naturi will touch you, I vow it."

As I spoke, a dark, feral need rose up in me. I needed to pull him down to me and drain some of the blood from his neck. I needed to feel his blood coursing through my veins, marking him as mine. I needed for all in the nightwalker world to realize that none should lay a hand on the hunter. He was mine.

Biting the inside of my cheek hard enough to taste blood, I released my hold and took a couple steps away from him. I shoved my hand through my wind-blown hair and drew in a sharp breath through my nose, pushing those feelings deep down inside of me. Danaus didn't need to know about such desires. It was a nightwalker thing—this strange need to possess and control. But he didn't belong to me; not as a friend anyway. He was simply my enemy put on hold.

"Will you let Shelly put you into a sleep spell?" I asked when I was back in control of my emotions.

"You make it sound as if I have a choice in this matter," he calmly said.

I smiled at him. "You do. You can agree to do this and we go about it calmly and quietly. Or, we fight it out until I knock your sorry ass unconscious and then Shelly completes the spell."

"But the sun is rising. There's only time for one thing."

"Please, Danaus, don't commit suicide out of fear. That's all this would amount to. You'd die because you were afraid to sleep for a few hours."

"I'm going to be helpless."

"But protected."

After a moment of tense silence as he turned the knife over in one hand, I knew he was drawing closer to his decision, though I wasn't completely sure that I would like it.

"Do it," he bit out abruptly, surprising me. I had thought he was going to force me to knock him out.

"You need me now?" Shelly asked, softly coming down the stone steps that led to the basement.

"Yes," I murmured, looking back at Danaus. "I need another sleep spell."

No one spoke as Danaus placed his knife back in the sheath on his belt and sat on the concrete ground next to Cynnia. He crossed his arms over his chest and stretched out his legs before him. His dark blue gaze never left me as I stood before him. My attention was torn between the hunter and watching Shelly as she pulled out her blue chunk of chalk and drew a circle around the hunter. It was outlined with a set of symbols I didn't understand and probably never would.

"You'll be safe," I said just before Shelly murmured the final word of the spell. Danaus's brilliant blue eyes slid shut and his head fell forward so his chin rested against his chest. His breathing was even, and I could feel a deep peace drift over him. A part of me wanted to reach over and push aside the dark locks of hair that had fallen across his face, but I couldn't break the seal. Something inside of me ached to see him like that, vulnerable to the world, vulnerable to my world.

"What do you want me to do now?" Shelly asked, drawing my attention back away from the hunter. She nervously turned the chalk over in her hand, waiting for the next spell that she was to perform. The tips of her fingers were a mix of black and pale blue from the ash and chalk she had been using around the lodge to protect us while we slept during the daylight hours.

"I'm guessing that you can't perform the same spell on yourself," I said with a frown. She shook her head and shoved the chalk into the pocket of her now worn and dirty jeans. "And there isn't enough time to teach me how to do it properly."

"What are you going to do with me?"

I sighed. I knew it was going to come to this, but we were left with little choice. I felt bad putting her in this dangerous position considering all she had done to protect us, but it was all I could think of.

"You have to sleep during the day with the others," I said. When she opened her mouth to possibly counter what I planned to say next, I held up my hand. "You have to sleep the entire day without moving or you could die. It's why you've put both Cynnia and Danaus in sleep spells. I need you to do the same, and the only way I can accomplish that is to hypnotize you."

"Why didn't you do that with Danaus?" she asked, taking a step back away from me.

"Because I seriously doubt that it would work on Danaus," I said, leaving out the part that I would not drink his blood. I might want to mark him, but his background with the bori meant that it was best if I avoided his blood altogether. Of course, it was highly unlikely that the hunter would allow me to drink from him anyway.

Shelly took a step backward again, holding up one hand to ward me off. "How do I know you're not just trying to kill me? I failed you on the island. Your people could have been killed because of me. I haven't been as useful as I should be. I'm a burden. This could just be your way of finishing me off." She edged farther away from me.

I matched her step for step, finally grabbing her outstretched hand with mine. Her fingers trembled in my grasp. "If I wanted you dead, I'd leave you alive to fuel the spell that Stefan and I are creating. I'd use your life to save us all. Instead, I'm trying to keep you alive because I'm going to need you to help me protect Cynnia for as long as possible tomorrow night. I'm not trying to kill you."

"Oh," she whispered. "Will it hurt?"

"You won't feel or remember a thing, I promise."

Before she could give me any further argument, I pulled her into my arms at the same time as I entered her mind in a single, quick thrust. She had left her thoughts a wide-open door to me in her confusion and fear, easily allowing me to take over. As my fangs sank into her slender throat, I was already sending through her body feelings of safety and serenity. I sent her images of being at home in her own bed, wrapped in a thick warm quilt. Shelly curled against me and softly sighed as her blood flowed down my throat in wonderful waves. I'd needed to feed again before I could complete the Stain with Stefan.

I drank as deep as I dared. I needed her to remain weak throughout the day, helping her to remain in the deep hypnotic state I was about to place her into. However, I didn't need her so weak that she couldn't function properly the next night.

Sleep deep, Shelly. I command you to sleep deep this day, I repeated within her brain, burrowing the thought into her mind so it was the only thing there. *You will sleep through the entire day until the sun sets on the horizon. You will remain asleep until I summon you. You will not move. You will not stir. You will not dream. You will sleep until I summon you.*

Quickly healing the wound on her neck, I gathered her up in my arms and carried her over to lay on the other side of Cynnia and Danaus. Around them, boxes of hotel supplies of different sorts rose up, obscuring them from view, protecting them in a type of cardboard fortress. It was the best I could do for now. Before the last of the night was through, I would join them in this little niche of the basement and offer up my own body as protection against the naturi.

Somewhat rejuvenated by Shelly's blood, I bounded up the stairs to find Stefan waiting on the front stairs leading from the lodge. The blue wall of flames was beginning to flicker and thin in places. The night was nearly gone, and my hold on both the blood and earth magic was failing. We needed to finish the Stain now if we were going to be able to complete it at all.

"Have your little ones been taken care of?" Stefan asked snidely.

"All of mine have been seen to. Have George and Bertha gotten everyone into the lodge?"

"Everyone has been settled."

"What about the humans?" I demanded, suddenly remembering the human guardians that were supposed to be arriving in the morning. If they came to the lodge, they'd all be killed just like the naturi.

"I've reached a few of them telepathically," Stefan blandly commented with an indifferent wave of his hand. "They've been told to remain at Aguas Calientes until after the sun sets. They are supposed to spread the word to the rest of the humans."

I was surprised that he had bothered at all, but then I was willing to guess he had a human or two within the group that he was partial to. As the old saying goes, good help is hard to find. And finding a human that you could trust to properly take care of your daylight needs took more than a few years of training.

"Then let's do this," I said, extending my hand to him.

Stefan smiled down at me as he took my hand and led me out into the open yard just in front of the lodge. "You make this sound so dire. Do you honestly fear the Stain on your soul?"

"We never expected the naturi to walk the earth in force again," I said when we stopped walking. "Do you not wonder if there are bori here as well? I have no desire to become a beacon to such a creature."

Stefan turned to face me and took my other hand in his. "Yes, I'd say you've attracted more than your share of attention already."

There was nothing to say after that. He was right. I was already a beacon to every dark and/or pathetic creature that crawled out of the night. I didn't need to draw the attention of anything else, much less the bori.

A creature that seemed more myth than reality now, the bori were the guardians of the soul. They gained their powers from anything that had a soul, and considering the number of humans that now occupied the earth, any remaining bori would be extremely powerful. While the lycanthropes had the dubious honor of being created by the naturi, according to legend, any nightwalker that wasn't in total denial was fully aware of the fact that the bori had created nightwalkers as a type of servant. We had freed ourselves from our masters centuries ago with the help of the lycanthropes, and were in no hurry to return to such servitude. The bori might be locked away, but the naturi had already proven that such a thing could be a temporary arrangement. I had no desire to have a Stain on my soul calling to them should the bori ever return. I had enough masters pulling my strings already.

With our hands clasped, I closed my eyes and opened my mind so I could easily hear Stefan's thoughts. I could feel his worry and his deep-seated frustration at being forced to protect me when he would much rather kill me for my seat on the Coven. I could also feel his confusion over Danaus, his curiosity over what he truly was and over what my fascination with the hunter.

There were no words for the spell. It didn't need them. After we both relaxed and opened our minds, the tendrils of our souls were free to wander and merge. The energy rose up between us and blanketed the area from one edge of the perimeter to the other, circling us completely. In unison, we drew in a breath of the cold night air, drawing our souls back into our bodies, creating the first step of the spell. Anything with a soul would have the energy immediately drained from its body if it stepped within the perimeter. Stefan and I then slowly released the breath, forming an invisible bubble between our two bodies. There, the energy would be stored until we released it the next night—the souls set free again to go to their respective afterlife.

I frowned as I slowly opened my eyes to meet Stefan's gaze. He was frowning as well because he felt the same thing that I did. When we started the spell, our souls had mingled together, and when we pulled our souls back into our bodies, they had not completely separated as we expected. I could still feel the cold touch of his soul within my body, and I had no doubt that he felt mine as well.

"It's like a fire burning inside of my chest," he whispered as he stared at me.

"And I now have a chunk of ice in mine," I replied.

"Interesting."

"Will it cause problems with the Stain?"

Stefan shook his head as he lead us back into the lodge, both of our hands still joined. "I would expect it to strengthen the spell. I have never done the Soul Sucking spell with another. I had not expected . . . this."

I paused at the doorway and looked back at the blue flames that ringed us. With a blink of my eyes and a smile, the fire died just as I kicked the door to the lodge shut with my foot. The spell was set. *Let them come.*

Stefan and I continued to hold hands until we reached the basement. There, our fingers slowly slid apart, releasing the invisible bubble so it was now housed in the relative safety of the underground room. I could feel its presence hanging in the air, but there was nothing else to indicate that it was there.

With my focus off the spell, I wavered on my feet and stumbled backward into the waiting arms of another nightwalker. The basement was crowded with bodies. I could feel a few on the upper floor, guessing they had preferred to find a hiding place in the closet of a darkened room or in the bathtub of a windowless bathroom. But most were in the basement with Stefan and me. If a fire started, the hope was that it would reach us last, buying us as much time as possible.

Exhaustion was starting to take its toll on me and everyone else. The nightwalkers around me settled on the floor, mindless of the dirt and the dust. They curled into balls like cats and hid behind piles of boxes. I didn't see where Stefan settled as I headed over to the corner that had been seemingly avoided by all the other nightwalkers—the corner that held Danaus, Cynnia, and Shelly. I settled on the floor directly across from Danaus. With my back against the wall and my ankles crossed, I stared at him, waiting for the sun to finally rise.

I could feel a tugging on my soul from the bubble in the center of the room. The naturi were close by, testing the perimeter burned into the ground by the fire. I doubted they would cross the line until after the sun officially rose, approaching at the safest moment for them. As my eyes drifted shut, a sleepy smile nudged the corners of my mouth. For a moment I wondered if Rowe would be among those to try to venture into the lodge to secure his lost princess. I honestly couldn't decide if I wished he would.

And then it no longer mattered. The sun cracked above the horizon and I was no more. At the last second, I felt a sharp tug on my soul as the spell was finally tripped. The naturi were coming, and there was nothing more I could do to protect myself or Danaus.

Twenty-Four

I awoke with a fresh scream lodged in my chest. Lurching upright, I dragged a deep breath into my empty lungs, preparing to set the scream free. As my mouth fell open, a pair of strong arms wrapped around me, pulling me tightly against a large chest. Blinking, I struggled for only a moment before the scent of the dried leaves wafted to my nose. I opened my eyes to find Stefan holding me. Never before had I noticed that he reminded me of fall itself.

"Are you all right?" he asked, slowly releasing me from his grasp when I finally stopped struggling and relaxed the tension from my arms.

I nodded, rubbing my forehead with the heel of my palm as he eased away from me. As I woke, I'd heard the sound of dozens of voices screaming, crying out in terror and pain. Now that I was completely awake I realized that it was the sound of the souls of the dead, trapped in the Soul Sucking bubble that was linked to my soul.

"Can you tell how many died?" I asked, sitting back against the wall. My thoughts seemed to blur and there was a strange buzzing in my head, as if something were trying to invade my thoughts but couldn't quite find the key to unlock the door.

"No, but there were a lot of them," Stefan said, shaking his head. He seemed to be suffering from the same mental distraction as I was. I looked around to find that none of the other nightwalkers in the basement had begun to move yet.

Putting my hand against the wall, I pushed slowly to my feet. "Let's pop this bubble and set their souls free so we can get back to the business of protecting the door."

"Agreed." Stefan rose as well and walked over to the nearly invisible bubble that hung in the air—a white mist that swirled and swam in an oval shape in the center of the basement; the souls of the dead.

Taking a deep breath, we both reached out a hand and ran our nails over the sensitive bubble, like a cat scratching the furniture. There was an audible pop, and a cool breeze swept through the stagnant basement as the souls of the dead finally ran free. I felt them push through and around me, carrying with them fear and anger and, for a rare few, relief.

Energy burned in my chest, filling me so that all the remaining aches, hunger pangs, and tendrils of fatigue were washed away. I looked up to find Stefan's blue eyes burning with a bright light. His head fell back as he drank in the power coming from the souls of the dead. He reveled in the power, while I felt only a tremble of fear. While the energy filled me, it felt as if a mark had been permanently tattooed onto my soul, a mark calling out to the bori to come and find me. Stefan believed there were no bori left to threaten us, but I knew better.

Out of the corner of my eye, I saw the blue dome that covered Danaus shiver, but then nothing more. Something ominous twisted in my stomach as I slowly walked over to the hunter. He had not moved an inch from where I had left him the moment the sleep spell took hold. His hair hung down around his face, and his chin rested against his chest, rising evenly with each deep breath. He was still asleep. But something was wrong.

"Is everyone awake?" I asked, glancing over my shoulder at Stefan as I continued to face the hunter.

"Yes. Why?"

"Have them go upstairs or outside. Check the area for any living naturi. See how far they got into the lodge before the Stain finally claimed them. I will wake these three."

"Why—"

"Just do it!" I shouted, including everyone in the vicinity, as well as Stefan, not caring how irrational I sounded. "Secure the area!"

There was a faint scurry of sound as the nightwalkers in the basement rushed to do my bidding. I might not have been well liked among my kind, but I was a member of the Coven and an able killer. They would follow and obey me out of fear.

I waited until I was totally alone in the basement before forcing myself to take those final few steps over to where Danaus slept against the wall. When I had chosen this path, I was afraid he wouldn't survive the day, that the sleep spell would not be enough to protect him from the Stain. Now I was afraid to awaken him, fearful of how the Stain might affect the bori part of his soul.

With the toe of my shoe, I smeared the pale blue chalk line that surrounded the hunter, popping the blue bubble that had protected him during the day. For a moment I thought everything was going to be okay. Danaus drew in a slow, deep breath, completely filling his lungs with air as he awoke from his deep slumber.

"Time to get up, sleepyhead," I forced myself to say in a lighthearted voice, still waiting anxiously to see that everything was truly all right.

But it wasn't. His second breath wasn't a breath of air at all. He had caught the scent of something and now he was sniffing for it. Suddenly, the hunter's head snapped up and his blue eyes glowed at me in the darkness. They had never glowed before. I took a couple steps back, away from him, but it was too late.

Pressing both hands against the wall, he launched himself at me. I never saw him get to his feet. In the blink of an eye he was across the room, one massive hand wrapped around my throat while the other hand was pressed to my chest as he held me pinned against the wall.

"I can smell them," he growled in a low, grating voice. He lowered his head so his nose was nearly between my breasts. "You've been killing naturi. Lots and lots of naturi."

"Danaus—" I tried to cry out, but his hand continued to squeeze my throat, making it difficult to talk.

"You've been killing humans too," he continued. He lifted his face so he was looking at me again. There was no recognition in his gaze, as if he wasn't seeing me, and I don't think he truly was. The bori inside of Danaus was attracted to the Stain that now shone so brightly on my soul. "Call them back for me before they wander off too far."

He pressed his hand harder against my chest, and I could feel an energy press through me, pulling all the souls that had escaped the bubble back in toward my body. Back toward Danaus and the bori that possessed a part of his soul.

A scream was lodged in my throat as I clawed at the hand pressed against my chest, but it wouldn't budge. The souls came slipping back into me one after another, and then into Danaus, where dark energy gathered and grew.

"Stefan!" I shouted both with my voice and my mind. I pushed and shoved against Danaus, but the hunter was suddenly stronger than me. He wouldn't budge from where he held me pinned to the wall. He was out of control and hungry for the power we had set loose.

I never heard Stefan approach, but he was suddenly there beside me. He wretched Danaus loose, throwing him to the opposite side of the tiny room, the hunter's large foot narrowly missing Shelly's head. The earth witch had yet to stir, and I was hoping she would stay that way until I got Danaus back under control, if that was at all possible.

"What's going on?" Stefan demanded, but any other comment was quickly buried under the low growl that emanated from Danaus.

"You've been killing naturi too," he said, an evil grin lifting the corners of his mouth. I had never seen that look on the hunter's handsome face, and it sent a shiver of fear down my spine. What had I set loose? "My children, you have done good work, but we need to call the souls back to me."

"Danaus, you have to fight this!"

"Fight what? What's going on?" Stefan demanded, his bright gaze darting from me to the hunter.

I didn't have time to answer, not that I knew what words to use even if I could have answered. Danaus reached out again, extending a hand toward my chest and Stefan's. The pulling sensation returned, and I could feel the souls of the dead rushing through my back and out my chest, being drawn back toward Danaus. Through our connection, I could feel the power growing within him, the darkness spreading across his own beautiful soul like a pestilence.

With a growl, I smacked his hand away and pushed him back into the opposite wall. Stefan quickly joined me when it became obvious that I wouldn't be able to hold the hunter in place. Danaus swung his fist at me, connecting with my jaw so that I was tossed to the ground like a rag doll. Stefan dodged the first blow, but a second connected with his stomach, sending the nightwalker to his knees before the hunter.

"Mira?" Stefan snarled.

"It's not his fault," I cried, slowly pushing back to my feet. My knees wobbled as the energy continued to pour through me, throwing me off balance. "It's the result of the Stain."

"The Stain shouldn't affect him!" Stefan shouted, pushing to his feet as well. We both attacked Danaus at the same time, throwing him back against the wall, pinning his arms beside his head. "It shouldn't affect him unless . . . "

I didn't look over at Stefan. I couldn't. I had no doubt that I would see horror shining in his brilliant blue eyes. He knew now that somehow Danaus was linked to the bori and that I had known before we even cast the spell.

For now, I ignored the nightwalker and turned my full attention to the hunter, struggling before me.

Danaus! Listen to me! You have to fight this! I shouted in his brain, since I no longer had a chance of reaching him with my voice.

Mira? His voice came to me from a distance, sounding confused.

Danaus, the demon has control of your body. It's destroying souls. You have to stop it.

Mira? Where are you? I can't find you.

"You can't have him back!" Danaus shouted at me. He pulled his one arm free and wrapped his large hand around my neck. His fingers squeezed impossibly tight on my throat until I was sure my neck would soon snap.

Follow the sound of my voice, I mentally said, ignoring the bori in control of him. *Reach for me. Please, Danaus, save yourself. Save us.*

There was a great roar that seemed to shake the boxes in the basement as the bori, Danaus, and I all screamed as we were ripped apart. Danaus was pressed into the wall, while both Stefan and I were thrown against the opposite wall. The hunter slumped into a sitting position, while I fell onto my hands and knees, heaving up blood into a pool between my hands as the last of the souls slipped back out of my frame and into the ether. Stefan knelt beside me, his trembling hand resting on my shoulder. The spell left more than a Stain on your soul. It served as a doorway for the bori to pull in the souls of the dead for energy.

Wiping my mouth with the back of my hand, I looked up to find Stefan hovering over me with a sword pointed at Danaus's chest. The hunter was white-faced and horrified as his mind attempted to process everything that had just happened between us.

"Put your sword away," I said in a rough, scratchy voice from where my throat had been crushed by Danaus's large hand.

"How did he do that?" Stefan demanded, his sword not wavering from where it was pointed at Danaus's chest.

"It was an accident. Some confusion from the sleep spell," I hastily lied. "Everything is fine now."

"I felt the souls too, Mira," Stefan pointed out. He roughly grabbed my elbow and hauled me to my feet again. "Our souls are locked together from the spell. Now and forever. I felt the pull of the souls too. They were called."

I pushed some hair out of my face, ignoring that some of it was now damp from the blood I had just vomited. "Part of Danaus's soul must have gotten stuck with some of the other souls locked in the spell. Something in the sleep spell must have tripped it up. Everything is fine now."

"Nothing is fine!" Stephan shouted, leaving me cringing under the weight of his anger. I didn't want him shouting anything that could be heard by the nightwalkers lingering on the upper floors. "He's a—"

"No, he's not!" I shouted back, desperate to keep the word bori from entering the air and causing a panic.

With this many nightwalkers, there was no way I would be able to protect Danaus. Besides, we still had to take on the naturi tonight. I couldn't waste my energy on this battle when another potentially waited for me.

"He's not," I repeated, lowering my voice. "One is tied to his soul. It reacted to the Stain. I had hoped it wouldn't but I was wrong. He has it back under control now. Danaus is still human for the most part."

"What have you brought into our midst?" Stefan whispered, the tip of his sword trembling as he stared at Danaus, who remained slumped on the floor. "Our greatest enemy sits before me and you want me to believe that everything is fine."

"He's not trying to control us. He's not trying to use us as pets."

"No, he just wants us dead!" Stefan snapped.

"But for tonight, he's willing to risk his life to save us from the naturi. We still need him alive."

"Let's just hope he remembers that he needs us alive to protect him as well," the nightwalker said through clenched teeth.

Stefan took a long look at my neck, which was undoubtedly red and bruised from where the hunter had grabbed me, then looked down at Danaus again. He slowly put his sword away as he released his grip on my elbow. "If I didn't know better, I'd say a bori had called those souls back. But then, we both know such a thing is impossible," he said, and then stomped back up the stone stairs, leaving me alone with a shaken Danaus.

"Just keep breathing," I said. "Everything is going to be okay." It was a lie. It was probably the biggest lie I had ever told. Stefan now knew that Danaus was part bori. If the nightwalker didn't immediately go running back to the Coven with that interesting bit of news, then he was sure to hold it over my head for the rest of my pitiful existence. Which, with the naturi lurking at Machu Picchu, wasn't going to be particularly long.

If the Coven discovered the truth of what was going on in Peru, I was so fried in the sun. Not only was the great Fire Starter toting around the younger sister of Aurora as some sort of prisoner/accomplice, but she was also protecting a bori. Or maybe just keeping him as a pet while she plotted to overthrow the Coven. Yes, I could hear those exact words leaving Stefan's lips as soon as he could steal away to get an audience with the Coven. I was toast and I deserved it. I was working with both a naturi and a bori. One race wanted to kill us all, the other simply wanted to rule us like a human keeps a cat or a dog. Neither existence was acceptable. And the Coven was going to have my head when it found out.

"Mira . . ."

"We can't talk here, Danaus, or now. The sun has set and the naturi will be preparing the sacrifice. We have to get to the top of Machu Picchu."

You knew! The two accusatory words rattled through my head, stopping me from smearing the chalk line that would end the sleep spell wrapped around Cynnia.

Knew what would happen? That you would attack me? No, I can in all honesty say that I had no idea that would happen, I mentally snapped back at him. Before he could continue, I smeared the blue chalk line with the toe of my boot, causing the little dome of energy around Cynnia to pop. The naturi stretched and yawned while I turned my attention to the witch.

A part of me tensed as I knelt down beside her and lifted her arm. I had felt her alive before Danaus attacked me, so I knew she had survived the night, but I wasn't entirely sure what kind of shape she'd be in. Beneath my fingers I found her pulse was strong and steady.

"Shelly, it's time to wake up. The sun has set. It's night. It's time for you to wake up," I repeated, resisting the urge to snap my fingers like some cheap magician. But I can't say that I wasn't more than a little relieved to find her stirring immediately. The hypnosis had worked.

Ignoring Danaus's dark look, I quickly pulled both Cynnia and Shelly to their feet. We needed to get moving again. We needed a plan.

"Shelly, take Cynnia upstairs. Raid the kitchen and see if you can find something to eat," I said, giving them a push in the direction of the stairs.

Shoving some hair out of my face, I turned to follow behind them, but Danaus stepped into my path. His large frame blocked the way through the boxes, and he kept walking toward me until I was backed against the wall.

"Not demon," he said in a low voice.

I frowned at him, finally coming to rest my shoulders against the wall. We were going to do this now. We didn't have time, but Danaus deserved an answer as to what he was, and I had been keeping things from him.

In Venice the hunter revealed to me that his mother had been a witch. While pregnant with him, she had made a deal with a demon for more power in an effort to extract revenge. For his entire existence, Danaus had thought his soul was tied to a demon. I knew better, but hadn't bothered to set him straight because I didn't think I had enough information. And because I was a coward.

"Not demon," I repeated. Biting my lower lip, I stared down at his chest, anywhere but at his fierce gaze. "As far as I know, there is no such thing as a demon. There are bori, however. Years ago they used to toy with humans to get access to their souls, their energy. They are the source of the old angels and demons mythology."

"So, I'm part—"

A scream rent the air, halting the words in his throat. We turned as one and went running across the basement. Danaus reached the staircase before I did and went charging up, with me following close on his heels. We found Cynnia standing at the top of the stairs, her shaking hands covering her face as she stared down at a naturi sprawled across the floor leading down to the basement. They had gotten close. Too close.

Grabbing Cynnia by the shoulders, I pulled her quickly through the lodge until we finally reached the kitchen toward the back. There were no dead bodies within the stainless steel retreat so I felt safe leaving her there for now, with Shelly to watch over her.

"So many dead. So many bodies," she kept repeating. Those words haunted me as I wandered through the lodge. I counted more than two dozen within the sanctuary and another dozen on the front lawn and in the garden. Rowe had forced close to forty naturi to their death in an effort to kill me and free Cynnia before he finally gave up.

Standing outside, I looked up at the peak of the lodge. It was blackened and smoldering slightly, but Shelly's protective spells had held. Amazingly, we had all survived the day, and it was now time to make plans for the night. I was beginning to believe that surviving thus far had been the easy part.

Twenty-Five

The stench of the burning flesh from the funerary pyre we had erected in front of the lodge crept through the closed windows of the bedroom. Staring up at Machu Picchu, I tried to ignore the smell as best as I could, but there was nothing I could do to push away the image of the enormous pile of bodies that kept flashing through my brain. Thirty-seven naturi bodies had been located around the confines of the perimeter of the lodge. They were scattered everywhere; in the garden and throughout the Sanctuary Lodge. In addition to the naturi, twelve humans had also been killed. Five of them were guardians that had come with the nightwalkers, but seven were tourists, from what we could tell.

The naturi had taken the time to tear open three of the humans and remove some of their organs. Another harvest. Rowe had proven on more than one occasion that he was apt at performing blood magic, some of which required the body parts of living creatures. I gritted my teeth, pushing back the swelling anger. I had a feeling that he'd killed the humans to simply prove he could, to prove that I couldn't protect them no matter how hard I tried.

When we awoke, the remaining naturi had retreated to

Machu Picchu. Tonight it was our turn to attack their stronghold and stop their plans.

Behind me, Danaus dropped his trusty black bag of weapons on the bed with an audible bounce of the springs. One of the humans Stefan contacted had been conscientious enough to grab it among the other bags we brought along. My small bag of clothing was missing, but I wasn't concerned. A few items of clothing, sunglasses, a hairbrush, and a toothbrush were all easily replaceable—assuming I survived the next several hours at Machu Picchu.

"We go forward with the original plan," Danaus announced into the all too silent room. I looked over my shoulder at the hunter to find him taking a quick inventory before deciding what he would carry. "We go to the top of Machu Picchu and stop the naturi from opening the door."

A fragile smile drifted across my lips as I turned and leaned my shoulder against the cold glass of the window so I could still watch the burgeoning night through the corner of my eye. The nights in Peru were growing shorter as they struggled to escape the bonds to winter's dark grasp and finally bloom into spring. Tonight was the spring equinox, here south of the equator in Peru—a time of new beginnings. Back in my home of Savannah, it was the first night of autumn—a time of endings and quickening decay. Either way, it was the key time for Aurora to return. Tonight, she planned to come through the door, triumphant, letting the change in seasons mark the beginning of her reign on Earth.

It seemed grimly ironic that man's savior would be the very thing that had filled his nightmares for centuries. But even that interesting twist of fate couldn't lighten my mood. There was no levity to be found tonight, and I just wanted to finally have it all done.

"And then we get back to the business of killing each other," I said, turning to fully face Danaus, trying to break the fear.

A crooked, half smile lifted his lips as he tossed me the gun holster he had originally given me months ago when we flew from London to Venice. "As God intended," he murmured.

During the next several minutes my fingers nervously slid over the various straps and buckles, checking that the shoulder holster was tightly cinched and that the sword lashed to my back wouldn't slip as I moved. I made these same adjustments over and over again. It kept me from trying to pace the narrow little room, already dominated by a double bed, a rickety dresser, and a pair of worn, high-back chairs. After the lavish opulence of our suite at the Hotel Cipriani, the little room seemed plain and coarse, with its burnt orange walls and worn carpet. However, it was more than adequate for our brief and simple needs.

Cynnia sat on the floor in the corner, her manacled wrists resting on her bent knees as she slowly rocked back and forth. The sight of her dead brethren had left her mute after her initial scream at the top of the basement stairs. Shelly sat silently on the edge of the bed. The index finger of her left hand kept tracing an infinity sign on the comforter. We were all lost to our own dark thoughts in these final hours.

An unexpected knock at the door caused me to jump. I hadn't been watching for anyone to approach. It was a good thing I wasn't holding a sword. I would have probably lost a finger. I nodded to Danaus and he rose from where he was seated on the edge of the bed to open the door.

Stefan stepped into the room as I fiddled with the Browning, his gaze carefully skipping over Danaus as he glided in. The handsome nightwalker wore a pair of jeans and black turtleneck against the cold wind, as if it could bother him.

"I see you've finally pulled your people together," he sneered. "We're ready to leave now."

I turned my eyes to Danaus, who was glaring at Stefan's back. "How many naturi?" I asked. I could vaguely sense them but had yet to hone that skill Danaus had obviously worked into a fine art.

Stefan finally turned and looked at the hunter, waiting for his reply. Danaus continued to glare at the vampire, but I could feel his powers sweeping out of the room, shoving aside Stefan's own powers as if they were an unwelcome guest. Stefan never moved, didn't even flinch. Was I truly the only nightwalker that could feel Danaus's powers? I didn't want to know exactly how deep this connection between us ran, but I knew no good would ever come of it.

"Almost fifty," he replied, his voice distant.

"Not bad," Stefan said, unmoved by the number.

"That's not counting the two dozen lycans they've summoned to the mountain," I added, dropping into one of the two high-back chairs.

"You're concerned about werewolves?" The laughter danced among his words as he arched one dark brow at me.

"In London they sent both wind and earth clan naturi," I said. "They will be prepared when we begin to climb the mountain to the ruins. Sending the lycans in is for their amusement, forcing us to kill our own allies."

"What are we facing now?" Stefan asked.

I looked over at Danaus, but he shook his head. "I can't tell which clan. It's just a band of naturi gathered on the mountain."

With my eyes locked on the faded burgundy carpet, I

frantically searched my memory. I'd spent centuries studying folklore and myth that had been handed down, looking for some kernel of truth to all the nonsense. The valuable information I had found within the journals kept by Jabari and a few of the other Ancients contained not only tales provided by the few nightwalkers that encountered the naturi and survived, but also information provided by the naturi themselves. Apparently, we had once been allies with the earth creatures.

"I don't know what we'll see," I said. "From what I've been able to gather, Aurora is a member of the light clan, while her consort Rowe is a member of the wind clan. So, I would assume most of the naturi on the mountain will be of the wind and light clans."

Turning, I looked down at Cynnia, who continued to stare off into empty space, oblivious to anyone in the room. I knelt down in front of her and grabbed her left shoulder, giving her a hard shake.

"Cynnia!" I snapped. "What's waiting for us on the mountain?" I demanded.

Her unfocused gaze finally moved to my face, her eyes slipping over my features for a moment before she finally recognized me. Her upper lip curled at me in disgust and she jerked her shoulder out from my grip. "Why should I help you? You killed them. You killed my people."

"What choice did I have?" I growled. "They were going to come during the daylight hours and slaughter every last one of us. It was the only way to protect us, to protect you. Weren't you the one telling me they thought you were a traitor and that they planned to kill you? Didn't I save your life?"

"But why did so many have to die?" she demanded, tears slipping down her face. "Couldn't you have done this some other way? Could you have at least warned them?"

"What? The blue-flame perimeter wasn't enough of a warning that I wanted them to stay out of the lodge? Yes, Cynnia, I set a deadly trap to save our lives. But Rowe is the one that sent one naturi after another into the trap. He is the one that kept sending them even when it became obvious that the trap couldn't be beaten. And when he was done, he decided to kill seven helpless tourists because he could. He killed the humans to get even with us!"

"But—"

"No!" I shouted at her. I leaned both my hands against the wall on either side of her head so she couldn't escape me. "There are no 'buts.' Yes, I am a killer of naturi. I'll kill however many naturi I have to, to protect what is mine, but what happened during the day—*that* was Rowe's choice. Blame him for sacrificing the lives of your people."

Shelly shifted nervously, drawing my attention away from the shivering naturi in front of me. "Why would he sacrifice that many?" she asked.

A smile drifted across my lips and I ran my tongue over my fangs as I looked over at Danaus and Stefan. "Because he's desperate," I said, slowly pushing to my feet again.

Stefan nodded, shoving his hands into the front pockets of his pants. "We need to get moving. They may have begun already."

"Agreed," I said, nodding. "Do you remember how to find the other entrance to the Incan Trail?"

"Yes."

"Take half of the nightwalkers and humans up the Incan Trail."

"And where will you be?" he demanded, taking a step closer to me.

"Danaus and I will take the other half up through the tourist entrance," I replied.

"My task is to protect you. That is all." Stefan stood a little straighter as he spoke, looking down his nose at me. If he thought trying to increase his physical presence would cow me, he was sorely mistaken.

"We have to attack them on two sides," I countered. "Their goal will be to delay us until they can open the door and allow reinforcements through. You will take your group up the Incan Trail to the Main Gate. From there, head east and we will meet outside of the Temple of the Condor. Human sacrifices used to be conducted there." I suppressed a shiver as memories of watching humans being slowly killed on a slab while their blood was captured in a basin swam to the forefront of my mind.

"Is that where they will open the gate?"

"I don't know," I admitted through clenched teeth. "My guess is that it will either be there, at the Sacred Plaza, or in the Main Plaza. I've scanned the area as best as I can from here. They have more than a dozen humans spread about the city, so I can't be sure."

"I will stay with you," Stefan said with a shake of his head.

I stepped away from Cynnia, closing the distance between us. Behind Stefan, just over his right shoulder, I could see Danaus taking up position, but I knew he wouldn't move until I signaled.

Standing so close to Stefan, I could easily meet his gaze, but he wasn't the type to back off either. We were both too accustomed to having our way.

"You are the oldest here," I said, "and the only one who knows both the city and the naturi. I need someone intelligent to lead the second group." He stared silently at me, carefully weighing my words. It was the truth. I could think of few others I would want trekking up the other side of the mountain. Stefan might not like me, but he had no problems ripping through the naturi. "If we attack them from two sides, it will force them to divide their people by thirds in order to take us both on and still guard the spell site. We'll be able to destroy more of them."

He smiled slightly at me. "I can see why everyone was so confident that you would take the open seat on the Coven. Giving commands comes naturally for you."

"I never wanted a seat on the Coven," I snarled. But it was too late for that. I was a Coven member, and it was time I started remembering it before it got me killed. But then again, my main concern was just trying to survive the next twenty-four hours so I could return to my own domain of Savannah.

"Good," he said, smiling wide enough to show off his fangs. That's what I thought. Stefan was simply aching to make the thousand-year mark. He had set his sights on Tabor's empty chair and had no qualms about taking the seat from me if I should fall during the fight with the naturi tonight.

I chuckled and turned my back to him, wandering back to my chair. I stood beside it, my left hand resting limply on the back. "You'll make an excellent Elder."

The smile instantly dropped from Stefan's lips as he tried to figure out whether I was mocking him.

"Mira." Danaus's deep voice drew my thoughts back to the task at hand. I looked over at the hunter and curtly nodded. No more talk. No more stalling, hoping for a last second miracle.

"Let's go." I was surprised. My voice sounded firm and strong, confident even. I was a better liar than I had thought. Maybe I would make an okay Elder too.

Twenty-Six

It was the summer of 1468 when I first saw the white-gray stones of Machu Picchu, more than sixty years before the Incans would be nearly wiped out by the Spanish conquistadors. The Incans had just finished building their city in the sky with its more than forty rows of crops stair-stepping up the mountainside and numerous thatched buildings. The enormous stones were perfectly cut and placed together like an intricate puzzle first designed by the gods and later pieced together by man. Up among the clouds, the Incans reveled in the sweeping vistas of great mountains, worshiped the sun, and paid homage to the moon.

However, that year, the Incan emperor Pachacuti anxiously watched the strange beings that had suddenly descended upon his mountain retreat. Their brown hair, golden skin, and amazing powers quickly marked them as great children of their sun god, Viracocha. Pachacuti was more than happy to serve the needs of the sun children, even if it meant human sacrifices. But these great beings had also left him in an awkward position. They held captive a daughter of the moon. While the children of the sun lounged in comfort around Machu Picchu, the moon's child was chained and blindfolded at all times.

During the day, I was kept deep in a dark, damp cave connected to the Temple of the Moon on the side of the mountain, hidden from sight and the far-reaching rays of the sun. And when I awoke each night, I was carried back to the funerary rock where I was tortured until dawn threatened once again.

Now, after five plus centuries, I found myself once again standing in the shadow of Machu Picchu, and I was terrified. The Sanctuary Lodge was the only hotel within walking distance of the Incan ruins. Most tourists were shuttled in from Aguas Calientes after making the long trek from Cuzco. So far the government had limited all development in the immediate area in an attempt to preserve the region and its history. But I was sure that would all change soon. It was becoming a hot spot for tourists, and the country was looking for ways to take advantage of the growing interest.

Stefan and I parted ways when we hit the road. I felt only a moment's hesitation when my foot touched the soil outside the lodge, but there was no power waiting to steal into my frame. Cynnia had given me back a sense of balance among the various powers in the air. The earth still tingled, vibrated, and roared with energy, but it was no longer trapped within my frame. The earth energy pulsed through my body, causing my bones to ache and a pain in the back of my head to throb, but it was nowhere near the pain I had experienced earlier at the Palace of Knossos or at the flow at Ollantaytambo.

As Stefan headed south to the ancient trail, I felt a good portion of the nightwalker horde follow him, along with their human guardians. Those that remained watched tense and silent from the shadows. They were uneasy about being near Danaus or Cynnia. Much to her chagrin, Shelly had been left behind at the lodge with the instruction to head straight back to Cuzco at first light and then on to the United States without looking back. She had done a good job in watching over Cynnia while Danaus and I were otherwise occupied, but she was in no way capable of handling the coming fight. Despite her protests, my conscience simply wouldn't allow it. And I knew Danaus wouldn't allow it either.

As I stepped through the tourist entrance, I pulled the Browning and Glock from their resting places beneath my arms, wishing I could actually clutch the sword still strapped to my back. Their cool weight felt surprisingly good in my hands. The guns might have lacked style and finesse, but they were still a deadly force. With them, I would take back control of my life one bullet at a time.

The trail up the side of the mountain was narrow, forcing us to walk in single file. I took the lead, followed directly by Cynnia and Danaus, who held a scimitar in one hand and a short sword in the other. He was also carrying a gun holstered in the small of his back, while an assortment of blades were strapped to his body. He hummed with barely controlled energy. I wanted to snap at him to bring it back under wraps, but I bit my tongue. Usually, the warmth of his energy was soothing, but tonight it was just a reminder of how my night would end, blanketed in his powers as they tried to rip me apart.

We proceeded slowly up the trail. The only sound in the cool night air was the crunch of gravel beneath our feet. I glanced up at the black sky and frowned. No moon shone above me. I never realized how lonely the night became without her there, throwing down her sweet, silvery light.

The region was pitch-black except for a faint glow of fire-light coming from the top of the mountain. There was a stir of magic tingling in the air, but not enough to indicate that the naturi had begun the spell.

Danaus suddenly grabbed my shoulder, halting me. He stood very still, his brow furrowed in concentration. Gazing behind him, I found the other nightwalkers watching him intently as well.

"Naturi?" I asked, my eyes slowly sweeping around us. We had just entered the lower agricultural sectors. There were a series of plateaus that had once been used for planting corn and other vegetables for the inhabitants of Machu Picchu. Little vegetation grew there now, just deep, thick shadows.

"No, but—"

"I know," I said. I could feel them too. They were coming.

As if on cue, the first wolf lifted its voice in song, baying at the moonless sky. The werewolf was soon joined by a chorus of his brothers and sisters, their forlorn cries filling the air. I didn't allow myself the luxury of scanning to see if Alex was among them. If she was there, I knew I'd sense it a second before I killed her.

Quickly returning my guns to their holsters, I drew my sword. The bullets weren't coated in silver. Without it, being shot would only piss them off. At the same time, the shadows lunged, converging on my little army.

"Mira?" Cynnia nervously said, staying close to my back as I continued to turn, searching for my approaching attackers.

"Can you control them? Can you stop them?" I demanded.

"I'm wind naturi," she snapped at me, grabbing ahold of my shirt as a shadow shifted close to my right. "I can't control animals."

"Not even a little?"

"Not at all."

"I'm not going to protect you up this entire mountain if you can't show a little resourcefulness!"

Low growls from both sides rumbled in the silence and then it began. A shadow jumped at me, but I sidestepped it, swinging my sword as I moved. I clipped its side, earning a sharp cry as it hit the ground hard. As it tried to regain its four paws, I slashed downward, removing its head.

I spun, slicing at a Mexican wolf with ruddy gray and red fur. Its sharp fangs and strong jaws were aimed at my throat. Dropping to my knees, I grabbed Cynnia's shirt and pulled her to the dirt as well. The wolf overshot me, landing on the other side of the trail in a spray of dust and gravel. He was quick to turn and make another run at me. I tried to dodge him again, but my foot caught on the body of the wolf I had killed moments ago, trapping me. The creature clamped down on my left arm with its teeth and nearly pulled me to the ground. Twisting, I plunged my sword through its ribs and into its lungs. With a yelp, it released me, pulling a chunk of flesh with its teeth. It tried to back off so it could heal from the wound I inflicted, but I was already there, removing its head.

The cut in my arm still throbbed, but it was healing. The flow of blood down it was stopping and would soon dry. I had nothing to worry about. I couldn't contract lycanthropy. Vampires were immune to the disease. Unfortunately, the scent of my blood on the air would attract more werewolves. I walked a little way up to the path, pulling Cynnia along as I went, trying to put a little distance between Danaus and me. The path was too narrow to allow the wolves to encircle us, but it also kept the nightwalkers trapped.

Our fighting was hindered as we struggled to not hurt our allies.

Screams and gunfire filled the air. Most of the humans had been equipped with night vision goggles and automatic weapons. The spray of bullets was slowing down the were-wolves a bit, forcing them to heal. The extra second allowed the vampires to pick the lycans off more easily, but in the end the humans were being torn to shreds. They should have never been brought. Like the lycans, they were only a distraction.

With a grunt, I eviscerated a wolf that lunged for my throat, its bowels spilling onto the ground. It howled once in pain before I took its head off. Behind me there was a brush of energy. Dropping to the ground suddenly, I rolled up the path a couple of feet, dragging a stunned Cynnia with me as best I could. Keeping her safely behind me, I stood with sword at the ready. The wolf that had launched itself at my back landed in the spot where I'd stood moments ago. It snarled and was about to lunge when Danaus drove his short sword through the creature's neck, severing its spine and piercing its throat.

"Showoff," I called, my bloody hands still tightly gripping my sword.

"They're coming," he said. With a jerk, he pulled his blade free, and the body of the wolf collapsed in a lifeless heap on the ground. By morning the mountain would be covered in naked human bodies. A part of me wished I would live to see the next day just so I could hear how our massive public relations group would spin this one.

"Let's get going!" I shouted. My group was finishing up the last couple of wolves. A dozen lycans were sent and all had died. I lost several humans as well. Several of the survivors would also grow fur at the next full moon. I was beginning to believe that this mountain carried some kind of curse with it. There was a price extracted each time someone set foot on her hallowed soil.

"Where's the other group?" Danaus asked, stepping over a dead wolf as he climbed the hill.

I started walking again, while my mind stretched out to find Stefan. His anger hit me first, causing me to stumble. His group was in the middle of a battle. Stefan felt my presence and sent back one word before pushing me from his thoughts: *Guardhouse.* I skimmed over his people. Most of the humans were dead and I felt only a light scattering of lycans, but there was still something wrong.

"Hurry!" I cried, jogging up the path while it was still clear. "Stefan's group is not far from the guardhouse. Something strange is going on. The nightwalkers keep thinking about rocks and the mountain eating them," I called over my shoulder at Danaus.

"It's the earth clan," Cynnia volunteered. She ran close to my side, staying on my left so it was easier for me to protect her. "They have the ability to move great boulders, or split the earth open and then close it again around their victim.

We had to hurry. While Stefan was encountering some interesting problems, he was farther up the mountain than I was. He was going to reach the Main Gate before I was in position to meet him. If the naturi were going to conduct the spell at the Temple of the Condor, Stefan needed more help if he wanted to survive.

I was about to ask what they were going to send at us when I felt something stir in the air. Not questioning it, I grabbed Cynnia's arm and pulled her to the ground with me. It was the same feeling I had moments before seeing the harpies at Crete. A shifting in the air, the feeling that something was about to land on your head from above. With a growl, I released Cynnia and rolled over onto my back. I reached for the Browning with my right hand and was about to raise it when I paused. They weren't harpies. It was worse.

Overhead, with a set of massive gray wings, was a creature that resembled a gorilla more than a man. Its face was large and flat, with a wide nose and fangs that protruded out from beneath its fat lower lip. In its arms it held a dainty woman with blue flowing hair. Her small, fragile hands rested against the pebbled skin of its arms and chest.

"Cynnia, what the hell is that thing?" I demanded, my aim adjusting to take in both the flying creature and its little treasure.

"In your language? An air guardian," she replied, seeming to back slowly away from me.

"Anything in particular I should know?"

"They're killers."

Keeping my back pressed to the ground, I fired at the air guardian as it swooped through the air. For something so large, it was amazingly fast, but I still managed to clip its wings. It roared in pain, wobbling in the air as it tried to lighten the strain on its wounded wing.

I tried to sit up to get a better angle on my next shot when a tree root erupted from the ground and wrapped around my chest, slamming me back down to the earth. I blinked against the stars exploding before my eyes. The root tightened around me, nearly crushing my ribs. I pushed against my earthy bindings, but these roots were controlled by magic, making them stronger. Another root near my foot sprung from the earth and grabbed my ankle, pinning me down. The earth clan naturi laughed from the cradled embrace of the air guardian as they hovered a few feet above my head. I struggled to cut through my bindings with my sword, but the progress was slow. In a moment my arms would break under the pressure and I'd be helpless.

"Come, little sister," crooned the earth clan naturi with a wave of her hand toward Cynnia. "You belong with us."

"Why? So you can kill me like the others tried to?" Cynnia snapped, crawling away from where I lay tied to the ground with a bunch of roots.

"You'd rather side with the nightwalkers?" the naturi gasped. She gritted her teeth and waved her hand toward the mountain trail. "Well then, I guess I'll leave you with no other choice but to side with us."

Down the line I heard a nightwalker scream seconds before his existence was snuffed out. From what I could tell, most of my kind were being tied down with the roots and then staked. A swell of panic filled my chest as I released my weapons. They were of no use since I couldn't lift my arms. With my palms open, I conjured up a wave of fire that covered the length of my body, biting into the roots that held me. The earth clan naturi above me squealed in frustration and tried to crush me with the roots, but they were already beginning to weaken. With my binding crumbling, I sent a fireball screaming through the air. The air guardian turned and tried to escape, but the flames engulfed him and the earth naturi in an instant. His tough hide melted, his flesh sizzling and popping in the night sky before he finally lost the ability to fly and tumbled back to the earth.

Pulling against my bindings, the roots snapped and broke. On my feet again, I lifted my hands and torched two other air guardians I could see in the air above me. Cynnia rose as well and called up a storm, bringing up a swell of air that kept the air guardians fighting to stay close to where we were located on the side of the mountain.

"With these iron cuffs, I can do no more," she confessed, holding her hands out to me.

"Betray me now and I'll destroy you," I snarled. With a grunt, I pulled apart the bindings of each iron cuff until they fell to the ground with a clatter. I prayed I wasn't about to regret this, but I needed all the firepower I could get. She could have gone with her own kind but had stayed with me.

Beside me, Cynnia drew in a deep sigh as she raised her arms freely up into the air. Black clouds swirled around us like a thickening witch's brew. I took a step backward and laid a hand on her shoulder, wary of what she was doing. In the flash of an eye two lightning bolts slammed to the earth, plunging through the two remaining air guardians before they had a chance to escape.

Along the path, the nightwalkers were breaking loose and getting back to their feet. Unfortunately, the humans had been quickly crushed and broken under the squeezing roots. I had also lost five nightwalkers. More than half of my army was gone now, and we had yet to reach the mountain ruins. I hoped Stefan was doing better.

Frowning, my narrowed eyes scanned the area laced with dancing shadows cast by the last of the burning roots. Danaus had disappeared from sight when the air guardians appeared. A chill ran up my spine. His name was on my lips when I finally spotted him sitting on the ground, his back pressed against the stone wall of the mountain. When I walked over, the harsh wheeze of his breathing could be heard over the crackling fires. Sheathing my weapons, I knelt beside the hunter. His throat was raw and bleeding.

One of the roots had wrapped around his neck and crushed his windpipe.

"Is it healing?" I asked. He tried to say yes, but the word never made it up his throat. I held up my hand, stopping him from trying again. "Just nod or shake your head." He nodded once, drawing in a sharp breath. I could feel the panic starting to swell in his chest. It wasn't enough air, not by a long shot. His body was healing, but too slowly, and soon he would suffocate.

"Anything else hurt?" I demanded. Danaus shook his head. "We'll wait," I announced, kneeling on the ground in front of him.

"What? Let's leave him!" snapped one of the other night-walkers watching our conversation. He was young and had no concept of what he would face at the Machu Picchu ruins.

"He's one of the few among us that can sense the naturi. I'm not going on without him," I said calmly.

"He's a hunter," the nightwalker sneered. His jean-clad legs were braced wide apart, as if he was about to pounce on Danaus.

"And at the moment he holds more value to me than you and your petulant whining. If you're anxious to move, take another and scout ahead." The vampire glared at me a couple of seconds before he motioned for another to accompany him up the path.

Kneeling before the hunter, I found that he was blinking rapidly, desperately trying to stay conscious against the crowding darkness. He would pass out soon if I didn't do something. I could now command the powers of both the earth and soul, but I lacked the ability to heal the human body. However, I did have a few other tricks up my sleeve. Not any that he would like, though.

I moved so I was directly in front of him with his knees on either side of my hips. He tried to shift and put some more distance between us, but I put a hand on his shoulder, holding him still.

"I can help you," I murmured, trying to keep my voice soft and reassuring. "But you have to trust me."

Danaus's frown deepened and his eyes narrowed. I think he would have told me to go to hell if he could, but instead he drew another ragged and fractured breath. He was running out of time.

Placing my left hand against the side of his face, I pressed my thumb against his temple. I captured his left wrist with my free hand and placed it against my side so he was grasping my rib cage. I held his hand there because I knew he would try to pull away when he figured out what I planned to do.

Closing my eyes, I relaxed the tension from my shoulders and mentally reached out with my mind. I let my thoughts brush slightly against Danaus's as a warning. He jerked away from me, digging his heels into the dirt as he tried to desperately push away, but I held tight to him.

"No," he rasped.

Relax, Danaus. I didn't use my voice, but sent the words drifting through his mind. If he hadn't been so weak already, I would never have been able to do this. When we had spoken telepathically in the past, it was sending a quick scattering of words across to each other. Our presence within each other's minds was at an absolute minimum, in an effort to give the other person a little privacy. At the worst, we received a flash of emotion from one another, but little else. But now was different. I was there within in his mind.

Get out of my head! He was livid, but over that was fear.

His fear of me and what I was doing was so thick it felt like I was slogging through a Florida marsh. Neither one of us had dared venture so deep, to places where we could hear thoughts and walk through old memories and deeply hidden secrets.

You have to let me help you.

Get out! I could feel the walls being thrown up around me as he tried to erect defensive barriers. He was using all of his strength to fight me, and left nothing behind to continue the healing process. I was only making matters worse.

Biting back a curse, I forced myself deeper into his mind, tearing down his walls. Before he could scramble to fight me, I slowed his thoughts, sending a thick fog across his mind.

Calm. Be at peace. Think only of healing, The words entered his brain as a whisper. He was trying to relax, but the burning in his lungs was growing.

Mira. My name came softly, weak and so fragile. He was reaching out, fearful and in pain. *Can't breathe.*

You don't need to. I'm breathing for you. As I sent the thought through his mind, I drew in a long, deep breath. His hand gripped my side tighter for a moment and then he relaxed. It was all a lie, an illusion that I was weaving for his mind. I couldn't breathe for him, but at the moment he believed I could and his panic waned, letting his body complete the healing process. The fear and panic subsided and all of his energy was redirected from trying to protect himself from me and the other nightwalkers toward healing the wound in his throat.

For a brief period of time I created an illusion of safety for him to mentally curl up in. At the same time, I opened the door to my own mind and powers, trying to push what energy I could into his body. I wasn't sure the energy would flow this way, but I had to try. I was willing to give him every ounce of energy I could spare, so his body could heal before he finally suffocated.

We stayed like that for another ten seconds. I sent soft, calming thoughts rippling through his brain with each deep breath I drew. But his thoughts were growing dimmer as the lack of oxygen was steadily stealing his consciousness. When I knew I could wait no longer, I released my mental hold on him.

Breathe, Danaus.

His first harsh breath shattered the pristine silence of the night. With both of his hands grasping my sides, he pulled me forward so he could lean his forehead against my sternum. My body had become his anchor to reality, and he was clutching me tight enough to create bruises.

I stopped breathing and absently ran my right hand over his hair, smoothing it as his own breathing slowly evened out.

Bitch.

I stumbled over that last thought as I pulled free of his mind.

"It was good for me too," I said in a husky voice before threading my fingers through his hair and pressing a kiss to the top of his head. I sat on my heels as his hands slid from my sides. He rested against the side of the mountain, tilting his head back so he could breathe more easily.

I could understand Danaus's fears, but I'd never tried to force my way into his memories, his secrets, until now, when I had controlled him, forcing him to believe in an illusion that could have killed him. His anger began to ebb, but his fear was still a tangible thing between us. In his moment of weakness I was able to enter his mind, which I would not have been able to do under normal circumstances. What's more, the direct path we had cut between our two minds was now stronger than ever. We could easily slip into each other's thoughts now, something I knew that neither of us wanted.

But for a brief moment in time it didn't matter. Tonight he would once again wield me like a sword in his hand. I might have briefly raped his mind, but I would repay that slight as his slave. We two were bound: vampire and hunter; monster and demon.

"We have to go," Danaus whispered.

"Soon. Catch your breath. Jabari would be sorely disappointed if you didn't make it to the ruins alive." The hunter drew in a deep breath, filling his lungs. He winced against the pain, but he was breathing again.

"Where's Stefan?" Danaus asked in a rough voice, pushing to his feet. I remained sitting another moment as I located the other pack of vampires. They were easy to spot, considering that they were currently fighting a group of naturi. The energy and violence in the air was building.

"They've just passed through the Main Gate. Let's move. We're almost to the top," I said, springing to my feet.

Twenty-Seven

We continued up the mountain in silence. Tension coiled in my stomach as I waited for the next roadblock, the next horde of naturi waiting to take my head off. We needed to punch through and finally crest the hike into the clouds. We needed to finally end this game.

A halt was called when we came to a final turn in the road. The two nightwalkers I had sent ahead stood with their backs pressed to the mountainside. The whiner was nearly doubled over, his arms crossed tightly over this stomach.

"What happened?" I demanded. The Browning was in my left hand, while my right hand was wrapped around the hilt of the sword. My legs were spread as I scanned the area, waiting for the next attack.

The other nightwalker held up an arrow between two fingers. "As soon as we turned the corner, they filled the sky."

"You'll heal," I muttered as I peered around the rock wall and up the hill. The firelight was brighter at the city entrance, but I still couldn't see anyone. A narrow staircase ran along the main wall surrounding the city, leading up to the rise that held the guardhouse. Stefan was still above us, but close. We had to take care of the army of naturi at the entrance before he and his band stumbled on them. "How many?"

"Fifteen," Danaus quickly answered.

"Know any good tricks?"

"No."

"But I do," Jabari said as he stepped out of empty air to stand beside me. Sadira stood in his arms, looking disoriented. Her skin was black and twisted, and her thick black hair was only now beginning to grow back. My maker and I had had a . . . disagreement while I was visiting Venice a couple months ago. The result had bathed her in flames, momentarily. In all honesty, it had been an accident, but I knew there wasn't a nightwalker in existence that would believe me.

Sadira wore long, baggy clothes, hiding her hideous appearance. Other vampires cringed and grimaced at the sight of her. Understandably, she refused to look at me, remaining huddled against the Elder.

"They have us pinned down," I said, looking back at Jabari. "Fifteen naturi with arrows. Earth clan naturi and air guardians are lurking around the mountain, giving us more than our share of problems."

"I will stop the arrows. We just need bait." Jabari smiled at me, his white teeth showing in the faint light. Any of the other nightwalkers would be fine for this task, but he wanted me.

I frowned and shook my head. "Yeah, I thought so." I turned to Danaus and handed him my Glock and Browning. He was a better shot than me anyway. "Don't miss. I'll know you hit me on purpose."

"I wouldn't dare," he replied, his rough voice dripping

with sarcasm. I must have looked nervous because he rarely stooped to jokes.

"Wait. I'm sure they'd be happy to carve 'Kick Me' into your back as well," I warned, forcing a smirk onto my lips.

"Mira?" Cynnia said, grabbing my arm as I prepared to step into the open. "I don't feel good about this."

"Do you know what they're planning?" I asked, cocking my head to the side as I waited for her answer.

She shook her head and bit her lower lip. "I don't know, but this just seems bad."

"I know it's bad, but I trust Jabari needs me alive for now," I said with a sneer as I looked up at the Elder.

Drawing my sword, I stepped around the turn and into the middle of the road. I stood waiting, but nothing happened. Tightly gripping the hilt in my right hand, I slowly trudged up, my left hand bathed in dancing flames. It wasn't possible to become a more visible target. I didn't know what Jabari's plan was, but I didn't trust the Elder to keep me completely unharmed. He needed me alive, but that left a whole gray area of what kind of condition he could put me in. To sweeten the deal, I was relying on a vampire hunter to watch my back; one who wasn't too happy with me at the moment. The only one that actually seemed concerned about my safety was the naturi. If I survived this, I was going to pay more attention to the type of company I kept.

Halfway up the path the first arrow floated through the air toward me. It arched high up in the night sky and I easily sidestepped it, dropping into a crouch. As I did, another ten arrows filled the sky, moving straight and fast for my new position. They were spread wide enough so that if I tried to dodge them, at least one or two would still hit me. I cringed, my muscles tightening as I waited for the impact, listening to Danaus fire at the naturi that had stepped into view. I mentally reached for the barrier spell that Cynnia and Shelly had tried to teach me in the woods, but my mind was a blank. I couldn't remember the trigger words, and the energy refused to come to my fingertips. As the poison-tipped arrows neared, I choked.

"No!" I heard Cynnia scream. I twisted around in time to see a white blur headed toward me. I was trapped between the arrows screaming toward me and something small and white. Raising my sword at the white blur, I flinched, prepared to take several arrows in my side and back. It was only a breath later that I felt Cynnia wrap her slender arms around me and pull me away before something else wrapped around us both. I looked up to find that a pair of perfect white wings had sprung from Cynnia's back and were now wrapped around us both in an effort to protect us from the arrows.

Amazingly, the arrows never touched us. They bounced off an invisible barrier inches in front of us and fell harmlessly the ground. I could feel more than hear Jabari's laughter. He had enjoyed my and Cynnia's momentary panic.

How sweet! A naturi protecting you. How ever did you manage that? he asked, his voice slithering into my brain.

I promised that I would not allow her sister to come through the door tonight, I replied in an equally sweet tone.

Sister?

Yes, she's Aurora's younger sister. A royal princess. A valuable commodity.

You are full of surprises, my desert flower, Jabari nearly purred.

For now, I was back in his good graces. Cynnia was truly a valuable item, and while I had my own uses for her, I would not be the one calling the shots at the mountain ruins. That would be Jabari—the puppet master. Any promises I made to the young naturi were null and void now that he was in control.

With a growl, I peeled Cynnia off of me and resumed my trek up the mountain. The naturi continued to fire arrows, but not one touched me. In return, I sent several balls of fire ahead of me. Danaus managed to pick off a few naturi, and I finished off the rest with a heady mixture of fire and steel.

Kneeling at the entrance to the city, I waited for my strength to return as Danaus and the others hurried up the mountain to join me. At the same time, Stefan appeared from the west. His group was battered and cut back to a measly eight. He was livid at being nearly defeated by the naturi, but still managed to stiffly bow his head to the Elder.

"We must keep moving," Jabari announced.

"Where are they holding the ceremony?" I asked, still not rising to my feet. I stared straight ahead at the stone walls closing in around me. I was in the city again. A tremor of panic ran screaming through me, tightening every muscle in my body.

"The humans have been gathered in the Main Plaza," Jabari replied.

"Let's finish this," Danaus said, extending his hand to me. I looked away from it, my body flinching. Warm energy radiated from his body, making my skin crawl. Finishing this also meant crushing me. In Venice, I had felt what it was like to have both the powers of Jabari and Danaus within me, fighting for control. It nearly ripped me to shreds. I couldn't imagine the pain that awaited me when the full triad put its powers through my body.

I turned my head to find Jabari holding his hand out to me as well. "I will not let them harm you again."

It was on the tip of my tongue to say that it was the harm he would cause me that was my concern. Instead I shoved to my feet unassisted and walked past them. "To hell with you both," I grumbled. With my sword in hand, I walked down the main street to the plaza. Jabari was correct. I could feel all the humans gathered together in the main plaza. We encountered only light resistance along the way, which was quickly dispatched.

At the edge of the plaza I came to a sharp halt. The night had been pushed back by dozens of flickering torches, reminding me of the scene laid out before me at the Palace of Knossos. The naturi had pulled back to the center of the large plaza to guard the sacrifice. A deep foreboding slipped into my bones and nagged at my thoughts. Five centuries ago they had needed only one sacrifice, a beautiful young woman with long black hair. She had been one of the emperor's daughters, and now played a starring role in my recurring nightmares.

Tonight, thirteen humans stood in the center of the grassy plaza, a mix of locals and tourists. They were arranged in a circle with their backs facing the interior of the circle. Each person's left hand was tied to another's right hand, keeping the circle locked in place. Their muffled sobs and pleading voices echoed off the surrounding stone walls and flew up into the cool mountain air. I felt no swell of pity for them. Their end would come quick. All that was needed was their hearts and some blood; the basic ingredients for any powerful spell.

Flexing my empty left hand nervously at my side, I tore my eyes from the human circle to Jabari. He was frowning.

Something about this little scene was bothering him as well. I had hoped it was just me.

"It's different," I said. He didn't reply, but his powers increased a notch, buffeting against my flesh. "Last time they had only one sacrifice; a woman. This time they have thirteen humans. Why?"

"They hope to summon more power this time," Stefan said, walking over to stand behind me. "We defeated them once. They hope to avoid such a humiliation again."

It almost sounded logical to me. More blood equaled more power, but why use thirteen? Why not two or five? Surely that would be more than enough. *Thirteen.* The number knocked around in my brain, teasing at some answer just beyond my reach. The number was significant. From a magic standpoint, twelve was a key number, but that was for a witch coven casting spells, not sacrifices. What's more, my earlier check revealed that not one of the humans was a magic user.

"This is wrong," I murmured, turning to look at Cynnia, who was hanging back. Her dove-white wings had been wrapped around her body, but now they were beginning to dissipate like grains of sand falling from her shoulders. "Do you know what is going on?"

"I—I don't know," she stammered, wringing her hands together. "I've never actually seen the ceremony for opening the doorway. I would never have expected that so many humans were necessary."

"You expect her to actually tell you the truth? Betray her people?" Stefan snarled at me, taking a step closer, so he was nearly standing between me and the naturi.

"She's helped us this far! She wants the same as we do— her sister caged! I'm willing to take any help I can get at this point." Turning to look over at Jabari, I motioned with my head toward the plaza spread out before us. "We've run out of time. It's time to act."

"Mira," Jabari rumbled in a low, warning tone.

I paused in the act of stepping onto the plaza as the naturi moved in front of each of the humans, short swords in hand. The screams and cries reached a fevered pitch. I raised my hands above my head, open and out, facing the night, but nothing happened. Had I truly reached this crossroad yet again? Just a few months ago I had been at Stonehenge and a woman was laid before me. The naturi were going to cut out her heart to break the seal that bound them. I killed her to stop the sacrifice. In Crete, I was prepared to do the same thing to three innocent humans, but I'd been too late. Now I stood on the edge of the plaza, the lives of thirteen innocent human beings in my trembling, bloodstained hands.

"Mira?" Danaus said, drawing my eyes back to his face. We both knew there was no saving the humans. They were dead whether by sacrifice or a stray arrow while we fought. "Do it quickly."

With a scream of frustration, I called up the energy to me, tapping only the blood energy that I had used for most of my life. I didn't want this fire to be tainted by the earth powers I had recently gained. If I was going to murder these people, it would be with my own abilities and the ragged remains of my soul.

The fire rushed into existence around the people, circling them for a moment. It happened so suddenly that their cries were instantly silenced. I could easily imagine them staring up at the yellow and orange flame in awe. I wanted to close my eyes. No matter how hot I made the flames, there was no way I could make it a quick, merciless death. They would suffer in their final minutes and would not know or understand that their deaths would save the human race.

Growling in pain and frustration, I moved my hands together, intending to close the circle of fire around them so it consumed the thirteen humans, but the flames never moved. I put more force behind it, pouring all of my energy into flames that crackled and snapped, but they never moved. However, six naturi with flowing blond hair stepped forward from the shadows. They waved their hands in unison and the flames disappeared as if I had never created them. I was outmatched.

Desperate, I was now willing to call on both the earth and the soul energy that flowed within me to finally end this standoff, but I doubted I would be able to take on six light clan naturi at once. I just wasn't that strong. And besides, we were out of time.

The moment the flames disappeared, thirteen naturi stepped into position before the humans with swords in their hands. I turned to Jabari, desperate for any kind of suggestion. We had come too late, too unprepared, and too undermanned. We had failed.

The surge of power rocketed outward from the circle, slamming into my back. I stumbled forward under its force, colliding with Jabari, who took a couple of steps backward. I looked around to find several other nightwalkers picking themselves off the ground.

Twisting back to the plaza, I found the naturi carving the hearts from the humans. They carefully piled them a few feet away, while several others chanted over them in their sweet, musical language. As the last heart was placed on the bloody pile, a white light hovered in the air near the hearts.

It looked as if someone had cut a hole in the air and was now pulling the seams apart. The door had been opened.

"Protect the triad!" Jabari shouted. He was finally ready to act. We stepped into the plaza as a group. Several naturi leapt away from the dead bodies and attacked, but the other nightwalkers maintained a wall of protection around us.

"What do we do?" I demanded, holding my sword so tight my hand began to ache.

"You do as you're told," Jabari said, standing directly behind me. Sadira moved off to my left shoulder, while Danaus stood at my right. I was about to comment that not one of them was close enough to touch me, but I soon discovered it didn't matter.

Jabari's powers hit me first, slamming against my spine like a sledgehammer. My body jerked and I heard my sword clatter against some stones on the ground. Sadira's power swept through me next, filling my body. With their energy came their emotions, swimming through my brain. I was drowning in their anger and fear. I could sense their feeling of betrayal and their uncertainty. Danaus soon joined the nightwalkers in my brain, pushing a scream from my chest. From the hunter came an overwhelming sense of peace and confidence. He believed in what we were doing. I tried to cling to the feeling of peace but was soon dragged under by Jabari's rage. He was fighting for control, sending more energy flowing through my limbs. I threw my arms out and my head fell back. My knees tried to buckle beneath me but I remained standing, crucified on the very air.

And then there was only light. I stood bathed in this beautiful, white light; brighter than fire, brighter than the sun. The door to the naturi realm.

Close the door.

The voice in my head was Jabari. Sadira was there, but I couldn't hear her. Danaus was also on the current, silent and strong. I mentally reached out to touch the door, but the second I did, it splintered. The shards jumped across space, forming thirteen separate shafts of blinding light. It all clicked at that moment. The twelve symbols carved in the trees around the world had been markers for the doors, with the thirteenth being the main one at Machu Picchu. They needed thirteen humans to open thirteen separate doors.

Close the door, Jabari ordered again.

I stretched out my focus and tried, but only succeeded in tearing another scream from my body. "I can't," I cried, my voice choked and shattered. "Too many."

Too many what? Jabari demanded, his anger and frustration sending another shockwave of power through my frame. I could no longer feel my body. There was only pain, as if my entire being were made of it instead of bone and sinew.

"Doors. Thirteen doors," I whimpered.

"Focus!" he shouted.

I cried out again as his power obliterated all thought. Now there was only light and pain. Somewhere in the light, I saw something move. I prayed it was death. I didn't care about the humans, the naturi, or my kind. I just wanted the pain to end.

"Mira," Danaus gently said.

He sounded close. I could feel his serenity, and struggled to grab hold of it. He carefully placed both of his hands on my waist, pulling me back into my body. I cried out again as the contact caused a brief spike in the power he was sending through me, but it soon evened out again.

"Can you hear me?"

"Please, stop," I pleaded. I was crying, but I couldn't feel the tears.

"Soon. We must close the doors," he said. He sounded so patient, as if he wasn't growing tired from the amazing amount of energy he was expending. He slowly slid his hands up my sides until they rested on my shoulders. His warmth was wrapping around me in a protective cocoon, and I clung to that small comfort.

"Can't. Too many."

"Can you close just one?" he asked. With amazing care, he slid his hands along my arms and threaded his fingers through mine, tightly clasping my hands. "Just close one door." His lips brushed lightly against my ear as he spoke.

Mentally pushing aside all the others, I chose one door and pulled the two seams together. A sob lodged in my throat when the door closed, and I felt Danaus give my hands a reassuring squeeze. We moved slowly from one door to the next, pulling them together like stitching together bits of fabric. We were on the last door when the power in my body sharply dropped. While my initial reaction was relief, I knew something was wrong. I could no longer sense Sadira. It was as if she had completely disappeared. The void was deeper than if she had just cut off the connection, but I couldn't hold onto the thought. It flitted away like a bit of stray paper caught up in a breeze, and my focus returned to the blinding pain that still beat through my entire body.

"Close the door," Danaus prompted me when I paused.

"I can't."

"Yes, you can. You are stronger than Sadira. You always have been. Close the door." His voice had taken on a new urgency. We were running out of time. I reached out with the last of the strength I could muster and pulled the door closed.

The white light disappeared and my vision slowly cleared. I saw Aurora standing there for the first time in more than five centuries. She looked like a sun goddess, with her long golden hair and perfectly tanned skin, regal in flowing white robes that danced about her in the wind. Staring at me, a malicious smile grew on her perfect face. She knew me; knew who I was and what I had done.

Still charged with the powers of Danaus and Jabari, I could sense the anger and fear of the naturi as they crowded around their queen. There were only a couple dozen of them, far fewer than they had hoped for. They outnumbered us. But we had closed their doors and defeated more than a score of them. I refused to believe that the entire naturi race had been able to run to freedom in the time it took me to close the doors. Most still had to be trapped on the other side. But then, I doubted that Aurora cared about those that had gotten left behind.

She was free.

Twenty-Eight

Conscious thought slowly leaked back into my sluggish brain, followed by the pain. My body hurt beyond belief, forcing a whimper between my clenched teeth. I reluctantly opened my eyes, somewhat surprised to find I was still here. I lay on the ground with a collection of rocks digging into my back. Around me, white-gray stone rose up, indicating that I was still in the Main Plaza. The sky was beginning to lighten from its endless black velvet to a murky slate gray. Dawn was coming.

Slowly, I turned my head, my eyes falling first on Sadira's lifeless body. She lay staring blindly up at the sky, an arrow protruding from her chest. Someone had gotten in a lucky shot, piercing her heart. She had died quickly.

As I turned my head back in the opposite direction, I felt an extremely sharp point dig into my cheek. My eyes continued in the same direction to find Rowe standing over me, with my sword pointing at me, the tip having prodded my skin. Not surprisingly, a wide grin was spread across Rowe's face. And why not? He thought he had won. But I wasn't ready to give up just yet. Not so long as I still had the power to move.

"Long time no see," I said in a low gravelly voice. My throat was still raw from the screaming I'd done earlier. As I spoke, hoping to keep Rowe distracted, I reached out with my powers. Danaus was close by—still alive. Jabari was also close, to my surprise. The Ancient nightwalker could have disappeared and reappeared in the relative safety of Venice and the Coven the moment the tide turned against us. He had stayed, but it didn't guarantee that he would be around for long.

"Yes, it has been too long, little princess," Rowe purred. "Sorry I couldn't make it to your little domain, but I had more pressing matters that needed my attention. But it doesn't matter any longer. I have you now."

"Let's see if you have the ability to keep me," I said, smiling back at him. Putting my empty hands on the ground on either side of me, I slowly pushed into a sitting position. My entire body screamed in protest at the movement, surrendering a whimper before I could stop it. Rowe followed my neck closely with the sword, ready to slice my head off in an instant if I moved too quickly.

"What are you going to do with her?"

It was a familiar voice, and I looked up to find Cynnia standing a few feet behind Rowe. Her beautiful white wings were once again exposed, partially stretched out from her back as if she was preparing to take flight. I think it was an anxious stance on her part. The dark horse she had bet on to win hadn't come through, and now she found herself standing with her own kind again—her fate hanging in the balance, just as mine was.

"Her Majesty wishes to see her," Rowe replied.

"And what will you do with me?" Cynnia asked.

"I imagine that Her Majesty will wish to speak with you

as well," Rowe bit out, refusing to remove his glare from me to the young nightwalker. I watched as Nyx silently walked over to us, a frown on her face.

"There's nothing for you to be worried about, Nia," Nyx calmly said, putting her hands on her sister's wings. She applied a gentle pressure, as if forcing her to relax her stance. "We all know that the nightwalker held you captive, forced you to turn on your own kind. Aurora will understand."

A dark smile crossed my lips as Cynnia finally looked down to meet my gaze. I knew we were both wondering the same thing: would Aurora buy such a story? Particularly when there remained some doubt in the air as to whether Aurora actually wanted her sister alive in the first place.

As we spoke, a large contingent of naturi walked over with their weapons drawn. There must have been something strange in their stance because Nyx moved Cynnia behind her as her right hand came to rest on the hilt of her sword. At the same time, Rowe's smile slipped into a dark frown. I was willing to bet that this wasn't the invitation they were hoping to receive from Aurora.

"The queen will see you and the nightwalkers now," said the lead naturi, pointing his short sword at the group of us.

"You and the nightwalkers," I chuckled under my breath around a grunt of pain as I pushed to my feet. "How does it feel to be included among the rabble?" I taunted Rowe.

The naturi said nothing as he tightened his grip on his sword and walked slowly over to the brightly lit area where Aurora had elected to hold court, at least for now.

The ruins of Machu Picchu now crawled with naturi, their crossbows and swords all held at the ready. They stood on walls and leaned against buildings, their eyes constantly watching the few nightwalkers still trapped within the city. I had no chance to take them all out, but then I didn't need to. I just needed to kill Aurora.

Behind me, I could hear Danaus slowly rising to his feet, a grunt of pain escaping him. We were all in extremely rough shape after expending so much energy to close the doors. I wasn't exactly sure how we were going to launch an attack against the queen of the naturi.

Danaus! I called, mentally reaching out to him as we marched across the field toward Aurora. *Do you have any energy left you can push into me?*

Some, maybe. But not enough to kill them all, he replied. Even his thoughts were coming through ragged and weary to me.

I turned my thoughts to Jabari and reached out to the Ancient. *Do you have any energy left?*

Enough to stage one last strike at Aurora, he admitted. *We will get only one shot—do you have a plan?*

Not yet, I regretfully admitted. I wished I had. Some great scheme that would not only wipe out Aurora, but all the naturi that were standing around us with their weapons ready to end our lives. I didn't want to just kill the leader of the naturi, I wanted to end this war for all time so I could go back to my domain and not have to look over my shoulder in search of a naturi waiting to kill me.

We finally reached Aurora, who was seated on a low wall at the edge of the Main Plaza. The remains of the humans who had been used for the sacrifice were now a massive, massacre bonfire lighting the ancient city. The flames danced in the winds, sending shadows swirling and stretching over the area like old ghosts woken from their centuries of rest.

The queen of the naturi glowed like a white beacon of

energy in the night. A part of me wondered how I had ever thought I could defeat something obviously so powerful, but I crushed the thought before it could fully form within my head. I had taken on the Coven, tried to destroy three of the most powerful nightwalkers in all of existence. I could take on the queen of the naturi, especially with the help of Danaus and Jabari. I could finish this. I had to.

Before me, Cynnia, Rowe, and Nyx all bent to one knee before their queen, while I simply smirked. Not surprisingly, one of the armed naturi hit me in the back of the head with the flat of his sword and then in the back, knocking me to my knees. He then kept the edge of the sword pressed to my neck, holding me down in a kneeling position. I wasn't about to willingly kneel before Aurora, not when I wouldn't even do so before the rulers of my own kind.

"Where is Rowe?" Aurora immediately demanded. Her voice was soft and yet firm, the voice of a creature long used to getting her way.

Next to me, Rowe sheathed his sword and smoothly rose to his feet. "Here my lady," he said. He opened his arms to her and took a step forward, awaiting his hero's welcome.

"No!" Aurora cried, recoiling where she sat. She held up one hand as if to hold him away if he tried to take another step toward her. "It can't be. My love is a handsome man of blond hair and clear green eyes."

"I am Rowe," he firmly said. His open hands curled into fists and fell stiffly to his sides. "I am the one who has dedicated the past five centuries to securing your freedom."

"What has happened to you? Did the nightwalkers destroy you?" she demanded. Her face was still turned to the side as if she could barely stand to look at him. Something twisted in my gut for the naturi that stood there under the horrified gaze of his wife-queen. He had dedicated his whole existence to her one wish of freedom and this was the welcome he received?

"Blood magic made me the way that I am." The words slipped out through gritted teeth. I looked up to find the muscles in his forearms tensed in his rage. "Blood magic has scarred me and darkened my hair so it is the color of the night. It has stolen my green eyes and replaced them with black. Blood magic made me the creature that stands humbly before you, because mastering blood magic was the only way to set you free."

"You've tainted yourself!" she cried, pointing one trembling finger at him. "You have turned from our ways and the embrace of the earth to learn the magic that has sustained the bori and the nightwalkers through the years. You have turned your back on our ways—"

"Never!" he shouted, taking a step toward her. At the same time, the guards on either side of Aurora took a step forward, their swords now pointed at Rowe's chest. "Earth magic would never have been able to break the seal and open the door. The original spell was woven with blood magic, and it had to be unwoven with blood magic. *I had no choice.*"

"There is always a choice, and you made a poor one by aligning yourself with those that are our enemies."

"I sacrificed all that I am for you!" he shouted, his hard voice ringing through the mountains until it reverberated in my hollow chest.

"We thank you for our freedom, but you are no longer one of us." There was a cold chill to Aurora's voice, an implacable tone that said nothing would move her from the course she had now set upon. "Because of your 'sacrifice,' I will let you live, but you are to leave here. Leave us. You are forever banished from our kind."

Banished. Banished from his kind forever. Rowe stood, unable to move, barely breathing as he listened to this sentence imposed upon him after everything he had done for her.

"Guards, get him out of my sight this instant," Aurora said with a wave of her hand as she moved to sit straight ahead on the wall again.

Rowe said nothing as several guards stepped forward and led him away. I watched him over my shoulder as he was led back across the plaza and toward the main entrance into Machu Picchu. I had a feeling they would lead him off the mountain itself.

A great bubble of laughter rose up inside of me and it was all I could do to swallow it back. Aurora had turned aside her greatest champion because of his scarred and dark appearance. She had turned him away because he had stepped too deeply in the dark side of magic for her. And in doing so, she had lost her staunchest defender. My main concern at killing Aurora had not been the horde of naturi that surrounded her, but getting past Rowe. She had completed that task for me in one quick swoop, and I was eager to see what else she would accomplish for me.

Maintaining the same cold voice, Aurora shifted her gaze to Cynnia and Nyx. Apparently, we poor nightwalkers were beneath her notice at the moment, and for now, I was content to keep it that way. The longer she took berating her own people, the more time I had to recover.

"Rowe is not the only one to disappoint me, from what I understand," she slowly drawled. "Defender of our people." Aurora pushed to her feet and took a couple steps toward where Nyx remained kneeling. "You were sent to secure our beloved sister and protect her from the nightwalkers, and yet I hear that she has spent her entire time here on earth as a prisoner of the Fire Starter."

"I tried to find her, but I could not," the dark-haired naturi said. "The Fire Starter must have found a way to keep her cloaked from me. I couldn't find her as you wished," she admitted, then reached across and took Cynnia's hand in her own, a fragile smile teasing the corners of her red lips. "But she's safe now. She is back home safe with us."

I saw Cynnia squeeze her sister's hand with both of hers as tears slid silently down her cheeks. There was relief in her expression. I knew at the end Cynnia had begun to wonder if her beloved sister Nyx was a part of the plot to kill her as well, but it appeared that Nyx was simply trying to protect her.

"You failed," Aurora snarled. "Your job as defender of our people is to protect us, especially the royal family. First, Cynnia was taken from her home and brought to earth, and then she was held prisoner by a nightwalker. Your existence is dependent upon the simple premise of protecting us and you failed at that, child who was never meant to live!"

"I did the best I could. I don't know how she managed to get to earth. I searched everywhere for Cynnia. I'd give my life for her," Nyx argued, pushing to her feet.

"And so you shall," Aurora said with a broad smile. "You failed to protect the young princess, so your punishment is death."

"Aurora!" Cynnia cried.

"You can't do this! I haven't failed you," Nyx argued, her right hand hovering near the hilt of her sword as if she was preparing to be attacked at any second. This naturi was a born fighter, and she was not about to go quietly into the night like her older sister wished.

Mira! What is going on? Danaus suddenly demanded from behind me.

Aurora is cleaning house, I replied. *I don't think she trusts those around her, and now that she plans to start a new reign of power here on earth, she wants to be surrounded by only those that she can trust.*

Turning my thoughts to Jabari, I repeated my guess at the situation, and asked, *Won't this leave her vulnerable?*

Possibly, he patiently replied. *Only if she doesn't have replacements already picked out. I've seen this done once before. A new Liege of the nightwalkers takes over and destroys the existing Coven, replacing it with members only he can trust as a way of solidifying his power. Aurora has two younger sisters who can claim the throne, and she no longer wishes to worry about the line of succession.*

To my surprise, Cynnia spoke up, in a cold, implacable voice that closely matched her sister's in authority. "You can stop the charade if this is the grand scheme you have concocted to eliminate both Nyx and myself."

Nyx twisted around to look at Cynnia, who was rising easily to her feet.

"Aurora's most trusted weaver Harrow said that she knew I wanted to go to earth and stop the war that Aurora planned to pursue," Cynnia said to Nyx. "She pretended to side with me and my wishes, so she was the one to take me through the barrier to earth. Once here, she tried to kill me, calling me a traitor to the crown." Turning her head to look at Aurora, I caught the flash of a dark smile that sent a shiver down my spine. "She admitted that it had been your plan to have me killed here and blame it on the nightwalkers. She told me everything as I slowly killed her."

Aurora said nothing as she returned to her seat on the wall, her guards closing in around her. Cynnia took a step closer to her sister. Her posture seemed straighter, her shoulders stiffer than I remembered. Looking at her now, I realized that I had been duped by the little naturi.

"Nyx couldn't find me because I didn't want to be found," she sneered. "I had no idea which naturi sided with you and would brand me as a traitor, which would try to kill me on sight. Your trustworthy consort Rowe? My own beloved sister Nyx? What wouldn't they do for you? So I hid." Cynnia turned and flashed me a wicked grin. In truth, I had to smile back at her. I saw her plan now and it was brilliant. She'd hid in the arms of her enemy, knowing that I would keep her alive as long as she proved useful. And as the sister of the queen, how could she not prove useful?

"Bravo," I murmured with a shake of my head. Cynnia acknowledged my comment with a slight nod before turning back to her queen sister.

"Silence!" Aurora shouted in a shaky voice. I wasn't sure if she was talking to me or her own sister. Her lovely face was flushed and her hands were balled into fists in her lap. "You are a traitor to the crown."

"I'm not a traitor because I want something other than the endless war with the humans and the nightwalkers that you have planned. It's not treason to want peace," Cynnia threw back at her.

"You cannot live in peace with the humans!" Aurora screamed, lurching forward to her feet. "They are destroying the earth and I am her protector. I have returned, and I will now return to the task of cleansing the earth of all human life so the Great Mother can once again flourish."

"You're wrong," Cynnia said, confidence overflowing in those two words. "The earth has picked a new mistress to protect her. Your reign is over."

"You conniving little witch! You will never succeed me as queen of the naturi!" Aurora roared.

"Yes, I will," Cynnia calmly said, then turned to look directly at me. "*After* the protector of the earth is through with you." It was only then that I realized she was talking about me—the new protector of the earth.

"Nyx, if you want to save Cynnia, I would grab her now," was the only warning that I was willing to give. Cynnia might have used me, but for now it appeared that we had a common goal. For that reason, I was willing to keep her alive, but my entire focus was on destroying Aurora.

Twenty-Nine

For the first time, Aurora met my gaze. In that moment, I saw all the hatred that she had harbored for me and my race boiled down into a single look. In the blink of an eye, I knew that she blamed me for the naturi's entrapment, their failure to escape for five long centuries, and now the loss of her sisters and her consort. I was the root cause of all her problems—the Fire Starter.

But the expression lasted for less than a second before her face was wiped clean of all emotion. It didn't matter. I had seen it, and it brought a broad grin to my face. I wanted her to hate me. I wanted her to hate me with the same mindless virulence that I hated her kind.

"She's the new protector of the earth? The Fire Starter? A nightwalker?" Aurora demanded, waving her hand toward me. "That's impossible. Nightwalkers have no tie to the earth."

"And yet she can control fire," Cynnia quickly countered.

"That is all she can control!" Aurora snapped, her temper flaring briefly before she tamed it. Watching her, I was beginning to see similarities between her and her younger brother Nerian. Both had a madness about them, a burning need for control of everything—situations and people.

"I know she can do more," Cynnia replied, growing calmer for each notch that her sister grew more irrational and desperate. "She can hear the earth speaking. How long has it been since the Great Mother spoke with you?"

What is she talking about, Mira? demanded Jabari mentally in a too sweet voice that had me cringing inwardly. A part of me didn't want to survive what was coming simply so I wouldn't have to answer the questions swirling around the Ancient's brain.

Are we three all who are left alive? I inquired, obviously avoiding his question.

No, there are several more, but we are surrounded and pinned down. We cannot hope to take them on directly.

I had known that much even before Jabari sent those few words skidding through my brain. We couldn't take them on directly. Kneeling as I was, I closed my eyes and reached down with my right hand to run my fingers through the cold grass. Beneath my hand I could feel the deep pulse of the earth beating up through the ground and into the surrounding air. The spell Rowe used to open the doors had not used all the energy in the area, as at past sacrifice locations. In fact, it felt as if the power was growing stronger the longer than I sat there. It once again pressed against my skin and demanded that I notice it, like a cat wanting affection.

Frowning, I opened my eyes again to find Aurora watching me closely. She realized now that something was off, and I smiled back at her. I wished I had more time to experiment with this new power, but there simply wouldn't be time to become an earth magic expert. Fire Starter was going to have to do.

"Can you hear her?" I asked, cocking my head to the side as if listening to a whispering voice. "She is pissed. And I mean royally pissed."

"Of course she's angry!" Aurora screamed, taking a step toward me for the first time. The guards followed beside her, while the one with the sword pressed to the back of my head shifted the edge of his weapon so it dug into the back of my neck. We were all balanced on a knife, and I was about to throw us off.

"She's no longer looking for a great protector, Aurora," I murmured, pressing my right hand flat against the earth. I closed my eyes at the same time I pressed my left hand against my chest, over the wound the Cynnia had made just the other night, essentially closing the flow through my body, forcing the energy to once again well up within me. "She's looking for an executioner. A weapon. And that is what I do best."

Get everyone out of here! was the only warning I had time to send to both Danaus and Jabari.

Rolling onto my side, out of the reach of the naturi that had been guarding me, I immediately set him on fire. The orange and yellow flamed enveloped him. He swung his sword blindly in my direction twice before falling dead. I tried to set more fires, but Aurora was there in an instant, putting them out again. Frustrated, I picked up the sword of a fallen naturi, determined to take out my opponents one by one. But we were outnumbered fifty to one.

Danaus, I need your energy! I cried out to him as I was surrounded by four naturi, each trying to decide who would attack me first.

It didn't work last time, he countered, sounding just as harried as me.

Push the earth energy out of me first. Just like at Crete.

The first naturi attacked, and I deflected the blow while dodging the second. I slashed at a third, cutting him across the stomach, succeeding in getting him to back off a step.

And then it hit me. The warm energy of the earth was flushed out of my body in a rush, followed by Danaus's own bone-crushing energy. I fell to my knees again as pain ripped through my body at an alarming rate. I screamed, letting the sword fall from my limp fingers. There wasn't time for thought or focus. I could feel the bori in Danaus, recognize it after our earlier encounter, and it was starving. His power consumed me and then flowed out across the field. I watched as the four naturi around me were instantly reduced to ash as we destroyed their souls in the blink of an eye. Twisting around, I located Danaus and Jabari several feet away from me, surrounded by naturi. A second later those naturi also went up in a puff of gray and white ash.

"Kill them! Kill them all!" Aurora screamed at the naturi that surrounded us.

"No!" Cynnia screamed at the same time. She tried to run toward me, but Nyx grabbed her arms, holding her back. "It's not supposed to be this way! You weren't supposed to destroy us all!"

I knew what she meant. She had expected me to destroy Aurora and the rest of the naturi nation that would follow her. She had not expected me to wipe out so many of her kind in order to get to her beloved sister.

And in truth, I knew that I was wasting time and Danaus's energy by killing all those naturi that surrounded us. Aurora was my goal. She always had been. Gathering up as much of the hunter's energy as I could, I turned my attention to the queen, who stood with her back to the wall, surrounded by a wall of naturi. Her beautiful face was twisted with rage as she shouted orders at her people to kill me. Yet after the display of power that Danaus and I had already shown, they now hesitated to approach us.

I let my eyes narrow and my senses reach out to the find the soul of the queen of the naturi. It wasn't hard to find. It was a great beacon of light in the center of all the darkness that filled that valley. The souls of the other naturi were just thin wisps of smoke in comparison to the light that emanated from her. With Danaus's energy balled up inside of me, I attacked the beacon of light. But nothing happened. I poured everything I had into crushing her soul, incinerating her from the inside out, but it didn't make a dent.

Behind me, I heard Danaus cry out, and at the same time his energy instantly left me. Before me, Aurora's laughter rang out across the mountain. She knew I couldn't kill her as I had killed so many of her own people. She was pure earth energy and couldn't be killed by something that was half bori and half whatever I was now.

"Kill her, Mira!" Jabari snarled from behind me. "You are the weapon of the Coven. I command you to kill her!"

"Kill me? You can't touch me, little nightwalker," Aurora mocked. "I am the queen of the naturi, protector of the earth. You cannot harm me."

Pushing to my feet, I swayed once and raised my head to look at the golden-haired woman that would be the scourge of my people. I mentally reached out for Danaus but could no longer sense him. A ripple of pain screamed through my chest and rage bubbled in my veins. The bori I had at my disposal that could have defeated her was no more. I had to turn to the other power I had at my fingertips and pray that it would be enough to destroy her. Maybe Cynnia was right, that I had been chosen by the earth to be her newest weapon—replacing Aurora. I could only hope so.

Drawing in a deep breath, I reached out to the earth energy I felt swirling around me, pushing against my skin and threading its fingers through my hair. I pulled it into my body, allowing it to fill in the places where Danaus's energy had once been. It pulled it in and mentally closed the hole that Cynnia had left in my chest, holding the energy within me so it filled my cells and poured into the marrow of my bones. The energy filled me until my soul was screaming and the monster that lurked inside of me cried out in pain. I felt as if I was killing myself with blinding sunlight.

With a sweep of my hand, the naturi that surrounded Aurora exploded in a roar of flames like a set of Roman candles. The queen screamed in frustration and surprise. I could feel her exerting her own energy to put them out, but I wouldn't allow it. I pulled more energy into my body and surrounded Aurora and myself with a wall of blue flames much as I had at the Sanctuary Lodge, setting up a perimeter. The flames reached more than ten feet into the air and separated her from the rest of her people. Around me, I could feel both Aurora and other members of the light clan fighting to put out the flames, but I was drawing the energy directly from the earth, fueling it with her anger. The flames never wavered.

"You will not touch me!" Aurora cried when I slowly closed the distance between us. She stood straight and tall, her back pressed against the nearby wall, her chin held high. "You cannot burn me."

Overhead, wind naturi had taken to the skies and were attempting to fly over the flames, but I stopped them with another wave of my hand. Their wings of feather and leather instantly went up in flames, sending them plummeting back down to the earth. No one was going to save Aurora.

Within me, I could feel the energy from the earth gathering, preparing for a final strike against the queen of the naturi. I smirked, briefly wondering if the earth wanted her dead as badly as I did. Yet, at the same time, I could feel the energy rising within Aurora. She was ready to protect herself.

A smile lifted my lips, exposing my white fangs in the flickering firelight. I closed the distance between us in a flash, plunging the dagger I had pulled from my side deep into her stomach. She had been expecting a magical attack, leaving her completely vulnerable to a physical attack. But then, I had always been more hands-on. I wanted to feel her warm flesh in my hands, her blood flowing over my hand as I slowly pulled the knife up from her stomach toward her heart.

Aurora gasped, her mouth falling open in a silent cry as her eyes grew wide with the pain ripping through her fragile body. The power that I had felt growing within her dissipated.

"Killing you is a lot like killing your brother," I sneered. "There's the same look of surprise on your faces."

Before I could reach her heart, a great stabbing pain plunged into my back, piercing my heart from behind. My focus had been so completely on Aurora that I'd let my guard down. Someone had gotten through the flames and stabbed me in the back.

"Release her and I won't cut your heart out, little princess," snarled an all too familiar voice. Rowe had come back.

I released the hilt of the blade and placed my right hand

out to my side, away from Aurora, who was now sliding down the wall. Blood soaked into her pure white robes, and her face was quickly turning a sickly shade of gray. She was losing blood too fast, but I knew how quickly a naturi could heal with proper help.

"She banished you," I rasped, as Rowe continued to hold the knife in my back, his left hand tightly gripping my left shoulder so I couldn't move. "She abandoned you after all that you did. Don't you think she deserves this?"

"She was my queen," he bit out, twisting the knife so that I cried out in pain.

"She turned her back on you. She doesn't deserve your loyalty."

"Sometimes loyalty is all you have," he said just before he ripped the knife out of my back again. He pushed me forward a few stumbling steps. I turned and fell to my knees with the intention of throwing a fireball at him, but Rowe had already taken to the air on a gush of wind. His great black wings were thrown wide like a giant raptor heading for the cover of the black clouds swirling overhead.

Kneeling on the ground, I lowered the blue flames that had surrounded Aurora and me. I was ready to die. I no longer had the strength to fight. The energy from the earth was still pumping through me, but it couldn't heal the knife wound in my back. Blood was pouring out of my body, weakening me with each second that passed. I was beginning to think that this weapon had finally reached the end of her usefulness.

To my surprise, as the flames died down, I discovered that a great horde of naturi wasn't waiting for me. In fact, only a handful remained. A scattering of bodies indicated that some had been killed in battle, but most were just missing.

A few feet away stood Jabari and Nyx. Both of their bodies were filled with tension, but neither was poised for the attack. Out of the corner of my eye, I saw a handful of naturi rush over to Aurora's side and gently lift her up. They carried her toward the entrance of Machu Picchu—the closest access to the surrounding brush and nature's bosom.

"Where?" I whispered, glancing around the now seemingly empty ruins.

"Cynnia has led many of our kind away from this place of death," Nyx answered, her eyes slowly moving from Jabari at her side to me. "Things are changing. Some are willing to accept her as the next queen."

"Aurora is not dead. At least not yet. She could still survive . . . " I said, drifting off. It was the second time in my lifetime I had failed to kill a naturi on this mountain. Five centuries ago I had left Nerian disemboweled here, assuming that he would never survive the wound. He proved me wrong. And now, I hadn't managed to cut out Aurora's heart before Rowe attacked me.

"Yes, she could still survive," Nyx said with a nod. Her voice was as soft and soothing as a forest brook running over smooth stones. "And some will follow her."

"And where does that leave us?" Jabari demanded.

To my surprise, a half smile tweaked one corner of her mouth as she looked from me to Jabari. "On hold."

"On hold?" I gasped. I coughed once and wiped some blood from my chin. My body wasn't healing. I was dying slowly on this wretched mountain.

"If Aurora survives, there will be two factions. The naturi will have bigger problems to worry about than nightwalkers and humans. You will not be our main concern, for now," Nyx said. She stepped back away from Jabari a few steps and bent forward as a pair of wings with rich black feathers grew out of her back in a matter of seconds.

"What about what Cynnia said? About me being the new protector of the earth?" I shouted before she could take to the air.

A light chuckle rose from Nyx and she shook her head. "I thought that was a nice ploy as well. Struck just enough fear in Aurora. She didn't get you caught up in that nonsense, did she?"

"It was something to consider," I admitted.

Nyx chuckled softly again. "A nightwalker protector of the earth? What a funny thought."

"Take my advice," I said, leaning forward on my left hand. "Finish off Aurora and save yourself the trouble."

Nyx again flashed me her enigmatic half smile and shook her head once. "I am the defender of our people. Not the weapon of the earth."

And then she opened her wings, catching the wind that was sweeping across the mountain, carrying her far from here. Leaving me alone with Jabari and my looming death.

Thirty

Jabari slowly turned to face me, a grim look on his handsome face. I forced a weak laugh up past my parted lips as he approached me. I couldn't imagine what he was thinking at that moment but I was about to find out. The wound in my back was beginning to slowly heal and the blood flood was ebbing. I'd survive the stabbing as long as I didn't sustain any more injuries from my beloved Jabari during the next few minutes. But I had my doubts.

"Protector of the earth," he murmured thoughtfully, scratching his chin as he looked down at me.

"Fanciful thoughts of a desperate naturi," I said, trying to easily shrug off the title. It had been something that Cynnia made up in order to strike fear into her sister. It also gave me the confidence to pull as much energy as I could from the earth to strike at Aurora and nearly win. "She needed someone to kill her sister. I was her best choice at the moment. Cynnia would have said anything to put some fear in her sister's eyes."

"Yes, but your display of power does raise some interesting questions," Jabari said. "I've never seen you control so much fire at once, and so deftly. One would think that you've

finally succeeded in mastering your skill. It's even more interesting that you managed to incinerate those naturi that
would have attacked you from above. Did you ever actually
look up at them or could you sense them on your own?"

"Jabari, this is all new to me," I quickly said. I pushed
my free right hand through my hair, trying to move it from
in front of my eyes, but pain sliced through my body at the
movement. My body was still healing. "I'm not sure what I
can do."

The Elder raised his hand above my head and I jerked to
my feet instantly, like a puppet on a set of marionette strings.
I hung in the air, my body trembling with his power pumping through it. A new pain wracked my frame, and it was
all I could do to swallow back a whimper. I was exhausted.
With Jabari's energy flowing through my body, there was no
way I could call in the power of the earth to even defend myself. It was either one or the other. The two could not coexist
within my system.

"What?" I snapped at him, lifting my head so I could
finally look him in the eye. "Afraid that you had lost the
ability to control me? No, I'm not that lucky! I'm still a puppet on a string for you."

"And this power from the earth you can now wield?" he
inquired, almost politely.

I shook my head. "Only under special circumstances,
like when they perform a sacrifice. I need there to be a lot of
energy in the ground for me to access it. I also can't control
it when a member of the triad is trying to control me. Blood
magic and earth magic just don't mix."

"Hmmm . . . " he softly said, cocking his head to one
side as he looked me over. I was ragged with my torn, bloodstained clothes. My skin was covered in blood and dirt,

while my hair was wind-blown and matted. I didn't look like someone who had defeated Aurora and the great naturi horde. Had I finally outlived my usefulness? Or could he still find some other dirty task for me to complete that put my life and the lives of those around me at risk?

"I guess it's lucky for you that the triad is no more." He lowered his hand and I collapsed to the ground like a heap of garbage. I watched him walk away a couple feet and then completely disappear. I noticed then that the sky had lightened to a pale shade of gray. The dawn was coming.

I lay on the cool grass, waiting for the sun to rise. I could feel no other nightwalkers in the region. But it didn't matter. At that moment I was ready for death. I had done my great deed; closed the doors and, if I was extremely lucky, killed Aurora. Whether I had earned Heaven or Hell, if they even existed, no longer seemed important. I just wanted to sleep, preferably forever.

"Get up, Mira," commanded an achingly familiar voice.

I tried to smile but it came off lopsided, as I could only muster the strength to lift one corner of my mouth. "Go away, Danaus. I'm not in the mood to kill you," I murmured, giving up on trying to open my eyes. I could feel him near me, standing a few feet away.

"The sun is going to rise soon," he reminded me, needlessly.

I ignored his statement. Why state the obvious? Jabari had left me to burn up in the sun. It wouldn't be that bad. I'd be asleep before the sun rose. I wouldn't feel a thing. There were worse ways to go. I should know—I'd inflicted a number of them on my own kind.

"I thought you were killed," I said, when I could finally speak past the lump that had grown in the back of my throat.

When his presence suddenly disappeared while I was fighting the naturi, I could only assume the worst—that he had been killed. There was no time to look around for him, no time to go back and check for a pulse.

"Knocked out," he said. He shook his head as he came into view, standing over me as I lay in the grass. "I think Jabari actually protected me a couple times," he admitted.

"I guess he still has a use for you," I said ominously, cracking my eyes open so I could look up at the hunter.

"I'm sure he'll have a use for us both until he has secured his total control of the Coven," Danaus said with a frown. "Now, get up."

My eyes fell shut as I thought about the world that still lay ahead of me. I was still the puppet of Jabari *and* Danaus. I was a member of the nightwalker Coven, upon which I had no doubt that both Macaire and Elizabeth wanted me dead. The naturi were running loose, regardless of whether they wanted us dead or not at this exact moment. Oh, and there was still Our Liege's plan to speed up the Great Awakening to this upcoming year, revealing to all the world that nightwalkers and lycanthropes truly did exist, creating a great war among the various races.

I felt weighed down, as if all the world were resting on my chest. I had no desire to move, no great desire to keep moving and fighting and risking death. I was tired. I was done.

"Go away, Danaus, please," I murmured with a soft sigh.

"You can't give up. The naturi are loose," he said. I heard him kneel beside me in the grass, his voice sounding closer.

Exhausted, I forced my eyes open to look at the hunter. His face was haggard and his eyes were tired, but somehow he found the energy to keep moving. "Go back to Themis.

Tell Ryan. Tell him everything," I said. The warlock had to know everything before it was too late. Ryan would be able to warn everyone about the escape of Aurora and the rest of the naturi. The warlock had to be told about Our Liege's plans for the Great Awakening. I didn't want a war, but the lycans and all the others couldn't be blindsided when naturi finally stopped fighting among each other and decided that it was time to attack the other races once again.

With a soft grunt, Danaus lifted me into his strong arms and stood. I cried out softly at the sudden movement and clenched my eyes shut again. I don't know how long he carried me; time seemed to slip away as I struggled to hang onto my conscious thought. The lodge was too far away to make it before the sun rose. It was only when the air suddenly became bitterly cold and it grew dark again that I realized he had taken me to the Temple of the Moon. It was on a cliff on the side of the mountain that rose up beside Machu Picchu, with caves reaching deep into its bowels. There, I would be safe from the far-reaching rays of the sun.

Danaus laid me on the ground and then sat down, heaving a heavy sigh. I opened my eyes but had trouble making out his face in the darkness. He slid his hand down my arm and took my hand in his, squeezing it lightly. There was no rush of power threatening to peel my flesh from my bone, just his warm skin pressed to mine.

"Our battles are not completed," he murmured. "But you'll have to take a rain check. I'm not up for killing you right now."

I wanted to laugh. The bastard made one of his few jokes and I didn't have the energy to laugh. The best I could do was pass out again, holding his hand.

Epilogue

Music screamed from the dance floor, throbbing against the walls with its deep bass, moving dancers who longed to forget about their broken hearts and disappointing lives. I stared at the black-clad people crowding the Dark Room. The dimly lit dance club was packed, but that wasn't surprising for a Friday night. I had come here to forget about what had happened among the white-gray stones of Machu Picchu. But I wasn't having much luck. The memories seemed to lurk around every corner of my brain. A phantom pain had even developed in my back from where Rowe stabbed me, even though the wound had healed, leaving behind only a pale white line to match the one on my chest left behind by Cynnia.

Two months ago I had awoken in the caves linked to the Temple of the Moon alone and sore, but still "alive." A testament to my own dumb luck. Stumbling down the mountain, I'd gotten back to Cuzco and grabbed a private plane back to my beloved Savannah. The world shuddered and bemoaned the loss of so many lives at the historic site, but the public relations engines were already churning. A group of political insurgents were blamed for the deaths at both Machu

Picchu and Ollantaytambo, and any questionable evidence, like the charred bodies of the naturi, was quickly swept under the rug. Questions were still being asked and the Internet hummed with speculation, but our secret was safe for now.

Yet even that certainty now hung perilously close to destruction. While the doors had been closed between our world and that of the naturi, many had still slipped through and were lurking in the shadows. Aurora was in our world. I knew she wasn't dead, no matter how much I wanted it to be so. Her people would have found a way to heal the wound. I cursed myself and my own weakness. I should have ignored Rowe and finished the job. I should have cut out Aurora's heart, leaving Rowe to cut out my own. But I was weak.

The queen of the naturi had yet to act, but I knew it was only a matter of time before she formulated a new plan of attack. She had her own kind to contend with at the moment. But I had no doubt that I was at the top of her to-do list. I awoke with a start every night, half expecting to find a naturi standing over my bed with a stake in its hand.

For now, my only concerns were staying "alive" and my newly formed family. Tristan remained sullen and dejected about Sadira's death. He was accustomed to playing the role of the doting servant. I didn't want anyone under foot and didn't need a servant. But I let him stay. Something in his eyes reminded me of Michael, whose body had yet to be found. I couldn't imagine who had taken it, and a part of me was waiting to see it suddenly appear, grossly mangled and decayed. It didn't matter. I couldn't save my angel, but I could try to teach Tristan ways to save himself. It would have to be enough.

Amanda and Knox had resumed their lives in Savannah with little change, even though they seemed to watch over me a little more closely than before. We all seemed more cautious now that the naturi were lurking in our world. No one appeared willing to hunt alone, and our relationship with the shifters was irreparably torn and shredded.

The song on the dance floor changed to something slower, more melancholy. I scanned the crowd. I wasn't in the mood to hunt and didn't particularly need to feed. Strangely enough, I was growing bored. I had missed my city, but now that I was here, I felt restless. I shut myself away from the rest of my kind but Tristan in an attempt to be alone, but I now felt an eagerness to be moving again. Too much had been left unanswered after Machu Picchu, and I was forced to wait for others to act. A part of me wished to see Danaus stride through the door, a frown on his dark face, with news that something horrible had happened. But even he disappeared after Machu Picchu.

A new emptiness had swelled in my chest when I thought of him. The world had grown colder in his absence. Somehow I'd become accustomed to the warm brush of power that emanated from him, the feel of his thoughts and emotions standing on the outskirts of my mind.

With a sigh on my lips, I was about to leave the Dark Room to look for a quieter spot to pass the evening when I felt someone vaguely familiar enter the dance club. Tristan stepped through the entrance and visually scanned the dimly lit club for me, but he wasn't the one that had piqued my attention. I paused and sniffed the air, catching the faint hint of a cologne I hadn't smelled in a while. Slowly, I lifted my feet from where they rested on a chair and placed them on the floor as I sat up. My eyes immediately fell on a slim face that put a smile on my lips. James Parker sidled past a large tattooed man with purple hair, his hand nervously straightening his dark blue and red tie. The gold-rimmed glasses of the Themis researcher glinted in the pale smoky light.

My tongue flicked across my teeth and I smiled, fangs slipping past my lips. Danaus would never have sent the Themis researcher into my domain. He would have come himself if he wanted something. However, the white-haired warlock Ryan could be interested in playing, and he would be the one most likely to send an emissary to fetch me.

Maybe my night was looking up after all.

JOCEYLNN DRAKE'S

NEW YORK TIMES BESTSELLING

DARK DAYS NOVELS

NIGHTWALKER
978-0-06-154277-0

For centuries Mira has been a nightwalker—an unstoppable enforcer for a mysterious organization that manipulates earth-shaking events from the darkest shadows. But the foe she now faces is human: the vampire hunter called Danaus, who has already destroyed so many undead.

DAYHUNTER
978-0-06-154283-1

A master of fire, Mira is the last hope for the world. Now she and her unlikely ally Danaus have come to Venice, home of the nightwalker rulers. But there is no safety in the ancient city and Danaus, the only creature she dares trust, is something more than the man he claims to be...

DAWNBREAKER
978-0-06-154288-6

Destiny draws Mira and Danaus toward an apocalyptic confrontation with the *naturi* at Machu Picchu. Once the *naturi* are unchained, blood, chaos, and horror will reign supreme on Earth. But all is not lost as a rogue enemy princess can change the balance of power and turn the dread tide.

Visit www.AuthorTracker.com for exclusive
information on your favorite HarperCollins authors.

JD 1009

Available wherever books are sold or please call 1-800-331-3761 to order.

SAME GREAT STORIES, GREAT NEW FORMAT . . .
EOS TRADE PAPERBACKS

THE UNDEAD KAMA SUTRA
by Mario Acevedo
978-0-06-083328-2

GODDESS
by Fiona McIntosh
978-0-06-089907-3

JIMMY THE HAND
by Raymond E. Feist
978-0-06-079294-7

THE SERVANTS
by Michael Marshall Smith
978-0-06-149416-4

DREAMING AGAIN
by Jack Dann
978-0-06-136408-2

JAILBAIT ZOMBIE
by Mario Acevedo
978-0-06-136408-2

THE NEW SPACE OPERA 2
Edited by Gardner Dozois and Jonathan Strahan
978-0-06-156235-8

Visit www.AuthorTracker.com for exclusive
information on your favorite HarperCollins authors.

Available wherever books are sold or please call 1-800-331-3761 to order.

EOT 0409